Golden Ribbons

Beth McMurchie

◆ FriesenPress

Suite 300 - 990 Fort St
Victoria, BC, V8V 3K2
Canada

www.friesenpress.com

Copyright © 2019 by Beth McMurchie
First Edition — 2019

All rights reserved.

No part of this publication may be reproduced in any form, or by any means, electronic or mechanical, including photocopying, recording, or any information browsing, storage, or retrieval system, without permission in writing from FriesenPress.

ISBN
978-1-5255-3686-1 (Hardcover)
978-1-5255-3687-8 (Paperback)
978-1-5255-3688-5 (eBook)

1. FICTION, COMING OF AGE

Distributed to the trade by The Ingram Book Company

Remembering Those Who Served
The Great War
1914 – 1918

RECOGNITION

A SPECIAL THANKS TO THE MAPLE RIDGE PUBLIC LIBRARY, WHERE a treasure trove of resources were available to me during the writing of Golden Ribbons.

Recognizing my daughter, Rhonda. Her contribution of practical support, and final editing, has been invaluable, and I believe she loves the characters in Golden Ribbons as much as I do.

Thanks to Rory for his graphic design.

Don, Jocelyn and Rich are a constant support in all things – Mother.

CHAPTER ONE

IT HAPPENED JUST AFTER ONE O'CLOCK IN THE AFTERNOON, October 15, 1898. The explosion at the coal mine had shattered the entire structure. The cave-in at shaft eleven was evident right up to what had been its entrance. Any thought of recovery was inconceivable.

"You are dismissed for the afternoon," Miss James announced to her class. "There has been a problem at the mine and you will need to be home with your families." Miss James understood all too well what the wail of the siren meant, having been born and raised in this coal mining community.

Rachael picked up her school bag and shawl and headed for the inside hallway – already crowded with children preparing to leave. She looked over the crowd but could not see her brother, Todd. *His class must have been dismissed.*

The old elementary school building emptied quickly. It had been an armaments shelter from an earlier time, but the old building had been restored to accommodate basic education for Scottish children of working-class parents. Carved into the splintered wooden doorframe: Locksbury Elementary School 1880. Locksbury was a coal mining burgh, connected by rail to Aberdeen.

Rachael and her classmate, Bessie, walked out to the road together. "My Da is off shift today, so he should be alright," said Bessie. "Is your Da in the mine today?" she asked.

Rachael did not answer Bessie's question. It was Rachael's birthday and, since there was early dismissal, she would take the longer sea front trail. *I want to think about being eleven years old today,* she thought, kicking stones along the way with her heavy rough shoes.

It was a clear and cold October day and she could see schooners off in the distance plying their way through the storm-tossed North Sea. She enjoyed thinking about their possible destinations: Norway to the north, or to the south of England? She loved the idea of travel. Geography was a favourite subject, and she would take every opportunity to have the one textbook all to herself. Todd also had hopes of travel and adventure. They would talk about it when they shared the seemingly endless task of carrying the big copper kettle of water across the roadway to be lifted onto the wood and coal-burning stove.

The family's source of water came from a communal tap secured to a block of cement, each tap spaced intermittently along the row of miners' houses known as Locksbury Gate. There was always water needed for laundry, bathing and cleaning. Todd had his own task of hauling wood and coal in a tarpaulin sling to keep the fire burning and the house warm. Coal and wood were provided by the mine owners, periodically dumped into a shed at the end of every block of houses.

Pete and Kate Atkinson had lived in this housing settlement since their marriage twenty-three years earlier. Their oldest child, Aggie, had married at age eighteen to a young coal miner, Robbie McNabb. They also lived in employee housing farther along the row. The younger couple had a two-year-old son, a baby daughter, and Aggie was into her third pregnancy.

The Atkinson dwelling was crowded now: the bedroom had been divided into two sleeping spaces separated by an old bedspread. The parents slept on one side, along with the twin baby girls in the old double crib. On the other side of the makeshift divide, Rachael and her two-year-old brother, Robert, shared a single bed. Twelve-year-old Todd made himself a private sleeping corner by pulling a chest away from the wall, allowing room enough to push in an old mattress. The older brothers, Billy and Joey – age sixteen and seventeen, slept on mattresses in the common living area. Their mattresses were propped against a wall during the day. Clothing was hung on a line of hooks around the room.

Each housing unit contained a coal and wood-burning stove with a small cupboard to one side, a table and benches, as well as two chairs. A coal oil lamp was used for lighting and was moved room to room as needed, and the bare wooden floor was scattered about with hand-made hooked rugs. Natural light came into the house on the east side through a low window.

A row of outdoor toilets, like soldiers on guard, paralleled the dwellings on the lee side. There were no trees, only the scrubby brush that bordered the sea. The coal mining town had, in addition to the primary school, a weekly mail service. The families paid for milk delivery provided twice weekly. Groceries and other needs were obtained from Aberdeen – an hour away by train.

The siren's wail continued as Rachael turned toward her home. She could see Todd rushing toward her. "Ma told me to come and meet you, and you are to hurry to be with the babes," he said breathlessly. "I've got to get Ma over to the mine right now. Hurry up!"

The children were in their beds napping as Rachael rushed in to look in on them. Kate looked at her daughter with impatience, but said nothing. Hugging her shawl tightly around her shoulders, she followed Todd hurriedly onto the road that led to the mine. Kate was a small figure next to her son - a detached looking woman of forty-one, pain and poverty had etched their patterns of grief and worry across her brow. Her only joy each day was to see her Pete walking up the path at the end of each working day. She could then relax knowing all was as well as had been the day before. Meeting him at the door with a towel to wipe the coal dust off his face, they would kiss tenderly, and finally she would help him out of his work overalls – giving them a hearty shake outside, and then hanging them on a hook behind the door. But this day was not as before. The siren wailed on and on, announcing another dreaded crisis that had held Kate in suspension between heaven and hell throughout the years.

It was then 3:30 in the afternoon. When the siren stopped, a deadly quiet descended on the mine site. Then the shouting began, and the terror of unknowing had taken hold. A list was posted on the door of the administration office and the crowd pressed forward as the announcement was read: "Those listed as working in shaft eleven are George Abelson, Mike Adams, Pete Atkinson …on and on." There were twenty-three names. Many more miners were injured as debris fell within a wide area. As quickly as these facts were revealed, it was announced that a time of remembrance would be held next day at 12:00 o'clock noon.

Kate stood staring at the chaos around her, seeing only the face of her beloved Pete as he would come through the gate toward her. Without a tear or a comment, she took Todd's arm as they made their way home past the stretchers bearing the injured on their descent to the infirmary, their wives and children following with water and bread for the expected long wait as each miner would be examined. Todd kept his mother on course as they proceeded down the hill and into their familiar neighbourhood of Locksbury.

———

Earlier, Billy and Joey felt the explosion as they were at their jobs of lifting peat onto a dray. Then they heard the siren, and they *knew. This would be their fate in a very short time: the dark, the filth and grime, and certain death.* Between them, the decision was made without further consideration. They would not return to their home that night.

———

Rachael had become the primary caregiver of the twin girls since their arrival six months earlier. Kate had tried to nurse them, but it soon became impossible with exhaustion and lack of nourishment herself. Milk was a precious commodity in the home. The twice weekly delivery had to be shared with three hungry little mouths whose bodies were growing and amazingly healthy.

When two-year-old Robert arrived, it was a pleasant shock as there had been no babies since Rachael was born. There was a scurry to find the crib and pram that had been lent out many times within the mining community. Baby clothing had been shared as well, and many an item came back home after it had been worn by other children.

When Kate became pregnant again it was more than a shock, delivery was difficult, and Kate did not cope well with the babies' care. Rachael especially loved the baby twins, she had been pressed into service for them almost immediately, and was even given the task of naming them – Joy and Jill. Rachael had only recently learned that there had been another birth, a boy between Joey and Todd. It was a previous summer day when she had been walking along the path bordering the cemetery that she noticed the row of small head stones. One in particular read: *Baby Atkinson – died in infancy – 1885*. Rachael was puzzled, and asked her mother about the discovery.

"It's no secret," her mother said. "I guess we just forgot to tell you about it."

Rachael wondered how a baby could be *just forgotten*. Although she sometimes resented the burden placed on her, she adored her small brother and baby sisters and couldn't imagine forgetting any one of them should they die. The three of them would always welcome her home from school with happy smiles and hugs, ready to go out for a walk with the pram, or play games in the common room that Rachael would make up for them. Robert would be eager for the surprise – laughing and jumping, and the twins would join in with clapping and giggles. These were Rachael's favourite times, marvelling how small children were always happy and loving. She wished they could stay that way forever.

Rachael could see the tragic news on her mother's face as she came through the door. She rushed to hug and comfort her but Kate made no response; she sat on the wooden chair by the low window staring out at the darkening afternoon. Motioning to Rachael that they would talk outside, Todd told her all that had happened at the mine site.

"What shall we do now, Todd?" she asked.

"We tend to all that has to be done here," Todd responded definitively, "then we help Ma into bed. Tomorrow we will all go to the ceremony of remembrance at the mine, and after that, I will not go back to school as Ma is very ill and she should rest before she can speak of all that has happened. She will have some direction for us. Aggie was at the mine and told me she had seen Billy and Joey," Todd continued. "They were there to say goodbye to her, and told her they would keep in touch with all of us. Their hope is to find jobs on sheep or dairy farms to the south."

Todd also told Rachael that Aggie had summoned a health visitor from Aberdeen on their mother's behalf. The visitor had been there a few days ago, but she would be back again soon.

"I will not go back to school either," said Rachael, "there will be a lot to do here."

As Rachael went about her chores the following evening, she reflected on her mother's reaction to the tragedy. *Ma didn't cry at the remembrance like the other mothers did,* she thought. Before it was over, Kate turned and hurried down the hill. Both Todd and Rachael, carrying the babies, had to run to catch up with her in case she would fall. When they arrived home Kate sat at the window, not accepting the food we offered.

Later, they encouraged her to bed, but she would not move. Rachael did hear her up in the night when she must have thought they were all asleep. Kate talked to Pete's picture – the one taken on their wedding day. Finally she went to bed.

As the days went on, Kate got up for short periods, but finally just stayed in bed. Todd and Rachael hoped the health visitor would return soon. Aggie came every day to help bathe her mother and attempt to offer her milk or water. It seemed that Kate was unable to swallow, and her breath came in gasps. Finally she talked to her children, saying the health visitor would be coming with a plan for them, and they were to behave themselves - accepting what she had to say.

Rachael recalled this moment so often later: *When the visitor arrived, Todd went to sit close by Ma's bed so he could hear what she was saying to the woman. Ma was so exhausted, she lay back in bed with her eyes closed. Finally, the woman spoke to Todd and me. She said Ma was so ill she would not be able to live at home anymore. The little ones would go to care homes until they could be adopted.*

I was so sad and shocked by this – Ma would never allow it! When the woman went to pack the children's belongings and we were alone with Ma, she finally spoke – first to me. I would go to live with Aggie now and help her with her babies. But I didn't want to live with Aggie, I wanted to stay at home with Todd! Ma also said that Todd, as well as Billy and Joey, would have to find work to support themselves. Todd seemed to understand this, but I could not. I was so sad and angry.

I could see Ma was sick, and so small. She was like a tiny lump of coal under all those blankets. But she did not speak again. As the health visitor came out of the bedroom, a child on each arm and carrying one of the twins along with a pillow case filled with belongings, it was clear to me that she was taking our babies away. How could Ma let this happen? But Ma had now turned her face to the wall. I grabbed the pillow case, but the woman knocked me backwards. "You, go behave yourself girl!" *was all she had to say as she hurried out to the waiting cart.*

"Alright, I will go find our babies and adopt them back, I will!" Rachael screamed as she sat at the edge of the road weeping and shouting as if her heart would break.

Todd came to lead Rachael back into the house. He tried again to move his mother so that she could speak to them, but her eyes were closed and she did not speak again. That evening, as Todd held her as if she were a child, Kate Atkinson died - and all of life in the home died with her. Rachael ran out into the street again, crying and calling to Billy and Joey, but they were gone – already far away from Locksbury and Aberdeen.

It was not long before neighbours came to extend comfort, but the door was closed to them. At Aggie's request, they were asked to summon the undertaker and local vicar. A few private minutes descended on Kate's children as they came to the realization that their mother was dead. Aggie went to collect her children so that they could see their Grandma for the last time and say goodbye, and then she would take Rachael home with her. But Rachael refused to go and stayed close to Todd as they stood vigil over their mother.

The undertaker and the vicar came and a few words of assurance were spoken over Kate's body. Then the two men carried her in her blankets out to the waiting wagon. The vicar spoke to Todd and Rachael, saying he would come next morning to see them. Kate's body would be buried that night. Todd held Rachael as she stood frozen to the spot in the doorway of the house. As the wagon pulled away, she had no more tears to shed. Hopelessness had crept into her soul.

As evening descended, Todd led Rachael onto the seashore. He wrapped her in their mother's shawl and, taking the rough blankets from the beds, they huddled into them next to a stone enclosure.

"You must go to Aggie's tomorrow, Rachael," Todd said gently but firmly. "Aggie will come to help me with removal of all we possessed in the house. She can take what will be useful to her, and I will keep two blankets and a nap sack. I'll try my luck at getting work – possibly in the city itself. When I have a place of my own, you can come and live with me." Todd was anxious that Rachael be left with some hope and direction, but he knew in his heart their futures were completely uncertain.

The next morning, as Todd and Aggie were busy cleaning out their old home, the vicar came by to offer his personal condolences. He told Todd and Aggie that many of the mine workers who were injured in the explosion were discovered to be at various stages of tuberculosis – some very seriously. It was his concern that their mother may also have been a victim of this contagious disease, consequently, before her burial, her body was taken to the morgue at the infirmary and an examination made of her throat and chest. Yes, it was believed the examination to be positive. At the direction of the infirmary resident doctor, the message was to be sent out that bedding and the mattress used by Kate must be burned. The vicar felt it was important to inform family members of the community that examination for signs of tuberculosis be carried out as soon as possible.

"Mine owners have been informed of this new information, and are fearful of panic and public outrage," stated the vicar. "They are at this very moment, clearing out records and sealing up the mine. I don't know what provisions they have made for the residences, but I have heard an unspoken rule that if a miner is no longer employed, the residence must be cleared in a fortnight."

"My sister and I are the only family members left in this house," Todd stated with finality, "and we will be on our way by tomorrow. There is no concern about eviction here. Perhaps the owners of the mine might have considered a mine closure because of this epidemic rather than allowing safety standards to slip to the point of disaster."

"Correctly stated," said the vicar. "These are very difficult times for all the families, and I wish you and your sisters Godspeed in whatever endeavours you choose." With that, he walked away.

Todd stared after the vicar for a moment, and contemplating the word *choose*. Such a concept at that particular time was beyond his ability to comprehend. A large fire was built from available wood and items remaining in the home were burned. Aggie rescued her mother's shawl from the flames and said she would boil and disinfect it for Rachael's use – something to remember of her old home. But Todd was glad that Rachael was not present to witness all that had to be done.

Golden Ribbons

Billy and Joey were eventually discovered – quietly huddled in a hayrack that was well on its way to Marywell. "Ya thought Ah didna know ya two lads were weighing down ma wagon, and Ah had hit ev'ry hole in the road ta git ridda ya," snickered the drayman. "Enna way, Ah'm about ta turn off now, and ya'd best stay on the main road ta git anither lift."

The brothers were grateful to get that far away from Aberdeen. As they tossed their light loads onto their backs, they thanked the drayman, and then headed off in an uncertain direction. As the late autumn sky darkened, they could see a barn ahead and hoped there would be some warm hay for beds. Next morning they would have to beg for food or find something edible in the fields – looking for work along the way. As it happened, the barn door was open, and they quietly made their way in the dark to what seemed like the steps to a hayloft. They were soon asleep.

Full of hope and determination, Todd walked the streets of Aberdeen. Darkness fell, but in the fading light he noticed an old man putting up a sign in the chemist's window: *WANTED for delivery and general cleaning. Must be eighteen years of age.* When Todd rapped on the window, the old man squinted into the dusk and pointed to the age designation at the bottom of the sign. Todd could not read it in the dim light - all he got from the sign was *delivery and cleaning,* but with a wide smile, he raised his arms to indicate strength.

The old man shook his head and was about to turn away, then changed his mind and spoke through a small slice of light at the door: "D'ye not see the sign? It says must be eighteen years auld! Ye're only a child."

"But I need a job to support myself and my sister, Sir," Todd pleaded.

"Where are ye'r parents, lad?"

"My Pa was killed in the mine explosion at Locksbury, and my Ma died too. I don't go to school now, but I learn quickly."

"Do ye indeed. Well then, Ah will take the sign down now until ye show ye'self at seven o'clock tomorrow morning. Good night, lad."

Todd was suddenly taken with hunger and exhaustion. He pulled the old blanket out of his nap sack, as well as the package of biscuits Aggie had given him, and was instantly asleep. He was wakened at first light by a dig in the ribs with the sharp toe of an enormous boot.

"Hey lad, no loitering in the street! What are ye do'in away from ye'r home at this hour?"

Todd was stunned by the awesome presence staring him in the face and for a moment was in a fog of confusion, trying to assess where he was. "I have no home, Sir. I'm starting a job at this shop at seven o'clock."

"Well then, ma good man," laughed the policeman. "I expect ye'll want to pull ye'self together as it's almost that hour now."

As Todd jumped up and threw off the blanket, the biscuits bounced across the road. Embarrassed, he rubbed his hands across his face and through his hair.

"My name is Sergeant McTavish, Aberdeen Sixth Precinct, boy, and Ah was about to stop next door for a cupa tea and a scone, if ye would care to join me."

Later, Sergeant McTavish went back to the chemist's shop with Todd at the appointed hour where the wizened shopkeeper stood at the window, WANTED sign in hand.

"No, No," said Todd, "I'm here and ready to work!"

With a look of doubt and resignation, the old man opened the door to Todd and the Sergeant.

"This young lad needs a job, Malcolm Murray. Will ye give him a chance? C'mon," he chided, "where's ye'r good Irish sense of humour? Just try it for a few days even."

With a nod and a sigh, the old man plunked the sign onto the counter.

"I'll be a good worker, Mr. Malcolm, you'll see," said Todd with conviction.

It was three days before Todd was able to finish his tasks early enough to make his way to Aggie's home and to see Rachael. He knew she would be anxious to see him and to hear of any hopeful news. Rachael met Todd at the door, bursting instantly into tears when she saw him. Aggie was away tending to another's laundry. Her husband, Robbie, was over at the mine site to find out what the owners were intending to do for the displaced miners.

Rachael blurted out all her frustrations and sorrows: "I don't love 'em, Todd, I can't love 'em – not like our own wee brother and sisters. I'm sorry for Aggie as she has a hard time of it working out and caring for her family, and I know she's hurt'n for Ma something awful, but I can't take it any longer. Robbie hates me, and I hate him. He says I'm a loafer and a bawl-baby. And, yes, I do cry a lot, thinking about our own babies – where they are, and are they crying too?"

Todd was sympathetic, but also firm. "We must not dwell on it, Rach, but let them go. Though we can't see them, we can send love to them with our thoughts."

"How do you mean – send love with our thoughts?" Rachael asked impatiently.

Todd sat down on the floor next to Rachael. "Do you remember the story book Aunt Aggie sent for all of us one Christmas? It was about how loving thoughts are like golden ribbons that can travel fast and to anywhere – even across the oceans, and a golden ribbon will attach itself to the one we are thinking of. When we think loving thoughts about our small brother and sisters, they will know we are thinking about them and we will always love them. Da and Ma always taught us to care for one another no matter what happens, even if we are separated. They did for us the very best they possibly could, Rachael, we must remember that."

"I will try to think that way, Todd, though it will be hard," said Rachael, pensively. "I will stay at Aggie's a bit longer and try to be cheerful, but I must think of leaving and find some work for myself – even looking after children in an orphanage, or something like that. I'm tall for my age. I have no clothes except what I'm wearing, but I could go to the charity for another dress and some shoes."

Todd thought for a moment: "I will talk to Sergeant McTavish about how we could do that."

Rachael then realized she hadn't asked Todd if he had found a job, and he was delighted to tell her about the chemist's shop, and that he would at least have a place to sleep and food, even if he did not know how much he would earn.

Rachael jumped up and clapped her hands. "I knew you could do it, Todd! I will find a job too – I just know it!"

Sergeant McTavish was pleased that Todd asked for his help, and he enlisted his wife, Daisy, to also help by referring Todd and Rachael to the Central Aberdeen Ladies Charity. After hearing their story, it was agreed that a one-time issue of clothing would be given. For Todd: shoes, stockings, knickers, a shirt and a woollen topcoat. For Rachael: a plain grey cotton dress, black stockings, some under clothing, black lace-up shoes, and a heavy cardigan.

Rachael was anxious to start looking for work immediately, and Daisy was able to direct her to the open laundry workroom which was a vacant warehouse off the main road of Aberdeen. A domestic supervisor and referral clerk, Miss Ellen Home, would speak to her. Daisy stressed to Rachael that she must be very polite and assume an air of confidence and maturity. *Her age is against her,* thought Daisy, but she did not speak of her concerns.

Rachael sat down in the last chair of a long row of domestic hopefuls, looking at each of them to see if any might be near her age. *Oh well,* she thought, *I'll speak clearly, as Daisy suggested, and try not to stumble over my words – keeping it short as possible.*

Miss Home, calling Rachael forward, said, "Oh, but you are just a child; do your parents know where you are?"

Rachael began her prepared speech: "My name is Rachael Atkinson. I am fourteen years old. My Ma and Da are both dead. I have some schooling, but not since my Da got killed in a coal mine explosion in Locksbury. I have cooked, cleaned, and cared for small children. I must have work to support myself."

Miss Home could see that Rachael was clearly desperate. It would be hard to find a placement for someone so young, even as she claimed to be older than she obviously was. Nevertheless, Miss Home was impressed by Rachael's response and felt some compassion for her. "I have a request for a kitchen helper, Rachael," she said. "It is at the manor home of the Marquis

Golden Ribbons

of Aberdeen. I am well acquainted with Mrs. Olson, the housekeeper, and I will say without hesitation that Mrs. Olson runs a very tight ship. One slip and a servant of any rank goes out the door."

As she wrote a reference slip for Rachael, Miss Home stressed the importance of this position, and that Rachael must be polite, alert, and willing to do all that would be asked of her. Rachael was surprised and shocked to be given a referral so quickly. Although anxious to be on her way with the note of introduction, she paused to thank Miss Home, who in return wished her well.

Rachael's confidence and gratitude began to wane as she approached the manor grounds. It was cold and beginning to rain, and she felt suddenly alone and frightened. She rapped on the wide oak door, and was shortly greeted by a tall, dignified-looking man who stated that one does not rap on the front manor door, but uses the bell that hangs on a cord to one side. When Rachael stated her reason for being there, the butler (she discovered later) directed her to go around to the back where she could rap at the door and be admitted to the manor's servant entrance and kitchen.

Maisie McLeod greeted Rachael warmly, introducing herself as the head cook at the manor. Rachael liked her right away, especially her inquisitive smile and rosy cheeks. In an adjoining room, Rachael could smell the aroma of bread right out of the oven. The sensation nearly made her faint. Maisie asked her to wait in the outer kitchen while she summoned Mrs. Olson, the housekeeper, for the third time that day.

Mrs. Olson looked Rachael over and smiled faintly. "What has Ellen sent us this time – a child?"

Mrs. Olson is obviously a person of authority, Rachael thought. She was awed at her stately appearance: her white hair was pulled back into a flawless bun, she was wearing a smooth black dress, and she had a pearl broach on her shoulder.

It was late in the day and Mrs. Olson was impatient to get this interview over with as quickly as possible. "What is your name, my dear, and do you have a reference? Better yet, just tell us quickly about yourself."

Rachael cleared her throat: "My name is Rachael Atkinson. I am fourteen years old. My Ma and Da are both dead. I have some schooling, but not since my Da got killed in a coal mine explosion in Locksbury. I have cooked, cleaned and cared for small children. I must find work to support myself."

"Well, there seems little else to ask, Rachael," said the housekeeper. "You have prepared yourself well. Would you kindly wait a few minutes while I speak with Mrs. McLeod."

The two women moved to the other side of the room. "I believe Ellen has pushed it to the limit this time Maisie. This girl is certainly younger than age fourteen. Still there is something very courageous about her, and I admire her directness. What do you think, Maisie? I am too tired to make an independent judgement this time."

"Ah feel we should give her a chance, Jean. She seems not the sort to present herself as something she is not, even if she is lying about her age. Ah say Yes!"

Turning to Rachael, Mrs. Olson nodded to her. "Very well then Rachael, can you begin immediately?"

"Yes, I'… ahh, Yes, Ma'm, and thank you." Rachael could think of nothing else to say.

"Mrs. McLeod will give you directions regarding your duties over the dinner hour, and she will show you to the room where you will be staying while serving one month's probation. You will receive only room and board during that time. If your work is satisfactory, you will receive a monthly sum that will be decided later on. Is that acceptable to you, Rachael?"

"Yes indeed, Mrs. Olson, and thank you."

"Very well then, I will see you at 8:00 o'clock tomorrow morning when we will discuss your duties more fully, as well as the routine of the manor. Mrs. McLeod will see if she can find a kitchen costume small enough for a girl your size." With that, Mrs. Olson turned on her heel and left the room.

Maisie motioned Rachael to follow her up two flights of stairs to the servants' quarters where Rachael was given a small but bright bedroom containing a chest of drawers with a mirror over it, a low wooden chair, and a cot laid out and expectant with a hand-made cover on top. A corner window offered a view of the back kitchen garden, and beyond it a wooded area stretched away as far as the eye could see.

Rachael stood at the window feeling happy, but also anxious and sad. *What if I make a mistake right off?* she asked herself. *I wish Todd was here to cheer me up. It seems a right nice place, but there will be so much to learn.*

CHAPTER TWO

MAISIE STOPPED BY RACHAEL'S ROOM TO TOSS A DUTY DRESS AND apron on the cot. As she touched Rachael's arm, she whispered, "Dinnae worry ye'self, lassie, ye will be helped along the way. Now change ye'r clothing and join the kitchen staff for a bite of sup. Sir Gordon has dinner later. Ye'll be called on to help with clean-up b'fore ye'r off to bed. Ach yes, forgot to tell ye the bathroom is at the end of the hallway that ye'll be sharing with Bronwyn – ye'll meet her later."

Rachael caught a glimpse of herself in a long mirror on the second floor landing as she descended to the kitchen. It seemed strange to be wearing such a costume, still she rather liked it. It was a bright green dress with white collar and cuffed sleeves to match the white apron. Arriving at the kitchen where she had first met Maisie McLeod, she was introduced to Bronwyn. *A girl about sixteen,* Rachael guessed.

Maisie explained that Bronwyn was cooking assistant, but would also be sharing kitchen and some household duties with Rachael. Bronwyn seemed pleased to have Rachael there. "Help at last," she smiled and showed Rachael to the long table where they would have their supper.

When the three had settled themselves they were joined by Clifford. Maisie gave a running record of all he attended to: the stable, the outdoor grounds, running errands, sometimes being a nuisance in the kitchen. Clifford laughed and showed his fists. Rachael enjoyed the fun moment, and she guessed Clifford to be older – about twenty.

A large bowl of beef stew with vegetables and dumplings had been placed on the table for self-serving, along with slices of the warm bread Rachael had detected earlier. Maisie explained that Mrs. Olson usually had dinner in her rooms. Rachael suddenly felt extremely hungry, and helped herself to a large portion of stew and bread. It was a hurried meal as Sir Gordon would be dining with two guests at 7:00 p.m. Serving would be Bronwyn's duty that evening with Rachael standing by to help with removal of the courses and later the clean-up. All would be completed by approximately 9:00 p.m. After everyone finished the meal the dishes were carried to a large sink, but dishes from Sir Gordon's entertaining would be added to it, and the clean-up done all at the same time.

Bronwyn asked Rachael to join her as she put finishing touches to the dinner to be served to Sir Gordon and his guests. She explained that it was a casual dinner and therefore Sir Gordon would expect the serving to be carried out quickly, and without special attention to elaborate table preparation. Rachael would remain at the entrance to the dining room and would respond when Bronwyn passed dishes to be carried to the kitchen. Rachael was dazzled with the china, glass and silver ware, but she also admired the ease with which Bronwyn went about explaining what had to be done. She also thought Bronwyn very pretty with her dark hair pulled back with clips, recognizing that her own hair must look ragged in comparison. She would ask Bronwyn's advice in having a change of hair style when they got to know one another better.

Later, when they were working in the kitchen, Bronwyn made little conversation, telling Rachael that Mrs. Olson would explain the duties of kitchen helper the next day and answer any of her questions. Rachael hurried up the stairs to her room as her first day at the manor ended. Then, thinking about the following day, she hoped her courage would not waver when she met with Mrs. Olson who she found frightening. But, remembering Daisy's words, she was determined to present herself as confident and capable as she possibly could.

Rachael lay awake for some time thinking about her family, especially her wee brother and sisters, wondering where they were. "I'll send loving thoughts to all of them," she said out loud. She closed her eyes and tried to picture their faces. *Strangely,* she thought, *I can't bring to memory the faces of Da or Ma.* With her face still damp with tears, she fell into a deep and exhausted sleep.

Golden Ribbons

Todd had lived and worked with the elderly chemist for three weeks. He was up to date with deliveries and had picked up a large parcel of orders from the infirmary. He had also fetched and carried groceries for the old man, as well as delivered his personal messages. The living quarters were cleaned several times each week, and were finally in a liveable condition. It was a small living space: a back room just big enough for Malcolm's single bed, a cold water bathroom adjoining - with a galvanized tub hanging on the wall. Todd slept on a cot in a utility room that consisted of a long table, two wooden chairs, an ice box, and a small range with a tiny cupboard above it.

One end of the table held a clutter of papers dating back many years. Todd had to check with Malcolm before throwing out even one slip of paper, so it took several days to clear the backlog. The shop itself was usually where Malcolm spent most of his waking hours, did his business, and occasional socializing. Though well worn, there were three fairly comfortable leather chairs in a semi-circle with a low table between them. A small hearth had to be kept stoked constantly to keep a chill off the room during the present early winter days.

Laundry was piled up in a corner. Todd was puzzled as he could not see a copper, or anything like it, that he had used at home. It was solved one day when a cranky-looking woman arrived at the door to collect the dirty laundry that had accumulated over the month. But when would it be returned? This apparently happened at the whim of the laundry lady. It was apparent from her manner that Malcolm was not a favoured customer. Todd decided not to offer another service before he cleared up the issue of pay with Malcolm. It was time to ask.

"Ah'm happy to give ye a bed and board, boy," said Malcolm. "What do ye need money for?"

"Mr. Murray, Sir," replied Todd, "if I'm not to be paid for the services I do, I will have to look for employment elsewhere. I have need of money, just as you do. I must also have time off each week to visit my sister to make sure she is well."

"Alright, alright, ye'll have three one-pound notes at the end of every month."

"Thank you, Sir, and time off?"

"Ah'll have to think about that" said Malcolm, as he sat down in his usual green leather chair, and scratched his beard. "Ye'll have Sunday afternoons, unless an emergency delivery."

"Thank you," said Todd. He was pleasantly surprised at the amount agreed on.

While cleaning the shelves and glass-fronted cabinets of Malcolm's shop, Todd was fascinated with the names of medications: "Sal Volatile, Mentholated Oil, Carbolic Soap, Mercurochrome, Iodine …" He had not heard of any of these preparations, and wondered what they were used for. While Malcolm had his regular afternoon nap, he tried to find the answers in the journals and notes piled on a shelf below the cabinets. He seldom found answers, but he enjoyed the search.

After breakfast in the kitchen, Rachael was asked to join Mrs. Olson for tea in her rooms. "Please sit down Rachael," she said, pouring two cups of tea and passing one to Rachael. "Did you sleep well? It can be difficult sometimes, in a strange place."

"Yes, thank you Mrs. Olson."

"Now Rachael, you can understand that I would be curious about your circumstances, and how you came to apply for a position here when you are so young. But be assured, no one will ask you to explain. Perhaps when you know us better you will want to share more of your story. You were hired because you presented yourself well, and both Mrs. McLeod and I felt you were being straight forward with us. We are a small number of servants in this manor home, and it works well because we have a policy of honesty and respect for one another. Have you been honest with us Rachael? Is the age you gave us exactly right?"

With this, Rachael burst into tears. "No, Mrs. Olson, I was not honest about my age; I had to lie to get a position that I need so badly. I wouldn't know where to go, or how to support myself otherwise," she sobbed, dabbing at her eyes with the back of her sleeve.

Mrs. Olson held out a hankie. "How old are you, Rachael?"

"I'm eleven years old. I don't want to go away, Mrs. Olson!"

As Maisie McLeod walked past the door, she turned and peeped in. "Wha's go'in on here, Jean, are ye pinch'in the lass?"

"Rachael is worried that she will have to go because she is only eleven years old, Maisie. When she stops crying, I'll explain that we had guessed she to be younger, but liked her and wanted to give her a chance."

Rachael was unable to stop crying. As Maisie put her arms around her, this was all that Rachael could stand: she buried her head on Maisie's shoulder and continued her choking sobs. "I'm sorry I lied, Maisie."

"There now Rachael, ye're a sad wee lass, but ye'll be treated kindly here. Lying is a hard burden to carry, and Ah feel there is more sadness beyond that. Ye go now and wash ye'r tears away and brush ye'r hair. Then, come meet me in the kitchen after ye feel better and ye will help me with the dinner veggies. It is Bronwyn's afternoon off and Ah will need ye'r help."

"Thank you, Mrs. Olson and Maisie," said Rachael, as she climbed the stairs to her room - sobbing until she finally felt some peace. *I will work hard, and I will always be honest. I want to stay here.*

As they worked together in the kitchen, Maisie showed Rachael where the vegetables were kept and she directed her with peeling and storing for later use. "Ye had some experience in helping Bronwyn with serving and cleaning last evening, did that go well?"

"Yes, Bronwyn told me exactly what to do. It went well."

"Sir Gordon will be dining out this evening, so the dinner ye are helping prepare is just for the servants," Maisie explained. "He will have guests later, and so will require refreshments then. Bronwyn will be back in time to take care of it this time. When ye have been with us a bit longer, Rachael, ye will take ye'r turn serving refreshments to Sir Gordon and his guests in the evenings."

"May I ask, Daisy, does Sir Gordon have a wife?"

"Ye're asking a good question, Rachael. Sir Gordon lost his wife to a serious fever about two years ago. He is still very sad, and all of us who serve here try to make his days as pleasant as possible. There have been many changes for Sir Gordon since her death, both socially and with his properties. But that is not a concern for ye or me. We only serve and get on with one another to provide a peaceful, if not happy, home for him."

"I will do my best, Maisie. I'm sorry his wife died."

"Mrs. Olson said she would speak with ye again this afternoon. Ye will change ye'r dress and apron after luncheon, and ye will get a clean apron ev'ra day. There will be an extra apron when ye are ready to serve dinner to Sir Gordon, or for refreshments in the later evening."

Rachael was overwhelmed by all the information coming to her, but she repeated it all to herself several times a day so she wouldn't forget. "I wish my brother, Todd, to know where I am, Maisie. Do you know how I could get a note to him?"

"Clifford may be able to deliver it, if not too far away."

"My brother works for Mr. Murray, the chemist on Stonehaven Road," Rachael added.

"Ye don't mean auld Malcolm! How auld is ye'r brother, and how long has he worked there? Malcolm Murray is a cranky auld sod, and doesnae get on well with lads who work for him."

"Todd is twelve years old, almost thirteen" Rachael added. "He says he likes working for Mr. Murray. He has been there for, I think, about three weeks."

"Verra well, when ye'r note is ready, Ah'll ask Clifford to deliver it on his round of errands."

Malcolm had to admit he was beginning to enjoy Todd's company. He was pleased that the shop and living quarters were kept clean and tidy, and as the weeks went by, gave him the task of filling repeat orders. Todd looked forward to Malcolm's afternoon naps when he would have a chance to look through the daily newspaper. One day, he was amazed to find that an English scientist had recently developed a way to refine the leaves of willow trees so that this analgesic could be more available and convenient in small tablet form. It was called *aspirin*. He wondered why Malcolm had not provided this new medication to his customers. When he found a convenient time, he thought he would ask. "Have you heard of the new discovery of aspirin, Malcolm? The newspapers have called it a wonder drug."

"Ah yes, Ah've heard," Malcolm grumbled. "Those quacks are always coming up with something that may do more harm than good."

"Should I read what the newspaper has said about it? That won't hurt. It says: *It had been used for centuries by native peoples in rain forest areas of the south hemisphere as relief in head ache, fever, muscle ache, and for a cold – just to feel better and to be able to sleep.*"

It was not long before the small bottles of aspirin were in the cabinet behind the counter, and Todd had designed a notice to Malcolm's customers that the miracle drug was available, noting the precautions to be taken.

One day Malcolm surprised Todd by commenting: "Ye're a bright lad, Todd boy, ye should be back in school. But," Malcolm continued, "Ah have to say Ah've been able to carry on the business longer with ye here. Ah'm an auld man now, and it's hard to keep up." Malcolm sat down heavily in his old leather chair, and Todd noticed there was a change in the old chemist's movement, as well as his tone.

"I've been glad to work with you, Malcolm," Todd replied. "You have taught me to be curious about medicines. I've been thinking that I would like to be a doctor one day, or a scientist to find cures for diseases. That's a long way off, but I will find a way …"

"Ah know ye will Todd boy. Yes, Ah know ye will! B'fore we tally up what has to be done today, I want ye to go out back of the shop to see a discovery Ah've made!"

Todd was curious to know what Malcolm meant by *discovery*, but leaning against the building was a new bicycle. He came back to Malcolm for an explanation.

"Ah've been reading the papers too, Todd boy, and a new safety bike has been invented by a fell'a, the name of Dunlop. It has new and better tyres – pneumatic tyres they call them. It's for ye to make faster deliveries. It's quiet here now, so have a go at it, then come tell me what ye think."

"I've never had a bicycle, Malcolm, but that one is a beauty! I will need some time to get on with it." Nevertheless, Todd went out eagerly, grabbing the bike by the handle bars and trying to get on several times - but without success. He felt he was missing a step that would get him on the seat and moving.

A young man, leading his own bike down the lane, noticed the trouble Todd seemed to be having. "Hello there," he called. "Can I help?"

"Sure could use some help. I've never ridden a bike before."

"You need to step on the pedal next to you, and slide onto the seat at the same time. Then, as quickly, get the other pedal going. It's tricky to start with, just be patient."

Todd had a few bad starts, but finally got the rhythm of it, pedalling a few circles around the lane and the roadway. "Hey, thanks for your help!" he called out.

After a few more circles, Todd rode cautiously down the lane, and then walked the bike across the road to the trail that followed the sea. Making a confident leap forward, laughing out loud, "I love this!" he called out.

When he returned to the shop, he found the old chemist dozing in his chair, but he started when Todd flopped down beside him – out of breath and smiling. Malcolm smiled too, and laughed. "Ah see ye didn't kill yer'self, Todd."

"It's wonderful, Malcolm. I've never had such fun in my life," Todd gasped.

"God bless ye, lad. There's a delivery to make, and ye can pick up some milk and bread for our supper." Todd was glad to hear Malcolm laugh and chuckle to himself.

When Rachael met again with Mrs. Olson, the most important matter to discuss was schooling. "Rachael, I'm sure you know that schooling is compulsory in Scotland until the age of thirteen," said Mrs. Olson, as Rachael nodded. "Since your parents are not living to see that this ruling is met, there may be another way to handle it and still keep you here. For now and until one month probation is served, we will just carry on as we are today."

"Thank you, Mrs. Olson, I would like that."

"Education is very important," continued Mrs. Olson. "I'm sure your parents would want more for you."

"Yes they would, as they had little education themselves. My Da was a coal miner, and my Ma died a few weeks after the mine explosion that killed my Da."

"I'm so sorry, Rachael, you are a brave girl to seek employment at your age. Do you have brothers and sisters?"

"Yes, I have," Rachael proceeded cautiously. "I have one sister, married to a coal miner, and I have three brothers. My two older brothers are looking for work on sheep farms or dairies to the south. My brother, Todd, is twelve years old. He works for Mr. Murray, the chemist."

"Oh yes," Mrs. Olson replied, "I know where that is. I hope one day we can meet your brother Todd."

"Yes, I hope so too," Rachael smiled.

Mrs. Olson then took Rachael on a tour of the rooms in the manor where she would be carrying out her tasks. As they passed through the main hallway, they encountered the man Rachael had spoken to the day she arrived at the front door of the manor. "This is Mr. Duncan McCabe, Rachael. Rachael has been hired as kitchen helper, Duncan," Mrs. Olson informed.

"Very good," said Duncan. "Welcome Rachael."

"Thank you, Sir," said Rachael shyly.

Mrs. Olson explained, as they went along, that Duncan, or Mr. McCabe until Rachael knew him better, had been with Sir Gordon for many years, and lives with his wife in a cottage on the estate. "Although visitors regard Duncan as an old-fashioned butler," she said, "he has many other roles, and Sir Gordon could hardly get along without him. So now, I believe you have met everyone except Sir Gordon, and you will have that opportunity soon.

"You may have noticed many unoccupied bedrooms on the servant's floor," Mrs. Olson continued. "That is because in days gone by, when Sir Gordon's wife was alive, the manor had many more servants, and there were a great many parties and dinners, as well as overnight guests to attend to. Sir Gordon does not require that any more, so there are few of us, but more variety in what we do. So, as times goes on, you will be performing many different tasks besides kitchen helper."

"I will like that."

As the weeks went on, Rachael became more and more enchanted with the manor. She especially liked the big clock in the main hall. She would listen after bedtime in order to hear the chimes for the hour and the half-hour. As she passed by the many rooms with heavy oak furniture and beautiful tapestries, she looked forward to the day when she could enter to dust and polish.

Malcolm was pouring over the newspaper, his spectacles creeping forward to the end of his nose. "Well, Todd boy, Ah think Ah've figured it out!" said Malcolm, pushing his spectacles back.

"What have you figured out, Malcolm?" Todd was busy dating and labelling bottles for re-shelving.

"We're soon into the year 1899 and, if Ah'm reading this right, ye can get into secondary school if Ah'm your guardian. It's all going to state support, and Ah'm a ratepayer," he exclaimed proudly.

"How do you get to be a guardian, just by saying so?"

"Sure, why not!"

"That's great, Malcolm," acknowledged Todd. "I do want to get back into school, so – as you say – why not!" Todd went to hug the old chemist.

"No use getting all mushy about it though," Malcolm mumbled. "So, Ah think all we have to do is go to the education office downtown and sign ye up! Ah'll take along ma tax papers, of course. No doubt there will be new forms."

"The only trouble is, Malcolm, I wouldn't be as available to work in the shop." Todd explained. "I love the job, and I need the pay."

"Auld Malcolm's not so dull, Todd boy. Ah have figured that one out too. Ye'll have the bike to get to school, and ye can be here after ye'r classes and carry on as b'fore."

"That's brilliant!" Todd said excitedly.

"Now," said Malcolm, "let's plan a day when we can close up for a few hours…"

Todd could hardly wait to tell Rachael the wonderful news. The next Sunday afternoon, he rode the bike to the manor and rapped on the kitchen door. Maisie answered the rap and was surprised to see a pleasant-looking lad before her.

"Please M'am, I am Rachael's brother, Todd. May I have permission to see her for a few minutes?"

"Ye certainly can, Todd. Why not come into the kitchen, we were about to take a tea break, and ye can join us."

"Thank you," he accepted with pleasure.

"Sit over here at the big table," said Maisie. "We'll give ye two some time to get caught up with ye'r news before Bronwyn and Ah join ye."

Rachael was happy with Todd's news. "Mr. Murray must be a wonderful man. I hope to meet him soon."

"You will, but first I have a birthday present for you." Todd pulled a package out of his pocket.

Rachael admired the package for so long he wondered if she would ever open it. "Oh, it is so beautiful! A clip for my hair is exactly what I would have wanted. Thank you."

Todd's next stop was to see Aggie and her children. His knock was answered by Robbie. "Ah see the auld man has given ya a bike. Next y'll be digg'n into his pockets," he said with a sneer, not moving to let Todd pass.

"Oh Todd, it's so wonderful to see you!" said Aggie. "Robbie doesn't mean to be rude, he's just worried about the mine closure, and not having a job."

"The bike is for deliveries, Robbie. It was not given to me. I'm pleased to be able to use it today, otherwise I would not be here," said Todd, not wanting to show offence.

Aggie hugged Todd warmly, as the two children, Peter and Mary, hid shyly within the folds of her skirt.

"I have a surprise for both of you," said Todd, as he pulled two small packages out of his pocket. The children approached him hesitantly, but accepted the packages and returned to their mother without opening them.

"So ya're a big guy now, be'n kind to poor folks on the dole," Robbie said again with sarcasm, and slouched lower in his chair.

"Please come again, Todd," Aggie said with sadness.

"I will do that, Aggie, and perhaps Rachael will be able to come with me," Todd agreed.

As Todd rode the bike down miners' row, he allowed despair to overtake him. He felt the hopelessness of Aggie's situation, and the day of celebration had been spoiled by Robbie's ugly tone. As he approached the trail bordering the sea, he quickened his pedalling. He was anxious to see Malcolm. *That is my home now,* he declared privately.

Beth McMurchie

Malcolm looked at Todd with anxious curiosity. "Ah know there's something bothering ye. Did something happen to spoil ye'r afternoon?"

"It was a day of celebration at first," Todd started. "I wanted to tell Rachael the good news that I would be going back to school. She was so happy for me, and I felt happy for her that she is well and contented among the people she works with at the manor.

"Then, I went over to Locksbury to visit my sister, Aggie and her children," he continued. "Robbie McCann, her husband, met me at the door and immediately noticed the bike, suggesting that I am using you, Malcolm. The small gifts I took to the children were also seen by him as evidence of a superior attitude on my part. I was very hurt and angry, and I did not spend the time to visit my sister as I had hoped to do. It was a shock to recognize Robbie's feelings, after all we have been through."

"Todd boy, how often have Ah seen hurts piled upon hurts in ma time," responded Malcolm. "Ye and Rachael are likely to experience this time and time again as ye both have moved on, without bitterness, to make a life for ye'rselves. Jealousy is an evil companion that will destroy ye'r brother-in-law, as well as his family. How very sad that is. Ah expect there are many miners out there who have not faced the reality of the mine closure, and will wallow in disillusion waiting for it to reopen. That, of course, will never happen. But Ah've seen it all b'fore! If Ah could take away your hurt, Todd boy, Ah would gladly do it, but it is ye'rs to recover from, and come out of it a wiser lad."

"You are so wise, Malcolm," said Todd.

"Wisdom comes with experience and suffering," Malcolm continued, "and sometimes with age, but if one auld man is exceptionally fortunate, it comes with the companionship of a lad like ye'rself. Ye'r hope, Todd boy, has rubbed off on me. Ah have found laughter, and a reason to enjoy living again that has been missing for too long."

"What made you lose hope, Malcolm? Do you mind if I ask?"

"Ah will tell ye, as it may hold a grain of wisdom that ye can recall in future years. Ah came to Scotland from Ulster thirty-two years ago. Ah was a broken and disillusioned young man, thinking that the awful hurt would go away if Ah removed ma'self from it," he continued. "That didn't happen, it only made me more closed and pitiful. Ah had married ma school sweetheart. We were so full of hope. After apprenticing with ma uncle in his business of pharmacy, Ah was ready to go it on ma own. Annie and me, we were expecting our first child, and so the future seemed as bright as anyone could expect. Then, in the agony of delivering a still-birth child, Ah lost ma Annie as well.

"The rest is history, Todd boy: thirty-two years of disillusion and anger. Ah tried to find some meaning in this shop, but even that fell short – all because of lost hope, and feeling that life had cheated me. Ah was very resentful." Malcolm paused in thought, and then brightened as he added, "Enough of that! Let's have a cup of tea, Todd boy, and maybe a tot of whisky to go along with it."

"Thanks for telling me about your losses, Malcolm," said Todd.

CHAPTER THREE

A LETTER CAME TO AGGIE'S HOME THE DAY AFTER TODD HAD BEEN there. It was from Billy and Joey.

> Dear Aggie: This letter is long in coming we realize, but it has been a time of dealing with the loss the family has suffered. How are you, Aggie? And how are Todd and Rachael? We felt it better to get away and find work immediately rather than hang around Locksbury and wonder what to do next. It was more sadness than we felt capable of handling.
>
> We are both employed with farmers in the Borders, a place called Melrose. I work on a dairy farm, and Joey works with sheep. We live in a bothy for single farm workers. There are eight in this particular one – more than there should be, but we expect to move later on. It was not hard to find work as men are leaving the country for Canada and Australia in large numbers. And this, too, is our hope. After we have been in this employ for six months, our employers will pay out what is coming to us. It should be enough to buy passages to eastern Canada.
>
> We have been to meetings and have met with people who are urging immigration of Scots to settle the southern prairies. They say that the Canadian Pacific Railway Company will transport us without charge from Montreal to the wide open prairies, known as Provinces of the Northwest Territories where there are large tracts of cheap land for the

taking. This is almost too good to be true, but no doubt we will be working for other farmers in the beginning until we can earn enough to buy supplies as will be needed. It's all very exciting and terrifying as well. I will enclose an address for you to use in replying to this letter. Next time, you will hear from Joey.

Love, from your brother Billy

"Can ya believe that Rachael! Ah can hardly keep up with her. She has a task finished b'fore Ah've asked for it!" said Maisie, to no one in particular.

"I like everything you ask me to do," said Rachael, beaming.

"Then, next ye'll take a list of errands out to Clifford at the stable. He should be finished tidying up out there by now."

Rachael found that the stable was just a pleasant walk from the manor. She was surprised to see Clifford outside polishing a black automobile. "I thought this was a stable."

"Hello Rachael! Well, it was a stable for many years, and still is a bit. Sir Gordon keeps a trap and pony for his own enjoyment when he visits the farms on his lands. Duncan drives this auto and chauffeurs Sir Gordon to official business and social calls in Aberdeen. It's a Benz, made in Germany. The original one was shown at the World's Fair in Paris in 1889!" Clifford said proudly.

"Have you worked for Sir Gordon long, Clifford?"

"About three years, I guess, but as soon as I have enough money I want to buy my passage to Australia."

"My older brothers are thinking of that too - they hope to go to Canada. I think it sounds so frightening, and so far away."

"That's true, Rachael, I feel that way sometimes," agreed Clifford. "But I don't have enough education to do anything interesting here, so I might as well take this chance."

"Thanks for the visit, Clifford, and here is your list. I must get back to the manor."

Rachael ran all the way back to the manor kitchen and was quite out of breath when she arrived. "I hope I haven't been away too long, Maisie. I had a visit with Clifford while he was polishing the auto."

"That's fine lass. It's good for ye to be curious about what everyone does here. Ye have assisted Bronwyn several times in serving Sir Gordon in the dining room," Maisie added. "Do ye feel ready to do that service yourself now, Rachael?"

"If you think I am ready, Maisie, I will do my best."

"Starting this evening then, ye can help Bronwyn with Sir Gordon's dinner as usual, and clean up. Then ye will be required to make tea later in the evening and serve it to Sir Gordon in his study. It may be late – even eleven o'clock, but it is part of all the duties we have here, and ye and Bronwyn will now take turns with it. If there is sherry or whisky to be served, Duncan will do that."

"What will I do between clean up and making tea?"

"There'll be silver to polish and Ah will leave a list for ye for a little while. When ye've been here for a bit longer, ye'll just know what has to be done. Mrs. Olson will make requests too."

"Goodness, there's no chance of being bored here, Maisie!"

"It will soon be routine. Ye're doing well, Rachael, but sometimes an easy task can bring unexpected problems. It's good to remember that," Maisie cautioned.

Later, as Rachael was busy polishing silver, Sir Gordon's bell rang for tea. She jumped up to put the kettle on and to arrange the tea service on a tray. Rachael was nervous, it was late and she was tired. When all was ready, she took a deep breath and hurried to Sir Gordon's study. As she entered the room her toe caught the outside edge of the carpet and she tumbled forward – tea tray and all!

"Ah, someone new!" said Sir Gordon.

Rachael scrambled to her feet, making an attempt to gather up the wreckage of the scattered tea tray.

"Duncan will pick this up, young lady. Did you hurt yourself when you fell?"

"No, Sir Gordon."

"You would not likely tell me if you were hurt, would you?"

"No, Sir Gordon."

"Come sit for a minute, then you can make more tea. I see you are limping."

"I'm fine really, Sir, and so sorry."

"Mrs. Olson told me there is a new helper in the kitchen. What is your name?"

"My name is Rachael Atkinson, Sir. I have been here for a month."

"Is that so. I'm glad to meet you Rachael. If you feel up to it, I would like my tea."

"Yes, Sir Gordon, I will get it right away!"

"But don't hurry Rachael, it's late and Duncan will not mind returning the tray to the kitchen."

"Yes, thank you Sir."

Rachael was so upset about dropping the tray, she was very careful with the second attempt. She found Sir Gordon bent over his writing and he did not seem to notice that she was back again with his tea.

"Good night, Rachael," he said, looking up. "I will leave a note for Mrs. Olson to check with you in the morning to make sure you are not hurt."

"Thank you, Sir. Good night."

Rachael slipped on her night dress quickly, and went immediately to bed. Her leg did hurt, but not as much as her spirit. *I wish Todd was here so we could talk about this.* She wept for her old home and her old life, but soon fell into an exhausted sleep.

The following morning as Jean Olson sat at her desk and read over the note from Sir Gordon, she pondered her role in speaking with Rachael. She had been to the place where Rachael fell and noticed the carpet had been dislodged that day by a trolley while moving a cabinet into Sir Gordon's study. It was easy for her to see how the accident happened. Jean also recognized her own responsibility in this incident by not checking to see the cabinet had been moved safely without causing damage. She had an uncomfortable responsibility, and she must deal with it directly herself rather than leaving it for Maisie to patch things up on her behalf as, she had to admit, often happened.

Jean rapped on the bedroom door and, getting no response, entered to find Rachael fast asleep. The trauma of the prior evening was evident on her tear stained face, with her hair tousled and bed covers right under her chin. "Rachael" she called softly.

Instantly awake, Rachael was shocked and frightened to see Mrs. Olson standing beside the bed, and she sat up with dreaded anticipation. Jean pulled the small chair over and sat to be close to Rachael. "I want to check to see if you have been hurt from your fall last evening," she said.

"No, I'm fine – really, Mrs. Olson," Rachael gasped.

"I'm not so convinced, and I want to explain that what happened is really my fault, and I need to apologize to you."

"You do?"

"Yes Rachael, I should have noticed the carpet had been pulled back when a trolley had been used to move a cabinet into Sir Gordon's office earlier in the day. Sir Gordon would not have noticed it either as he enters his study by another door."

"I see, Mrs. Olson, and I am grateful for your apology," Rachael said with relief, "but I need to watch where I'm going as well."

"I must also ensure that the late night tea-time for Sir Gordon is thought out in a better way," continued Mrs. Olson. "I know, from what Maisie tells me, you are wearing yourself out trying to accomplish more than your share each day. I can understand why you are doing that, but it is not necessary or expected of you, Rachael, and we will try to correct what is not working. I will speak to Sir Gordon about this incident as well, he is a fair man."

"You are brave to do that, Mrs. Olson, and I respect you for it."

"So, no more worries, and let's see how your leg feels when you stand."

Nothing more was said about the unfortunate tea-serving incident, but Rachael felt more trust and good will toward Mrs. Olson. This was valuable to her as she felt supported and her self-confidence grew along with her comfort in being a member of the household staff.

After her meeting with Sir Gordon, Jean Olson was given the Christmas envelopes to be distributed to her staff, and she was pleased that Sir Gordon had remembered to include one for Rachael.

In a casual moment, Jean Olson told the staff of Sir Gordon's wish to have a New Years party to entertain his friends of former times. Duncan and his wife, Margaret, would assist him as hosts, Jean and her staff would be on hand throughout to ensure the party's success as well as to feel part of the celebration. Jean and Maisie were delighted. Once again, the manor would be a place of entertaining and excitement. They would begin planning with Sir Gordon immediately.

The manor kitchen was all a bustle as Maisie prepared for the annual baking of Christmas cake as well as her famous Plum Pudding with Brandied Cider Sauce. She reserved Bronwyn and Rachael's exclusive time for three days; they would carry, chop and stir, ready the pans and assist with the delicious task of icing the cakes with almond paste. Next would be the wrapping and packaging of the individual cakes for Clifford to begin his delivery rounds to resident farmers. Duncan would make deliveries to friends and associates of Sir Gordon. As well, the manor staff would each receive a cake and a plum pudding.

On his next visit to the manor, Todd found Rachael in happy spirits, and she asked if they could go to visit Aggie. She had arranged to have some time off the following Sunday afternoon and she would take her Christmas cake and pudding along as gifts. At the manor, Rachael had been introduced to the special Scottish word – Hogmanay, and the traditional gift of cake for the New Year. It would be exciting to take the train to Locksbury with Todd, and to feel the excitement of the approaching New Year 1899!

The following Sunday, as they walked to the train through the falling snow, Rachael was bursting with happiness to be with her brother on this excursion. She had bundled herself in her mother's shawl and she was wearing the butterfly clip Todd had given her to fasten her long hair back, as Bronwyn had suggested. She chatted with Todd about the wonderful gift from Sir Gordon, and about the excitement the staff felt with the plans for a New Years party to be hosted at the manor.

Todd was quiet as they trudged along; he didn't want to share his anxiety about going to Aggie's home, and to be confronted again by Robbie. He wanted the afternoon to be special for Rachael.

As they approached the miners' row, Todd and Rachael felt a sharp dislocation and the day seemed suddenly colder and more dismal. It was all such a sad reminder of a family split apart, and how difficult the past few months had been.

As Aggie responded to the rap on the door, she was overjoyed to see her brother and sister smiling happily in greeting. She clung to them until she finally realized they would be only with her for a few hours and there was so much to talk about. She shared the latest letter from Billy and Joey, and all were amazed at how a new life had evolved for their elder brothers. Rachael couldn't wait to tell Aggie about her work at the manor and how everyone was so kind to her. She gave the gifts to Aggie and told her that she had helped make the cake. Aggie was in tears as she heard all of this wonderful news, and she wished she could keep these two loved ones closer to her. She was so proud of them.

Aggie explained that the children were having their afternoon nap. She wanted to relate all that had happened since Todd's last visit, but didn't want the children to overhear it. She shared that Robbie was not there now and had not been home in more than a fortnight. He had left as soon as Aggie began having birth pains, and she had to ask her neighbour for help. As the day wore on, it was evident that there was a problem with the birth, and the neighbour summoned the resident doctor at the infirmary where Aggie was admitted overnight. In the morning, the child came but only lived for a few minutes. "The tiny boy was buried next day beside his Grandma Kate," Aggie sobbed.

Todd and Rachael sat in silence and desperate sympathy for Aggie, knowing there was nothing they could do to help. Aggie then told them that she had contacted their Aunt Aggie in Dundee to explain her plight. A messenger had come that very morning with an envelope containing train fares to Dundee for Aggie and the children, and Aggie supposed this was the only choice she had - she would start getting belongings together next day, and they would go.

"But," she said, "you are here now and we must enjoy each other for the rest of your visit." She made tea, and Rachael cut pieces of cake.

As the train made its lumbering way toward Dundee, Aggie was filled with mixed emotions. Desperately poor as she was in the mining community, it had been her home. She had her children to care for as she saw fit, there were problems to solve, and she had the distinction of being the eldest child of her parents.

She also knew her mother recognized all that her sister, Aggie Sr., had given up to run the family home after their mother died. She had taken over smoothly, doting on her father as her mother had done, as well as raising three siblings as if they were her own. But Aggie's mother was the independent one and wanted to be out from under her older sister's care and domination. Her marriage to a coal miner was not looked on approvingly, but Aggie Sr. was a welcome visitor to the home, and the children always looked forward to her arrival.

When Aggie's grandfather died, she had been with her mother to attend the funeral. That was the only time she remembered visiting her mother's family home in Dundee.

Taking the omnibus from the train, she hoped she could remember what the home looked like, but as soon as it came into view she recognized the old grey stone house immediately. Any misgivings she had about the reception she would receive evaporated as her aunt enveloped Aggie and the children in her arms. Aggie knew this was where they needed to be. Her children, Peter and Mary, would be safe and well cared for here.

The manor's great room was reopened, and Bronwyn and Rachael were occupied in a flurry of activity as lounges and chairs were uncovered, tables and cabinets as well as the grand piano were dusted and polished to a brilliant shine. Clifford was recruited to help lift the heavy carpets for airing out of doors, and they were then carefully put back in place. Mrs. Olson and Maisie poured over the elaborate menu for the banquet, as well as planning an assortment of hors d'oeuvres to be served in the later evening. Duncan inspected the wine cellars for the best in vintage wines and spirits. Flowers needed to be ordered, and a harpist chosen to play the classics as well as the best in Scottish tunes throughout the evening.

Rachael was overcome with the splendour of it all. Bronwyn and Rachael were to wear white cotton serving dresses with ruffles at neckline and sleeves, complemented with tartan sashes. Maisie's serving dress would have a plain neckline, and would have a tartan shoulder sash. Mrs. Olson would wear her best black formal gown with a necklace of pearls. She would be in charge of comforts for the ladies, and Clifford would wear a new tartan scarf as he tended to the carriages and horses of the guests. Duncan, of course, would be in formal attire. Sir Gordon approved of all these plans and spent his time with Duncan and Mrs. Olson going over the guest list. The gaiety was infectious and Sir Gordon contributed details as well as accepting gratefully all the plans proposed by the manor staff.

New Years Eve was clear and cold, with a full moon and newly fallen snow. "This is so exciting," exclaimed Rachael to Bronwyn.

Bronwyn agreed, but with less enthusiasm. "I must stay, of course," she said, "… but I was hoping to spend this New Year celebration with my friend, Geordie. He will be going away the end of the week to find work in the south of England."

"Do you mean Geordie is like your beau?" Rachael asked.

"Well, yes that is true, we have talked of marriage when I am eighteen, but that is still a year away."

"But what a lovely time to look forward to, and he will write to you often. The time will go quickly," assured Rachael.

"I hope you are right," said Bronwyn, "but for now, we must get our special serving costumes on and decide how we would like to wear our hair. I will brush your hair, Rachael, and it will look lovely with your special butterfly clip holding your hair at the back."

"Thank you, Bronwyn," said Rachael, as she reminded her friend of Maisie's request to meet with them before the guests started to arrive.

After the party moved from the banquet to the great room, Rachael heard the piano being played and a lady with a lovely voice singing a song she had never heard before. She entered the dining room again so that she could get closer to the music and, as she strained to listen, the words became clearer:

Oh, my love's like a red, red rose that's newly sprung in June;
Oh, my love's like a melody that's sweetly played in tune.
As fair art thou, my bonnie lass; so deeply in love am I,

And I will love thee still my dear, 'till a' the seas gang dry.
Till a' the seas gang dry, my dear, while the sand o' life shall run.
And fare thee well, my only love, and fare thee well a while!
And I will come again, my love, tho' it were ten thousand mile.

Rachael had never heard anything as beautiful as the song; the words and music lingered with her as she lay in bed that night. There was a lightness of heart she had not felt in a long time.

The first day of classes at South Aberdeen Secondary School found Todd in a quandary of feelings. He hoped the day would not be too long and tiring for Malcolm; at the same time he was apprehensive about fitting into the practical and social milieu of the school. After formal on-site registration, he was directed to a classroom on the first floor where the students were welcomed back after the holiday break. His name was called, among a number of other newcomers, which he happily acknowledged. The routine began, and as the last class of the day ended, he headed out immediately and biked as fast as he could to Malcolm's shop.

Malcolm met Todd at the door, handing him a delivery request. "Hurry back Todd boy," he said. "I want to hear all about the first day at school. Mrs. Cronin has fixed a special supper for us, and a birthday cake has been delivered from Rachael!"

When he returned to the shop, Todd was anxious to tell Malcolm about the events of the day, but he wanted to know how Malcolm got along without his help.

"Ah did fine, Todd boy, it was pretty quiet here. But let's talk about school and birthdays – thirteen is it? Ah don't have much for ye, except that the bike is ye'rs, for your birthday."

"You have been so kind and generous to me, Malcolm. I accept the bike with great pleasure; it will be treasured forever."

"So, let's enjoy this wonderful dinner and the cake Rachael has made," said Malcolm, moving slowly to the table from his leather chair. "Later, we'll have tea and a drink to the great future Ah know ye'll have."

"You are such a big part of my life now, Malcolm, it will be your future too."

Todd noticed that Malcolm ate little of the dinner, and shortly left the table, returning to his old chair looking tired and pale. Todd did not comment on what he was observing, but got up and put the kettle on for tea. It was time for Malcolm to be seen by a doctor, but he knew it would be useless to mention it to him.

As the days moved along in the New Year 1899, Rachael became more confident and efficient about her work – but always remembering, with a sad smile, the evening she stumbled over the threshold of Sir Gordon's study, spilling the tea tray. One evening as she was serving him his late tea break, he looked up and acknowledged her and asked how she enjoyed working in the kitchen. She, of course, assured him that she enjoyed it, and that it was nice to work with such pleasant people.

"I want to tell you, Sir Gordon: I happened to hear the song that was sung so wonderfully at your New Years party. I thought it was the loveliest music I had ever heard."

"Well, that's so nice of you to comment on it, Rachael! The singer was my sister, Bonny. I asked her to sing a Robby Burns poem set to music. That particular one is my favourite. Are you familiar with the writing of Robert Burns?" he asked.

"To tell you the truth, Sir, I've never heard of him. There was no music or poetry taught at the school near my home."

"Oh, that is a shame, Rachael, and a great failing of our education system!" exclaimed Sir Gordon. "I have several books of Burns' poems in the library that you are most welcome to read when your duties are finished for the day."

"Thank you, Sir."

When Jean Olson was summoned to Sir Gordon's study, she was surprised to find that Rachael was the subject of his enquiry. "This young girl should be in school, Jean; we could be in a bit of hot water if it was evident we are

Golden Ribbons

paying for her services in the kitchen. This has to do with the new child labour laws that, incidentally, I have been a proponent of for a very long time."

"As you know, Sir Gordon, Rachael is an orphan. I have no idea what status that gives her with the school system."

"It should give her every consideration, but rules are cast in stone. I will check to make sure, but I believe there is a ruling now of *half-timer* that enables children under the age of thirteen to attend school minimally, and still contribute to the paltry income of so many households. I am frankly impressed with that young lady," continued Sir Gordon. "She shows a keen interest in literature and music, and I'm sure she excelled in all of the three R's when she did attend school. What a tragedy to be left on her own at that age!"

"Yes, and she is an excellent worker – so willing to accommodate to any changing situation. We all enjoy her youth and enthusiasm."

"So Jean, let's see what we can work out. Rachael will need a few shillings of her own, so we could call that her *half-timer* wages. I would certainly not want to see her thrown into an elementary classroom with children who are just waiting to leave school permanently. We should have a meeting again in a few days, so come back with some ideas," directed Sir Gordon. "This matter must be settled for Rachael very soon."

Malcolm decided to pay a call to his old friend, Doctor Henry Wilkins at the infirmary. "Wonderful to see you, Malcolm!" said Doctor Wilkins. "I've been wondering how you've been getting on with that new lad you have working for you. He certainly knows how to conduct himself when making medication deliveries – always enquiring as to the patient's well-being, and they appreciate it! He is making himself very popular with the medical staff here as well."

"Ah'm glad of that, Henry, and it's working out well for me. Ah do have a reason for ma long over-due visit today," Malcolm explained. "Ah'm not feeling that well these days, and maybe it's time to have a check up to and see what's the matter with me."

"Can you tell me more about it?" asked Doctor Wilkins.

"Ah'm just tired most of the time, no appetite, and upset stomach. Maybe just getting auld and worn down."

"I don't want to see you worn down, Malcolm, you are just too important to us here at the infirmary," assured Doctor Wilkins. "You are also highly respected in this city and I suspect we are neglectful in showing appreciation most of the time. So let's see what can be done about making you feel better; ...suppose I could recommend a tonic of some kind to give you a boost, but let's talk a bit about how you're living these days.

"I hear you have sponsored Todd to enable him to attend secondary school, and that's a wonderful thing you've done," said Doctor Wilkins. "But Malcolm, this whole relationship you have established with Todd is a major change in your life! A wonderful change of course, but you have had such an isolated existence for so many years, it would be tough on any of us old gents to move into what is essentially a parent role. I appreciate you coming to talk to me about it, Malcolm, because that's what is needed – talking about it. Not only that, but when was the last time you set a foot out of your shop? I prescribe a good half hour walk outside every day. How about if we meet at the pub periodically for a cup of tea – or anything else you would like, say in the late afternoon when Todd is home from school. Todd might like some time to himself as well," he suggested. "No doubt he will have reading and assignments to attend to. Perhaps you two can sit down together and work out a new schedule in the interest of both."

"Ah'm sure you are right, Henry, but don't think it will be easy for me to change ma ways," sighed Malcolm. "Who would have thought Malcolm Murray would find himself in this position!"

"Well," said Doctor Wilkins, "miracles do happen. Let's keep in touch."

"I will do the deliveries when we are finished eating, Malcolm," said Todd. "Is there anything I should pick up for you?"

"No, Ah'm fine, Todd boy. Ah will get out of ye'r way this evening and go for a walk. Have they loaded ye down with home study and assignments?" asked Malcolm.

"Actually they have," agreed Todd, "but nothing too serious yet."

When Jean Olson next met with Sir Gordon regarding Rachael's, and their own, predicament, it was recognized that Rachael would require someone to be her guardian until age thirteen, and even beyond. "If Rachael is to remain here," said Jean Olson, "I'm afraid that *someone* must be yourself, Sir Gordon, since this is your home and you are the ratepayer that is specified in the rule book."

"I was afraid that might be the case, Jean. There is no way around it," said Sir Gordon. "I certainly don't want to turn Rachael out onto the streets; therefore, the only other option would be to hire a tutor and for Rachael to do her lessons here. It would be none of the Education Department's business who is paying for the tutor - I think we could by-pass them altogether."

"That sets up a strong obligation, Sir," Jean cautioned. "I suppose we must see what Rachael thinks about the plan."

CHAPTER FOUR

A NOISY SCUFFLE COULD BE HEARD AT THE FRONT MANOR DOOR. "A good Happy New Year to ye, my Duncan lad! Is Popsy at home?"

"I don't believe Sir Gordon is expecting you, Mr. Blaine."

"Goodness, Duncan lad, of course Popsy expects me at any time, this is my home!"

Brushing past Duncan, the unexpected visitor rushed down the main hall and right into Sir Gordon – knocking him against the wall. "Popsy! How are you?" Blaine exclaimed with his hand outreached.

"What are you doing here, Blaine? I told you never to enter this house again," Sir Gordon said, with controlled outrage.

"But Popsy, this is my home. What would Mumsy say about your rudeness?"

"You didn't even come back for your mother's funeral. I'm not worried about what she would think of you, I did not want to ever see your smirking face again."

"Now Popsy, I didn't want to embarrass you," stated Blaine. "After all, I am a bastard. What would your noble friends think?"

As Duncan moved forward in an attempt to physically remove him, Blaine ducked farther down the hall into the kitchen. Jean Olson's back stiffened as she recognized Blaine's voice from the front hall, and the sadly predictable clash with Sir Gordon. Blaine had not been back to the manor since before his mother's death.

"Mrs. Olson! Come give us a big love," said Blaine, holding out his arms in an exaggerated manner.

"Watch your attitude around my staff!" Mrs. Olson said angrily.

"Ooo, how important we've become. Now, who is this gentle rose?" said Blaine, looking at Rachael.

Golden Ribbons

"One who can prick!" Rachael said firmly.

"How feisty for a lowly kitchen wench," said Blaine, with surprise.

As Blaine moved to approach Bronwyn, Rachael blocked his way with the toe of her boot and Blaine stumbled forward – hitting his head on the cutting block's jagged edge.

"I'll get you for this, you sodden little trollop!" he shouted. His forehead was bleeding and he grabbed a kitchen towel to cover it. Turning, he was about to raise his fist to Rachael when Duncan appeared to grab Blaine's jacket from behind.

"Blaine!" roared Sir Gordon. "Get back here and deal with me directly and finally!"

Blaine was now bleeding profusely as he charged back into the hallway. "Oh, you'll deal with me alright, Popsy!" he said. "Remember now, I am your dearly beloved bastard step-son. I'll be demanding my bounty from the spoils you leave behind – which to God will be sooner than later!"

As Duncan and Clifford each took an arm to lift him off the floor, Blaine was rushed out the door and down the walk to a waiting carriage.

"Take him to the railway station immediately, and see that he has a one-way ticket to London," Duncan ordered. "I will follow along to pay, and to see that he is on his way."

Blaine called out finally: "See you in Court, Popsy, you old goat."

By the time Duncan returned to say that Blaine was well on his way, Sir Gordon had composed himself sufficiently to ask that all the staff meet him in his study. "First of all," said Sir Gordon, "I want to apologize to all of you for that inexcusable and outrageous incident. For the benefit of our new staff members, I will explain that the intruder was my late wife's illegitimate son. When you love someone as dearly as I did my wife, one is inclined to disregard undesirable attachments that come with a marriage commitment. I tried to build a parental relationship with Blaine but, as he was already fourteen years of age and had built up long standing resentments and lack of trust, I finally conceded that our relationship would always be troublesome. Duncan and Mrs. Olson can attest to the many unpleasant encounters with Blaine over the years."

Speaking to Duncan and Jean Olson, Sir Gordon added: "I have appreciated your loyalty through it all, and I speak of Maisie as well, since she is not here today. Actually, Maisie could always put Blaine in his place," he smiled, "She may wish she had been here to confront him today."

No more was said about the incident, but Rachael was uneasy about it. She wondered how Sir Gordon could possibly have treated Blaine badly in the past. The conflict between the two must surely be with Blaine. She would not forget Blaine's look of anger as he turned to hit her, but there was also a look of fear. As she thought about that later, she felt sorry for him.

"Atkinson, could I ask that your paper be read to the class?" asked the head master. "I'm referring to the one you wrote about the mutation of bacteria causing infectious diseases."

"Yes, I don't mind, Sir, bearing in mind that my guardian is a chemist and there are excellent journal resources in the shop."

"I understand that, Atkinson, but I happen to own the article you refer to. The class can be assured that this is an authentic paper – no plagiarism here."

Taylor glared at Todd with pursed lips, and signalled to two others.

Todd was determined not to show uneasiness around Taylor whose feelings were becoming obvious. At close of class for the day, Todd left first, saluting the others and wishing them a cheery good afternoon. "See you tomorrow," he said.

"You bet your boots you'll see us, Atkinson!" Taylor smirked, as he poked ribs of the other two, who laughed on cue.

Todd asked Malcolm if he would like a companion on his walk that late afternoon.

"Why, o'course, Todd boy, Ah would like that very much," said Malcolm.

As they headed off toward the sea trail, Todd found that Malcolm was moving along at a good pace. "I'm glad you seem to be feeling better, Malcolm."

"Yes, Ah am, and Doctor Wilkins' prescription to walk daily has given me a lot more energy. But he didn't say when Ah could quit!" Malcolm laughed.

Golden Ribbons

"I'll keep watch over that," Todd returned. Todd was so happy to find their friendship easy and relaxed. He was feeling that he loved this old fellow.

"Malcolm, I think I'm headed for trouble with this lad, Taylor, at school. He makes no secret that he would like to harm me in some way."

"He has a following no doubt," suggested Malcolm.

"Yes, it would appear that way. He can be very threatening to them as well as to me."

"About all ye can do, Todd boy, is to watch out for him when ye're coming and going, and he will no doubt try to push it as far as he can. He is probably jealous of the attention ye are getting – especially as the head master has made an example of ye'r work. Not really a wise thing to do to a new lad, in ma opinion. But, just be ye'rself, Todd boy, you can't do better than that."

"Thanks old friend," said Todd, his arm on Malcolm's shoulder.

―――――――

"Gosh, I like your bike, Atkinson," said Taylor. "I sure would not want anything to happen to it, for your sake, of course."

"Of course," said Todd, moving to his seat.

At the end of the afternoon class, Todd felt he would get away safely as he waved the class good-bye. *Maybe lucky this time,* he thought.

As Todd was about to swing onto his bike, Coach Robinson stopped him to enquire about his classes, and if he would have time to try out for the soccer team.

"Thanks for asking, Coach Robinson, but believe I will leave that until start of the fall classes. I'm still becoming oriented to the school routine."

"We'll talk about it then," agreed the coach.

Todd pedalled the bike along faster than usual as he knew Malcolm had an appointment and would be expecting him back in time to watch the shop. As he turned swiftly around a sharp corner, bordered on each side by tall hedges, he suddenly lost control of the bike and was swept backward – crashing hard against the cobblestone street.

"Ha, ha, ha," came cackling laughs from one side. But suddenly it stopped; it was apparent that Todd was not getting up. Taylor and his friends disappeared as a carriage and team of horses came around the bend. The driver pulled back sharply and narrowly missed where Todd was lying. A passenger got out of the carriage and began to see what could be done. Todd appeared to be unconscious. Asking for assistance from another passenger, he immediately asked that the back of the carriage be let down, and the two men carefully put Todd inside and headed for the infirmary.

"This is not like Todd to be late when he knew he is needed," thought Malcolm. Pacing back and forth, he wondered what had happened when he noticed Sergeant McTavish walking up the path.

"Todd had an accident after school, Malcolm. Come along and Ah'll try to explain as Ah take you over to the infirmary."

"What happened?" whispered Malcolm, clearly distressed.

"It would seem that he lost control of the bike and flipped backwards," explained the Sergeant. "A carriage was just coming around that particular sharp bend and it narrowly missed him. Ah got the report of it from the carriage driver. We will investigate later."

"Dear God!" said Malcolm, "and Rachael must be told."

"Ah have already been over to the manor," said the Sergeant. "Mr. Duncan said he would take Rachael to the infirmary directly. She will be there with Todd now."

"Thank you, Sergeant," said Malcolm.

"Hello, Mr. Murray," called Rachael. "Todd has still not wakened, but he will Mr. Murray, I just know it! Todd can survive anything. We both love him so much."

Malcolm nodded, his head bowed.

"This is hard news, Malcolm," said Doctor Wilkins, as he put an arm around his old friend. "It's a bad concussion but we will hope the very best for this wonderful young man. You will want to stay, as Rachael is. I will get blankets, and there are two arm chairs here. Perhaps you both would like something from the kitchen?" Malcolm shook his head.

"Thank you, Doctor Wilkins," said Rachael.

Golden Ribbons

The hours passed, and still Todd did not respond to the strong light focussed on his eyes. Doctor Wilkins came back before midnight and found Rachael asleep, but Malcolm sitting up – his eyes had never left Todd for a moment.

"He is a strong lad, Malcolm, and I believe he is giving it all he has to regain consciousness," assured Doctor Wilkins. "His blood pressure and pulse are good and no sign of fracture. You must get some rest, or at least go outside for a bit to get some fresh air."

Malcolm nodded and moved to the door leading to the front street and the familiar trail along the sea. He recalled that just the previous evening he had walked the same winding trail with Todd. As he stood looking out at the North Sea, an unusual calm on the waters, he was suddenly overtaken with fear and panic.

"Whatever ye'r name is up there," he shouted, looking up into the starry sky, "surely ye'r not going to let me down again!" Then he sunk to his knees and wept, "Dear God, please don't let Todd die."

Later, as he rose to his feet, a faint light was glowing along the horizon. "It's almost morning," he said. "Ah must get back."

> *I'm coming down to get you, Da!* Todd was slipping down and down, faster and
> faster. *It's too late, son, don't come down. You get on home now, Todd, you will be needed at home. Go home Todd ... Go home Todd ... Go home Todd.*

"Oh Todd, you are awake!" cried Rachael. I will get Doctor Wilkins, but I don't know where Mr. Murray is." Rachael rushed away to find the doctor.

Malcolm found a strange peace and lightness in his bones as he crossed the street to the infirmary. "Ah know Todd is awake!" he exclaimed.

The evidence was not too difficult to see. A rope was dangling from the hedge on one side of the road; on the other side, a branch of the hedge was broken away. Todd's bike had been removed and was propped against one side.

"The frame is badly bent, but nothing that can't be fixed," said the Sergeant to the accompanying officer. "We can drop it off at the repair shop. It would seem that we should pay a call to the school this morning."

"Hello Todd, it's Doctor Wilkins. Do you remember me?"

"Yes, of course, Doctor Wilkins, but what am I doing here?"

"You had a bad fall, Todd, and you've been unconscious for about twelve to fourteen hours. But I'm glad you were able to recognize me so soon after wakening. We're moving in the right direction. I am going to assign a resident to be with you for the rest of today to guide you gently back to full consciousness, and we will keep you here for two more days after that just to make sure you are fit to go home. Do you understand that, and feeling alright about it?"

"Yes, but I …"

"Actually, I would prefer you not talk right now, and not move any more than you have to," interjected Doctor Wilkins. "The resident, Tom is his name, will be asking you questions slowly and monitoring your responses. In a little while he can tell you all about your accident. He will also get you to the bathroom and back into bed whenever the need arises. Good going, Todd! We were all very worried about you. It was a bad concussion and we want you to have a full recovery without any setbacks. Rachael and Malcolm have been coaxed into leaving you for today, and they will come back tomorrow."

Todd's homecoming was a special occasion for Malcolm, he could hardly suppress his joy. Todd was glad, as well, to get back home and to a normal routine, even though he knew that both Malcolm and Doctor Wilkins would be determining the day of his return to school. Gifts for Todd arrived at the shop: fresh baked scones, knitted woollen socks, as well as many good wishes from Malcolm's grateful customers who were concerned about Todd and had missed his delivery visits.

Sergeant McTavish returned the bike from the repair shop, waiving off the fee. "Ah'm just glad ye're still with us Todd," he said.

"These lovely scones will come in handy when we have Rachael here for tea today, Todd boy," Malcolm said, as casually as he could manage.

"You mean Rachael will be here today!" Todd was delighted. "But how will she get here, and back to the manor again?"

"Auld Malcolm figured that one out all by himself," he chuckled. "The boy who works there – Clifford, will walk with Rachael, and then Mr. Duncan will call for her after he has delivered Sir Gordon to the theatre at Cowdray Hall."

"Brilliant!" said Todd.

The three happy spirits sat around the hearth in Malcolm's shop enjoying each other's company over tea and scones, reliving Todd's accident, and expressing relief with his recovery.

"Ah'l just get away now and have ma walk while the day is still warm," said Malcolm. He felt Todd and Rachael should have some private time together before Mr. Duncan would call for her. The days were getting longer, with buds appearing on the trees along the sea trail. Malcolm was full of joy with the approaching spring.

Identical letters were sent to Aggie, Todd and Rachael as their brothers, Billy and Joey, sat in The Tub of Ale, a cosy pub on the outskirts of Melrose.

"Here, you copy this first page while I write the next, and then we'll switch around," Joey suggested to Billy. "Before we know it, the letters will be posted and on their way."

Joey reflected, with the miles between them, how vitally important to keep in touch with letters, that there could still be an Atkinson family after all. He looked across at Billy and thought, but could not put into words, *How lucky I am to have a brother with me, and that we have the same goals and outlandish dreams! Alone, it could never happen.*

> Dear Aggie (Peter and Mary), Todd and Rachael. It's my turn to write again. We brothers are sitting in a most jolly pub on our Saturday afternoon from work. Saturday afternoons, as you can guess, are special times to get together and plan. It is also an occasion to remember all of you, and we enjoy your letters more than you can imagine.

Our plans have taken a turn lately, and we will now leave for Canada sooner than we originally told you. There are small steamers coming and leaving regularly from the Clyde that connect with larger ones at the main port of Liverpool. We hope to be on one of them by early summer. These are cargo ships as well as mail carriers, and we can pay our way by loading coal into the big ovens that keep the ship going. We will be assigned shifts to do this work once we are on board ship. This may, or may not, get us to Montreal and the long train trip to the prairies while there is still some warm weather, or at least before winter. We are hearing rumours of winter temperatures falling as low as minus forty degrees. Hopefully that is only a rumour, or at least rarely happens.

This is great news, Todd! We hope the best for you in secondary school. Please keep us posted about your plans. And darling Rachael: how proud we are of you, but most of all that you are happy and working with kindly people. Aggie: Our love and thoughts go with you and the children as you make your way to Dundee. We send our love to Aunt Aggie as well. PLEASE, keep the letters coming. We will do the same.

Love from your brother Joey

Jean Olson caught up with Rachael as she was peeling potatoes in the pantry off the kitchen. "Could you come now Rachael, and meet with me and Sir Gordon. Don't bother to change your apron – just a quick meeting in Sir Gordon's study."

"Oh certainly," said Rachael with surprise. "Are you sure about the apron? This one is a bit dirty."

"That one will be fine - you will be right back here again in a few minutes," Jean answered. Rachael smoothed down her apron, took off her hair covering, and looked at the state of her hair in the big copper kettle as she hurried along after Mrs. Olson.

"Please sit down, ladies," said Sir Gordon. "First of all, Rachael, I hope your brother is back to his old self again. That was a nasty situation."

"Yes, Sir Gordon, Todd is back to school again, and all going well, thank you."

"Rachael, I have met with Mrs. Olson recently to discuss your schooling if you are to remain with us at the manor." Rachael looked up anxiously.

"And, yes, we want you to stay," he assured her. "It will involve a commitment from you as well as from Mrs. Olson. This is what we are proposing: instead of returning to school for half days, a tutor will be hired to instruct you two afternoons a week, for two hours of each day that a tutor is available. This will allow us to legally have you work at the manor as a *half-timer*, as the Education Department calls it. The schooling through a tutor will include the basic education, just as you had before. I want you to think about it until tomorrow and then tell us what your decision is. I have to say, Rachael, that everyone wants you to stay here, and that includes me."

Rachael sat motionless for a few moments, fighting tears. "I am so happy at the manor, Sir, I hardly know how to answer. I appreciate having a day to think about it, but it will certainly be yes! How can I even express how thankful I am?" she sobbed.

Sir Gordon offered his handkerchief. "Let us hear from you tomorrow then, Rachael."

Later, as Rachael had a chance to digest the offer given to her, she realized that she did have some questions about it. "Mrs. Olson, may I speak to you for a few minutes?"

"Certainly, come in," invited Jean Olson.

"I was just wondering about the offer given to me, and how it would affect my duties here at the manor."

"I'm so glad you are asking that question," Jean replied. "It is important that we understand how this plan will work, although it's something new for all of us. We will start out with tutoring as we suggested in the meeting. What I'm hoping you will do is design a typical day for yourself, and then let us see what you believe will be workable. Does that seem fair to you, Rachael?"

"That sounds really quite interesting. I will work on my response this evening in my room."

"Good for you, Rachael! This is the kind of working arrangement that will be most successful." Jean Olson smiled.

"Good to welcome you back, Atkinson," said the head master.

"Thank you, Sir,"

Todd was happy to be back at school, although he noticed that Taylor and his two friends were no longer there. *This is unfortunate,* he thought. *I wish none of that ugly situation had happened. I guess it's just another topic of discussion with Malcolm.*

"This is an excellent response from you, Rachael," Sir Gordon said. "It's very ambitious as well. Do you actually feel that your school work would not affect your duties at the manor?"

"I do, Sir Gordon, but it would have to be put into practise before I would know for sure," Rachael explained, "and there would also be the unexpected."

"I am a strong believer in expecting the unexpected, Rachael," Sir Gordon stressed. "Mrs. Olson will attempt to hire a tutor immediately."

Aggie watched as her children, Peter and Mary, played out in the garden, her aunt nearby. It was apparent her Aunt Aggie delighted in the children, and in turn they had grown rapidly within such a short time - both physically and socially. Before she joined the jubilant group, she paused to read the newspaper just delivered. Inside was an article written by a local doctor stating his delight in announcing there would be a school of nursing and midwifery built adjacent to the Home Road Hospital, construction to commence immediately.

At least I've had enough experience with home nursing and midwifery, thought Aggie. *But this would be excellent training, and working as a nurse almost too exciting to think about. I will mention it to Aunt Aggie when the school's construction is actually underway.*

Todd began to work on his assignment at the long table in the kitchen where he could spread out all his references. It was a big assignment this time and would take several evenings to complete. "Sorry I can't come along on your walk this time, Malcolm."

"Business b'fore pleasure, ma boy," replied Malcolm, as he pulled on his old jumper and headed out the back door. The daily walk with Malcolm was something Todd looked forward to. There was always something to talk over with him, and walking along together seemed to be the right time to do it.

As Todd poured over his books, a shadow crossed the window blocking out the light. A familiar face appeared and a fist started rapping at the window. "Oh No, it's Robby!" said Todd out loud. Opening the back door slightly, "What are you doing here, Robby?"

"Wha, Ah'm here ta visit ma fav'rit brother-in-law," Robby scoffed, as he pushed past Todd into the kitchen. "Ah know you took Aggie and the bairn out of the house on me, so you's better admit it and make it up to me."

"I did not take Aggie and the children away, Robby, and you know it! You abandoned them, even when Aggie was about to deliver the baby. You can get yourself out of here, and don't bother me again!"

"Ahh, big talk! Ah'm here to get paid out! The dole's been chopped in half with them's out of the house. How's a man to live, Ah'd like to know?"

"How about getting a job, like any useful person?" Todd's anger flared.

"Wha you… Let me help with your homework, Toddy baby," Robby sneered sarcastically, as he flung himself across Todd's papers – scattering them on the floor. "Ah know the old man is out for a walk, and that will give me time to find the cash box. And don't tell me you don't know where it is!"

Todd stood at the door of the shop in an attempt to stop what the next move appeared to be, but Robby knocked him to the floor as he rushed into the shop, looking wildly around for the counter. As he leapt over it, he started opening cabinets and throwing contents in every direction.

Malcolm returned, quietly opening the back door. "Get outa here, NOW, before Ah blow ye'r brains out!" roared Malcolm, holding a revolver straight at Robby.

Robby did exactly that, straight past Todd and out the back door. Todd was stunned by this turn of events. He looked at Malcolm's angry face, the revolver still in his hand. "I didn't know you owned a gun, Malcolm. And I didn't expect you back so soon, but thank goodness you did come back – just in time."

"Ah'v seen this bludger walking past the shop several times, and looking this way as though he might enter. Ah expect he's kept track of ma walks and how long Ah usually stay away. There was just a feeling this time… We'll leave the mess just as it is, lock up, and get on over to the precinct. Hopefully McTavish is there, but a constable can start tracking this tramp down, and he'll be charged with break-in and vandalising."

"I just seem to be causing you trouble all the time, Malcolm," Todd stated regretfully.

"That is trouble Ah would not be without, Todd boy. A slap at ye is a slap at me, that's the way friends operate. But let's talk about guns on another walk together, Todd boy. Ah'm guessing ye are puzzled that Ah own one. There are times when Ah wonder why Ah own one as well. Ah need to know what ye think about it."

"I'm just glad the gun scared Robby off," Todd replied, "but how I feel about it in a general way… I don't know."

"I have a sad announcement to make," said Jean Olson. "Bronwyn will be leaving us. She is planning to be married."

"That is wonderful," said Rachael, "but, of course, we will miss you."

"And I will miss all of you," said Bronwyn.

Rachael recalled Sir Gordon's words to always expect the unexpected. *I guess this is one of those times, though it is painful,* she thought. *Mrs. Olson will be hiring someone new, and that is too sad to think about.*

Golden Ribbons

"You look downcast, Rachael," Sir Gordon remarked. "Is something wrong?"

"It's just that Bronwyn is leaving and I will miss her," said Rachael, choking back tears as she served Sir Gordon his evening tea tray.

"Change is always painful, Rachael, especially when it is a relationship that we have counted on to always be there. But, one day we will all part company. In this house, we have had many partings. Then along came Rachael, and the sun came out again."

"You are so kind to say that, Sir."

"Are you finding interesting books to read, Rachael? Mrs. Olson said she had gathered a few she thought you would like."

"Oh yes, she has! I have just been reading the stories written by Han Christian Anderson. One in particular - <u>The Ugly Duckling</u>. I wonder, Sir, would Hans Christian Anderson be talking about himself in that story?"

"That has always been my thought about it. In what I have read about him, he seems to have been a person who felt he had no home, and he wasn't from anywhere."

"It's hard to imagine someone so famous thinking that of himself."

"It's often people who think deeply about life who also feel they are not at home in it. Does that make sense to you, Rachael?"

"Yes, I think so Sir."

"You might like to start selecting books yourself, Rachael. I feel you should have better access to books that appeal to you personally. Some of those volumes have been there since I was a child," Sir Gordon continued, "and others added throughout the years. I will be in my study around one o'clock tomorrow and I can show you the categories of books – that will narrow your search. That place is like a mausoleum, no one goes in there except me, and occasionally Duncan. Next day when your tutor comes, perhaps we can find a spot in the library that would be more inspiring for learning than getting together in the kitchen."

"That sounds wonderful, Sir. I have been in the library only to dust, but I have to admit I have lingered to admire the beauty of it."

"It will be my pleasure to share it with you. Good night Rachael."

"Good night, Sir."

As Rachael prepared for bed that night, she puzzled over her reaction to Bronwyn's leaving, and she felt Sir Gordon was trying to cheer her up by offering her the freedom to use the library at the manor. It did cheer her up, but still heaviness remained in her heart. Then she remembered that it would be her baby twins' birthday tomorrow, and they would be one year old and walking by now. Also, Robert would be three years old, and she had not remembered his birthday. She was so busy and happy helping with the New Years party, she had forgotten.

This is not right, she thought. She decided then and there to always send those dear ones loving thoughts every day. *They must think I've forgotten all about them, and then they will soon forget about me.*

"I am concerned about Rachael, Jean. She was on the verge of tears last evening. I think something about her family is bothering her or she would not be so upset about Bronwyn leaving."

"Yes, Sir Gordon, Maisie saw this as an over-reaction, and she hopes that Rachael might now feel like sharing more of her story. In addition to that Sir, I believe she is ready to take on more responsibility in the kitchen. I would like her to work more closely with Maisie in food preparation and baking."

"Good plan, Jean. Let's give her that chance and see how she gets on."

As they greeted each other the following morning, Jean Olson informed Rachael that she would be working more closely with Maisie from now on. "This is another wonderful opportunity to learn, Rachael. The manor is the envy of most other estates of the nobility in Aberdeenshire. Maisie is a well-known chef, and she could have a position anywhere, but chooses to be here - not only because of Sir Gordon's kindly nature, but because he treats all of us as a team, and we are to feel that this is our home."

"I'm happy to know all these things, Mrs. Olson," said Rachael. "I have so much to learn, aside from catching up with schooling. How wonderful it will be to work directly with Maisie!"

The following Sunday when Todd called for Rachael, she was able to relate the news that she would be assisting Maisie with cooking and baking from now on. "I guess one could say it is kind of a promotion, but I am happiest about spending more time with Maisie. She seems to understand me when I'm feeling sad. Do you ever get sad about the family, Todd, especially about our babies who we will never see again?"

"Yes, I think about them, but I try really hard to put all that behind me. We have our whole lives to look forward to, Rachael, and it's not that I don't care about family, it's just that they have their lives too. Would we want them to be often sad, or would we want them to remember us as we were at home?"

"Thank you, Todd, I do need to think that way. I guess I just need more time."

"So, shall we take a longer walk today?" suggested Todd, with an effort to cheer. "I read there is a band concert in the park today. It's the first one of the season!"

"Yes, Yes! I would love that."

"I wonder how we could get you a bicycle," he continued. "That way we could go exploring farther away than just this part of Aberdeen. I will ask about it at the bike shop, and of the people where I make deliveries. Someone may know of an opportunity to get one at a reasonable price. I have a few pounds saved up."

"And I would add to it all the money I have," said Rachael. "What a wonderful idea!"

"Another surprise, Sir Gordon," Duncan announced. "Clifford will be leaving us the end of May. He will help his mother to get settled with her sister, and that will enable him to be on his way to Australia. It does seem, Sir, that gone are the days when a young man would stay with a position all of his life!" he reflected sadly.

"Changing times, Duncan! The colonies and the United States continue to lure our good and capable men away from our shores for better opportunities elsewhere. But, if they are brave enough to start out and begin again, perhaps we as a country need to evaluate what such a loss is meant for all of us. One way we can start making this right is to have open access to education for all," Sir Gordon stated with a note of grim determination.

"Indeed Sir," agreed Duncan. "At the moment though, Sir Gordon, I believe it is my duty to find a replacement for Clifford's position. That will be a difficult task."

CHAPTER FIVE

RACHAEL WAS WORN OUT AFTER THE LONG WALK TO THE PARK and back to the manor, but she was happy and rewarded Todd for his good idea by giving him a hug.

"I guess Malcolm's resistance to *mushy stuff* is rubbing off on me, Rach," he said, pulling away.

"Okay, just on special occasions then," laughed Rachael. *I guess Todd is growing up and getting self-conscious,* she thought.

"Oh yes, Rachael, I must tell you: I promised Malcolm that next Sunday I will unpack a box of medications having just arrived. They will need to be labelled and shelved."

"Never mind, Todd, I will just read during my free hours."

"I have an idea: why don't you plan to read at the shop, you can read aloud to Malcolm while I'm working. He never reads books anymore because he says the print is too small and is a strain on his eyes."

"Alright then, I will enjoy reading to Mr. Murray."

"Before I go, how are you getting on with the tutor? Someone nice I hope."

"Oh yes, and you won't believe that it is Miss James, my teacher at Locksbury School!" Rachael exclaimed. "Many families have left because of the mine closure, so the school also closed. Miss James does not have another position, so she thought she would try tutoring. We were both surprised to see each other on her first day at the manor. It has worked out well as she understands my weak subject is the sums. We're concentrating on that."

"Sums!" remarked Todd. "How can that be? Sums are so easy."

"Maybe for you," Rachael sulked.

"Well it's important to be interested, so get interested! Spend more time on it, rather than having your nose in a book in your free time."

"You don't have to be so bossy!" Rachael said, as she hurried into the manor. She did not want Todd to see that she was hurt by his comments.

"How was ye'r afternoon, Todd boy?"

"Oh, alright I guess," Todd said despondently.

"Do ye want to talk about it?" Malcolm asked with concern.

"Well, I feel badly because I hurt Rachael's feelings," Todd confessed. "She told me the tutor plans to concentrate on the sums, Rachael's weak subject, and I told her she needs to - in not so many words - get on with it, and not have her nose stuck in a book all the time."

Malcolm put his hand to his head in a gesture of dismay. "Todd boy, that wee girl worships ye as if ye are a saint of some kind. It was not kind of ye to hurt her, but at the same time she has had a jolt to earth, and ye are wobbling on the pedestal at the moment. This has to happen so that she will put her trust in others, not just in ye'rself.

"When Ah think of that lass, at her age, impressing folk at the manor enough that they would take her on, - well Ah think she is a wonder - even if she doesn't understand the sums. She has her special gifts, and it just may be that one day ye will need her strengths even more than she needs ye'rs now. It will all come out well, but it doesn't hurt for ye to examine how ye are feeling about everything once in awhile."

"Thanks Malcolm, I needed that. I will get on with some work I need to have accomplished for tomorrow's class."

"Aye lad. Ah will get the tea ready."

Rachael flew up to her upstairs room. "I will not cry over Todd's rudeness to me! I will not cry!" She stamped her foot and pulled at her shawl and dress, throwing them across the room. "I will not cry!" she repeated over and over as she dressed hurriedly into her kitchen costume and apron. "There are other people important to me now … like Maisie, Mrs. Olson and Sir Gordon. So why should I go bawling around about Todd? He's only a *know-it-all* brother, and Mr. Murray has spoiled him rotten."

Rachael brushed her hair hard, washed her face and hands, and decided that she would not wear the butterfly hairclip, she would instead make a braid to hold her hair back. Walking confidently down to the kitchen, she found Maisie busy making last minute preparations for Sir Gordon's dinner as well as two invited guests.

"May I help, Maisie?"

"That would be lovely, Rachael. Ah'm a bit short-handed today with Bronwyn away sick. Ah will ask ye to prepare the vegetables, and then start arranging the table in the large dining room. We'll use candles, and Mrs. Olson is gathering some of the early flowers from the garden. It's an anniversary, you see, of Sir Gordon's sister and her husband."

"How wonderful!" exclaimed Rachael. "I will begin immediately."

Rachael decided to take a moment to ask Maisie about a new kitchen dress. "I have grown out of this one, Maisie."

"So ye have indeed! And ye are becoming a lovely young lady. Let's have a look in the closet here to see what might fit ye better."

"I would like to make myself a new dress for summer," Rachael continued. "Would you know where I might be able to purchase the fabric, Maisie?"

"Oh, of course, let's plan a day to go shopping. Ye will need matching thread as well. An'a thing else can be found in the sewing room on the second floor of the manor. Have ye used a sewing machine, lass?"

"Thank you, Maisie, I will look forward to an outing with you. But a sewing machine! Will you show me how to use it?"

"Indeed, Ah will do that, love. We'll get Mrs. Olson to mind the kitchen while we are away. Duncan will'na mind dropping us off at a linen store, and fetching us back later."

Maisie arranged a day and a time that was suitable for everyone. "Ah'll just get ma coat and hat, and we'll be away," she announced.

"Well, that certainly didn't take long. The fabric and trimming will be great fun to work with," said Rachael, admiring the sky blue cotton with tiny raised dots, and the white lace trim.

"We still have almost an hour before Duncan comes back. Wha don't we treat ourselves to a cupa tea and a scone," suggested Maisie.

"That will make this wonderful afternoon of shopping complete."

As they looked out onto the glorious late spring day, Rachael felt it might be the right time to ask a personal question. "Is it proper to share sorrows with people you have known only for a short time? I mean, you and Mrs. Olson, as well as Sir Gordon and Duncan, are like family to me now. It doesn't seem right that I keep sorrows to myself when I want to share with people who are important to me."

"Ah do agree with ye, Rachael love. Ye have become verra special to all of us as well."

"I have to tell you about the sorrow I carry in losing my small brother, Robert, and twin baby girls. I loved them like my very own children. Before my mother died, she arranged with a health visitor that they would go into care homes, and wait there to be adopted. I have forgiven my mother, as I know now it was only the practical thing to do, and it took great courage on her part. At the time, though, I could only think of myself."

"Ahh Rachael, what a burden to be carrying. Ah'm so happy ye've found a time to share this with me. But ye can continue to love them, keeping them in ye'r thoughts. After all, ev'ra one of us is but the sum of our memories. Those of us who serve Sir Gordon are from poor homes, and we have our memories too, some are happy and others painfully sad. Sir Gordon has shared many of his sorrows with us, and we try to always be patient and understanding of him. He is a very kind man, and special to all of us."

"Thank you, Maisie. I have been very selfish, thinking I am the only one who holds a painful memory. But I do feel better in sharing it, and I'm grateful for your listening and sympathy."

Maisie smiled, patting Rachael's hand.

Rachael realized she had something else to ask. "I have wondered about Mr. Blaine, Maisie. I know you were not there when he paid a most unwelcome visit to the manor, and his conduct was quite terrible. Still, I have the memory of his sad and fearful face. Is it true: we cannot judge an act of such insolence without knowing all the reasons for it."

"Quite so, Rachael. Ye are a sensitive and compassionate young lady, and those are qualities to protect and practise at all times. Just remember, not all that seems either right or wrong can be judged by our own narrow standards."

Golden Ribbons

Todd had trouble getting on with his assignment. He understood what Malcolm said, but at the same time he was tired of the emotional load Rachael seemed to dump on him every time they met. All he wanted was to get on with life – after all, his older brothers seemed to be happy in their freedom. Malcolm said he should examine his own feelings. Alright, he was examining them, and he realized there was some resentment in being the one left behind to take over after his parents died. *Did my brothers, Billy and Joey, think it was easier for me, and they had a right to just take off and think only of themselves?*

Todd was becoming more angry and frustrated by the minute. "I'm just tired of it all, and I'm tired of all of them!" he fumed, as he shoved his books to one side.

"Not going to have breakfast b'fore going to school, Todd boy?" Malcolm puzzled.

"I want to catch the head master early," Todd explained. "My assignment is not ready, and I need to plead for more time."

"You have never been late with any deadline, Todd," said head master Jenkins. "How about catching up with it in the library this morning, and give it to me before you leave for the day. That way you won't lose any marks."

"Thanks, Sir, I can use a break right about now."

"I hope you are feeling well, Todd. You have had a rough ride this term."

"I think this will be very helpful to you," said Miss James, as she looked over the chart of weights and measures Maisie had given Rachael. "It's so much more interesting to study a subject when it can be put to daily use. When I became a teacher, I had trouble staying awake when it was time to introduce sums – especially when the sun shone through the open windows," she laughed.

"I'm surprised to hear that. I have always thought teachers must love everything they have to teach."

"Not so, Rachael, we have to take the bitter with the sweet, as in all occupations. Some day, it is hoped that women can follow a passion and make a living at it. As it is, there are few options open to us. Teaching and nursing are old standbys, but neither of those pay enough to live on – less than half of what a man would earn in the same occupation."

"I'm shocked to hear that, Miss James. Who decides such things, and why?"

"That is a very big topic, Rachael, old as time itself. When you are a fully adult person you will encounter many such discriminating practises. However, we are living in fortunate days, where brave and prominent women are addressing the very questions you are asking, and asking more strongly every day! The National Council of Women, an organization founded here in Aberdeen, is one of many like groups around this country, as well as in England. Each organization raises issues publicly concerning what they see in their own communities as the most pressing needs. For instance: access to a higher level of education for all, especially for women. As well, they argue for improvements to health care for everyone, but again – especially for young mothers and their children."

"These subjects were never talked about in my home, Miss James. I suspect my mother's concern for a family of eight children was to simply survive."

"Your family was no different than many others who still struggle. The issue is to get beyond the need to simply survive, and have the time and energy to pursue a better life. But we have done well for today, Rachael. I brought along some reading you may find interesting; I think it's important to keep up with more recent authors. It is <u>Kidnapped</u> by Robert Louis Stevenson, and you are welcome to borrow it. After you have read it, I would like you to prepare a synopsis of the book. I have an example here that you can refer to. It will be your first literature assignment, and a change from the sums," she smiled.

"How about accompanying me on my evening walk?" suggested Malcolm.

"I'd like that," agreed Todd.

Golden Ribbons

They walked in silence for several minutes – each staring out at the open sea. "I felt pretty miserable last evening, Malcolm," Todd began. "It sure was a bad feeling, but one that's hard to shake."

"What were some of your feelings, Todd boy?"

"Oh, anger, resentment, and I had to dig for these – fear and loneliness. Now how could I feel lonely when I'm living with a great chap like you? But there it was."

"Ah can only offer sympathy, son. I've been there ma'self. It takes time and a lot of looking out for blessings. We have to stack them up against the miserable stuff."

"Did you realize you called me *son*, Malcolm?"

"Oh, of course I realized it! Are you offended?"

"Certainly not!" Todd stated with conviction. "You are a father to me in every way."

It was Sunday afternoon again, and Rachael assumed her time with Todd was still on. She couldn't stay mad at him very long, but she hoped he was in a better mood and would not lecture her about the sums. She would definitely not hug, he was very sensitive about that.

As she looked out her window, she could see Todd walking toward the manor – but with two bikes! "What has he been up to?" she gasped, as she bolted down two flights of stairs to the kitchen, and out to the back garden.

"Well, what do you think? Is the colour right?" Todd asked.

"It's beautiful! Where in the world did you get it?"

"That's between Sergeant McTavish and me. It's not new, but with the coat of paint, it's good as new!"

"I like it very much, and thank you Todd. Thanks to Sergeant McTavish as well," said Rachael. "Of course, I'll have to learn how to ride it."

"Well, if you had some comfortable knickers and a warm top, that would be a start," said Todd.

"When I finish sewing a new dress, I'll rip this old grey thing apart and make some fancy knickers. I can't wait to get on that bike and fly away! But first, I'll have to find a place to store it."

"While you're doing that," said Todd, "I have to gather the orders from the infirmary to take back for Malcolm, and then get on with unpacking that box. I'll be right back."

Rachael found Clifford at the stable, and asked if there would be room there for her new bike.

"Certainly, Rachael," he said, admiring the bike. "That one looks just fine."

"Will you help me get started with it when we both have some free time?" she asked. "I want to be ready to take a long bike ride with Todd next week."

"Sure, sometime on our breaks. Everybody needs a bike, Rachael, I'm so glad you have one."

When Todd returned, they walked together back to Malcolm's shop. "I've a synopsis of a new book, <u>Kidnapped,</u> by Robert Louis Stevenson. I could read that to Mr. Murray while you are working," suggested Rachael.

"That sounds about right. There is not much left of our afternoon, but let's be ready next Sunday to take that bike ride together. I have some ideas for a destination."

Arriving at the shop, Malcolm was delighted to have a visit with Rachael, and he was especially pleased she brought along some reading to share with him. Seating herself close to his chair, she began:

> "A synopsis of the book <u>Kidnapped</u> by Robert Louis Stevenson
>
> "This book is a work of fiction; it is the memoirs of the adventures of David Balfour in the year 1751. David Balfour was a sixteen-year-old orphan, kidnapped by his villainous uncle, but later escapes and becomes involved in the struggle of the Scottish highlands against British rule.
>
> "As penned by the author himself: *The characters took the bit in their teeth; all at once they became detached from the flat paper, they turned backs on me and walked off bodily; and from that time…it was they who spoke; it was they who wrote the remainder of the story.*
>
> "As stated in this author's declaration, the era of the adventure novel presented hope, risk and opportunity - contrasting

with the earlier years of this century, which reflected a society broken by the impact of famine, and mass removals. Robert Louis Stevenson has left a lasting legacy of an earlier time, as well as providing a look into this present period of transformation in Scotland. His life and work will be remembered fondly for many decades to come. Robert Louis Stevenson died in 1894.

"A literature assignment, prepared by Rachael Atkinson, May 1899"

"That is verra excellent, Rachael! Ah see ye haven't missed a beat with having lost a full term of schooling."

"You wrote that?" asked Todd in amazement.

"Well yes, thank you for asking," said Rachael with as much haughtiness as she could muster without bursting into laughter.

"Well done, Rachael!" Miss James exclaimed. "I see a writer in you that must not be put off by anyone or anything. You have a gift that honours the language, and reflects your ability to encapsulate a major work in a few sentences. Congratulations!"

"Thank you, Miss James, though the assignment made me very sad to learn that Robert Louis Stevenson has died, and so recently. How I would loved to have met him."

"The wonderful thing about this quality of writing, Rachael, is that the work continues to inspire. You will be able to meet this author through the years, time and time again - every occasion to get to know him better. Now, we'll just get on with the chart of weights and measures, just to see how you are progressing there. Remember: the bitter with the sweet."

"A letter just arrived from Mister Blaine's solicitor, Sir Gordon," Duncan announced with a measure of personal interest.

"I suppose he intends to contest my application to disinherit him."

"That can be a nasty business, Sir. Shall I contact your solicitors in Edinburgh?"

"No Duncan - not yet. I'm in the midst of negotiating the sale of two connecting farms near Waterwell at the moment. The sale will possibly pay all the taxes for this year; the farms have not been profitable the past few years, better to get rid of them while I can."

"Indeed, Sir. There may be an opportunity, with that transaction, to fill the vacancy left by Clifford. A married couple have sublet one of the farms in question, but now that may leave them without a livelihood."

"Let's keep that in mind, Duncan. They would need a place to live, and there is a vacant cottage available – similar in size to your own, but badly in need of repair I'm afraid. Take a look at it, will you, Duncan, and assess what needs to be done. Then, we need to meet with Mrs. Olson. This couple you mention may fill the kitchen need as well."

Rachael spent every free moment in the sewing room until her dress was complete. *Oh, but the knickers,* she pondered. *Pretty funny I guess, but I'll ask Todd if we can take back roads for our first biking adventure. With this cast-off sweater from Bronwyn, I should be reasonably respectable.*

Bronwyn stopped by and took a peep at the sewer as she bent over her project. "How is it going, Rachael?"

"I'll let you be the judge of that, dear friend."

"You are indeed a brave girl," said Bronwyn smothering a laugh. "Perhaps you will start a fashion trend. I have seen many women on their bikes with skirts bunched up at the back of the seat. This is certainly more practical."

"I will take that as approval then."

Sunday afternoon arrived with threatening clouds overhead, but Todd was insistent that the biking activity begin. "Now don't laugh," said Rachael, as she met him in the driveway with her bike.

"Why would I laugh?"

"Well, the knickers, you silly. Will they start a fashion trend?"

"Oh that! Of course, and I think they look just fine. Much more comfortable than a big floppy dress," agreed Todd. "We'll proceed north along the sea trail, and then turn west about one kilometre. Hector Abbey is said to be haunted and in complete ruins. How is that for a start? It will be fun to uncover some gimmick that has been set up to scare people off."

"May I lead the way? I may fall off my bike and need to be rescued."

"Alright – this time," Rachael was pleased to find that she was soon into riding along smoothly. She relaxed and began to hum a lively tune she had heard Clifford whistling as he worked about the manor.

"I see the place just ahead," yelled Todd. "We'll walk our bikes as we leave the path; there is just stones and deep grass at the approach."

There was a clap of thunder followed by a streak of lightening, and the two brave adventurers stumbled along to the shelter of a strange looking overhang to the ruins. As they got closer, they could see that the overhang was laden with hooks, wires, and other paraphernalia that seemed to have no relationship one to the other. The rain fell heavily as they moved closer to the strange object, and just as they scrambled underneath it, the overhang swung down and projected them - with a mighty crash, into the space that appeared to be an interior of some kind. The floor was uneven and there was a rocking motion as they moved forward.

"Are you still with me, Rach?" asked Todd.

"Something banged my head, but I'm right behind you."

The interior was black as ink until they adjusted to the sudden change. A jagged hole in the ceiling gave them the perspective of an old chapel that had been turned on its side and put back upright again. Seats were tangled together, but the alter appeared to be in one piece. What may have been intended as holy water in the baptismal font was slopping back and forth with the rhythm of the rocking floor. It was the assortment of objects on the alter that caught the adventurer's attention: animal bones, old shoes of various shapes and sizes, a baby buggy, an open casket with a mass of dark hair tumbling over one side, and other objects that defied inspection.

"I think we should get out of here," said Rachael, "...and look! The way we got in here is now part of a wall, there's no door!"

"You're right, but there must be another way out. I'll just see if I can't find my way around the inside walls to check for another door," Todd remarked bravely.

Rachael tried to steady herself by leaning against a bench. There were scampering noises around her feet that gave her the creeps. In an attempt to get her feet off the floor, she slid onto the bench and then looked along the length of it to find a horrifying figure sitting at the other end. The figure was staring at her behind the hood of an oversized black cloak. "What are you doing in my house?" it said, letting out a most hideous screech of a laugh.

"You must be the ghost gimmick we've heard about," answered Rachael. "I hope you are getting paid well for it. What an ugly place!"

"Here now, young lady, I certainly am a ghost, and from hell, thank you very much." Once again, it let out a hideous screech.

Rachael put her hands over her ears. "That is a most dreadful noise."

"Well I suppose we could call it a hell of a noise," said the figure – not taking its beady eyes off of Rachael for a moment. "But, you see, that's why I'm not in hell today, but back here in this boring old wreck. The Devil sent me back because I was scaring my hell-mates to life."

"I thought hell was as bad as it could get," exclaimed Rachael.

"Oh, my no, little one," it replied. "I made it much worse with my screeching. The sad part is that I miss my old hell-mates, and I want to go back. The only way back is to keep burning down the old wrecks they send me to. That's why I will burn this one down today. I'm afraid that you, and that funny-looking boy you're with, will *go down with the abbey* as they say."

Todd approached, saying with a firm tone, "You're no ghost, even if you have a hellish laugh. You're just an old tramp!"

"Now, listen here, you! In two minutes this edifice will go up in smoke, so you'd better say your prayers!"

The hideous laugh reverberated off the walls and the whole structure was shaking. A torch appeared from under the black robe and a flame went up from a pile of rags near Rachael's feet. She snatched the hood off the black robe the old tramp was wearing, and began to strike the flames. Meanwhile, Todd grabbed part of a broken bench and chopped a hole in the wall where they had entered. They could try to get out that way.

Then, with a final screeching laugh, the mysterious figure jumped up to release a hinge, and the wall caved in all around them. Todd and Rachael managed to claw their way out before the ceiling gave way. Crawling their way to a reasonable distance from the flaming ruins, the two adventurers pulled their bikes out of the surrounding rough grass, and hurried out to the path.

"Whew," breathed Todd. "That was a close one; still we might as well stay and see the end of it."

The old abbey put on quite a show with flames shooting high into the air – and strange objects flying out from nowhere. Just then bells of the Aberdeen fire brigade could be heard coming from the city, and Todd and Rachael were able to relate their adventure to the chief and the firemen.

"We've been trying to catch the fire bug going around burning down these old abbeys," informed Fire Chief McNibbon. "But glad you two are none the worse for your adventure today." As the two bikers made their way up the path toward the sea trail, they noticed a figure running across the field, black robe flapping in the breeze.

"I'm filthy!" Rachael exclaimed with disgust. "I must get back to the manor. I'm helping Maisie prepare dinner, and I will be serving it to Sir Gordon and a guest. A quick bath would be in order."

CHAPTER SIX

"ALRIGHT THEN," SAID TODD. "IT WILL BE PRETTY HARD TO BEAT today's excitement, but there are other places just as mysterious. Would you like to take turns planning our outings? How about you plan next week?"

"Okay Todd. I have been asking some questions about one-day excursions and Clifford mentioned that there's a carnival going on every weekend throughout the summer - about half way between the outskirts of Aberdeen south and Stonehaven. Would you be interested in something like that?"

"Sure, let's give it a try. Perhaps start out a bit earlier than usual."

After Sir Gordon shared interviews with Jean Olson and Duncan, the displaced farm couple, John and Rebecca Neilson, were hired to replace Bronwyn and Clifford, and the cottage was quickly made ready for their arrival. It was Jean Olson's idea that Rachael now move down to a second floor bedroom. The one next to Maisies' rooms could be made ready for her.

"It would not be right to have you on the third floor all by yourself, Rachael," Jean Olson said. "Come along, see what you think of it - or perhaps another would suit better. We will see about new curtains and other coverings to match."

"Oh, Mrs. Olson," Rachael exclaimed, "This one you've chosen is perfect. It's so big, and the furniture is wonderful. May I help to choose colours, and assist with the sewing?"

"Certainly, Rachael. You will find that our new kitchen helper has many skills that will be very useful to us, and you will be able to count on any help you will need to make it your place. Then, in turn, we'll all pitch in to make the cottage a cosy home for John and Rebecca."

By the end of summer, Rachael's new bedroom was a delight to the eye with all the wonderful matching and blending colours she had chosen. As well, the new employees, John and Rebecca, were becoming used to their new surroundings. John proved himself to be not only a capable stable and grounds keeper, but carpentry was a learned trade and he was anxious to use his skills. Rebecca transformed the kitchen garden into a collection of unique vegetables and herbs that challenged Maisie and Rachael with the capability of many unique menus. Jean Olson was pleased with this effort as well; it gave her household budget a welcome boost, and orders to the grocer were becoming less frequent.

Todd arrived at the manor bright and early on the next Sunday afternoon. It was a clear sky, and a pleasant summer breeze. "Off we go then, I expect this carnival to be about three kilometres from the southern border of Aberdeen."

"I believe we can follow along the sea trail most of the way," Rachael added.

The carnival could be seen from a short distance and there appeared to be a sizable crowd gathered to take in all the events. "I'm glad I remembered to bring along a few extra farthings," said Todd, as he spotted booths with line-ups of children and young people willing to take their chances for a prize.

"I see a performance of some kind going on over there," said Rachael, as she pointed to a stage that had been set up, with a shelter covering one side. The other side open to an audience seated on rugs covering the grass. "Do you mind if I go over there, Todd, and we can meet up a bit later?"

"That sounds okay with me, as long as you don't wander too far away. I don't want you getting lost."

"Oh you are such a worrier, Todd! I will be fine, and I can watch to see where you are going."

As Rachael approached the stage, she felt some recognition of the main character in the play. With her bike beside her, she found a spot for her small rug and sat down as close to the stage as she could. It was obviously a comedy, as children were laughing and clapping at the same time. "Oh gracious!" she almost exclaimed out loud. "I believe that main character to be Mr. Blaine, Sir Gordon's step-son."

"Ladies and gentlemen, our next performance will be in twenty minutes," announced the stage director. "That will give you just enough time to get your ice cream and come right back."

Rachael was mesmerized by what she was witnessing. Becoming aware that everyone in the crowd had disbursed except herself, she got up hurriedly from her rug and prepared to move away.

"Do little kitchen maids enjoy country fairs, as well as tripping people and sending them off to patch up their wounds?" asked Blaine, as he moved toward Rachael.

What should I do now? Rachael thought. *Should I let him know I recognize him, or get out of here as fast as I can?*

"Now, don't you go running off, fair rose. I deserve a full accounting from you, not to mention a most sincere apology."

"Alright," said Rachael, "I had hoped to escape, but now here I am in front of a person I do recognize - and with great surprise. But should you not be the one to apologize?"

"Indeed not!" said Blaine, laughing. "I carry a scar on my forehead that will be with me forever, as a reminder of the fair rose who is responsible."

"I am indeed sorry that your head met up with the chopping block, Mr. Blaine, but you must admit to having been a most obnoxious intruder."

"I was just having a bit of fun with Popsy, and – gosh – everyone took it so seriously," teased Blaine. "But you seem to remember my name, so we are off to a great start. If you would tell me your name, I will invite you to be my guest at the next performance."

"I admit to being curious, so I'll accept your invitation," said Rachael. "But first, I must spot where my brother is in the line of booths, and let him know where I am. My name is Rachael, by-the-way."

"Hurry back, Rachael, the show must go on!" said Blaine, with flamboyance.

Noticing that Todd was engrossed in the games of chance, Rachael decided not to bother him. As she moved back to the stage area, she found a spot to the side of the stage and settled in for the performance.

"Ladies and gentlemen, and my special guest, Rachael: You are about to witness the most remarkable and outstanding of acrobatic wizardry in all of

Great Britain!" With that, a pyramid of young men formed, with Blaine at the top. First: standing on one leg, then flipping upside down, a one-hand hold, and finally a leap to the stage, with cart wheels all around. The sequence was repeated until the pyramid collapsed, but with Blaine calmly standing on the stage - as though he had been there all along. The crowd was delighted, and Rachael applauded enthusiastically.

"And now, for a musical treat I know you will enjoy," said Blaine, as he walked down from the stage and took a place on the lawn beside Rachael.

"That was quite unbelievable, Mr. Blaine."

"Just Blaine, please, Rachael. I've never been a Mister, or a gentleman for that matter. But let me explain a bit about myself."

"You don't have to. I have no business in Sir Gordon's affairs, and your relationship with him has nothing to do with my enjoying a most wonderful display of talent. Is this a summer placement for you?"

"Fair enough, Rachael. Yes, it is a summer fill-in," Blaine proceeded. "I do musical theatre in Glasgow and London on a more regular basis. But I'll share this one thing with you Rachael: my mother was, before she met and married Popsy, the beautiful star of a musical theatre company in Glasgow. Because she left such a sparkling career to become the wife of a staid and boring old aristocrat, I could not adjust to so much humiliation, and consequently became a problem child. Does that make me any less of a monster to you, Rachael?"

"I did not regard you as a monster, Blaine, - just an angry young man. I enjoyed your performance; in fact I've never seen anything like it!"

"Right then," said Blaine, "and I'm happy you are here today. It has bothered me that I left the manor as a common tramp. I hope you will visit one of the performances in Glasgow or London in the future, and be my special guest."

"I certainly hope that may be possible, Blaine. But now I see my brother coming over this way, and I must introduce you to him." Rachael waved Todd toward her, but as she turned around she found that Blaine had suddenly disappeared.

"Who was that you were talking to?" asked Todd

"Oh, just one of the theatre's performers," she said, surprised at her own disappointment.

"Well I guess we'd better be heading home, Rach. I've lost all my spare change, but I had a great time. Thanks for the idea of this outing."

"I enjoyed it too," said Rachael, with a secret smile.

With summertime adventures ending, there was a feeling of reluctance, but expectation too, as Rachael and Todd recognized the coming of fall meant a return to regular routines. With the collaboration of Jean Olson and Malcolm, they were each given four days vacation time to visit their sister Aggie and her children in Dundee. Their Aunt Aggie had supplied the train fares.

The reunion was special, and they were grateful their Aunt Aggie had made it possible. As it had been more than two years since they had seen their aunt, they were astonished at how she seemed frail and so much older. In confidence, their sister shared that Aunt Aggie was not well and her care becoming more demanding. Difficult though it was, the younger Aggie was grateful for a loving home, and that her care was needed. Peter would soon be in nursery school, and that would add another dimension to their permanence in this old family home.

That first evening, the three siblings gathered in the front parlour of the old home in Dundee to read the latest letter from Billy and Joey, received August 20, 1899.

> Hello Aggie: As we know that Todd and Rachael will be visiting you within a fortnight, we decided to make it just one letter this time, and to all of you. First of all, we hope Aunt Aggie's condition is not worsening and that she is not in pain. How fortunate you are there to assist her, Aggie. We send her our loving wishes, and extend to you a wish for strength and courage as you meet the coming difficult times. Please tell Mary how much we enjoyed the picture she sketched of her cat, Sandy. We have it pinned to the wall above our bunk beds. Good luck to Peter as he begins nursery school.

The activity here has been non-stop as we complete our work every day and make plans for our departure approximately August second. We will take a small steamer from the Firth of Clyde that will meet up with a larger merchant ship at the Port of Liverpool. Our fares have been arranged with the Canadian Pacific Railway, covering transportation from Montreal directly to a small community in the southern prairies. The merchant ship is called *The Pride of Dundee*. We are assuming a connection to the huge cargo of processed jute made into bagging and carpeting that will come from that city. Locomotives and hydraulic equipment, Singer sewing machines, as well as the usual in textiles - cotton, linen and woollen products, will be on board. However, let us not forget all the coal that has to be stored - later to be shovelled into the huge ovens in order to keep the boilers going and the engines fed.

Now for the most newsworthy of our letter: we will be joined by a third partner. Her name is Maggie, a dairy maid on the farm where we are employed. As we became friends with Maggie, she eventually asked if we would consider taking her along, as a full partner, on our journey to Canada. She is somewhat older than we are, well - age twenty, and has worked on the farm for six years. She wants to leave and sees this as a chance to claim a life for herself and not be under the domination of a task master. It is evident to us that women who do this work are treated with little consideration. This is a situation we hope will one day be rectified, but probably not soon.

So, after thinking about it for awhile, we decided that - yes, we would be happy to have Maggie as a third partner. A second decision had to be made in this regard, however, as the law states that women immigrating to the colonies must be married. Guess who is the lucky bridegroom in this *marriage of circumstance*? Of course, it's Billy, as he is the elder, being eighteen.

Maggie has insisted that this arrangement be contracted and officially signed by a Justice of the Peace, with all the conditions spelled out. She will be a partner in all endeavours and will pay her own way in outfitting the farm we envision. You will probably be amazed at this turn of events, but we are certain that Maggie will be an asset to our farming operation. She has a very agreeable disposition and possesses the strength and endurance that pioneering will require. She is also an excellent cook!

Please direct all messages and letters to the office of the Canadian Pacific Railway in Glasgow, mentioning The Pride of Dundee as it will be our home for many weeks. We will mail letters at every opportunity along the ports of call.

Our love and best wishes to you all, your brother Joey

As Aggie, Todd and Rachael sat in a fog of utter amazement – each afraid to make the first comment, it was Todd to begin: "I can't believe what's in this letter - Billy in an arranged marriage!" Then he began to laugh until he was weak with exhaustion.

"I think this is wonderful and courageous of all three of them, Todd," said Rachael, "and you are very rude to laugh. I'm happy for Maggie, and I know Billy and Joey will be good and considerate of her. I plan to add a note to Maggie along with my next letter to my wonderful brothers," she declared with assertion.

Aggie simply smiled, "This is sometimes where it all has to begin with women of courage and determination. I'm very happy and hopeful for Maggie, and I'm proud of my brothers."

Realizing he was completely outwitted, Todd excused himself to go out for a walk, hoping that he might more objectively digest the new information.

Golden Ribbons

As their departure day approached, Todd and Rachael spent time with their Aunt Aggie, telling her about their lives and the people who brought them both friendship and opportunity. Their aunt, in turn, responded with her feelings of love and appreciation for their sister, Aggie. She spoke with affection for Peter and Mary and how they have brought so much joy into her life. It was evident to Todd and Rachael: they would not see their aunt again, and this made the final hours difficult.

Aggie was distressed to see them go, but promised to return to Aberdeen with the children sometime in the future to take care of unfinished business. Peter and Mary hugged and blew kisses to Rachael and Todd, after Todd had lowered Mary from his shoulders as the train came into view.

"It looks as though many of our customers were happy ye were having a short vacation, Todd," said Malcolm. "There are just a few deliveries and there are no prescriptions to pick up at the infirmary."

"Nice timing then, Malcolm. I hoped we would have some free moments to get caught up on the news from both here and Dundee."

"Ah expect ye would have to be away for six months b'fore Ah would have anything new to report," Malcolm said, jokingly. "But Ah am sorry to hear of ye'r aunt being so ill. It would seem that ye'r sister, Aggie, is often called on for her nursing care in the most urgent of cases."

"That is certainly true, Malcolm. Aggie has been the rock of our family, and I hope that one day she will be able to legitimize her nursing skills through formal training. But for now, in addition to caring for our aunt, she must raise her young children. Peter and Mary are doing well, their shyness has disappeared and they are friendly and engaging."

"Ah'm glad to hear that," said Malcolm. "Are ye looking forward to classes starting next week, Todd?"

"Yes I am. I will enter into it with a lot more confidence than last term. That was a social disaster, but I expect – necessary."

"Ah believe that's true, son."

As Jean Olson had been busy getting the cottage ready for the new members of the manor staff, as well as coaching them regarding their duties, she almost forgot to contact Miss James and to enquire if she would be available to continue tutoring Rachael. But, yes, Miss James would be back in early September. She could not guarantee her services beyond January first, but with all the activity at the manor, even this shorter space of time was acceptable.

"After completion of your basic requirements, Rachael, have you given any thought to entering the apprenticeship program?" asked Miss James. "It's almost a *given* that the brightest young ladies will enter this program and then go on to one of the normal schools to receive certification as a qualified teacher. I was a product of that program, and at least it guarantees employment."

"Yes, I have given it some thought, Miss James, and I only have a bit more than a year before my thirteenth birthday to make the decision, but I'm inclined to pass it by. There is so much opportunity to learn here at the manor," Rachael shared. "I'm delighted to becoming a professional cook under such pleasant coaching as Maisie, and the skills of dressmaking and design are available here too. The sewing room is equipped with all the most up-to-date equipment, and of course I don't have to tell you how happy I am to live here and be provided with every opportunity to advance in the areas I enjoy. So, for now, I want to just stay here and remain in the company of the people I most enjoy and appreciate."

"In addition, your literary skills will always serve you well in the future. Have you been writing stories of your own lately?"

"Yes, I actually have started doing some of that. In the company of my brother, Todd, and our biking adventures together, I've accumulated some interesting subjects - with a focus toward children. I don't see why young people and adults should have all the fun of adventure reading."

"You might enjoy entering one of your stories in the occasional competition that is sponsored by the new community libraries, Rachael. We can thank Mr. Carnegie for these wonderful libraries, as well as his other gestures of generosity."

"Yes," said Rachael, "Sir Gordon told me about Andrew Carnegie not long ago, saying he was a philanthropist. Such a big word, but for the big cause of education! Sir Gordon is also of like-mind."

"I have heard that is true, Rachael. He is respected for his opinions regarding inclusive education. Of course, there are opposing views - as always!"

Dear Maggie: I am enclosing this note in a specially sealed envelope along with a letter to my brothers. I want to express my good wishes to you and to assure you that my brothers, Billy and Joey, are very special people and will be considerate of you. What a brave woman you are to start out on a voyage to a strange place, and to toil along with the men in making a home and a living for yourself. I hope you will consider me a friend back home in Scotland, and that you will write to me sometimes when you feel like having a chat. I will surely answer and write to you regularly.

With very best wishes, Rachael Atkinson

As Rachael sealed the envelope addressed to Maggie, she was overwhelmed with thoughts of the impending hardships that will be faced by all three travellers. "As well as for all my brothers and sisters, Maggie will now be on my list to receive loving thoughts."

When Todd called at the infirmary for the weekly orders, he was met by Doctor Wilkins. "Hello Todd, I was hoping to catch you today as I want to let you know that Malcolm will shortly have to give up his business at the shop. He is suffering from irregular heart beat," Doctor Wilkins shared. "If such a routine is kept up, it will certainly have severe consequences. His daily walk, though, should be maintained as long as possible, it gives him so much pleasure."

"I've been aware that this would be coming, Doctor Wilkins. I will not leave Malcolm as long as he lives and needs me. I'm glad you are his doctor as well as a good friend."

"I'm pleased to hear that you will stay on with Malcolm, Todd. I felt you would do that."

"Thank you for the information, Doctor Wilkins." Todd was close to tears and left hurriedly not to show how distressed he was.

"Ah hope Doctor Wilkins hasn't been filling ye'r head with nonsense about ma giving up the business here at the shop," announced Malcolm. "Ah think we're doing just fine as it is, don't ye Todd boy?"

"No Malcolm, Doctor Wilkins is right. I want you around for a good long time, and I'll make sure you follow his instructions. He is a good friend to you, and I respect his judgement. I will never leave you, Malcolm – not ever."

"Thank ye, son," said Malcolm, with relief and resignation.

"I understand that the infirmary is planning to install a pharmaceutical dispensary on the premises," said Todd. "It will take some time to make this transfer as they have counted on your service for so long, but if we get started right away it will be less confusion for their staff as well as for the patients. Do you think I would be suitable as a *go-between* in the meantime Malcolm?"

"Of course, Todd, of course."

"Are you finding any reading of interest in the library here, Rachael?"

"I certainly am, Sir Gordon. Ever since I read Robert Louis Stevenson's Kidnapped, I've been looking for more of his books, and I've found that Treasure Island is among your collection. Also works by Margaret Oliphant."

"Do you know about the author, Stevenson, himself? In his later life he went to live on an island of the Pacific – the Western Samoa Island I believe, and he is buried there."

"How fascinating, Sir, I didn't know that."

"Mrs. Olson tells me you have been doing a bit of writing yourself, Rachael."

Golden Ribbons

"Yes, my brother Todd has joined me on our Sunday afternoons this past summer, and we have made several interesting bike trips. I am using those experiences as the back ground of writing stories for children."

"If you want to enter one or two of your stories in the Carnegie library competition, Rachael, I would be pleased to assist you in paying for printing."

"I would appreciate that so much, Sir, the world of printing and publishing is somewhat of a mystery to me."

"Just let me know when you are ready to have your stories printed."

"Thank you Sir Gordon. I believe that will be quite soon."

After removing Sir Gordon's tea tray to the kitchen, Rachael reflected on Blaine's assessment of Sir Gordon as a staid and boring old aristocrat. *Well, I certainly don't think that. Sir Gordon is just reserved and very much a gentleman, as I'm sure he was brought up to be. Still, he does seem detached and troubled a great deal of the time lately. I wish there could be something that would cheer him up.*

"Welcome back to all," said Head Master Jenkins. "This fall term, it's my hope that some thought be given to school spirit. If any of you have suggestions as to how this might be achieved, please bring it forward for discussion. I know Coach Robinson is looking forward to a full complement of soccer hopefuls, and what better way to start off the term than with an active sports program!"

As Todd was leaving school for the day, Coach Robinson approached him and asked if he would like to be part of the soccer program.

"I certainly am interested, Sir. The only reservation I have is the practise schedule. Malcolm is not well now, and I must not leave him alone for any length of time."

"Let's give that some thought, Todd. I certainly want you on the team, and it wouldn't do for you to be distracted or worried during a game. If I know Malcolm, he would want you to take part in all of the school's activities that interest you. After try-outs, we'll be working out a practise schedule, and hopefully it will accommodate both Malcolm and yourself."

"I hope so too, Sir," said Todd.

When Todd met with Rachael the following Sunday, he told her of his dilemma. "If you have a Sunday practise, Todd, or one in the late afternoon when I'm not serving dinner at the manor," suggested Rachael. "I could at least look in on Mr. Murray for a time while you are away."

"That's good of you to offer, Rachael. If I may then, I will put you down as an option. I don't want Malcolm to feel he is being a detriment though. If he even thought that might be so, he would argue endlessly that he is one hundred percent safe and capable of looking after himself. But I have a feeling other options will work out as well, my sister. I do want to play soccer."

Sir Gordon met with Clifford a final time, after assisting him with immigration papers and other matters to end his employment at the manor. Clifford would be met in Melbourne by relatives who had immigrated several years earlier, clearly an advantage. Sir Gordon offered a substantial valise, and Duncan would drive him to Glasgow, where his journey would be finalized.

With a sigh, Sir Gordon then turned his attention to letters and documents that had piled up on his desk. The letter from Blaine's solicitor had to be responded to, and that would require getting in touch with his own solicitors in order to deal with this personal entanglement. But another letter from Blaine's solicitor had arrived that day, and Sir Gordon imagined that time was running out for resolution to the matter. To his amazement, the current letter was short and impersonal: "In regard to the pending legal arguments to be made on Mr. Blaine Arbour's behalf, my client now withdraws his contest of your application to disinherit him, and to put an end to this matter as quickly as possible."

It was a load lifted from his shoulders – certainly, but at the same time Sir Gordon's dispute with Blaine had, in some ways, kept a channel open where memories of his beloved were kept alive. A wave of long-held despair and loneliness swept over him. It was now finished.

CHAPTER SEVEN

RACHAEL HAD CREATED HER FIRST ATTEMPTS AT AUTHORSHIP, THE manuscripts carefully rewritten and proofed. *Would anyone want to read this? Oh well, here goes! Sir Gordon may even offer some suggestions before they go to print,* she speculated.

"I find these stories very lively, Rachael, and enough suspense to keep children on their toes and wondering what comes next. It shows that you have been a keenly objective reader of other works. Front covers are very important as well, and I am acquainted with a printer's expertise in having a cover designed that will attract and tantalize. I will send a message to a local printer, and an appointment will be made for you to present your work. Do you feel confident enough to handle an appointment on your own?"

"I believe so, Sir Gordon," Rachael said hesitantly. ". . . if I may ask for a further consultation with you beforehand."

"Certainly. I am very proud and happy to be of assistance."

Rachael was delighted with the friendliness of the printer's staff member. The cover suggestions were ones that she never would have thought of, but found to be unique to the targeted reader - with colours and shapes to attract the eye. When the copies were printed and delivered back to her, she could not wait to show them to Sir Gordon.

"I think this is the best effort possible." said Sir Gordon, admiringly. "Do submit a copy of each to the competition. Then we'll await the outcome."

"Thank you, Sir." said Rachael, glowing with happiness.

Beth McMurchie

August 12, 1899 Dear family: In just a few minutes we will be heading out of the French port of Les Sables d'Oionne Arcachon. Sacks and hydraulic equipment have been unloaded and sold. Wines and cheese have been picked up here for trade elsewhere. So far seas have been fairly calm. Joey and I are getting used to the movement of the ship, but Maggie is having more difficulty. As we are on hand to shovel coal into the ovens in the hold, we seldom see her, except at meal times. She was snapped up right away when she applied to be cooks helper.

Our accommodation is very cramped, as expected – and we thought the bothy was small! A package of your letters arrived, just in time, before we boarded ship in Liverpool. We were pleased that you had a good visit with Aggie, and that Peter and Mary are thriving. Sorry to hear that Aunt Aggie's condition is not improving.

Maggie thanks you for your letter, Rachael; it meant a lot to her, as there is no one she will be keeping in touch with back in Scotland.

Love to all, Billy

"It will be an exciting term ahead, Todd," said Malcolm. "Ah'm so glad ye're interested in soccer. When will practises start, son?"

"Try-outs this week, then I expect it will be in full swing."

"Ah can't wait to hear all about it, and Ah'll be at all the games, of that ye can be sure!"

"Terrific, Malcolm; let's enjoy it together."

"Ah see ye have a letter that's come from France today."

Golden Ribbons

"That will be from my brothers. They have started out on their voyage with a cargo steamship, and there will be other letters coming from different ports. Their job is to keep the coal shovelled into the ovens, and the boilers producing steam to keep the ship moving along. I'm sure it will be tough going, Malcolm, but I hope they have a chance for some sight-seeing too."

"What brave lads they are. No doubt there will be some weeks before they arrive in Canada?"

"My brother, Billy, states the time to be thirty-five to forty days. I'm very proud of them – in every way."

"By-the-way, Malcolm, Doctor Wilkins suggests we should be thinking about an estimate on the sale of your business. Perhaps your solicitor can help you there – it sounds complicated to me. Since the shop is your home, the business is the number of clients you've served over the years, and your reputation in the community."

"Well, Ah've never heard of such a thing! But Ah will talk to ma solicitor and find out about it."

"If you'll write a note to your solicitor, I'll deliver it to him and he can suggest a time when he can come here to see you."

"Thank ye, son."

"I would like to welcome all of you budding writers to this closing of the literary competition," the librarian, Miss Applegate, stated with exuberance. "Judging was a most difficult task; the level of plot development was at a very high standard, as well as language use and grammar," she continued. "So, if a grand prize escapes you this time, there will be other competitions in the future, and what you have learned from this first attempt will give you confidence to reach out a bit further next time. The prizes will be awarded with certificates of merit first, and then the three top winners: Third, Second, and First."

There was shuffling of feet, and nervous coughs among the ten contestants, as all looked up expectantly awaiting the announcements. The seven certificates of merit were presented, followed by generous applause and smiling congratulations from fellow contestants.

"And now, said Miss Applegate, the third prize goes to a most lively and entertaining story written by John McMaster – <u>An Unforgettable Vacation at Bridlington.</u> Congratulations John, and keep up the good work!" John stumbled forward amid wild applause.

"Second prize goes to Rachael Atkinson for her remarkable use of dialogue and descriptions in <u>A Country Fair.</u> Well done, Rachael!" As Rachael accepted her second prize envelope, there were happy smiles and congratulations all around.

Then, with a tone of excitement, Miss Applegate announced: "While you're still standing, Rachael, I'm pleased to also award you first prize for your wonderful, but scary, story – <u>The Ghost of Hector Abbey.</u> I'm sure we will be hearing from you again in the future!"

"Thank you so much Miss Applegate," said Rachael. "I'm honoured to have had such wonderful writing companions in this exciting competition."

Jean Olson had accompanied Rachael to the awards ceremony. "We are all so proud of you, Rachael," she said. "Sir Gordon must be told this wonderful news immediately; I know it will brighten his day."

"How are the practises going, Todd?" asked Malcolm.

"Oh great, Malcolm! We generally have a quick meeting before to decide who would like to change a position – just to get the experience."

"Do you have a preference?"

"No, not really, except I would not like goalkeeper on a regular basis. I prefer to keep moving around the playing field all the time. It's a great game, and I'm so happy to have the chance to play it," replied Todd.

"Ah'm happy about that too," agreed Malcolm.

"There will only be two regular games this fall since so many of us are beginners," said Todd. "I think the first one is to be mid-October. I hope you will be up to attending – at least part of it. It might get a bit tedious toward the end of the game, unless the score is very close, or we are winning.!"

"Ah will do ma best, son. Ah would love to see ye play."

"Have you thought about an official date for your retirement, Malcolm?" Todd enquired. "Just before the final date, we could put a fancy ad in the newspaper where you would make your announcement and thank all of the people... Well, you know, sort of a testimonial in a way," he continued. "You have been a big part of a lot of lives here in this part of Aberdeen. Why don't we keep an eye out for similar announcements, just to get some ideas. I think yours should be very special."

"Ach yes, this is a big step for me, son, but one that Ah welcome too."

"Congratulations, Rachael!" said Sir Gordon. "Now that you are a prize winner, I believe both stories should be published. Let's look and see what publishers there are in Glasgow who might be interested."

"Gracious Sir! This is all going so fast, I feel like it's just a dream."

"These opportunities must be happily acknowledged Rachael, and then start moving on to yet another level," encouraged Sir Gordon.

"All the help and encouragement you've given me, Sir, has helped so much to make this happen."

"The joy has been mine," said Sir Gordon, sincerely.

A letter came from Aggie, but Todd decided not to open it until he saw Rachael, and they could read it together. Aggie wrote:

> I am so sad to report that your Aunt Aggie died last evening. I was with her right to the end, and that has given me some consolation.
>
> The children, of course, are having a hard time understanding how someone they have become so close to has suddenly left us. This will take ongoing talking to them until it is somewhat resolved in their little heads. Please drop them a line when you have time so they will know there are still family members who think of them and love them.
>
> There will be a small funeral. Uncle John and Aunt Mary will be attending, I sent a telegraph message to them this

morning, and they have replied. Uncle John will be a great help to me in settling the estate; it is small, nevertheless the home has been left to me and I am grateful for it.

With loving wishes, your sister Aggie

"Aunt Aggie's death is so sad for all of us, Todd - especially for Aggie and the children. We must plan a visit to them soon."

"I agree, but it may be early in the New Year before it can happen. We both have school, and I have Malcolm to care for as we prepare for his retirement. Then there is soccer."

"Let's keep it the New Year then. I will write to Aggie for both of us."

"But I must not forget the wonderful news about your literary prizes. Congratulations Rachael!" exclaimed Todd.

"Thank you. Yes, it is very wonderful, and Sir Gordon has been such a help. But now, I must ask you about Mr. Murray," said Rachael, with concern. "I am so sorry he is ill - is it very serious?"

"Yes, I'm afraid it is, and we will announce his retirement very soon. I believe he has decided it will be October 31st, and then perhaps he can relax knowing the shop will be closed after that date. This is a very big and emotional change for him."

September 12, 1899 The Port of Lisbon, Portugal

Dear Family: This will be the last letter for awhile, as we push off shortly to cross the Atlantic. Besides the regular trade, we have picked up bales of cork and cases of wine – mostly port this country is famous for. Coal is scarce here as there is only one active mine left in the entire country, but at least we have been able to replace what we have used so far for the long journey ahead. There are two apprentices (that's us), as well as six able seamen, and we will now take regular four hour shifts to keep the ovens stoked constantly. With the heat and the energy required to carry on this work, four-hour shifts are seen as the maximum. Billy and I have asked that we take two four-hour shifts in a twenty-four hour period so that we can always work together.

Maggie is certainly appreciated in the ship's kitchen for all the good work she does. However, she is ill much of the time, and we have been worried about her. Finally, last evening, as we had a few hours to go ashore here and walk along the dock, she shared that she is pregnant, a victim of rape by the dairy farmer's son. This was very difficult for her to share, but it finally became necessary to tell us. She was worried that we might now regret our decision to take her on as a partner, but we have assured her that we are now even more aware of her bravery and her decision to leave Scotland at the earliest possible time. There would be no sympathy for her back home, and certainly no recourse in advising the employer of her plight. Oddly enough, now that she has shared her story and we still want her with us, she feels much better and she can withstand the journey and face the future with a bit more spirit.

We are hoping that the time frame for the trip to Canada will remain as close as possible to the booking agent's assessment, and that the child can be born after we arrive at our destination. There is a ship's doctor if his services are required, but we hope it will not be needed. God's blessing to us all. The voyage will take possibly three weeks, but the captain hopes for less.

Love, your brother Joey

The Aberdeen Chronicle October 1st, 1899

Mr. Malcolm Murray of number 190 Stonehaven Road wishes to announce his retirement October 31st, 1899. The shop will be closed at the end of that business day, and a new pharmaceutical location will be opened the following week at the Aberdeen South Infirmary.

"It has been with a great deal of satisfaction that I have served this neighbourhood for more than thirty-two years. I thank you for your patronage."

With affection and good wishes, Malcolm Murray

"Well, what do you think, Todd Boy?"

"I think it's perfect, Malcolm. There will be many tears shed when this announcement comes out in a few days. How about we have a short stroll along the sea trail before dinner tonight? Mrs. Cronin has prepared a special dinner surprise for this occasion."

"That sounds like a splendid idea, and we need to get caught up on a lot of news. What about Rachael? Ah'v wondered about the library competition and how she fared with it."

"As it turned out, Malcolm, she fared very well indeed – taking first and second prizes," Todd said, proudly.

"How wonderful! Ah hope to see her soon so Ah can congratulate her in person. Then, another matter: how about soccer, son? When is the first game to be played?"

"It will be October 10 – a home game. We are playing against a Secondary School from Peterhead."

"How exciting for you, son!"

"It will be just a quick visit this Sunday, Rach. I've soccer practise at 2:00 p.m. Are you still up for staying with Malcolm, at least for part of the time?"

"Certainly, Todd. But I will have to leave for the manor by 5:00 p.m. as I'm helping Rebecca serve dinner to Sir Gordon and his guest. It will be her first time doing this task."

"I hope to be back by 5:00 p.m., but if not – shortly after. Would you mind riding back to the manor on your own?"

"That should be alright, Todd. It's not so dark yet at that time of afternoon."

Golden Ribbons

"Ah'm not so sure Ah think this is such a good idea for ye to ride ye'r bike alone, Rachael, especially as it is getting dark so early these fall days," Malcolm said, with concern.

"I'll be very careful, Mr. Murray, and I'm sure Todd will be along any moment. He can come along later if he wants to. It's only a half-hour ride."

Malcolm stood outside the doorway of the shop until he could no longer see Rachael. She waved to him as she turned a corner out of his sight. A dark figure suddenly stepped up in front of Rachael, grabbing the bike's handle bars and stopping her with a jerk. "Wall now, if it isn't little bawl-baby Rachael, and her riding a nice red bike. Did ya hit up the old man fer that one too, sweet'art?"

"What are you doing out of prison, Robby? Get out of my way, right now!"

"Now, now, is that ena'way ta treat y're dear brother-in-law? Leas' you could do is lend me ye'r new bike – just for a day or two."

"No! Now get out of my way!" yelled Rachael as she pushed the bike forward.

"Naw, you get outa ma way, bawl-baby," barked Robby, as he pushed her off onto the street and started pedalling away.

"Hey! What's going on here?" said a constable, pulling up along side on his giant gelding.

"That man knocked me to the ground and grabbed my bike, officer. He might already be far down the street," Rachael called out, with fearful indignation.

"I'm after him then," said the constable.

"What happened here?" yelled Todd, as he pulled up beside Rachael.

"Thank goodness you're here, Todd. It was Robby. He jumped out of nowhere, knocked me to the ground and took off with my bike. The constable, on horseback, is after him."

Just then the constable came back with Robby in tow, a rope around his neck and leading the bike.

"Thank you, constable, for being here when this happened," said Todd. "This ruffian is unfortunately our brother-in-law and he has caused trouble before – raiding Mr. Murray's shop."

"Ah yes, I heard he got away," stated the constable. "He and I will just take a nice little trotting journey to the precinct, and he will be charged and held a little more closely this time. Glad to have been a help." Todd and

Rachael looked on as Robby had to run at top speed to keep up with the mounted policeman.

"I'm sorry this happened, Rachael," said Todd. "Will we ever get Robby out of our lives?"

"Not if he has anything to say about it, I'm afraid. Now, I must get to the manor quickly, and you can accompany me this time. I think Mr. Murray will be worried until you get back to him."

"Yes, I'm sure he will be," agreed Todd, "but we have had very little time together lately, so let's walk our bikes to the manor. I can do a speed trip back to Malcolm."

"I know you have been very busy, Todd, and I have too. Mrs. Olson asked me to spend time in the sewing room to make new kitchen costumes for Rebecca and me. Mrs. Olson doesn't sew, so she is helping Maisie in the kitchen and getting Rebecca used to her duties. So we have all switched around, and it does get confusing."

"I do want to ask you, Todd: do you think I am selfish in wanting to spend my prize money on a new coat and shoes?"

"Certainly not, Rach! You have earned that money, and it should be spent on anything you would like. I'm saving up now for some good soccer shoes."

"Do you think we could go shopping together soon?" she asked. "You can help me pick out a coat, and we can get shoes for both of us. I would have enough money for that."

"Well, I sure would be happy to borrow some money from you, Rach, so that I could have the soccer shoes right away. I hate to ask Malcolm for extra money, he is always generous as it is."

"Well then, let's take a few hours for shopping next Saturday."

"Saturday sounds good, and I'll tell Malcolm about it this evening. By-the-way, did you get the latest letter from Billy and Joey?"

"Yes, Todd. Isn't it amazing how our brothers react to new circumstances! I'm sure Maggie must appreciate their consideration."

"I am indeed amazed as well as awe-struck," he agreed. "The three of them together will make a great team."

Bundy's Department Store was, as always, crowded with shoppers on a Saturday afternoon. "This is the type of long coat I like, Todd. What do you say – the blue, or the red one?"

"I would definitely say red, Rachael," said Todd, as he inspected the array of coats. "Malcolm was mortified that he had not thought to give me extra money for soccer needs, so I'll not have to borrow from you after all. That being the case, I would like to buy you a scarf to go with your new coat. It will be an early gift for your thirteenth birthday next week."

"Thank you, that's so thoughtful. I did admire the black one with red and white embroidery."

"Then, the black one it will be. We did well to pick out shoes so quickly, so off we go and we can catch the last omnibus of the day. Will you be able to come to my first soccer match Monday afternoon, sister?"

"I would like to, Todd, but with all the changes in our daily schedule at the manor, I can't be sure."

"Well, I'll hope to see you there," said Todd. "Doctor Wilkins is attending with Malcolm. He is such a wonderful friend to both of us, and he is making this special effort to accommodate Malcolm's wish to be there for part of the time."

"Good evening, Sir Gordon, and here is your tea tray," Rachael said, with a smile.

"Can you stay and chat a while?" he asked.

"Of course I can, Sir. You seem to have been away a lot of the time, and we have all missed you."

"That's kind of you to say that, Rachael. I'm hearing wonderful things about your stories that went to the publisher in Glasgow, and they are apparently hoping for more."

"Yes, that is wonderful news, Sir Gordon, and I am grateful for that opportunity. However, it will be January before I feel there will be anything to submit on a regular basis. My tutor, Miss James, has accepted a full-time teaching position in January, so my time with her will soon be finished. She feels there is little more she can add to my schooling. Since I will be thirteen next birthday, she said she would write a letter to the Education Department stating that, from her assessment, my basic education is complete."

"That is very good of her, Rachael. Do you feel that her tutoring sped up that process?"

"I believe it did, Sir. One-on-one is far better than one-on-thirty, and I'm grateful to you for giving me that advantage."

"You are very welcome, Rachael. Now about my being away: I am negotiating more sale of lands, and that does take time and travel. As a result, I will be away most of the time until the year end. I'm sure you will all be kept very busy keeping this place going. However, I always leave knowing the manor is in capable hands. I will say good night then."

"Good night, Sir."

The soccer game commenced promptly at 2:00 p.m. Todd was playing forward, and as he ran onto the playing field with his team mates, Malcolm could hardly contain his excitement. "Ah think Todd looks splendid, don't ye Henry?"

"Indeed Malcolm, you have good reason to be proud. He is a fine lad, and a credit to you for all your support and encouragement."

At the mid-time break, Malcolm became agitated and pale. "I believe we should go, Malcolm," remarked Doctor Wilkins. "Todd can tell us about the remainder of the game when he gets home." Malcolm nodded. They walked slowly to the exit where a waiting hansom returned them to Malcolm's shop.

"I'll just slip this tablet under your tongue, Malcolm, and you should feel a bit steadier in a few minutes," assured the Doctor.

"Thank ye, dear friend. It was wonderful to see Todd on the playing field, and ye were so generous to accompany me today."

"That was my pleasure, Malcolm. It reminded me of my own lads when they participated in the game a few years ago before entering university."

"Yes, Ah remember those boys. Ah regret not having the spirit at the time to attend such wonderful events. Before Todd came along, Ah was a miserable auld sod, right Henry?"

"I guess you were," Doctor Wilkins laughed. "But, now is the time to be thankful that some joy crept in to change you before it was too late. We two are old friends, Malcolm, and we can speak openly about the number of days you have left on this troubled old earth."

With stethoscope on Malcolm's chest, he added: "I count two minor strokes in the past few hours. You must remain quiet and rested as much as you possibly can, - not for your sake, but for Todd's. He must be prepared for the day when he will lose you. I'm sure you have thought about how he should carry on?"

"Oh, indeed, Ah have, Henry. My solicitor has all the information. Ah have tried to think of everything that will guide this young man after I am gone. Somehow, Ah do not feel that we need to have a talk about it. We both know that all will be his, and we have trust that the future will progress as we would both want it."

"That's wonderful, Malcolm. Now, I must slip away to the infirmary," said the doctor. "When Todd comes home and has any concerns, he should come get me immediately. You get some sleep now."

As Todd took a quick look up to the stands where Malcolm and Doctor Wilkins had been seated, he realized they had left because Malcolm was not feeling well. *What would Malcolm want me to do now?* he thought. But the answer was clear: he should carry on with the game and put his full attention on it.

"I'm afraid they shut us out the last play, Malcolm," Todd reported. "But it was close, and our team was satisfied that we played well."

"That's the main thing, son. Ah surely did enjoy the game."

"Thanks, Malcolm, it was great knowing you were there. The return game is next Monday in Peterhead, about two hours travel time - both to go and come back again. I believe Mrs. Cronin plans to drop in a time or two throughout the afternoon."

"Then Doctor Wilkins will come for a bit in the evening," Malcolm added, "until ye get home."

"Now that my basic education is complete, I'm sorry that we have to part, Miss James. Can I offer you some tea before you leave?"

"Thank you, Rachael. I have enjoyed our times together, but we both must move on. I am looking forward to a full classroom again."

When Rachael returned the tea tray to the kitchen, she found Maisie bent over some writing. "Ah'm just getting a note off to ma brother in Montpellier, France," explained Maisie. "He operates a school for deaf children there."

"Goodness, Maisie, my world gets smaller all the time as I hear of our own people doing wonderful things in other countries."

"Come sit with me awhile, Rachael. Ah've made a decision today – not an easy one. Ma brother has often suggested to me that Ah consider moving to Montpellier to be with him and his family, best of all to assist in the school. And so, Ah'm dropping a line today to say – yes. It will be wonderful to be near my brother again, and an opportunity to do something new and useful."

"Oh, Maisie, I can hardly imagine what the manor will be without you. But I do understand that such a challenge is a necessary part of life. I will wish you all the joys this new experience will bring. How can I adequately express my love and gratitude to you for the times we've had together. But, when will you be leaving?" asked Rachael.

"Ah should have ma affairs in order by the end of February, so Ah will be leaving sometime soon after that."

"I am so happy and excited for you, Maisie!"

Rachael pondered over this latest news. She had lived in this special place such a short time, and yet it had revealed so much to her about her own life, as well of those who had become precious to her. *To stand still is never acceptable,* she thought. *Sir Gordon has reminded me of that truth so many times. We must embrace change and welcome it.*

CHAPTER EIGHT

MALCOLM AND TODD HAD TEA AND SCONES FOR THEIR BREAKFAST before Todd left for Peterhead with his team mates. Malcolm got out of his chair, slowly, and made his way to his usual green leather chair. Todd brought a blanket to put around him.

"Now, are you warm enough?" Todd asked. "I will just stoke the fire one more time to make sure. Mrs. Cronin will be asking about your needs."

"Ah'm just fine, son. If ye would just fetch me ma notepad and a pen, Ah have another journal entry before it is taken off to the pharmacy."

"Now, you rest well today, I will be thinking of you at various times of the day, and I will play hard, just for my dear friend, Malcolm."

"Ah know ye will strive to the best of ye'r ability, son, just as ye have done since the day Ah first laid eyes on ye. Do ye remember? It is just over a year since we met at the door of this shop, and Ah almost turned ye away."

"That would have been most unfortunate for me, Malcolm. You are the best friend I have ever had."

"As for me, Todd boy, ye are everything."

"O.K. then, if that's the way it is, I abandon myself to *mushy stuff*, and tell you that I love you, Malcolm. You are my father."

"Now Todd boy, ye know I don't…" Malcolm's voice faded away.

"I know you don't go in for *mushy stuff*. I'll let you off this time. So dear friend, I'll leave you for now." Todd was choking back tears; as he opened the door to leave, he gave a smile and a victory sign.

Malcolm gave a weak cough and mouthed, without sound, "I love you, Todd."

Riding swiftly away on his bike, Todd resolved: *I will only think of Malcolm today when there is a happy moment, or if the sun comes out on this dull day. Or if we win!*

When Todd returned home at eight o'clock in the evening, he noted the lamps were burning in the shop. Doctor Wilkins met him at the door. "He is gone, Todd. Mrs. Cronin said he died peacefully while she was here with him."

"I guess I knew he would not be here when I got home. I appreciate that you have stayed to tell me, Doctor Wilkins. Still it is very hard."

"Good night, Todd, I will see you in the morning. I want to assist in any way I can."

"Good night, Doctor."

Todd tossed his school bag onto the small table in front of the hearth and sat down in Malcolm's old green leather chair. *We won, Malcolm! That was for you.*

The notebook and pen were open on the floor beside the chair. Todd knew it would be a letter to him.

> Dear son Todd: I feel that a welcome closure is coming today. I rather think that you know it too. Please drop in to see my solicitor as he is in charge of settling all accounts. Everything else belongs to you. As well, do sell the shop when you are ready to leave yourself.

Reaching toward a lump at the side of the chair, Todd smiled when he saw that a flask of whisky was kept there. As he remembered: it was not yet October 31st, Todd pulled out the CLOSED sign, hung it in the shop window, and went to bed.

"Good morning, Todd," greeted Doctor Wilkins. "Were you able to get some sleep last night? Yesterday was a very heavy day for you."

"Yes, Doctor, I was able to sleep knowing that Malcolm is safe now. The past few weeks have been so hard, watching his decline every day."

"Did Malcolm mention to you that there should be no funeral," asked Doctor Wilkins, "and also that he is to be buried at Hillside Cemetery?"

"It was like him not to mention it, Doctor Wilkins, but thank you for telling me his wishes now. Those would have been very hard decisions to make."

Doctor Wilkins continued, "Todd, I would like to speak to the school about Malcolm's death on your behalf. You will need the rest of the week to attend the burial tomorrow morning, and then to meet with the solicitor – all in good time."

"Thank you Doctor, those are matters I would not have thought about. I'm in a bit of a fog right now, and I appreciate all that you are doing for me."

"Todd, I have to tell you that, until a few weeks ago, I had no idea of the depth of the relationship you and Malcolm shared. It was father-son, friend, companion, confidant, all rolled into one. It was a very unique relationship, indeed, and one that many fathers and sons could only dream about."

"Yes, that's true, Doctor Wilkins. And I believe it has not ended. I will always consult with my memory bank before making any big decision. What would Malcolm think or say?"

"That is very remarkable. Do you plan to remain here for a time, Todd?"

"Yes, for now. I have to complete the transfer of records, and usable medications to the new pharmacy. I will not mind living here a short while, Doctor. I think Malcolm would want me to do that."

"Then, I will see you at the burial, Todd."

"Thank you again, Doctor Wilkins."

As the Doctor left, Sergeant McTavish arrived to extend condolences.

Todd acknowledged the expression, relating Malcolm's high regard for the Sergeant: "He always called you *McTavish*, which to me meant you were more than the neighbourhood law enforcer, but someone to trust and appreciate. But, could I ask a favour? I would like a note sent over to Rachael, telling her of Malcolm's death."

"Certainly Todd," the Sergeant agreed. "Just bring the note over to the precinct whenever it is ready."

And so it went throughout the morning. Mrs. Cronin came to give Todd a motherly hug, which he gratefully returned. "Mr. Murray was a dear man," she said. "He left me £40 to see that you are fed regularly."

"Ah think Ah can manage the Christmas cakes and puddings, with Rebecca's help," said Maisie. "You have been kept busy in the sewing room, Rachael, and that will be enough for you to handle."

"I will miss that baking fun this year, Maisie, but no doubt there will be fewer cakes and puddings required now that so many of the farms have been sold."

"Ah am sorry to say this is verra true. Sir Gordon is being taxed even more heavily this coming year. John will be working on expanding the old stable into a more accommodating one for a carriage and one more steed; the Benz will be next to go. Ah believe Sir Gordon is happy with that decision, not so for Duncan, however," smiled Daisy.

"Ah did hear Malcolm Murray has died, Rachael. Ah expect your brother will be sorry for his passing."

"Indeed, that is true, Maisie. They have been like father and son. I loved Mr. Murray too."

September 26, 1899 Port of Spain, Trinidad

Dear Family: Well, here we are on dry land again, and it does feel good. This is a beautiful port on the north westerly tip of South America. It was an excellent voyage: mainly clear skies, light winds, and many sightings of sea animals. To see a school of whales spouting as they break through the surface of the water is an awesome sight!

The cargo taken on here is sugar cane, coffee, cocoa, and various varieties of nuts. We are trading in sacking, of course, and hydraulic equipment. Textiles and Singer Sewing Machines are being saved for New York, although those commodities could have traded anywhere along the line.

We will leave this port in two days and ply our way around the Windward and Leeward Islands to the next port of call in the Bahamas. We are all well, and send our good wishes to all of you.

Your brother, Billy

Todd took time every evening to walk the sea trail that had been such a pleasure with Malcolm. It was this activity of walking together at the end of each day that he missed most. It was almost finished: the tasks of sorting and packing for himself, and for Malcolm's usable clothing and furniture to be sent to the charity. It was not home anymore, but he would stay on until after the New Year holiday in Dundee. When he went to see the solicitor at the end of the week, he would enquire about the process of selling the shop in the near future.

"I have to tell you, Todd, that Malcolm was not a man who spent a great deal of time counting his money," said Mr. Thomas Ross, the solicitor. "He had on deposit far more than he realized. What he has arranged for you is an annuity of £150 to be paid out annually until you have completed secondary school. He assumed you would then go on to University; but, in any case, the remainder of the estate will be at your disposal at age eighteen.

"I understand you may be running a bit ahead of the age seventeen leaving age, therefore I have permission to grant you whatever your needs are until age eighteen. That may be up to a period of two years. You will get a full accounting of what will be paid out on behalf of Malcolm's final expenses, and a chequing account will be set up in your name. And, yes, I am sorry to say there will be death and inheritance taxes when all is completed. But for now, Todd, just get along as best you can knowing that Malcolm is looking out for you as we speak.

"This is much to be digested, Todd," the solicitor went on, "but Malcolm was confident you will make good use of all he has left to you. He even made a suggestion that gifts be made to your sisters, as well as an investment toward your brothers' farm operation in Canada. He was completely enthralled and passionate about their courage and daring – setting off with only determination and reputation for hard work. This is, of course, discretionary on your part.

"You asked about the sale of the shop," continued Mr. Thomas Ross. "For now let's just keep that as it is. It may be that the old building being sold will only add to your tax burden and you might be wiser to simply donate it to the City of Aberdeen. Please drop in any time if you have questions regarding this last will and testament."

I have questions about everything, thought Todd, as he later started out on the familiar walk. Bringing Malcolm to mind, he blurted out loud, "Malcolm, please tell me what to do next!" It became clear to Todd within minutes: he would get back to school the following week, and simply carry on. *Just be yourself, Todd boy, that's the very best you can do,* came the memory of Malcolm's voice.

You are nearer to me now than before, old friend, thought Todd.

The weeks sped by for Todd with school, soccer, and shopping trips with Rachael. "I believe two toys for each child should be enough, Rach. We must not spoil them, although we would like to."

"That is so true," agreed Rachael. "The holidays tug at those impulses. I am sewing a dressing gown for Aggie, I know she will love it. Of course the cake and puddings will be packaged up and taken along as well. I want this New Year to be special for us, Todd, and also for Aggie and the children. There should be letters coming from Billy, Joey and Maggie soon. I hope they bring in the New Year at their own home, or at least close to it. It seems so incomplete now to just refer to Billy and Joey, it is like Maggie has always been part of the team."

"I know what you mean, I feel that way too."

Excitement was building at Aggie's home as they awaited the visitors' arrival. The house was decorated with coloured streamers, and the smell of good cooking wafted throughout from the kitchen. As the train pulled into Dundee station, Aggie and the children were there with outstretched arms. It was a joyous reunion.

During the special dinner, Aggie could wait no longer to share her good news: she had been accepted into the new school of nursing, beginning in early January.

"That is such wonderful news, Aggie!" exclaimed Rachael.

"Congratulations, Sister," said Todd, as he circled the table to give Aggie a hug. "You will be a marvellous nurse!"

"There is no doubt, I have you both as my inspiration," Aggie responded.

With dinner cleared away and the children tucked into bed, the others settled into comfortable chairs in the parlour of the old home to read the letter received from their brothers and Maggie.

November 15, 1899 New York Harbour

> Dear family: Because of heavy storms and cross winds, we had to bypass Central America altogether, so now we are in New York. There are line ups of cargo steamers and combination passenger-cargo ships in the harbour, and so we wait our turn to unload and to trade. Passengers on the other ships are from all over Europe – men, women and children.
>
> As each lighter or steamship moves its cargo to shore, the waterfront is a bedlam. Clattering wagons swerve around heaps of boxes and crates as newsboys and peddlers compete with the crying children. The passengers are somehow moved through this maze to immigration on Ellis Island – a short ferry ride. We are glad to be moving on to a smaller port of demarcation.
>
> The ship is now two regular seamen short, but a very large black man has been taken on to fill their places through to Montreal. He has already been helpful in getting our cargo stationed on the ship so there will be less confusion when

it is finally moved ashore. His name is Joshua, and Joey and Maggie have had an opportunity to meet him. They have learned that Joshua has been around the dock waiting for an opportunity to board a ship going to Canada.

Maggie has been a brick through all this waiting and confusion, but we hope to be on our way by tomorrow mid-morning. We have urged Maggie not to carry on with her work in the ship's kitchen, but she is determined to continue until we land in Montreal. Maggie has brought us good luck in so many ways, and yet again she has surprised us: she has convinced the captain and purser to allow her to purchase a Singer Sewing Machine and a bolt of flannel from the ship's cargo. This is a special favour; her faithful service as a cook's assistant has been rewarded and these items will accompany us when we leave ship.

You will not hear from us again until that happy day when we are on dry land. We are glad to know you will all be together to bring in the new century.

Our love and best wishes to each of you, your brothers Billy and Joey, and from Maggie

---

Smoke from the jute mills had been cleared as the New Year approached. It was accomplished grudgingly, but the residents of Dundee were happy that pressure put on the owners finally made them concede - the mills were shut down for the prior eight hour shift. People from every corner of Dundee were lined along the hills above the Firth of Tay, it seemed the whole city was out that evening to celebrate and welcome in the new century. When the siren ended its five minute wail to indicate midnight, followed by a few minutes of thunderous fire works that lit up the sky, a great cheer was heard and all joined hands to sing the hymn of the old national bard:

Should auld acquaintance be forgot
And never brought to mind?
Should auld acquaintance be forgot,
    And days of auld lang syne?
(refrain)
For auld land syne, my dear,
    For auld lang syne.
We'll take a cup of kindness yet
    For auld lang syne.
We two have run about the braes,
    And pulled the gowans fine,
But we've wandered many a weary fit
    Since auld lang syne.
And there's a hand my trusty fiere,
    And give's a hand of thine,
And we'll take a right guid-willie waught,
    For auld lang syne.

When she could be heard, Rachael asked: "What in the world is a guid-willie waught?"

An old man with a cane stepped forward and called out: "Wha it's a 'good will drink' ma good lass!"

This time, with arms linked together, the refrain was sung again, and with gusto:

"We'll take a cup of kindness yet, for auld lang syne!"

"I liked the fire works best," said Mary.

"What is a century?" asked Peter, "I thought it was New Years!"

"It is both, Peter," explained Aggie. "The new century is the beginning of the next 100 years, just as the last one was. That's why this New Year celebration is so special – the start of the next 100 years."

The New Year 1900 brought a heavy snowfall to Aberdeen. When Todd returned to the old shop after school each afternoon, he felt confined and missed the use of his bike. "Now I can appreciate that bike more than ever,

Malcolm," he said to the old green leather chair. "Perhaps, if the cold and snow continues I may find another place to call home; Mrs. Cronin has offered a room and that may be an option. But then again, Malcolm, I miss being busy with deliveries, and why would I keep house here when you are not here to keep house for?" As Todd began to spread his notes and books over the table, he heard a knock at the front door.

"Hello Todd, and Happy New Year!" said Doctor Wilkins.

"Nice to see you, Doctor. The same good wishes to you. What brings you out on this cold and stormy afternoon? Come in and get warmed, I just built up the fire."

"Well, that's just the point, Todd. I sure would not have ventured out except to say that we could use your help over at the pharmacy. Two of our people there are down with influenza-like symptoms, and the orders are piling up. I'm hoping you can come over to straighten them out for us, and prioritize the serious ones. Unfortunately, the streets as they are – covered with snow and ice, you would have to walk to make the deliveries where necessary. We hope there are not too many."

"Certainly, Doctor Wilkins!" Todd replied, trying not to sound too eager. "I was just in a mood to find something useful to do."

"That's wonderful, Todd. You can plan to have your evening meal with those of us who are marooned at the infirmary this evening. I have a carriage waiting outside, so let's go!"

Todd put his coat on quickly, then took a backward glance at the old green leather chair, and smiled.

It was a delight for Todd to be back doing the tasks he knew so well. He set to work immediately sorting the orders and within minutes he had three scribbled repeats set aside; each one was for ladies he knew from his time at the old shop; Malcolm would tell him that these ladies just wanted to have him come by on his bike to share a cup of tea. Todd often felt this was true. Miss Hickson greeted him warmly suggesting he stay awhile to warm up.

"I'm sorry, Mam," said Todd, "but I have two other orders to deliver and I'm on foot, for – as you see, biking in this weather would be quite dangerous."

"Of course, I do see that Todd. I hope you will be making deliveries for the new pharmacy in the future."

"Actually," said Todd, "I am just helping out this evening."

The other two repeats were of a similar nature; certainly not urgent, even though that was reflected on the order. Todd felt sad for these ladies who were obviously lonely and wanting company, even that of a delivery lad. Sad, yes, but at the same time impatient with people who waste others' time for their own solace. *There are so many real needs around us, and so few who are called to respond,* he thought. *Then there is Mrs. Cronin: she always put herself out to be kind to Malcolm, even when he was, at one time, a cranky old man.*

Huddled in his coat and cap, Todd was back at the pharmacy where he was greeted again by Doctor Wilkins. "It seems, Todd, we can't get along without you. I realize you still have many matters to clear up since Malcolm's death, but whatever time you have in the future – well, let's discuss how we could work it out." After a good but hurried meal with the infirmary staff, Todd made his way home again feeling that, once again, Malcolm was setting a new path for him.

As the day of Maisie's departure approached, there was a reluctant scramble to redesign household duties at the manor. "We must plan a suitable send-off for Maisie," said Jean Olson, speaking to Rachael and Rebecca, "so that will be our first task. Then, we'll have to see how we can get along without her."

"I have a suggestion for the short term," said Rachael. "With Rebecca's help in planning meals for Sir Gordon, cooking and table setting can be less elaborate and we can work out between the two of us how we will rotate clean-up. We should also consult with Duncan to see if he might take over late night tea time, as he is here at the manor at that time anyway. Housekeeping will have to be shared; perhaps the rooms can remain without dusting and mopping for an extra day each week."

"Thank you Rachael for laying that out so simply and completely. I have been, quite frankly, at a loss to even be able to contemplate the change. So, indeed, we will talk to Duncan about tea time. Let's not forget that Sir Gordon may also have some ideas."

Rachael realized that she must put aside her own feelings of loss to accommodate Mrs. Olson in every way possible. After all, Mrs. Olson had worked with Maisie for more than twenty years and they were also close friends.

Sir Gordon arrived home from his business travels the end of January. He was noticeably ill, and looked very tired. "Of course I want to be part of the send-off for Maisie," he said. "What has been planned so far, Rachael?" he asked, as she served him tea and a peppermint brew.

"We thought a late family dinner with all staff attending, Sir. I will team with Rebecca in coming up with the best dinner we know how to prepare, and we will also do the serving - just like a regular family."

"Yes, and I must find an appropriate gift. Perhaps Mrs. Olson can help me there, I will speak to her about it. I hope the remaining staff people will not find the work too heavy with one important one missing."

"I believe we have it covered for now, Sir. Once Maisie is gone, we will consult with you regarding the closing off of some of the large rooms on the main floor to save housekeeping and heating."

"That's excellent Rachael! We are definitely in economy mode now, and I must explain fully to all the staff the financial position in which I now find myself," said Sir Gordon, looking defeated and sorrowful.

"You can count on very strong support, Sir. We all respect and admire you. Meanwhile, all our attention and love will go toward Maisie, and we will wish her much happiness in her new life."

"Indeed Rachael. She has been as faithful as any household member could be. Please keep me informed of the time and day you plan this farewell dinner. I will not be available in my study tomorrow; I must rest in my rooms for an important meeting the following day."

Rachael spoke to Mrs. Olson concerning Sir Gordon's state of health and spirit. "He does seem very ill."

Jean Olson nodded in agreement, but did not speak.

CHAPTER NINE

A LETTER FROM THE SOLICITOR ARRIVED FOR TODD, AND HE WAS quick to open it. He had not heard from Mr. Thomas Ross for several weeks.

> Dear Todd: Pursuant to our visit following Malcolm's death, I enclose a full accounting of all expenses incurred both before and after that sad event. Please call in to see me as soon as possible, Todd, there are matters pending that call for immediate attention.
>
> Yours, Thomas Ross

"Hello Todd! I'm glad you could come straightaway," greeted the solicitor. "There are several items on the agenda for attention. First: recalling our conversation regarding disposal of the shop, you will be surprised, as I was, to have a prospective purchaser come forward with an offer. The gentleman in question is a relatively young man who is interested in converting the shop into an ice cream parlour! He, along with his young wife, would completely renovate the building – both inside and out. I have his cheque for £200 to hold the property until speaking with you, but he hopes to take possession at the earliest possible date.

"If this seems a reasonable offer to you, Todd, it also means that the contents of the shop must now be removed as soon as possible."

"Yes, Mr. Ross, I believe that the contents of the shop can be removed at any time. I depend on you, as Malcolm did, to have done the necessary research into property values to make an informed recommendation. Therefore, I believe that Malcolm would approve this sale. The thought of breathing life back into the old shop, rather than having it weather away to nothing, is something I personally find very exciting as well as practical."

"Another matter, but related," stated the solicitor, "is Malcolm's wish to provide gifts to your sisters, Aggie and Rachael, and also to administer a boost to your brothers' farm operation in the form of an investment. My feeling and recommendation in this matter is that £50 each be immediately given to your sisters in accordance with the overall worth of the estate at this time.

"We might also consider the sale of the shop as a trade-off to an investment in the farm operation. I recommend, no - insist, that an investment certificate be drawn up, with all parties signing. In matters where there is an exchange of money, it is necessary to do so – especially between family members. Even if the operation is not a success, and this happens, then at least a formal process was followed. But we are assuming it will be a success and that you, on Malcolm's behalf, will be a shareholder."

"I approve those measures as well," said Todd.

"Very well then, I will have my assistant write two £50 notes, credited to your sisters, and if you can wait fifteen minutes, it will be accomplished right away. You can sign for them and then deliver them personally. Is that satisfactory?"

"Yes, thank you Mr. Ross."

"An investment certificate will take longer to prepare and execute," the solicitor continued, "but I understand that your brothers are either on their way, or have barely arrived at their destination. This will provide you with enough time to inform them of Malcolm's interest in their future. When I know that this information has been received, you will be asked to sign the investment certificate and this will go along with a money transfer made through one of our banks to the Imperial Bank of Canada in Calgary. After the certificate is signed at that financial location, and it is returned to my office, your brothers can then use these funds that, I'm sure, will be most welcome."

"Once again, Sir, I am very satisfied with this process, and I will write to my brothers immediately."

"It is a pleasure working with you, Todd," said the solicitor. "Please don't wait until you hear from me. If you have a question or concern, do not hesitate to contact me immediately."

Golden Ribbons

As Todd waited for the gifts to be prepared for Aggie and Rachael, he felt again the presence of Malcolm. He was at peace knowing that Malcolm's final wishes were being honoured. He could now get on with the business of accepting Mrs. Cronin's kindly offer of accommodation, and he would arrange for a dray to pick up what remained in the old shop.

Rachael went quickly to the watch maker's shop. She had enough money now to make the final payment on Todd's birthday gift, and she was excited about presenting it to him. *Oh, I hope he likes it,* she said to herself. *When he comes to the manor on Sunday, I will suggest we have tea and cake at a nearby confectioner.*

"This was a good idea, Rach. I have a million things to tell you."

"First of all, Happy Birthday, Todd," said Rachael as she brought the package out of her reticule and placed it on the table.

"My goodness, Rachael, I had forgotten all about it. Here I am an old man of fourteen! Should I open it now?"

"Well certainly, go ahead," urged Rachael.

"It is wonderful, I mean beautiful, my sister! Do I deserve such a handsome pocket watch? I never imagined I would have one. Thank you so much, Rachael, I'm overwhelmed. I love the engraving of the sailing ship on the cover."

"I'm so glad you like it, Todd. I don't know if you deserve it, but it is given because you are a special brother, and I love you to pieces."

"Thank you, thank you," he repeated, giving his sister a rough hug. "Ahh, Wow!" He stood gazing at the watch several minutes before he reluctantly placed it carefully into the front pocket of his trousers.

"With all this excitement, I almost forgot what I have to tell you. Malcolm has left a gift for you and Aggie. I have yours in my satchel. Here it is – all yours, from Malcolm."

"Oh, from Mr. Murray!" exclaimed Rachael. "How wonderful of him to do that, and it's such a big gift!"

"He enjoyed your visits so much, and was always interested in the details of your life. Though he hadn't met Aggie, he heard about her and felt he knew her. I'm sure his gift will greatly ease her financial burden right now."

"Oh, of course it will, Todd."

Todd finished the visit by telling Rachael about the proposed ice cream parlour, and his decision to live in Mrs. Cronin's home. There were more items for discussion than there was time to spend together. Arm in arm, chatting noisily, the brother and sister returned to the manor in time for Rachael to prepare the evening meal. As he rode away on his bike, Todd waved to Rachael then displayed his new pocket watch, clutching it to his heart.

Rachael laughed and waved back.

December 07, 1899 On board the immigrant train, out of Montreal.

Dear Family: We are on our way west, and it will take about a week, as long as there is no problem with heavy snow on the tracks. You will not believe this, but we are sitting comfortably in the club car, awaiting the first call for dinner. Our complementary tickets cover one meal a day on board the train. We decided to ask a compartment for Maggie; she deserves good rests and the conveniences that will certainly not be available at our destination.

I must speak now about our new friend, Joshua, and the trauma of boarding the train. We were sorry that our acquaintance with him would be so short, assuming his point of departure being Montreal. As we started out on the long walk from dock to rail station, trolleys of baggage, crates and boxes following behind, Joshua swept Maggie swiftly into his arms and strode off toward the train station like a man with a mission. We lagged behind with our loads, wondering what Joshua was doing – he certainly didn't have a ticket to board. He paused on the station platform to let us get closer, and we could see he was talking earnestly with Maggie. She nodded her head in agreement.

"Gangway you people," he hollered, as he quickly boarded the train. "This little lady is about to give birth. I am a doctor, and I require four seats together to make sure all will go well."

The porters departed quickly, having collected tickets from the startled passengers already seated. Joey and I managed to squeeze our way onto the train that was filling quickly, and then looked around for Joshua and Maggie. Moving from car to car, we finally found Maggie sitting alone in the last car. The other passengers looked relieved as she came along with us to a forward car where we had reserved seats. We have no idea how long this charade can be kept up, but Maggie finds the incident hilarious. The only explanation Joshua offered her was that he planned to accompany us to our destination, and he would see us again when we arrived.

The adventure continues! There may be a possibility of our arriving at our destination by Christmas.

Love to all, your brother Billy. Joey and Maggie send good wishes.

Sir Gordon was seated at the head of the long table in the main dining room, with Maisie beside him. The others seated themselves as they felt comfortable. Duncan served wine as Rachael and Rebecca hurried in with platters of succulently prepared beef and duck, as well as a vast variety of fragrant side dishes.

"This is a wonderful meal prepared to honour our long enjoyed friend, Maisie," said Sir Gordon. "How we will miss you, Maisie, but wish you all of the good things that your new life will bring." Raising his glass, he added: "To Maisie!" All responded with clinking of glasses, good wishes and cheerful conversation.

Rachael was pleased that Sir Gordon felt well enough to attend the parting occasion for Maisie, but it was noticeable that he had made a special effort to be there. He was pale and exhausted, excusing himself often to cough.

The next day, Jean Olson accompanied Maisie to her port of departure at Dover. Watching from the library windows as the carriage pulled away, Rachael decided to let herself cry. *It's hard to be cheerful when there have been so many partings,* she sobbed.

"What I can offer you, Todd, is a choice of one of the two attic rooms," said Mrs. Cronin. "The front one is the largest, so I expect that would appeal to you. It has a large window, and faces the front street. I would have to ask you to help me move all the items from one room to the other, I'm afraid I've been very neglectful in cleaning out these spaces regularly."

"I see no reason to worry about that, Mrs. Cronin, I am more than happy to move items around, and the space you describe sounds quite acceptable."

"Then, we will go have a look see, before you make your decision."

It was a narrow staircase to the attic, but Todd was delighted to see what was there. "I like this front-facing room very much, Mrs. Cronin. I hope you will give me a free hand in designing the space for myself. I plan to keep Malcolm's old green leather chair," said Todd, as he pondered its place in the room.

"I am delighted to have you here, Todd," assured Mrs. Cronin, "and you just do whatever will make this space home. No doubt you will need another strong person to help you move the old green chair up the stairs, but we can work that out."

"It's a deal, Mrs. Cronin!" exclaimed Todd.

As Todd returned to the shop, he remembered that he had packed all of Malcolm's belongings into boxes, all except the gun. "I will go to see what Sergeant McTavish would recommend about that," he muttered. Placing the gun gingerly into a paper sack, Todd headed out toward the precinct.

"Well now, Todd, what have ya got there?"

"It's Malcolm's gun, Sergeant, and I wonder what I can do with it. I certainly don't want to keep it."

"Just you come with me to a back cupboard here," said the Sergeant. When unlocked and opened, the cupboard contained shelves of various types of ancient fire arms.

"This is a little hobby of ours here at the precinct, Todd. Whenever someone wants to turn in a gun, we check to see how old it is and, if it meets the *ancient* category, we place it with the rest in this cupboard. It would be a pleasure to have Malcolm's old gun; it must be at least 100 years old, and possibly from Ireland."

"I think Malcolm would be honoured to have his gun in such a place. Can we say you will take it?"

"We surely will," agreed the Sergeant. "I hear you are moving over to Mrs. Cronin's home. I think you will like it there. Is there anything I can do to help?"

"Coincidentally, yes, Sergeant," said Todd. "I want to keep Malcolm's old green chair, and I need a strong helper to get it up the stairs to the front attic room of Mrs. Cronin's home."

"Consider it done, Todd. One or more of us here at the precinct will be happy to do that for you. Just let us know when it is ready to go."

So, Malcolm, will your old green chair be comfortable here? I think it looks wonderful in front of the window where we can keep an eye on the shop to see how the ice cream parlour is progressing. Looking further around the room, Todd could see all the possibilities with the furniture available: a good bed, an old door that could be made into a desk, and a comfortable chair.

Tomorrow he would unroll the large hooked rug. *I have lots of evenings to sort this all out,* he thought, *and I must get into the habit of letting Mrs. Cronin know what I'm doing, and when she should expect me for meals. It's all so different now, Malcolm. There seemed no need to explain anything. I do miss you.*

Since there was still some of the winter afternoon available, Todd decided to drop into the infirmary. Perhaps Doctor Wilkins would be in.

Todd made himself comfortable in the manor's kitchen for his Sunday chat with Rachael. "I'm sure you miss Maisie," he said, with concern.

"Oh yes I do, Todd, but the good thing about being so busy, as we are now without her, it's impossible to think much about it. We all look forward to the first letter coming from Montpellier.

"I do have a matter to discuss with you today, Todd. I have received a letter from the publisher in Glasgow where my books were sent for review. It states the books are selling well in a number of shops, and a small payment was received in receipt of them. This Mr. McWiggins suggests that I arrange a visit to his office in Glasgow soon to discuss the possibility of writing a series of adventure books for children. This is very frightening, Todd, I have never been to Glasgow. Do you think you might be able to take a day or two from school," she asked pleadingly.

"Oooeee, Rach! That does sound exciting! But, Rach, you need some time to think about it. Do you want to do it, and also – do you have time?"

"Thank you, Todd. Meanwhile, I will discuss this with Sir Gordon when he is feeling better."

Rachael found Duncan sitting in Sir Gordon's study at an extra desk set up for him. "Hello Duncan," she greeted, "do you think Sir Gordon would feel well enough to speak to me for a few minutes?"

"Oh I believe so, Rachael. He is out of bed now and dressed. Just give a rap on his door."

"Come in, Rachael, it is good to see you," said Sir Gordon. "I'm feeling like a prisoner since the doctor came around to see me. But at least I can get up and read for a while."

"I'm glad to hear that Sir. We are at the end of February now, and soon the days will be longer. Perhaps a short walk in the sunshine will be something to look forward to."

"That does sound good, and I would enjoy it that much more if you could take that short walk with me."

Golden Ribbons

"I will make sure of that, Sir," Rachael smiled.

"What can I do for you today, Rachael?" Sir Gordon asked.

"Well, it's not about the household, for a change, Sir. I have received a letter from the publisher in Glasgow. You remember referring a McWiggins Publishing to me regarding the books I wrote for the library competition?"

"Oh, yes – yes, of course."

"Mr. McWiggins asks that I consider writing a series of adventure books for children. He asks, also, that I make a trip to Glasgow soon to talk with him about it."

"Oh, that's a publisher for you! They stamp every piece of paper that passes across their desks with URGENT!" Sir Gordon made a sweeping motion, fist on table, to demonstrate the rubber stamp routine. Rachael laughed, sensing that Sir Gordon must already be feeling better.

"I would recommend that for now you simply acknowledge receipt of his letter, and indicate you will consider his request. Just take your time with this, Rachael, there is nothing urgent about it. At your leisure, think about the possibilities that lie within this offer. Knowing you, as we all do, I expect you will come up with a counter proposal that will dazzle him. But, remember, all in good time."

"Thank you, Sir. My position here at the manor will always come first. But, I will consult with you about this matter from time to time, if I may?"

"I am always pleased to chat with you, Rachael. It has brightened my day just having you come to see me today."

"Todd, you know the routine side of this operation better than we do," expressed Doctor Wilkins. "I would like you to come along to the pharmacy whenever you can. We need to know how to do things better."

"I have to tell you, Doctor," Todd responded. "Had Malcolm lived, there would have been changes made. Most obviously, deliveries needed to be phased out - unless in unusual circumstances. When you think of it, Sir, the patients are receiving their orders right here at the infirmary, then they can then walk a few steps to the pharmacy and have their order prioritized along with others. I would think they could have their medication in as short a time as fifteen minutes, just by waiting for it. But this would be a big change from having a delivery boy at the door, and for the people to accept."

"Yes, indeed it would Todd. By giving patients the option of waiting," Dr. Wilkins continued, thoughtfully. "Well, we would have to try it, one patient at a time, and you can certainly help us by passing the word *change* along gently."

Miss Hickson finished seeing her doctor at the infirmary, and with medication order in hand, she passed it quickly to the pharmacist. "Hello," she called to Todd. "I'll see you later."

"Hello Miss Hickson," greeted Todd. "You might have noticed, with your last order, a note saying that the pharmacy no longer delivers orders, unless in unusual circumstances. I'm sure if you take a seat, your order will be ready in a few minutes and you can take it home with you."

"Do you really think Mr. Murray would have approved of this ridiculous idea, Todd?" Miss Hickson said hotly.

"Yes, he would have, Miss Hickson, and, had he been able to carry on in the business, the change would have been implemented in his shop as well. For many years Malcolm always put the patient's welfare ahead of his own, and his health reflected the ongoing demands placed on him."

"Nonsense! He never complained to me," said Miss Hickson hotly.

"If you will take a seat, your order will be ready shortly," Todd continued with conviction.

"But I do feel weak after a doctor's examination, Todd, - my heart, you know. If I walk home right away it usually passes."

"Just sit down," said Todd, patiently. "If you suddenly feel weak, I will be able to find a nice cup of tea for you."

Miss Hickson folded her arms in defiance just as the pharmacist said, "Your order is ready Miss Hickson." As she grabbed the package from him, he added. "It has been a pleasure to serve you."

"Well, that might be *one down* Todd," said Doctor Wilkins, when he heard about the incident.

"We would like to think that, Sir," returned Todd.

Dundee. February 23, 1900

Dear Todd: You have no idea how welcome Mr. Murray's gift will be! It is like a miracle. Without this kind gesture, I don't know how I would have paid for Mary and Peter's care while I am in day classes. His regard for you, Todd, must have known no bounds.

God Bless you and those whose lives you touch.

Love, your sister Aggie

As soon as her letter of acknowledgement to Mr. McWiggins was posted, Rachael began to put a plan together regarding the adventure series proposed to her. *Let's see now,* she pondered. *I would think a girl of my own age the best option. I would relate to her dilemmas, her likes and her dislikes.*

Now, for a name: I like Polly as a character name; it sounded open, friendly, a bit mischievous, as well as impulsive. The last name should also be a 'P': Poffenroth, Purkins, Preston, Pringle, Peters ... Which first and last name is a good match? All of a sudden, it became obvious: "Polly Peters!" she exclaimed. "Yes, that's it: <u>The Adventures of Polly Peters</u>." Rachael decided to consult with Sir Gordon before proceeding further.

December 22, 1899 The Homestead, near the hamlet of Airdrie, Northwest Territories

Dear Family: Well, here we are! As hoped, we arrived before Christmas. The immigrant train rolled into Calgary on December 15, and we were met by our neighbour, Mr. George Donaldson - a mild-mannered Scot and very helpful. This seems to be the routine: the earlier pioneers take it upon themselves to meet and welcome the new ones. So we will also do our neighbour greeting in the future. It seems a very pleasant way to settle an area.

Calgary is a very busy and noisy place - wagons, horses and people everywhere. Even at 7:00 p.m. in the evening, when we arrived, the Hudson Bay Company store was still open, and we were able to purchase much of our immediate needs. It was fully dark when we were finally loaded into Mr. Donaldson's hay wagon (on sleds for winter). He had included blankets for our use, and that was a blessing as the night time temperature was twenty degrees below zero. It took four hours to get to our homestead and we were very tired and glad to get here. But, in spite of the hour, Maggie was enchanted with the snow-covered countryside that was lit up by a full moon. The only sound was the puffing of the horses as they plodded their way over rough ground.

Billy accompanied Mr. Donaldson into Calgary a few days later. After we had a look around this abandoned home to see if anything usable was left behind, much more was purchased. (Briefly, the folks who occupied this rough dwelling went back to England last summer because of family complications). Billy was able to get a small short-term loan at the bank, and this, along with what we have, will get us through the winter and early spring. He also investigated the process of getting two heavy horses that we will need in the spring for ploughing. But, for now, we will buy an older pony to pull the cutter that we are presently building. The snow is very deep here; we continue to shovel every day hoping to find a suitable site for the stable.

I will speak again about our new friend, Joshua. Sure enough, he was at the train to meet us. We asked no questions, and he offered no explanation about how he found his way to Calgary. During their wait, he had charmed Mr. Donaldson with his good will, and informed him he would be staying nearby the homestead and would be helping us settle in any way he could. Mr. Donaldson has already recruited Joshua to help replace a barn roof that was torn away by strong winds. We are unaware of where he sleeps, possibly in an out building at the Donaldson farm, but he does join us at mealtimes – usually a wonderful dinner concocted by Maggie out of thin air!

The dwelling here is adequate and a shelter from the long winter days and nights. It is banked by hay bales, and the roof is of single wood covered with sod. Best of all is the large fireplace, and Mrs. Donaldson has kindly supplied a hearth rug. Two lamps were left behind – fuelled by coal oil. Joshua has already made wooden frames for each of our mattresses of straw, and Maggie went to work immediately putting the bolt of flannel into service as covers for each. Even a small frame with tightly packed straw is ready for the baby when he or she arrives.

And so we wish all of you: Aggie, Todd, Rachael, Peter and Mary, a Happy New Year full of all the good things that 1900 can bring.

Your brother, Joey

It was routine now for Todd to bike directly from school to the infirmary. *I guess, Malcolm, as time passes, new things take shape. It has been hard, but then, you have had the same – with a new dimension to adjust to. I have to tell you, although you know, that Aggie and Rachael were so grateful and happy to receive your wonderful gifts. Rachael loved you just about as much as I did – or do. Someone told me: love never dies. I believe that's true.*

CHAPTER TEN

AS TODD ENTERED THE INFIRMARY AND HEADED TOWARD THE NEW pharmacy, he *knew* there was something in the air, like a shock or a surprise. It certainly was a surprise, as above the entrance was painted in large letters: The Malcolm Murray Memorial Pharmacy! "What a wonderful honour for Malcolm!" Todd exclaimed, as he stood gazing upward.

Doctor Wilkins was there to witness the occasion: "Malcolm deserved this honour, Todd, and so do you."

A table was set up in the seating area of the pharmacy and refreshments served in celebration of the official opening of the service. Todd took the opportunity to speak with people whose homes he had called on with deliveries. The message passed along was generally well received, but Todd could sense that the change was a loss as well. He noted the present occasion was an opportunity in late winter for neighbours to reacquaint socially. It seemed amazing to realize that his former deliveries had served a social as well as a medicinal need. *Having an ice cream parlour in this community is a great idea,* he thought. *I hope it works out well for the people who are taking it on.*

Thank goodness Mrs. Olson is coming home today, thought Rachael. *What a wonderful help Rebecca has been, but we've never had a minute to sit down to a cup of tea!*

Jean Olson had a lot of catching up to do: overdue accounts and marketing to take care of. She also realized the responsibility of the kitchen and housekeeping had fallen to Rachael, and she was determined to make it up to her. "Would you like a bit of time for yourself, Rachael?" she suggested.

"That would be a help, Mrs. Olson."

"Then, consider the rest of the week yours."

What an opportunity this is! thought Rachael. *I can start working on the Polly Peters adventure series right away.*

"This is still at the idea stage," Rachael shared with Sir Gordon, as they made their way around the garden and out to the manor grounds. "I believe twelve might be a good number of issues for the Polly Peters series. What are your thoughts about that, Sir?"

"Yes, I agree with that, Rachael. Knowing the limit of your interest, and communicating that to the publisher, would get the matter settled on a firm footing."

"I also believe an illustrator's work would be of value - right from the beginning. I'm certainly not an artist, and the story will require action breathed into it."

"Oh absolutely!" agreed Sir Gordon. "That is something that should be decided on with the publisher. The illustrator's availability and your timing should match perfectly, and you must be satisfied that his or her work to be of the standard you require. Most illustrators have a portfolio to review."

"Goodness, Sir Gordon, what would I do without your advice and ideas!"

"Well, Rachael, if experience counts for anything, I'm happy to share it."

"I hope you are feeling better, Sir. I don't want to take you on a longer walk than you feel up to."

"No worry, Rachael. It's just a pleasure to have good company on walks that will surely build up my strength. I see that Mrs. Olson is back from her sending-off mission with Maisie. I know she appreciated the opportunity to go, but I hope it was not a heavy burden for you to carry on as you did."

"It was busy, Sir, but I was happy to see Mrs. Olson accompany Maisie. It was important for both of them since they have been friends for so long. I've been given some time for myself since her return."

"That's excellent, Rachael. Now, as we arrive at this particular pathway and look out on the fields beyond," Sir Gordon continued, "I must tell you that it is of significance. I have now disposed of all my lands except for the ten acres where we live. I felt I wanted to share that with you first, Rachael, as you have an understanding and compassionate nature. Those qualities are of value to me in this transition period of my life."

"But, I don't understand, Sir."

"The truth of the matter is: I have been over ruled in what was my hope that all my lands would one day be held privately by the farm families who have always been there," Sir Gordon continued, with regret. "But international investors have come along to take it all, and I have not had an option but to let it go to them.

"You would probably not know, Rachael, but land holders, such as myself, have been under a great deal of pressure to relinquish property or be taxed beyond reason. This would include even the manor and grounds around it. The government feels the land is not being farmed efficiently and that new ways must be implemented. I guess one would call that progress, but my burden and heartache has been for the farm families. Ultimately, their option will be to go to the big cities and work in industry. I shudder to think what will happen to them."

"But, Sir, surely the farmers have had adequate time to prepare for a future that includes competition with other countries," stated Rachael. "My brothers left Scotland to have a hand in providing that competition, and they with only small savings and a willingness to work the clock around to make it happen."

"I have needed to hear that, Rachael. I am a fine one to lecture on change and how we must welcome it. Did I not, even courageously, lecture you in the matter of loss and change?" Sir Gordon stated, with humble recognition.

"Hardly a lecture, Sir," Rachael laughed, "but, yes you did. Most of us are inclined to correct others on attitudes we have ourselves."

Sir Gordon and Rachael walked slowly back to the manor, each in their own thoughts. "May I make a suggestion, Sir?"

"Of course, Rachael."

"We all had such a happy time at Maisie's farewell *family dinner*, would it not be possible to have family dinners on a regular basis, Sir. It could be a time of sharing new ideas and supporting each other. Since John and Rebecca live in their own cottage, we don't have the same opportunity to get to know them well and to hear some of their ideas, and they are good ideas. I'm afraid they are not people who will sit around and wait for someone else to tell them what to do. On the contrary, they have made many improvements with the grounds, and also with the kitchen garden - especially in the fall to make it ready for spring planting. Family dinners would bring them out of their cottage to meet with us regularly. These are just my thoughts, Sir Gordon, you may want to discuss it with Mrs. Olson."

"I have been so occupied with land issues, I'm afraid I haven't taken the time to see what wonderful things are going on right here in my own home. I will discuss the *family dinner* idea with Mrs. Olson immediately. This would be a great change for her as she has lived as an aristocratic servant for many years. I will not mention that you have spoken with me first, Rachael. We aristocrats are very sensitive about protocol," he said, with a smile.

As Rachael entered the manor kitchen, she found John and Rebecca sitting with Mrs. Olson at the large table. The couple were discussing the possibility of enlarging the kitchen garden – in fact, making it a full-fledged market garden operation, not just for consumption at the manor.

"I will speak with Sir Gordon about this," Jean said. "He is very accustomed to seeing the layout of the grounds much as it has been for many years. It is the aristocratic way."

Rachael smothered a giggle as she heard this last statement, then went about the business of preparing the evening meal.

January 02, 1900 The Homestead near the hamlet of Airdrie, Northwest Territories

Dear family: Another letter, but full of good news and thankfulness. First of all: our new family member is Niall Paul, born the afternoon of December 24, 1899. (Niall is a favourite name, and Paul for Maggie's brother who was killed within the first few months of the South African conflict). Niall is a healthy baby, and mother Maggie is doing well. Mrs. (Katherine) Donaldson insisted that Maggie move over to their home whenever she felt the time was near. She could not feature a birth taking place in a straw bed. Katherine also has experience as a midwife, so lucky we are again! To tell the truth, Billy and I never thought about the actual birth and who would assist – we only knew it would not be either of us!

But along with Niall has come your wonderful letter, Todd, telling us about Mr. Murray's wish to invest in our farming operation. Need I tell you what welcome news that is! When the investment certificate arrives at the bank in Calgary, Billy and I will be there to sign, and it will be returned to Mr. Murray's solicitor.

When an unexpected gift like this happens, it seems the first reactions are disbelief, panic and fear. How best can we use this wonderful expression of confidence? As the days go by, I feel we will be better able to digest this miracle. Of course, we did not have the pleasure of meeting this man, but your speaking about him assured us that he was very special in your life. God bless you both.

Katherine decided that Maggie must stay at their home for ten days to recover and get used to being a mother. We certainly have missed Maggie, and we will welcome her home later today – along with this new and precious little fellow. Joshua has a surprise for Maggie: he has worked every evening, and often long into the night, building a proper kitchen with a large space open for a big McClary Range (some day). As well, he has found some pieces of beautiful maple wood, and has made a rocking chair for her. The natural wood has been polished to a high shine.

Love and best wishes to you all, Your brother, Joey

"We will have company with us for our evening meal, Todd," said Mrs. Cronin. "The folks who have purchased Mr. Murray's old shop have arrived, and they want to get started with renovations immediately. For a few weeks, until they have sleeping provisions over at the shop, they have asked to stay here. They will sleep in my tiny guest room downstairs. A right nice couple, I believe."

"I will be pleased to meet them, Mrs. Cronin, and I can possibly be of some help to them in getting set up."

Rachael had taken a day to make Rebecca's summer frock, making one similar for herself. Finally, she could start thinking about the Polly adventures. *I just have a feeling that the first book in the adventure series should be about an eventful, or possibly disastrous, biking journey. Thinking about those ugly knickers I wore every weekend last year... No, this one must have class!*

Taking her own measurements, Rachael decided to travel by omnibus downtown to a fabric shop. The light-weight cotton tweed for the biking costume was just as she pictured it should be. As soon as she arrived back to the manor, the scissors were out and the new costume took shape: knickers with smart cuffs, a short fitted jacket with silver buttons. The hat should have a wide brim, turned up at the front, and decorated with a narrow leather band, and a small green and gold feather.

I like this a lot, thought Rachael, smiling. *Of course it will not look so classy after Polly pulls herself out of that murky creek!* With costume almost complete, and an outline of the first story underway, Rachael was beginning to see the possibilities of the venture. *Oh yes,* she remembered, *... the illustrator.*

Wondering who might lead her to the right person to illustrate her books, Rachael remembered the printing shop, and the fine work that was done on the covers of her previous writing. *I must tell Mrs. Olson where I'm going,* thought Rachael. *She is, after all, responsible for me, and I don't want to get her into any difficulty with Sir Gordon.*

"Can I help you, young lady," said the friendly clerk.

"Actually, I am looking for information," said Rachael. "I wonder if you would know of a commercial artist in Aberdeen who might be interested in illustrating a proposed series of books for children?"

"There is an art school in just the next block, above the milliner shop. You might try that; I believe they are open weekdays. Are you the young lady I met before? We did some printing for you, and we made coloured covers."

"Yes, that's right," replied Rachael, "I recall the work was accomplished most satisfactorily."

"Thank you for mentioning that, and you might also inform the art instructor of the school that I referred you there. My name is Robert Milton."

"I will certainly do that, and thank you for the information Mr. Milton."

Reaching the milliner shop, Rachael found that she had to reach the art school through their premises, and up a rickety set of stairs. It was an open space without a door to close it off from the rest of the building. She entered and found a young gentleman doing a sketch on a large canvas. The room was filled with light that came from windows on three sides of the open space. With his back to her, the man appeared not to realize she was in the room. "Yes, what can I do for you?" he asked, continuing his work.

Clearing her throat, Rachael replied, "I have been referred to this art school by Mr. Robert Milton of the printing shop."

"That was generous of Robert to call this an art school," said the man, standing back a little to gaze at his work. "Are you interested in art lessons?"

"Actually, no, I need to collaborate with an illustrator who has the necessary skills to enliven a set of children's novels," explained Rachael.

"Really!" said the man, finally turning around to look at his unexpected visitor. "But surely not for yourself! You are just a little girl," he said in surprise.

"Not such a little girl, Sir," Rachael said, with emphasis. "I am twelve years old, almost thirteen!"

"Indeed, a young lady who makes her wishes very clear. I don't suppose Robert mentioned my name. It is Terrance Gibbons - Terry for short, and budding artistic genius. I have no students, but pretending this is a school allows me stay here under these fantastic conditions!" said Terry, with an expansive arm gesture. "The light is terrific."

"I rather think I might have been misled by Mr. Milton," said Rachael. "It would appear you are more of a classic artist, rather than commercial. I will just let myself out through the store."

"No, now wait just a minute. Please tell me more about these novels. I assume you are the writer."

"Yes, I am the writer, and I have one story in outline and almost completed. I also have a costume made that would be worn by the character in the book throughout the story."

"How very interesting," said Terry. "I assume you have a parent or guardian and a home where we might meet, and I to better understand the skills you require. At the moment, I am not run off my feet with commissions to paint portraits of famous people."

"Well, yes, I have a guardian. I'm sure it would be quite acceptable for you to come to my home, and we can discuss details there. I live at 90 Marquis. Would you be able to come tomorrow, say 2:30 p.m.?"

Flipping absently through his appointment book, Terry acknowledged, "Yes, I will be there tomorrow at 2:30 p.m. Now, your name?"

"It is Rachael Atkinson. Please mention my name when you are greeted by a Mr. Duncan McCann."

As Rachael hurried to catch the omnibus back to the manor, she was unsure how she should mention this visitor to Mrs. Olson.

Jean Olson was in agreement with Rachael's appointment the following day. "Please, just mention to Duncan who it is coming to see you, and he can arrange an appropriate meeting place. Do you need a table, paper and pencils – that sort of thing?"

"No, thank you. I believe the gentleman coming will have a sketch pad and pencils with him, but a table would be useful. I would appreciate it, Mrs. Olson, if you could be on hand to meet this gentleman. He was curious to know if I had a parent or guardian, but he does not need to know our special relationship."

"A good idea," said Jean Olson, "I believe we forget what relationships we have with each other. We are all just family."

"I like to think of it that way. This is certainly my home, and I can tell anyone that without hesitation."

Todd was delighted he could be of some use in the tearing down and construction phase for the new ice cream parlour, and Matthew and Molly McPhee were also pleased there would be a helping hand so close by. They understood Todd's connection to the old building, wanting him to feel part of the excitement this project would create in the neighbourhood.

Doctor Wilkins was sympathetic to Todd's wish to be relieved of duties at the infirmary. "I can understand, Todd, there is nothing new here for you to learn. But I do appreciate your efforts in making the transition to the new pharmacy such a success. Please keep in touch socially. If we can maintain our friendship, it will be like a bit of Malcolm still around."

"Thank you, Doctor Wilkins. I know Malcolm would like that link carried on. As you know, I am going to pursue medicine in the future. I would appreciate your advice and insight into any hurdles that may come along."

"Count me in, Todd. Are you still playing soccer?"

"Definitely, Doctor, I can't wait to get started. A practise schedule will be set next week; I enjoy the practises just as much as the games."

"Let me know when there is a game planned," said Doctor Wilkins.

"I apologize for the hand-written outline of the first book, Mr. Gibbons. I thought we might go over the parts that will require illustration for now."

"Please call me Terry, Rachael. For now then, I will make a few quick sketches with captions below to keep me on track. We can meet then, say - in one week, so that you can approve of my approach to this assignment."

"That sounds very agreeable. Next week then: same place, day and time."

Rachael decided it was time to discuss her writing project with Jean Olson. "There is so much to consider, Mrs. Olson. I need to get advice, from both you and Sir Gordon, about timing, and any steps to be taken I am not aware of. As well, it has to be of a nature that does not interfere with my duties here at the manor."

"This is a very ambitious project! Sir Gordon has discussed it briefly with me, and we agree that you should be encouraged in every way possible. My opinion is that you should take your time and not be hurried about any of the steps involved. The stories are, of course, the most important part. If this Mr. Gibbons has the talent to create illustrations that will enhance your stories, and you are happy to work with him, then it is up to him whether or not he will commit time for the whole series. You are just at the beginning of this project, Rachael, and you want to enjoy the journey."

Golden Ribbons

As late winter turned into early spring, Rachael and Todd began to talk about a trip to Glasgow together. "I know you are busy with school, soccer, and with helping at the new ice cream parlour, Todd, but I wonder if we could go to Glasgow about the final week of June? I should write to Mr. McWiggins soon to ask if our plan might coincide with his schedule."

"That should work well for me, Rach," said Todd. "School and soccer will be finished until fall, and the grand opening of the ice cream parlour is scheduled for July 15. I certainly want to be on hand for that occasion!"

Todd was fascinated to hear about the innovations planned for the ice cream parlour. An electrician and plumber were contracted to modernize those necessary aspects of the building. "We hope to keep the front of shop as close as possible to the original," said Matthew. "I think it is important for folks in the neighbourhood to recognize it as it had been, and the fireplace, being of vintage design, will definitely stay."

"This will be an excellent addition to the neighbourhood," said Todd, "giving both the elderly and young people a place to socialize."

"When we start tearing down the back part of the building we can certainly use your help, Todd," said Matthew. "If you could tell me the times you will be free to help, it will give me some idea of how many others to bring on."

"I will certainly do that, Matthew," agreed Todd. "The afternoons between soccer practises will be free, and on Saturdays."

"Let's just visit here in the kitchen today," suggested Rachael. "We can have tea and chocolate cake. It has been a challenge, Todd: trying to balance my manor duties with writing the stories, as well as maintaining the appointments with Terry, the illustrator, but I will have two stories, and the accompanying costumes, ready to take to Glasgow."

"That will be fun, Rach!" said Todd. "Let's try to make it a holiday, as it seems we will both have a busy summer ahead of us. Matthew and Molly are great people, with wonderful plans for the ice cream parlour. Unfortunately, they are having trouble lining up workers so that the store will be complete on schedule," he informed. "If you hear of anyone who might like to commit time to help, they should go to see Matthew."

"I will mention it at our family dinner this evening. John has finished enlarging the stable. He might welcome some extra work."

"I believe it is my duty to welcome all of you to the first of many *family dinners*," said Sir Gordon. "I have spoken privately to everyone, and it seems all are pleased to have this time to dine together and talk over the adjustments that will be necessary in order for each and every one of us to remain here at the manor, and to call it home.

"I have dreaded the time when I would have to share my dilemma of shutting down the manor. But with your ingenuity, it seems we can stay here, cooperate and even thrive. Thanks to everyone. I am humbled and grateful for your willingness to give it a try. So, getting started, has anyone something to share?"

"Yes, I have, Sir," said Rachael. "As most of you know, the old chemist shop - formerly owned by Mr. Malcolm Murray, has been sold to Matthew and Molly McPhee. They have a project planned to renovate the old building and to make it into an ice cream parlour. In order to meet their hope of opening July 15, they will need a helping hand in this work. My brother, Todd, is helping when he has free time, but that will not be enough."

"Well John," Sir Gordon acknowledged, "this might be an opportunity to use some of your wonderful carpentry skills. If you are interested, I would encourage you to see Mr. McPhee about hours required. We can make adjustments here. I believe the important word here is *opportunity*. No longer can we wait for possibilities to fall out of the sky; we must actively seek out ways to grow in areas of interest, and profit by them."

"I will certainly ask Mr. McPhee about helping with that project," replied John. "I would like to make a suggestion, Sir, regarding the carriage horses

Golden Ribbons

as well as the pony. There is land available for a paddock and the horses need space for exercise and grazing."

"Right you are, John. We'll take a walk out there to see what land can be effectively used for that purpose."

"As we conclude for today," said Sir Gordon, "I need to say that I include myself in making this place a living and working family home."

"We have so many things to talk about today, Todd. Let's take our bikes this time, and we can stop at the bench enclosure along the sea trail."

"Sounds good to me, Rach," agreed Todd. "Better wear a big hat, it's going to be a warm afternoon!"

"First of all," said Rachael, "I think Niall is just the nicest name! I wish we could see this little fellow."

"Yes, and arriving Christmas Eve has made it so special. Perhaps we can send a gift to Niall from the two of us."

"That's an excellent idea. But, now, I have to tell you I have a very capable illustrator lined up for my books, Todd. I'm sure two books will be ready for the trip to Glasgow in about two weeks."

"I'll be ready for that, Sis," agreed Todd.

"Another thing, Todd, - if you can you believe it! Sir Gordon is going to open up the big rooms of the manor for public events, like lectures and recitals. We will all have a chance to contribute our ideas about this project," Rachael related, with excitement.

"I think that is extremely innovative," said Todd.

"Now, I must tell you my news, Rach: the work on the ice cream parlour is progressing with great speed," said Todd with excitement. John, from the manor is a talented cabinet maker, as you know. He is already working on a long curved counter, and has offered to build the small tables and stools back at his shop at the manor. They will then be installed when everything else is finished. Painting is coming next, I hope I can be trusted with a brush and a pail of paint!

"But before we part for this time, Rachael, I must also inform you that there will be two soccer matches scheduled before the school term ends. Both are here in Aberdeen. I hope you can come to one of them."

"Yes, Todd, I will certainly attend one of your matches. I'm so proud of you. As well, I believe the ice cream parlour will certainly be a wonderful success."

February 23, 1900 The Homestead near the hamlet of Airdrie, Northwest Territories

Dear family: We are experiencing our first Chinook-winds today; the mountains loom clear and magnificent! I have taken Maggie and baby Niall for their first outing in the cutter. At home, we have had a competition going: the first one to get a smile out of Niall. Of course, it was Joshua who has a smile that lights up the darkest corner. But you should witness Joey's behaviour! He can't take his eyes off this baby, taking every opportunity to hold him. I guess we are all besotted.

It was time to have Niall's birth registered. I had the forms handy for several weeks, but found it hard to bring up the subject with the others. Then it dawned on me: I want Niall to have Atkinson as his last name, and I want Maggie to be Atkinson as well - my real wife this time. As we gathered around the table one evening, I put it simply: "I want to marry you, Maggie, and I want Niall to be my son." It never dawned on me that she would refuse.

There were a few moments of hesitation, . . . then she said, "Yes, Billy, I will marry you."

What a burden to be lifted from my shoulders! But, of course, I had to check with Joey as well. It had been decided long ago: we would never make a decision without a discussion with the other. Joey was agreeable as long as he has certain uncle privileges, that of consulting about Niall's future. Maggie and I agreed. Then we had a group hug to seal the deal - with Niall squished in the middle.

This may not sound like a romantic beginning, but I do love Maggie, and I love Niall. *Why wait any longer?*

We all await your good wishes.

Love from your brother Billy

———

"Todd! You were terrific today!" called Rachael, as Todd beamed toward her.
"What a game, Rach! You picked a good one! I really thought we were finished, then two goals in a row! Could that ever happen again, I wonder?"
"It was so exciting! Now I will want to get to all your games."
"That sounds good to me, Rach," said Todd. "I think you brought us luck. Now let's get biking over to the manor so I can have some of your maple walnut truffle, and several cups of tea."
"Trifle, Todd, trifle!" yelled Rachael, bumping her bike into his.

———

CHAPTER ELEVEN

SIR GORDON CALLED TOGETHER ALL THOSE WHO HAD SHOWN AN interest in his project of opening the manor to public events. "I very much welcome suggestions and ideas from all of you," he said.

Jean Olson was the first to respond to the invitation. "I believe, Sir, before an actual event takes place, it would be prudent to have an open house – say, about two hours on a Sunday afternoon. I'm sure the citizens of Aberdeen have wondered at times just what kind of a home this manor is. An open house would give them an opportunity to gaze into the various rooms, and to get a feel for the kind of events that will follow.

"You would be correct, Sir, in assuming that I have given this matter some thought," Jean continued. "I can envision Duncan in his usual place, greeting people at the front door. From there, you and possibly me, to be tour guides and have two groups moving around consecutively. I place myself in this position because of my length of service to the manor, and I know and love every picture, tapestry, name and type of furniture, and any other bits of interesting information."

"Jean, I am overwhelmed!" replied Sir Gordon. "Once again, I have not acknowledged the level of commitment you have given to the manor over the years. Of course, you are to be a tour guide! I will likely be asking you questions in regard to those interesting bits of information you refer to. I need to be brought up to date, and that is something we can work on together. Are there any thoughts in reference to Jean's proposal of an open house?"

"I think it's brilliant, Sir!" said Rachael. "I'm thrilled and excited about all that Mrs. Olson has proposed."

"Rachael," said Jean gently. "Please call me Jean. We are all, now, co-workers in a grand scheme."

"Thank you, Mrs…I mean Jean. It will be hard at first, old habits die hard. But, yes, I would be honoured to call you Jean."

"Right then," said Sir Gordon. "We are off to a great start. I'm sure ideas will be trickling in."

"Mr. McWiggins has confirmed our timing of June 25 to 27 in Glasgow," said Rachael. "He looks forward to greeting you, Todd, and further recommends, if possible, that Terry Gibbons also attend. He has emphasized that effective illustration is an integral part of children's literature, and must be given a prominent place in a contract agreement."

"That will be good for Terry to know his rights, and to have a part in the agreement. But I am only your travel companion, Rach," emphasized Todd. "This is your meeting, and I don't want to interfere in any way."

"I'm sure Mr. McWiggins understands that, Todd, but I will appreciate having you close by. In addition, Mr. McWiggins has offered connecting rooms at a near-by rooming house for both of us - at his expense. He would also like to provide us with complementary tickets for a tour of the City that begins at George Square mid-afternoon of our first day," Rachael announced, with mounting excitement. "Sir Gordon has informed me that this is all part of public relations in business and I am to accept graciously knowing it is not personal but part of a developing contract relationship."

"Wow, Rach!" exclaimed Todd. "This all sounds so grown up."

"That is certainly the way I feel," Rachael agreed. "I will speak to Terry about his availability to attend the meetings next time we meet."

"I do like your aunt's idea about Polly's hat," said Rachael. "It has more of a jaunty look, and I believe that's what would be more appropriate for her."

"I think so too, Rachael," said Terry. "My aunt has offered to make the necessary alternations to the hat you made."

"That is so good of her," said Rachael. "The swimming story and costume are almost ready. I will drop them off at your studio next Tuesday."

Rachael was always pleased to speak with Mavis Gibbons every time she passed through the milliner shop on her way up to Terry's studio. Miss Gibbons expressed her interest in Rachael's writing project, and of her gratitude that Terry was an important part of the finished products.

"Terry is so talented," said Rachael. "I'm the one to be grateful. Every story is greatly enhanced by his work."

"We are moving right along with the third book. I think each issue in the series should be a bit more outrageous than the one before. Do you agree, Terry?"

"Definitely, Rachael," agreed Terry. "I'm having a great time experimenting with these drawings."

"I think they are wonderful, Terry. Polly jumps right out of the pages!"

"Do you have a time budget for further books, Rachael?" asked Terry. "My father has enrolled me in a six-month course at some kind of school of economics in London. It will begin January, 1901. I don't want to keep you or the publisher waiting on my account."

"No worry about it, Terry, but I'm glad you shared this news with me. I will see that another three stories are ready before the end of the year. After that, it will be one step at a time."

"Thanks Rachael, I can assure you: I will make this collaboration a priority. I'm not at all interested in Adam Smith or economics!" Terry added.

"I want to thank you, Rachael, for sending me a preview of your first book," said Mr. McWiggins, "as well as Mr. Gibbons' illustrations under caption headings. It has given me a chance to peruse the effort you and Mr. Gibbons are making together. I would say it is a very excellent collaboration, and certainly one that doesn't easily happen. You are both to be congratulated."

"Thank you, Sir," said Rachael. "Mr. Gibbons and I have two packets with us this morning for your inspection."

"Excellent!" Mr. McWiggins responded. "As you are both aware, publishers are in the business to make money by getting good products on the market, and by ensuring they are sold in great quantities. So, that's my role in this agreement. Since this is probably the first assignment of its kind for both of you, I will explain briefly how royalties work. However, if you feel an independent legal opinion is required before the agreement is arrived at, I will certainly understand.

"I believe this is all that we need to take care of initially," said Mr. McWiggins. "I would like to continue meeting with both of you throughout <u>The Adventures of Polly Peters,</u> but we will keep in touch by mail in the meantime. A copy of the agreement will be ready tomorrow for your inspection, and even if you decide to sign tomorrow, you will have ten days to rescind the agreement. That applies to either one of you, or both."

Terry and Rachael shook hands with Mr. McWiggins before leaving his office. Then, as Todd was summoned from the outer office, he stood to shake hands with Mr. McWiggins, expressing the pleasure both he and Rachael had in seeing Glasgow for the first time.

"You are most welcome Todd," said Mr. McWiggins. "You have a very talented sister. It has been a pleasure to meet all of you."

Rachael and Todd parted with Terry out on the street, and arranged to meet with him again the next morning to review the agreement. "Have fun shopping, you two," said Terry. "I must find my father now and get my annual lecture on the merits of sons following in the footsteps of their fathers." He waved and walked hurriedly over to a building opposite.

Todd crooked his arm toward her. "Mrs. Cronin, may I be the first to escort you to the new Ice Cream Parlour."

"Oh my goodness, Todd, it has taken such a short time for everything to change at the old shop! I'm not sure I can handle the emotion of it. I'm sure to break down and cry."

"Well then, if you do, I'm sure a nice dish of ice cream will surely fix you up."

"Such blarney, then," Mrs. Cronin scolded in fun.

It was a delightful scene: all the colours of the rainbow, in fact a rainbow had been painted on the wall behind the fireplace. Matthew and Molly, dressed in starched white jackets, were behind the counter - metal scoops in hand and ready for the first customers. "On the house today!" called Matthew. Within a half hour, the ice cream parlour was packed, and excited chatter filled the room that suddenly seemed so much larger than it had been before.

"Do you think Malcolm would like it, Mrs. Cronin?" Todd asked.

"Ach, Todd, he would love it!"

"I have looked forward to this second planning meeting all week!" exclaimed Sir Gordon. "Jean has been coaching me toward being a successful tour guide, and teaching me about everything in this home that has thus far evaded me. It is a magnificent place."

"My pleasure, Sir," Jean smiled.

"I would like to offer my services for an evening in mid-September to honour Sir Walter Scott, the Scottish and most normal of geniuses," said Sir Gordon. "I would like to invite Rachael to co-host this event with me."

"I would enjoy co-hosting with you, Sir," said Rachael.

"Thank you, Rachael," acknowledged Sir Gordon.

"I would like to prepare an evening focussed on the manor gardens, as well as the various plants and herbs we are experimenting with," said Rebecca. "I would like to have Mrs. Olson co-host with me."

"Thank you, Rebecca, I would love to co-host with you. The gardens will be particularly lovely in late September."

"Since there are no other ideas forthcoming, and so few of us, perhaps announcing two events will be sufficient for now. Another can always be added later," stated Sir Gordon.

Golden Ribbons

March 12, 1900 The homestead near the hamlet of Airdrie, Northwest Territories

Dear family: Last week we were sorry to say goodbye to our good friend Joshua. He felt he should be moving on out west. George Donaldson offered him a ride for a short way, as he had to deliver some hay to a ranch in the foothills. I'm not sure if we would have a stable now if it had not been for Joshua's help, but he would take no pay from either the Donaldsons or ourselves.

Joshua felt a strong kinship to Maggie. He shared with her that he was from a small city in South Carolina, and asked her to write a letter to his wife telling of his love for her and the children, but that he must keep moving. He instructed that Maggie must wait two weeks before writing the letter to the address of his mother-in-law, who would then forward it to his wife. We are concerned about Joshua, as this final request did indicate some serious trouble in his past. We can only remember him with good wishes and a hopeful resolution to his problem.

On a happier note, Maggie and I will be married March 25 in Calgary. It will be a private wedding in the accompanying chapel at the Knox Presbyterian Church. That same Sunday, Niall will be christened. George and Katherine Donaldson will accompany us, and of course Joey will be there, his pleasure being to hold Niall and to accept his role as God parent.

We have obtained two heavy horses and, for now, a hand plough. Maggie would like us to build a hen house, and for a short time that will mean having baby chicks in a box close to the fire to keep them warm. I think Niall will love them!

With love to all, your brother Billy

"Where has the summer gone!" exclaimed Rachael, as she enjoyed a dish of her favourite strawberry ice cream, served with an elegant flourish by her brother Todd.

"It's been pretty active for both of us, Rachael. But I am happy to be getting back to school."

"And soccer, no doubt."

"Oh yes! I will be happy about that too."

"I hope you can attend one of the events at the manor this fall, Todd. I am co-hosting with Sir Gordon as we talk about Sir Walter Scott. I will let you know the date."

"Well, I don't know about that one. I'm not too interested."

"You're not interested! Well get interested, instead of kicking an old soccer ball around all the time!" Rachael yelled, as she tried to hide her laughter.

"Okay, okay, I get it," said Todd reluctantly. "Touche."

After rehearsals and much laughter, Sir Gordon and Jean were ready for the open house, and their respective roles as tour guides. Duncan decided to have carafes of sherry or port on hand should the crowds exceed the required ten for each tour of the manor, and there would be necessity to wait. The people did come, and the afternoon was heralded as a big success. There were questions about the events to follow, and even suggestions for the hosts to consider. As the afternoon ended, Sir Gordon and Jean Olson collapsed in the most comfortable chairs in the great room, and Duncan served them celebratory glasses of sherry. Shortly the others joined them, with hearty "Congratulations!"

Sir Gordon held up his glass of sherry and declared, "To this wonderful family: health and happiness."

As the weeks went by, the manor home evenings were seen by the public as complementary events to those presented at Cowdray Hall. Soon, requests for intimate manor evenings called for a more formalized booking system, and Jean Olson filled that administrative function without question. Individual piano recitals brought noted performers to the magnificent grand piano in the great room, and chamber groups were also attracted to the intimate setting provided by the manor.

As cinema began to replace musical theatre, its former patrons were happy to see many of their favourite performers back again at a manor evening. By the end of the year 1900, the project to open the manor to cultural events was seen by the manor family as a worthwhile, and early success.

"I see no reason to hold you back, Todd," said head master Jenkins. "Even with the rigid schedule of soccer practises, you are well ahead of your classmates, and I expect you to have your leaving certificate by the end of the spring term. University entrance is, however, very rigid. I wonder if you might consider one of the apprenticeship programs - just for a change of focus, and until you can enter University at age seventeen."

"I will certainly look into that, Sir. I have heard the Naval Academy offers such a program, and that would be one interest."

"Take your time, Todd. I would think that early January, 1901 would be ample time to make application."

Todd decided to walk the sea trail on the late golden afternoon. *Our visits will become more frequent in the next few months, Malcolm. I need to talk with you about this new opportunity.*

As the year 1901 came to a close, the manor family had changed, and was attempting to rearrange itself. A matter that had been previously seen as of little importance suddenly became top of the agenda at *family supper* conversations. The change to *family supper* rather than *family dinner* came about as all members were usually engaged in their special, as well as regular, duties until late evenings.

Following Duncan's retirement the previous month, Jean Olson took over many of the duties left unattended. The bell that had formerly hung on a cord by the side of the front door was replaced by a bell which, when initiated, resounded loudly throughout the manor. Initially, it was to be Jean Olson's task to answer the bell. However, this system broke down when it was found that Jean spent less time at the manor than the others. She was now the one to honour outside appointments, in addition to her usual attention to the household budget and shopping. Failure of this first scheme resulted in an attempt at a second: the person nearest the door when the bell rang was obliged to answer it.

The second attempt was generally acceptable, except when a visitor would be met by a family member with coat and hat on, just preparing to leave. On other occasions, duties of the kitchen had to be abandoned, and the visitor asked to wait while the greeter hurriedly went to wash hands and strip off apron and hair covering.

"It seems that the door bell has taken over our regular routines," declared Sir Gordon. Just as he made this statement, the door bell rang. Each one looked at the other, but finally Sir Gordon got up and went to answer the summons. He was surprised to find a lonely-looking old gentleman, asking directions to a nearby address. "Goodness, my good man, you do look chilled to the bone. Do come in and warm yourself by the fire in the parlour. If you will excuse me, I will find someone to keep you company until you can better orient yourself."

Sir Gordon summoned John, explaining the situation to him, and then went back to resume the supper topic. "This is a most unfortunate situation that John has graciously responded to," he related to the others. "The answer to the problem of the door bell must be found immediately!" he ordered, as he walked quickly away from the family supper meeting.

When John returned to the meeting, he found it had disbursed, and Sir Gordon had retired to his study. "I will accompany the elderly gentleman to his destination," he reported.

"Thank you, John," Sir Gordon said. "Let me know how it turns out."

Sir Gordon remembered that Rachael had requested to see him briefly, following the meeting. She wanted to update him on the amazing reception her books were receiving, and to thank him for all his encouragement now that the series was complete. The Adventures of Polly Peters series had exceeded Mr. McWiggins' expectations of its selling potential. Some months later, the book's popularity was greatly enhanced by an offer from Bundy's Department

Store to stock replicas of the costumes that Rachael had designed for each book in the series. A local clothing manufacturer had been approached to produce as many costumes as the publisher estimated the demand to be, and the book sales doubled when the costumes became available.

"I seriously do not understand why any young girl would want to own one of these costumes let alone wear it," Rachael laughed. "They were, after all, designed for their comic affect."

"Rachael, it has been my impression over the years, that certain well-to-do parents will do anything to please their children. It is assumed by these parents that children must have what they want in order for the parents to have what they want – mainly peace and quiet. I would think that might be an aspect of society you know little about."

"That is true, Sir Gordon," responded Rachael. "It sounds like a dual to me, and if that outcome is as you suggest, it makes me feel responsible for it."

"That is one of the dilemmas of life, Rachael. Undoubtedly, if it was not one of your designed costumes, it would be something else as a bargaining tool," said Sir Gordon, with sarcasm. "But, did you not tell me: part of your decision to feature your costume design was to boost Terry Gibbons' portion of the profits, now that his father has cut him off from all support? That was generous of you, but it was Terry's decision to leave the economics course before it began. We live by the consequences of our decisions."

"That is giving me something to think about, Sir Gordon," said Rachael. "If, as you say, Terry must live by the consequence of his decision, then so must I as a consequence of my regard for Terry's commitment to our collaboration agreement. But thank you for your comments, Sir. Good night, Sir Gordon."

"Yes, good night, Rachael."

As she went to her bedroom that evening, Rachael thought about the dilemmas of life. "What was wrong with thinking of Terry's welfare when he was brave enough to release himself from his father's domination so that the collaboration agreement would not be disrupted?" she pondered. Rachael had a sad feeling of discomfort in disagreeing with Sir Gordon; she hoped it would not affect their friendly relationship. At the same time she felt, uncomfortably, that it would.

Later, in his rooms, Sir Gordon thought about the issue of the door bell. "Duncan is gone, but not forgotten." he recognized. "Foolishly, I felt it was an insignificant part of his duties, and I don't recall ever giving him special thanks for it. I never thought for a moment that this function should have been given consideration before he left."

As Sir Gordon began to settle in for the evening, a rap came at his private door. "Sorry to disturb you, Sir," said John, "especially on your one evening free of an event, but the gentleman who arrived during our supper meeting is still here. I went with him to the address he indicated, just a short distance away. The place was deserted and obviously had been for some time. Then this gentleman - Angus is his name, shared with me that he was not surprised that this was the case, but he stopped at the manor feeling, with so many lights on, it must be a welcoming place. He obviously has no place to stay tonight, and I wonder, Sir, if we might put him up in the day room for tonight. There is a fold-down cot in the closet, and I can find a pillow and blanket somewhere . . ."

Sir Gordon felt he was getting a headache. "I leave this to your good judgement, John," he said sharply. "We can deal with this man tomorrow. Good night for now, John."

"Good night, Sir," returned John, closing the door softly behind him.

When John arrived at the manor the next morning, he found that Angus was up and active. The cot was put away, and he had made a search of the broom closet. There being a late dusting of snow on the walks, he was busy clearing it away. "That is kind of you to help us out, Angus," said John. "When you have finished, come along to the kitchen and you can share a light breakfast with me. Sir Gordon will be available shortly, giving you a chance to explain your situation fully for us."

Sir Gordon decided not to waste a lot of his time attending to Angus. It was obvious that he was a homeless person, and once contact was made with a social worker, he could be on his way. "Could you briefly tell us something about your situation, Angus?" Sir Gordon began. "We can then be in a better position to refer you on to people who may be of help."

"Well Sir," said Angus, "I am in rather a pitiful family situation at the moment. I am retired, and since my dear wife died a few months ago, my son insisted I give up the family dwelling and move into his home. When my son went on a business trip this week, my daughter-in-law stated firmly to me that she did not approve of my being in her home. I was basically

Golden Ribbons

in the way - sitting around all day. I had hoped desperately to find my friends still living at the location I had formerly known, but unfortunately, as John will tell you, their home was closed. It was a wild act of desperation when I approached the door of the manor. I hope you will forgive me for the intrusion."

"I hope you don't mind telling us, Angus, the type of work you did before your retirement?" enquired Sir Gordon, "and if you are in good health? John tells me you were up this morning and out sweeping the walks. That was a kind gesture, and I thank you for it."

"I do like, perhaps need, to be kept busy, Sir," said Angus. "I am in sound health, and I certainly didn't enjoy *sitting around*, as stated by my daughter-in-law, any more than she did. It was simply not working out. I had to leave. You asked the nature of my employment before I retired: I had served for forty years at the elegant Royal Albert Hotel here in Aberdeen. I was a lift operator."

"We do have a need here that might interest you, Angus," explained Sir Gordon. "Our faithful butler and administrative helper retired recently, and this left us in a quandary regarding some of the tasks he performed that were simply automatic and taken-for-granted. Now we need someone here to answer the door bell on an ongoing basis. We could not offer remuneration, but room and board in this comfortable setting would have to compensate for it. If you would like to stay on for a week as a trial, Angus, it may relieve your situation somewhat in the short term."

"I will accept your offer, Sir, with appreciation," said Angus, wiping a tear away and blowing his nose. "I am at your service in any way that is helpful."

It was not long after the first week that Angus was proving himself to be of enormous help at the manor. Asking that his clothing and other personal belongings be sent to the manor, it was found that Angus had a most acceptable wardrobe to be serving as a greeter. He quickly became acquainted with everyone at the manor, recognizing the position they held and their daily schedule. On evenings when an event was held, he was first to set up chairs in appropriate settings, and he made thoughtful suggestions regarding every aspect of the front-of-house role. Sir Gordon was pleased that at least one problem was solved.

Todd was approached by Coach Robinson as he left school for the day. "I understand you will be leaving secondary school soon. I would just like to tell you that we are often approached by the manager and coaches of the Rangers Soccer Club to recommend one or two of our graduates as back-up players. It's an opportunity to gain some experience and recognition with the professionals, should you be interested in playing at that level in the future."

"I will certainly consider that as an option, Coach Robinson, but for now I am just happy to continue playing with my team mates that I know so well. Even after leaving school, I hope that I can continue playing with the school team as long as possible."

"Of course, I'm happy to hear you say that, Todd," said Coach Robinson. "I just wanted to let you know another possibility exists."

Speeding his bike along the sea trail, Todd stopped at a bench along the way to gaze out at the open sea. *Well, Malcolm, now I have a choice of two options.* Thinking back on those enjoyable walks along this trail with Malcolm, he remembered again the words, spoken so often: *Just be yourself, Todd boy, you can't do better than that.*

Actually, I think I have the answer. Toss realized that soccer had become a big part of his life, and he loved playing every minute of it - but it was for fun and companionship. I'm not so sure I would find that within a professional setting. So, I guess I have made a choice – the Naval Academy it is! Todd sped away to his attic retreat, feeling that the right choice had been made.

CHAPTER TWELVE

"You seem a bit detached and unhappy today, Rachael. That's not like you. Want to talk about it?" asked Todd. The Sunday meeting place had evolved to be spent at the Ice Cream Parlour when the shop was closed at three o'clock, and Todd had finished serving customers.

"Yes, I do, Todd. There has been a difference of opinion between Sir Gordon and me, and that has changed our friendly relationship. I feel that the change of philosophy at the manor, where we are now all family, is not as straightforward as before. Speaking for myself, I'm not sure where I stand in the grand scheme of things, or if there is a grand scheme. I am thinking of leaving, Todd. It's heartbreaking to consider such a move; I love the manor as I always have, but as we are now to consider ourselves equal in every respect, something has been lost. I can't explain it exactly."

"I will try to put myself in your place, and that might be helpful," said Todd. "I'm not sure that equality can exist for long in such a major transition. The manor is still Sir Gordon's home, even if not in reality. He has been lord of the manor far too long to suddenly be put into the position of being just one with the family. I can't say that I'm surprised that this is happening, Rachael. But I know you will use your maturity and good sense to know when you must leave. I only want you to be happy and at peace with the world, as I know you feel the same way about me."

"Yes, that's true. We will always have each other to turn to at moments like this. Thank you for being my brother," said Rachael, her eyes betraying her sadness. "Let's get on our bikes and ride along the sea trail until it ends. By the time we get back again, I will feel much better."

"Good plan, Rach, let's go!"

Several weeks passed before Rachael felt she must speak to Jean Olson about her uneasy feelings. Since their exchange there had been no late evening chats with Sir Gordon, she would simply go to her room after an event and the great room had been tidied. Sometimes she would chat a while with Angus who was experiencing a high point in his time at the manor. He was so happy to be needed and useful again, he could hardly contain his level of energy.

"May I see you for a few minutes, Jean?" asked Rachael, as she entered with a tray containing a fresh pot of tea and two cups, as well as some oat cakes.

The desk was not in its usual uncluttered state, but piles of papers were lined up in front of Jean. "Certainly, Rachael!" she said. "I can use a break and to share a cup of tea with you."

"You have a heavy load to carry these days, we hardly ever see you."

"That is unfortunately true," Jean sighed, "and I miss the occasions when there was time to have a chat during our regular routines. But I hear your childrens' series is complete now, Rachael. Do you miss it, or is it good to have more time for other things?"

"I did miss it, and I felt happy that the task was complete, but I'm not here to talk about that, Jean. I feel there is a change that has come over Sir Gordon; we had a disagreement that I felt was quite unreasonable on his side. As a result of the exchange, I sense a chill as I move about the manor. I am planning to leave, Jean, as soon as my brother, Todd, is away to Dartmouth and starting his apprenticeship with the Naval Academy."

"Oh Rachael, I can hardly take this in. How can I, or any of us, get along without you! I realize that Sir Gordon is finding the schedule of events heavy, but that is what we had hoped for – it's been a success! I'm tired too, and some days I wonder if I can keep up with all the extra tasks I've been handed. Have you been offered another position, Rachael?"

"No, Jean, this will be a time to evaluate where I've been, and where I want to go in the future. If I did not love the manor so much, this would be so much easier. As it is, it's a heavy weight to carry, but I feel I must soon move on."

"And you at such a young age, Rachael," said Jean Olson. "I can't express what an impact you have made here! We all love you, and I feel that includes

Sir Gordon. I must speak to him about this, Rachael, but I'm not looking forward to it."

"I have learned to love you too, Jean, just as I did Maisie – perhaps too much. When I came here, I was a little girl looking for - not only a job, but love and security. All were provided to me in good measure. I have got to learn to find that security within myself now."

The door bell rang and Angus rushed to meet a delivery lad carrying a large bouquet of roses and daisies. "For Miss Rachael," said the delivery lad.

Angus found Rachael in the kitchen taking loaves of bread out of the oven. "For you, Miss Rachael. Somebody loves you!" teased Angus.

Rachael was puzzled over this bouquet, and wondered if the delivery lad had made a mistake and it should go to someone else. "No, Miss Rachael, it most certainly is for you," said Angus. Reluctant to leave, Angus heard the bell again and rushed off to answer it.

> Dear Rachael: I am sending this gift along to you as an expression of thanks, in some small way, for the help and inspiration you have given me over our collaboration with the *Polly* series. You may be interested to know that I am now working with Robert Milton at the printing shop. I have my own little corner with a drafting table and a high stool. I pay the rent on this space by designing the occasional layout for Robert, and illustrations of course. In addition to that I am taking assignments from other businesses. I am happy and optimistic about all that is happening. Please drop in to the printing shop when you are passing by, Rachael.
>
> Kindest wishes, Terry Gibbons

Sir Gordon sat quietly for several minutes, attempting to grasp what Jean Olson was telling him. "I'm tired, Jean, and I know you are too. How did we get to this place, and where is it leading us? I'm sure Rachael is very serious about her decision to leave. She is not the type to make a decision and then change her mind. Did you say she would leave toward the end of May? That gives us some time to evaluate how and if we can carry on. The summer months will be quiet."

"Yes, Sir Gordon, she plans to attend her sister's May graduation from nursing school in Dundee, and spend a bit more time there than she has in the past. Then she will come back to Aberdeen before her brother goes away to his apprenticeship at the Naval Academy. Knowing our Rachael," Jean Olson expressed, "she will have assessed her own position by then, and will be involved in something worthwhile."

"Yes, I'm sure she will," said Sir Gordon, with resignation, as he got up from his chair behind the desk and walked slowly toward his private rooms. "Thank you, Jean."

In Duncan's absence, Jean Olson was obliged to report on the manor's financial position regularly. As it was April first, she gathered up the notebooks and ledgers to be reviewed by Sir Gordon that afternoon. Jean was shocked to see her employer and friend slouched at his desk, looking haggard and dishevelled. "As you have requested, Sir, I can give you a quick accounting of the bank balance, which at this time could possibly cover the manor expenses throughout the summer months."

"It seems, Jean, you are the only one I can depend on and trust," Sir Gordon responded. "What are we paying Rachael and the Neilsons for the services they are supposed to be doing?"

"You must surely recall, Sir Gordon, that I am the only one on the payroll now that Duncan has left us. Rachael, as well as John and Rebecca, have received no remuneration for over a year. That was at their request."

"But are they of any help, Jean? Rachael is off marketing her books and costumes without a thought to her duties here. And the Neilson's – I'm sure they are profiting greatly from their garden operation, and neglecting the duties they were hired to do."

"You are wrong, Sir Gordon! Rachael works long hours in the kitchen, and then helps Rebecca in maintaining the housekeeping at its usual level. As for John and Rebecca, they are certainly providing for themselves, but they are also keeping the household budget low by supplying all of the garden produce needed at the manor. John is an excellent grounds-keeper and, you will have to admit, he meets all your transportation needs. If you have been out to the back garden lately, Sir, you would have certainly been amazed at what John and Rebecca have accomplished."

"I have no intention of going out there, parading around in wellingtons, as of a common servant! And while you are here, Jean, I want you to notify the local police, and have them investigate a theft of my wife's jewellery that I have always kept in my office safe. I believe Duncan has made off with all of it."

"Again, Sir, have you forgotten that the jewellery was sold last year in order to reduce some of your personal debt? The receipt is in the record book that Duncan has so meticulously kept in order." Jean rose to leave. "I'm sorry, Sir, but I cannot sit here and listen to this slander against the very people who have supported you faithfully throughout this - your financial crisis!"

Jean hurried out to find John, and asked that he summon Sir Gordon's doctor immediately. "I will have a note for you to deliver," she said. "There is a problem with Sir Gordon, and we all must be on guard for a further outburst of his irrational thoughts and behaviour."

"I will have Sir Gordon admitted to hospital this evening, Jean," said Doctor Brooks. "He seems to be having a mental breakdown, and will require complete rest for an extended period of time. If you could have John assist him with preparations to leave, I will have the hospital emergency staff on hand to transport him safely to the Middletown Infirmary. He will be given a sedative to calm him until we can conduct a full assessment.

"For now, Jean, I would advise little action on your part, or of any member of the household staff. I will let you know as soon as we have something reliable to report. I would advise that Sir Gordons' lawyers in Edinburgh be notified in a day or two, and follow-up given to them as the days go on," Doctor Brooks continued. "They are well aware of the financial situation here, and if the court application to appoint an official receiver is made farther along into early summer, then even a small delay gives you good people here more time to adjust to your own futures. I know Sir Gordon very well, and he would want as much consideration given as possible."

"Thank you, Doctor," Jean acknowledged, as she went on to attend to related matters: cancellation of the evening's program and meeting with the others to pass along the current information.

As the staff met over a simple supper in the manor kitchen that evening, there was shock and sadness in hearing what Jean had to tell them. But there was relief as well. Each one had felt the intense stress Sir Gordon was experiencing, and that somehow they were individually responsible to alleviate it. Their plans, as a group, need only to be in the short term now and for each one it was a reprieve.

Only one issue was in need of discussion that evening: could they carry on with hosting the evening events that were currently in planning to the end of June? All were in agreement that, yes, they could. It would be easier to carry on to the end of season, rather than having to notify presenters as well as the patrons. Angus was especially pleased to hear that the events would carry on a while longer. A sociable person by nature, he relished the greeting and escorting of the patrons to their seats. But, he missed his old home too. There would be time to give notice to the renters living there, and he could move back where he belonged.

As everyone disbursed to their own private quarters, Jean approached Rachael. "May I count on you to be with me until this matter is resolved, Rachael?" she asked.

"Of course, Jean. Let's sit a while in the front parlour while it's still warm," Rachael suggested, "and if Angus comes along to attend to the embers still burning, that will be quite acceptable. How strange it is to be relaxed and accepting now that Sir Gordon is away and getting some help. In reality, I suppose we of the household staff have been the *family*. Sir Gordon's station in life could never allow him to be part of it."

"I see that too, Rachael. It clarifies so much, doesn't it: Blaine's position within the manor is certainly one issue that comes to mind, and dear Duncan! What a revelation to find that, in his quiet way, he ran the manor for all those years."

"Do you have any idea what your plans might be, Jean?" Rachael asked.

"Yes, I believe so. I have been very close to my husband's aunt and uncle over the years, and they have often suggested I live with them whenever the time came that I would leave my position here. As they are older people now, I'm sure my help will be appreciated. I still need to be needed, Rachael, as we all do."

"I'm sure they will love having you with them, Jean. May I ask how you became a widow?"

"My husband was with the English Navy, and was killed within the first few days of a training exercise that involved explosives; a *readiness for war* they called it. We had just been married a short time," said Jean with regret. "I believe it was a time to grab happiness, knowing how soon it could slip away. In your short lifetime, Rachael, you have not experienced war. I hope you never have to."

After a fortnight had passed, Dr. Brooks made a return visit to the manor, asking to speak to Jean Olson. "I'm sorry to report, Jean, that our efforts to lessen Sir Gordon's anxiety have not been successful. Periods of lucidity are becoming less frequent, and he wanders about for hours until exhaustion finally overtakes him. Then he will often sleep up to sixteen hours, but wakens dazed and incoherent. Initially - after I had examined him, he requested if he should be near death, he be allowed to die in his own home. This is not a judgement I can make at this time, Jean, as we never give up hope that a patient will return to normal functioning. But, I want to honour his request," continued Doctor Brooks. "I only ask that the manor staff bear with us until such time as Sir Gordon's condition is deemed irreversible.

"We in the medical profession can often cure a physical ailment, and sometimes a mental disturbance can be alleviated with rest. But the realm of the spirit is beyond our level of understanding. As personal physician and friend to Sir Gordon, we developed an intimate dialogue over the years that included matters of a wounded spirit. I believe this is one of those periods of his life where the spirit cannot be at rest. It's just a matter of waiting, I hope no more than a week or two. I am here to request your indulgence in this matter, and when Sir Gordon does come home, he will be accompanied by a medical attendant."

"Thank you Doctor for coming and sharing this information," said Jean. "You and Sir Gordon can count on our support."

Jean felt it was time to get in contact with Sir Gordon's lawyers once again, giving them specific details of Sir Gordon's condition as it was related to her. Speaking individually with each of her staff, all assured her that they would stay on to see this unhappy time to its conclusion. "This is so very difficult for you, Jean," said Rachael. "Is there anything I can do personally to help you through it?"

"How thoughtful Rachael. Just as you were the problem solver when Maisie left, I know I can count on you. All I need is for you to be here."

As the days went on without further reports from Dr. Brooks, the manor staff often sat in with the patrons when an evening event was of particular interest. Jean Olson would introduce each program and graciously explain to the patrons that Sir Gordon regretted his unavoidable absence.

"It does seem strange to have ceased wearing my identifying kitchen costume as I move about the manor," said Rachael.

"Yes, I'm sure it would seem that way," Jean responded. "We are not servants to each other, and I feel we no longer have to continue as before. When will you be leaving for Dundee, Rachael, and – more importantly, when will you be back? You have no idea what a comfort it is to have you here."

"I have discussed this with Todd, Jean, and we will leave for Dundee the day before Aggie's graduation, and return the next day. I hope this will not leave you in an uncomfortable position," Rachael said, with concern. "I'm sure Rebecca and John will be on hand to help in any way that is needed."

"Of course, Rachael. Do give my best wishes and congratulations to your sister, Aggie."

It was a sunny and warm graduation day in Dundee. The outdoor ceremony was colourful and festive in every way, only eclipsed by the sight of fourteen angels in long white nursing dresses and soft white veils, as they made their way to join the glowing faces of family and friends. "There's Mommy!"

whispered Mary, as she sat close between Rachael and Todd. Peter sat on the edge of his chair, his face full of wonder and pride.

"You will excuse me, ladies and gentlemen, but I am choked with emotion today," said the medical director. "Our very first graduation class, this May 15, 1902! We are into a new era now: a future of medical practise that will bring a level of comfort and healing never experienced before. Congratulations to each and every one of you dear ladies!" he said, presenting the individual scrolls tied with blue ribbons.

Sir Gordon's wish to die at home was honoured, and his passing was as quiet and dignified as his life had been. That evening, when the staff once again gathered at their evening meal in the kitchen, there was little conversation. Jean suddenly rushed from her seat and ran into the empty formal dining room. Following in alarm, Rachael found Jean seated at the long table, her head down and her shoulders racked with uncontrollable sobbing. Rachael put her arms around her friend, "Oh Jean, you loved him too."

"Yes, Rachael, I loved him too."

Within a week, the appointed receiver, and his three assistants, descended on the manor. "We are not here to remove anything, Mrs. Olson. Our job is to record and give a value to each item located in every room. It will be a painstaking process, but we will try not to disrupt your regular routines any more than absolutely necessary. We will be here at 9:00 every morning, and will leave again by 4:00 p.m. We understand there are still a few evening events planned, and that you and your staff are committed to fulfil Sir Gordon's arranged schedule."

"Yes, that's true, Mr. Bryce," said Jean. "I hope you will be in a position to share when the manor is to be shut down."

"Indeed we will, Mrs. Olson. My instructions are: when our task is finished, two weeks notice of eviction will be given to you and your staff."

"Thank you, Sir. I have one concern regarding John and Rebecca Neilson, who are grounds and house keepers," stated Jean. "They have established a very extensive market garden operation on the property. John has spoken to me about the feasibility of their leasing the portion of this property that includes their market garden as well as the paddock, the stable, horses and vehicles. They would appreciate having that notation on your records."

"I will certainly do that, Mrs. Olson. However, I am not in a position to foresee the outcome of the manor's disposal. I am assuming it will revert to the Crown, or in this case the City of Aberdeen, and that decision will be revealed in due time. The nearest relative is Sir Gordon's sister, and she will be consulted regarding her interest in purchasing items, before it is given over to public auction. In returning to Edinburgh," assured Mr. Bryce, "I will encourage the same courtesy be granted to Sir Gordon's faithful household staff."

With his departing good wishes, Mr. Bryce gave Jean Olson a copy of the listing of household goods available for sale within the following two weeks. "It would be tempting to simply say: 'I don't want anything,' out of sympathy and respect for Sir Gordon's memory," stated Jean to the gathered household staff, "but we have been given the opportunity, and I believe – with Sir Gordon's blessing, to choose items that can be useful to us, and that would serve as a memory token as well."

As she tidied up the sewing room that afternoon, Rachael suddenly had a sad feeling that this would be the last time she would have the opportunity to enter this delightful work place. *But wait a minute,* she thought, *I wonder if I could buy the sewing machine? In fact, I want everything in this room! I have kept Mr. Murray's lovely gift – perhaps this would be an investment he would approve of. I will consult with Todd about this later today."* After speaking to Jean Olson about her idea of purchasing the entire contents of the sewing room, she offered to be available for Mrs. Gilbert's visit.

"Yes please, Rachael!" said Jean, "There is no question – I will need you here."

Golden Ribbons

"On behalf of the household staff, I want to offer my sincere condolences to you, Mrs. Gilbert," said Jean. "This must be a very difficult time for you."

"Indeed difficult, Mrs. Olson, and furthermore, embarrassing! I had no idea Gordon was in such financial difficulty. I expect it was that common woman he married that set this downward spiral in motion. It is indeed a blot on our family's good name. But I'm not here to air my disfavour. I will just roam about and choose as I go. If there a trolley available, perhaps your girl here can follow along to assist me?"

"I would like to introduce Rachael Atkinson, who has remained here at the manor to be a support to me. I see you have your daughter with you, perhaps she could help you."

"Mrs. Olson, you seem not aware to whom you are speaking! My daughter will not assist me, as it is not her place to do so," Mrs. Gilbert stated firmly.

"Neither is it Rachael's place to serve you; there are no servants in this home. We have all stayed until resolution of this unhappy situation, out of respect for Sir Gordon. Go ahead and decide what you want to take, Mrs. Gilbert. I will remain here in the day room, and before you leave I will record your choices, and inform you of the amount you will be expected to pay. I am under the direction of the court appointed receiver to do so."

"Well!" said Bonnie Gilbert, in disgust. "I have no intention of paying for anything I want in this manor. This is my family home. I will have my husband take care of this, and our solicitors will deal with it directly. Come Penelope!" she ordered.

"I want a drink of water, Mommy. The girl can get it for me," whined Penelope.

"I will show you to the kitchen, Penelope," said Rachael flatly, "and you can get a drink of water for yourself. Come along then, if you wish . . ."

"Hurry up then, Penelope!" Mrs. Gilbert said impatiently. "I will wait for you in the carriage."

Penelope stood in the doorway of the kitchen, her hands folded in front of her. "The water glasses are kept in this cupboard," Rachael pointed. "Water comes out of the tap, or you can get it from a jug in the ice box." Rachael stood to one side, waiting for Penelope to move.

"Alright," said Penelope, as she moved awkwardly toward the cupboard. Then she turned the tap and filled the glass to overflowing. "Ouch, that's hot!" she yelled. "Are you trying to trick me?" Penelope threw the glass into the sink, and stomped out – not remembering the pathway to the front door.

Rachael moved back to the day room, telling Jean that Penelope was loose in the manor. "How much time should we give her, Jean?" she laughed. "By now she should be wandering through every open door."

"You can be a very naughty girl, Rachael," smiled Jean Olson, "… but delightful."

As the visit to Dundee came to a close, there was again the familiar sadness in parting, as well as good wishes to Todd as he would be going to Dartmouth in a few days. "Please write soon, Todd," said Aggie. "We will be so anxious to hear about this new adventure."

Todd reminded that he would be back in eighteen months. "Hardly time to get sea legs," he laughed.

"I think it's wonderful you are investing in such a practical endeavour, Rachael," said Todd, "but where are you going to put all of this sewing equipment?"

"Well, I have a week to find that out, Todd," Rachael replied with uncertainty.

"I could ask Mrs. Cronin for you, if you like," suggested Todd. "It could possibly be squeezed into my attic room."

"I will think about that as a last resort, Todd, but I do have an option to explore, and I will let you know about it tomorrow," Rachael said, smiling.

"I have made all the necessary enquiries, Rachael," said Mavis Gibbons. "There seems to be no road blocks to your leasing the second floor space here. Actually, I'm very excited about what you are proposing."

As Rachael stood on the railway station platform, waving Todd good bye, she suddenly realized he would not be within her reach tomorrow, and so many of the following days. *I should be getting used to this by now,* she thought. *But, this is Todd leaving!* She decided to get right back on her bike, and ride to the end of the sea trail. That activity never failed to make her feel better.

Mrs. Cronin welcomed Rachael, as she had Todd, after Malcolm's death. "You may use my little guest room, if you wish," she said. "I don't believe Todd was here long enough to make his room very homey. And you know, of course, Todd has paid six months of your room and board. I will miss him, but it is a welcome treat to have you take his place while he is away."

"Thank you for being so flexible about the change, Mrs. Cronin," said Rachael. "We seem to be a family of change," she added, with a note of apology. "But, as with Todd, I will not be here a great deal. I appreciate the offer of your cosy guest room, but I believe for now I will occupy Todd's attic space. When the weather turns cold, I will be most happy to move down to be near your warm fire."

"Just as you wish, Rachael," agreed Mrs. Cronin pleasantly. "But let's have a cup of tea, and you can tell me about your plans for setting up a dressmaking service, in combination with Miss Gibbons' millinery shop."

"I am happy to share the plan with you. It will take a few months to settle into a new and challenging working partnership for both Mavis Gibbons and myself," said Rachael, "but I'm looking forward to it, and excited about working with lovely fabrics and creating outfits that will be pleasant and colourful to look at."

"Perhaps I will ask you to design and sew a dress for me, Rachael, and Miss Gibbons to complement it with a hat," suggested Mrs. Cronin. "I will be attending a niece's wedding in late summer. A new dress and hat will make the occasion even more enjoyable for me."

"And that is exactly what the aim of this service will be. It will allow women the privilege of choosing what is right for them, and not to be carried along with current trends in fashion – just because a few people in industry decide what that should be."

"Wow, Rachael!" said Terry, as he leapt into the open second story room. "This is going to be a happy work place."

"Thank you, Terry," said Rachael, "and, thank you for your work in helping Todd move all this sewing equipment up those stairs. I do appreciate the incredible light of this room – as you drew my attention to so long ago, but I will allow you to come occasionally," she teased. "You can sit quietly in a corner with your sketch pad."

"Oh, thank you!" said Terry, with pretend annoyance.

Rachael received a note from Aggie:

> I have a few free days in late July. I hope it might be convenient for the three of us to visit you for two days – July 25 and 26.

Rachael was delighted with the plan to show Aggie and the children the places where she and Todd had lived and worked. As well, they would make an attempt to find out if Robby was still in Aberdeen. It was arranged that Aggie and Mary share Mrs. Cronin's guest room, but Peter was anxious to sleep in Uncle Todd's room in the attic. A small cot was brought forward from the back attic room that served his need quite adequately. The search for information about Robbie was a bit more challenging, but Rachael decided that a visit to Sergeant McTavish at the South Aberdeen Precinct could prove enlightening.

"Let's see here, Rachael," said Sergeant McTavish, as he thumbed back through several pages of the giant record book. "Ah yes," he noted: "January 5, 1900, Robbie McNabb agreed to exchange his prison sentence for one-way passage to Australia. He would be assigned to a hay ranch in New South Wales. He is not seen as a danger to re-offend."

Rachael thanked the sergeant for the information and, as she took Aggie's arm - returning to the street and the bright sunshine, Aggie said, with sadness, "At least I know where Robbie is now. I hope he has found a place where he can be content."

Rachael looked around her with delight, as she sat with Mavis Gibbons over a cup of tea in the new upstairs workroom. "Thinking of this combined effort, Mavis," she asked, "how do you see this dressmaking and design workroom as a complement to your activities downstairs? I realize you already have a comfortable gathering of clientele, but will dressmaking be seen by them as an opportunity to engage in a coordinated presentation?"

"Believe me, I have thought about it," said Mavis. "In fact I've put myself in the place of every client as they leave my shop with a hat they absolutely love. But, what will they wear with it? That bothers me because, if what they are wearing does not complement the hat, it is a reflection on my skills as a milliner. This new approach will take time to be accepted, Rachael. But, from what I had observed from your collaboration work with Terry, I became convinced that we could work together in a coordinated effort. Then, you came along and made the suggestion, and I was ready for it!"

"Thank you, Mavis," returned Rachael. "Your experience and insights will help me to prioritize the steps so that I'm not wasting time, as well as investment money, and I will welcome your suggestions."

"We can share the expense of items that overlap our services," suggested Mavis. "One item could be a mannequin to show an example of what we are attempting to accomplish. But let's, for now, give planning top priority, then moving ahead slowly – one step at a time so we are not overwhelmed by matters we are not prepared for."

As Rachael returned to Todd's attic sanctuary that evening, she noticed Malcolm's old green leather chair for the first time. It was tucked in a corner with an unobstructed view of inside, and, through the big window, the outside – taking in the movements of a quiet neighbourhood as well as the occasional burst of excited laughter as people entered and left the ice cream parlour. "What a wonderful place to think, dream, and write," thought Rachael. "Perhaps making these lists will not be as scary as I had thought."

Dartmouth, August 12, 1902

Dear Sister Rachael: Here I am at the Naval Academy. So far I feel ignored, and disoriented. This <u>is</u> England, after all! I rather think they will soon get around to noticing me, and it will be *full steam ahead!* Then there is the English food! Sausage and thick white bread for tea! How I miss Mrs. Cronin's cooking; please tell her so.

Other than that, the sky is grey, the water choppy, and there are about thirty ships out there - doing whatever it is that ships do. I wish my bike was here, but perhaps I will rent one when there is some time off. I miss you Rach, and I miss our bike rides together. But that will happen on your first visit - I'm already plotting...

Love from your brother Todd

I did not expect a note from Todd quite so soon, Mr. Murray, Rachael said to the old green leather chair. *I'm sure he is homesick, and I miss him too. But I will send your love along with my own when I post a note back to him tomorrow.*

CHAPTER THIRTEEN

"I CAN HAVE YOUR PACKAGES DELIVERED, MRS. CRONIN," RACHAEL said, as she put finishing touches to the autumn gold afternoon-dress that would accompany the hat, with coordinated colours.

"Thank you Rachael and Mavis," said Mrs. Cronin, obviously happy with her new outfit, "but I believe I will take them home with me in the hansom."

"So, we can call this a *dry run* Rachael," laughed Mavis. "Our collaboration has been put to the test with a friendly client."

As one satisfied client referred three more, Rachael and Mavis were working long hours, and beginning to feel the strain of keeping up with the demand. "I believe, Rachael, that some of these dear ladies are going to have to be scheduled to our timetable, not just their own. It could be that what we offer is novel, although not in the larger cities, and the big wave will soon be just a trickle. So, let's not allow that to happen. We could ask Terry to help us out with a very attractive layout for the newspaper, something like: *Booking now for those New Year parties*," she suggested.

"I do agree, Mavis. However, it just dawned on me: we don't have a name. What are we calling our service?"

Whenever Terry had a few minutes in his day, he would drop in to see how the new business partners were getting on. "Why don't you simply call it *The Ensemble*?" he suggested. "If you like that name, and I notice you haven't come up with another, I will design and install a sign for above the door. And, at your request, I will also start on a dazzling layout for the newspaper."

"There were certain matters we didn't consider," said Rachael, "and Terry has been that objective observer who has just the right suggestions."

As team work at The Ensemble progressed at a more reasonable pace, Rachael and Mavis took time to consider improvements to the physical space where they would greet clients. Rachael had an uncomfortable feeling about the mannequin. *There will be times when I will not agree with Mavis, or she with me,* thought Rachael. *I'm afraid this one of those occasions. I might as well speak about it, and get it over with.*

"You spoke earlier about buying a mannequin, Mavis," Rachael began carefully. "But I do not think one of them would benefit our shop. I have seen them in the windows of Bundy's Department Store, and I find them grotesque."

"Do you have another idea for a window display, Rachael?" Mavis asked guardedly.

"Yes, actually, I do. I can envision a sitting room arrangement where the fabrics themselves can be displayed, and where two of your lovely hats would be available to lend the coordinating colours."

"You have obviously given this quite a lot of thought, Rachael, and it does sound original. Could we ask Terry to sketch the scene you describe?" asked Mavis. "Like the children who are attracted to your books and costumes, Rachael, I am a visual person - having to see the arrangement before I can commit to accepting it."

"That sounds reasonable, Mavis. I will get in touch with Terry, and I hope we will come up with a scene you will like."

Rachael and Terry met that evening at the ice cream parlour. "You should not worry about Mavis, and her old fashioned ideas, Rachael," said Terry. "She was raised with convention, as I was – although longer, of course. She is very artistic in my opinion," Terry continued, "but it's been suppressed. It's very good for her to have you as an associate; I can tell she has already relaxed some of her opinions. So, tell me what your idea is about a window display."

As Rachael presented her plan in as visual a manner as possible, Terry was already way ahead of her. "Hmm, yes I can see it clearly," said Terry. "It's a marvellous idea, Rachael! I believe we should paint the backdrop, and I can do that," he offered, as he began his sketch. "Now, about the furniture: I would think two rather attractive chairs in good condition, a small table to set just behind them, flowers, a window …"

"That is just what I had in mind, Terry!" exclaimed Rachael. "We seem to occupy the same brain – only in different spheres," she laughed.

"It will be like stepping into a drawing room," said Terry, "and, yes, we do seem to occupy the same brain in so many ways, Rachael. Thanks for asking

Golden Ribbons

me to help. I've been in need of your inspiration ever since we said good bye to the *Polly* series."

"I hope I can always be that kind of friend, Terry," said Rachael, as she lifted her ice cream spoon in a toast.

"To our friendship – always!" Terry responded, with a clink of his ice cream spoon against hers.

"Your name is Atkinson - Todd, is that right?" asked the captain.

"Yes, Sir," responded Todd.

"My name is Captain Jim Patton. We've actually been looking for you, and then realized you had been referred to the wrong dormitory. Sorry about that."

"Your apology accepted, Sir," said Todd with good humour.

"Never mind, then," said Captain Patton. "We will get right on with it. You will be in dormitory three, and your supervisor First Lieutenant Peter Crandall. We do indeed welcome you post-secondary school lads to Naval Academy, although for a short stay. But our hope, always, is that one day the navy will become a career choice," Captain Patton emphasized. "I expect it was explained to you:" he continued, "when you return home to university you will be cast as *reserve,* and will be required to report to a naval base for three weeks of further training every two years."

Todd was taken to dormitory three, and to meet First Lt. Crandall. "Welcome Todd," said Lt. Crandall. "It's about tea time around here. Would you care to join us, and you can meet some of the other lads in the program."

"A pleasure, Sir," said Todd.

"It said in your referral letter, Todd, that you had made quite a name for yourself on the soccer field at your home secondary school," said Lt. Crandall. "We always look forward to new recruits. Actually, there are two teams in this program at the present time, and it's great to have a match or two here on the grounds of the Academy. It happens rarely," continued the lieutenant, "but if one team outshines the other there is an opportunity to travel out of our encampment here and to have a match with lads elsewhere."

"That sounds most interesting," replied Todd. "I enjoy playing soccer."

"Right then," said Lt. Crandall. "Now I'll just go over the program as a whole..."

Dartmouth Naval Academy September 10, 1902

Dear Sister Rachael: My life here is beginning to make sense, as I know where I'm supposed to sleep, who is in charge, etcetera. Best news is that soccer is played here - in fact two teams! Anyway, I've had the program explained to me and it seems like the days will be pretty busy. I am officially a naval cadet, but not in reality; the status is somewhere between cadet and midshipman. A cadet can be as young as twelve, then after completing secondary school here at the academy, moves on to the Royal Naval College, and at sixteen can be designated as a midshipman. So, you can see where I stand, being fifteen – well, as you know, sixteen in January!

I'm glad you and Miss Gibbons are getting along well, and you are creating wonderful gowns for lucky women. I agree with you about the issue of the mannequin, I always think they look like dead people. But knowing you, I'm sure the issue was resolved peacefully.

Love from your brother Todd

p.s. I know Malcolm is happy you are there, in the attic room, taking my place.

"I hope you will have a wonderful New Year visit with your sister and her children, Rachael," said Mavis Gibbons. "After four months as co-workers in this world of fashion, I would say we are off to a good start."

"I agree, Mavis. It has been very rewarding to work with you, and I look forward to a new season of spring fabrics. It does seem, though," continued

Rachael, "these ladies are not taking our ads seriously about booking in advance. We are still working on their time schedules."

"Yes, I see that too," said Mavis. "I suppose it is something we must suffer through until they realize we are a credible service. I expect that may take longer than four months to establish."

"I'm sure you're right. I guess I'm just a little impatient with people who expect so much in so little time."

"We are dealing mainly with upper-class women, Rachael," said Mavis with sympathy. "Unfortunately, most of them have a choice to take their business to Glasgow if we are not serving them as quickly as they would like. It's sad to realize that women of a lower class cannot afford our service."

"That is sad, Mavis, and one I must come to terms with. After Sir Gordon died and the manor was closing, I came to understand the nature of class distinction, and I was, quite frankly, discouraged with a state of affairs that separates one group of people from another. I want the world to operate differently, Mavis. I don't want to simply give way, and settle into a morbid attitude of acceptance."

"That's what makes me admire you so much, Rachael. You are so young to be dealing with these issues, but I have a feeling your heart will not allow you to settle into that *morbid attitude of acceptance* you have just stated. But, let's have a joyous New Year – 1903! No matter how difficult the road ahead may seem, the good will ultimately always win."

Is there truth in what Mavis just said, Rachael pondered. *Will the good ultimately win, or should we not keep trying to push against the difficult road?*

Rachael had just enough time to finish sewing a spring dress for Aggie, and her new valise was jammed with outfits for each of the children, as well as a doll for Mary and a game for Peter. *I guess it's a loving thought for Todd this New Year, Mr. Murray,* she said, sadly, to the old green leather chair.

As she was leaving her attic home, Rachael noticed mail left for her on the landing. *I will read this on the train,* she thought, as she waved good-bye to Mrs. Cronin and rushed to catch the omnibus to the train station. Rachael relaxed into her assigned seat on the train and watched the dismal winter scene passing by. She could not get the thoughts from her mind: *So many women out there, this frosty New Year's eve, will not have a new dress to make her smile, and to lighten here step as she prepares for another new year.* Then, as the porter asked for her ticket, she remembered the mail tucked into her leather case.

A beautiful card, containing loving thoughts from Todd, was the first to be opened. The second letter was from Mr. H.B. McWiggins, the Glasgow publisher.

> Dear Rachael: I sincerely wish a bright and happy New Year to you, and that 1903 will be a time when you will consider honouring me with more of your writing. The Polly Adventure books continue to sell well, especially at this season of the year when parents are searching for both amusing and interesting reading for their children.
>
> I would, however, like you to consider writing a contemporary novel. Serial novels are becoming popular, as that can be one-at-a-time buying which is more in line with the household budget. I find that readers are looking for every-day stories of every-day life - something they can relate to. Please consider these ideas for a writing project in the coming year.
>
> Kindest regards, H. B. McWiggins

I will, indeed, Mr. McWiggins.

Dartmouth Naval Academy December 20, 1902

I am sending a New Year greeting to all of you in Dundee, and wishing I was there. Preparations for the holiday seem to be quite different from our own in Scotland. The mess hall has a Christmas tree decorated with coloured balls, and even candles. Christmas in England seems to be more of a family time, where there are gifts exchanged. New Years Eve, I will be joining the lads in the program for an evening of games and some entertainment. The officers and their wives or girlfriends will be attending balls or other small parties.

My classroom time will change to training onboard ship in early February. I am looking forward to that, but I am quite happy and fascinated with everything so far. The winter months are warmer here than in Aberdeen; consequently soccer is played almost year-round.

With love, from your brother, Todd

November 30, 1902 The Village of Airdrie, Northwest Territories,

Happy New Year to all! You will be missing Todd this New Years, and I'm sure he feels the same. It seems strange to think of Todd way down there in Dartmouth, England, but I'm sure he is making good use of the time as naval cadet. The Canadian Prime Minister, Sir Wilfred Laurier, has argued for, and won, a program to replace British soldiers with Militia under Canadian command, and there will also be an official Canadian navy in the near future. This is all very exciting for us. We are beginning to feel *Canadian*.

Our grain crop was of a good grade, and so it was a successful harvest. We are very thankful and hope for the same in 1903. Most of the profit will go toward improvements in the home: wood flooring, a big window on either side of the fireplace, and a large order has been placed with the Eaton's Catalogue (it has everything!) for many smaller needs that we felt we could not afford before now. George Donaldson is encouraging us to purchase another quarter section of land that is adjacent to what we presently farm. He feels that with more homesteaders coming every year, the price of land will certainly rise. We are giving this advice serious consideration, and if it goes ahead, will again be thanks to Mr. Murray. Maggie, Billy and Niall are well and send their love. Spring will bring a new blessing as we await a wee brother or sister for Niall.

Love to all, your brother Joey

Rachael was happy travelling to Glasgow on such a sunny and warm June day. She would take the final draft of her first book in the three-part serial, <u>The House on Cobblestone Lane</u>, to be reviewed by McWiggins Publishing. *It has been such fun to write again,* she thought, as she watched the fields slide by in full summer glory. *I can understand why my brothers, and Maggie, are so thrilled to be growing crops on their very own land, though it's sad to think of them so far away.*

The spring rush had finally passed at The Ensemble, and Rachael and Mavis could take time off to enjoy the summer months, staying open for business only three days a week. Rachael had plans to visit Todd in August when he would have some time away from the naval academy. "We will stay in the village," he wrote, "and bikes can be rented so we can tour some of the ancient sites on the moors."

The excitement of looking forward to a holiday with Todd, and packing up some of her favourite outfits, kept Rachael's troubled thoughts at bay. Her smart new biking costume was given a special place in her valise. Changing trains in Edinburgh, she realized she had never been to this beautiful city before. But there it was - Edinburgh Castle! She would certainly come back another day to see it up close, and to tour the many brilliant rooms.

Arriving at Dartmouth train station, Rachael looked around frantically for a glimpse of Todd – not noticing that he was standing right behind her. "Can this beautiful girl really be my sister?" Todd asked with admiration and pride.

"Oh Todd, how I've missed you!" said Rachael, trying to choke back the tears, as she rushed into his arms. "I don't care if you object to mushy stuff," she laughed.

"No objection, my sister, I've been looking forward to this moment for days. Let's get going into the village. We can find a pleasant spot to sit and have a cup of tea before I show you to our lodgings." There was so much catch-up news, the brother and sister found themselves chatting longer than they realized. "We'd better hurry along, Rach," Todd urged, "or the lodging house proprietor will give our rooms to someone else."

"You look so wonderful in your naval uniform, Todd! So grown up!" chattered Rachael.

"Yes, but look at you!" Todd returned. "Such a smart travelling suit and with your hair piled up under your hat! Wow!"

"Let's just say we have both undergone a transformation," said Rachael. "But really, I can't wait to get into my biking costume, and let my hair down again," she laughed.

"Tomorrow morning - bright and early! I've reserved the bikes for nine o'clock!"

The days passed too quickly as Todd and Rachael made up for lost time with bike travels, long walks, and just enjoying each other's company. As the day approached for Rachael to once again return to Aberdeen, she reluctantly changed back into her travelling suit and hat. When she met Todd in the lobby of the lodge, he had also changed back into his naval uniform. "I have to get right back to the base, Rachael, so I might have to leave you at the train stop a bit early," he said with regret.

"That's fine, Todd. You will be back in Aberdeen in a few months, and after this time we've had together, your being away will then seem so much shorter. Thank you for an amazing holiday my dear brother," she said, giving him an expected hug.

"Picture, Sir?" the street photographer asked, as he approached Todd and Rachael.

"Yes, please!" said Todd, "and make it four copies. I will pay you now, and you may mail the prints to the naval college." After presenting his card to the street vendor, Todd was off – turning once to give Rachael a smile and a wave.

"We must mail our order for fall and winter fabrics right away, Rachael," Mavis said. "Then, let's try our promotional advertisement again; perhaps the ladies will notice and be more cooperative this season."

"There is still a lot of fabric left over from our order of last fall, Mavis; we can cut back a bit."

"I'm afraid not, Rachael. Not one of our clients would appreciate having a gown or hat made with last year's fabric. The very idea would be an outrage to them. It does seem a waste, but we more than make up for it with our charge for service. It's just part of an exclusive appointment."

"I suppose the left-over fabric could be sold at a consignment shop," Rachael further suggested.

"Can you imagine what that would do to our reputation if a common woman was seen wearing a gown or hat of similar fabric to one that we designed especially for that one lady the prior season!" said Mavis, with finality.

"Yes, I see," said Rachael.

I wish I had discussed this matter with Todd, thought Rachael. *I cannot go along with this line of reasoning; it goes against everything I believe in.* As she walked slowly up the side street to catch the omnibus to Todd's attic room, she decided to see if Terry was still at the printing shop. "I must talk this over with someone," she said out loud.

When Rachael expressed her need for a serious talk, Terry suggested they have tea together at a nearby sidewalk café. "I have involved myself in this cooperative venture, Terry, without realizing that it would end up being exactly what I would hate – pleasing snobby women, and charging more than any fool would expect to pay for the service," said Rachael, with a combination of regret and disgust.

"I can only listen and sympathize, Rachael," said Terry. "You are a friend that I value more than any other, and you have helped me break a deadlock with my father by urging me to follow my own way. For that I will be forever grateful. Mavis is, however, my aunt, and she has encouraged me in a similar way. I only suggest," Terry continued, "you speak to Mavis very frankly about your feelings; she would certainly realize that your work would suffer if you remained."

"Yes Terry, and thank you. I guess what you have said is what I already knew to be true. I have no option but to follow your suggestion."

"I love you as a dear friend, Rachael," said Terry "even though I do not fully understand your feelings. I have not lived your life; if I had I would be in a better position to empathize and be of more help. Only remember: I am here for you – always."

"I felt this was coming, Rachael," said Mavis. "You have a heart for fairness in society that I cannot share – I don't have the background and insight that you have. I can grasp the political and social protests of women in Aberdeen who labour long, and with great courage, to see that equality in those spheres come about. But, I feel you have a much deeper social conscience, and I can only bless you with all my heart."

"Thank you for planting seeds of opportunity in this field of fashion design – just as you helped Terry take the leap of faith and follow his own way," Mavis continued. "You will have my full cooperation in the timing of your release from our work together. It will be hard to replace someone as talented as you are, but I will do it now that you have given me the confidence to know that it can be done."

Rachael had an opportunity to transfer the lease of the upstairs workroom to the incoming seamstress, as long as the sewing machine and cutting tables could be sold to her in the deal. *Giving up the sewing equipment is a sacrifice,* she thought. *It's all I have to remember the manor.* At the same time, Rachael could see it was a practical offer, and she would always be able to buy a new, or used, sewing machine whenever she was settled.

I suppose this is another one of Sir Gordon's dilemmas of life, thought Rachael. *Here I am, right back where I started, after leaving the manor. But, I'm sixteen now, and* old enough to lease a flat of my own! If I am to write every- day stories of every-day life, then I had better plant myself where I can observe it — at least observe the folks who live in my serial novels* The House On Cobblestone Lane.*

Before Rachael left the attic apartment to meet Todd at the train station, she made the space look welcoming and in good order. *I have enjoyed living here these past months, Mr. Murray,* she said to the old green leather chair. *But, Todd will be home today, and that will make both of us very happy.*

It was a balancing act: continuing to work with Mavis until the New Year holiday, satisfying Mr. McWiggin's urging for that second book in the serial, and settling into her flat, located above a greengrocer. Ethan and Rosalyn Schwartz had welcomed her warmly, and Rachael felt right at home. *There will be neighbourhood people coming and going,* she thought, *and I will get to know as many as I can.* The flat was partially furnished, but there was enough for immediate living, and it was clean. Her bike could be kept in a storage shed behind the shop, and Ethan Schwartz gave her a key, so the small building could be opened to her at any time.

Todd had no time to waste: he had an entrance exam to prepare for, and he had to take care of all those other entrance papers that universities are famous for. *Can you believe it, Malcolm!* said Todd. *Five years ago, I didn't know where my next meal would come from. Now I'm going to university, and it's all thanks to you, old friend.*

Todd noticed a note had been left for him on the landing to the attic room.

> Dear Todd: Could we meet this evening at the corner of Melrose Street and Crosstown. I hope 6:30 will be convenient. I want to show you my new flat. I love having you back home again; I'm sure Malcolm is pleased too.

"This flat is great, Rachael. It is You! But for now, we have two days before we head off to Dundee and the New Year holiday. Can you handle that short space of time?" asked Todd.

"It is time enough, Todd. I will meet you at the train station the afternoon of December 31, 1903!" said Rachael. "I will run everywhere I have to go, and not sleep – if necessary."

As Rachael approached The Ensemble for her final round of fittings and sewing, she was thankful for the insight this opportunity had given her. *I will, never again, stoop to serve as a servant to anyone who perceives themselves as superior,* she thought.

Rachael and Todd found Aggie to be in good spirits as she welcomed them with outstretched arms. It was apparent that her work at the hospital was satisfying and rewarding. Peter and Mary, at ages seven and six, were becoming independent and helpful.

"May I take your cases upstairs, Auntie Rachael?" Peter asked.

"Yes, thank you Peter," said Rachael, noticing how grown up he had become. Aggie had made the old house a festive array of flowers and streamers, and with a formal dinner awaiting their enjoyment. Gifts were exchanged, with thanks, smiles and good wishes. The children were allowed to stay up until midnight to welcome in the New Year, and they could join the grownups for sharing in the news coming from Canada.

> December 02, 1903 The Village of Airdrie, Northwest Territories
>
> Dear family: We join you across the miles in welcoming in 1904! How wonderful you are all together again for this special time. Our little daughter, Katherine Rachael, is now seven months old. One thing about the arrival of a second child, we realize this little one won't break, and she can become a solid and strong member of the family right away.
>
> We are thankful for a successful harvest again this year. A McClary range has been added to the kitchen; we wish

Joshua could be here to celebrate this wonderful addition to the kitchen he built for Maggie. Speaking of Joshua, George Donaldson mentioned to me a few days ago that two officers from the Northwest Mounted Police had been along to his place, asking about the black man who had been seen working in this area. It seems Joshua's problems have been settled without his knowing about it; a second jury trial in South Carolina had acquitted him of being the prime suspect in the murder of a local politician. George was able to tell the mounted police that Joshua had headed west, and the approximate date. With this news, we hope Joshua will soon be found, and the good news related to him.

Rather than adding rooms to the main floor, we have decided to raise the roof to make a second story. This will make a very active summer, but we hope to make it happen quickly. Niall is looking forward to having his bed, and all his precious belongings (stones and odd pieces of wood), in an upstairs bedroom.

Congratulations Todd, in achieving the rank of midshipman, and thank you for the delightful street picture of you and Rachael; we have it on our new mantle above the fireplace, along with the lovely graduation picture of Aggie, and of Peter and Mary at ages six and seven. We delight in the images of our family every day!

Maggie is especially anxious to receive copies of your serial books, Rachael. The ladies in this community have organized themselves as, officially – *Women's Institute*. There is opportunity for a book exchange, and yours will be added to it.

With our love, and every good wish for the coming year, your brother Billy

Golden Ribbons

With little time to relax on the train before arriving back to Aberdeen, and busy days ahead, Rachael and Todd made a pledge that the tradition of Sunday afternoon visits be faithfully kept. "Classes start in a week," Todd announced. "It's certainly an exciting time, and I will want to find out if soccer is an organized extra-curricular activity."

"Oh, you would!" teased Rachael. "I will have serial book number two ready by mid January. Would have time to go along with me to Glasgow?"

"Don't count me out just yet, dear sister."

Between writing and organizing her small flat, Rachael took time to roam about the neighbourhood of small shops, interspersed with family dwellings of one and two stories; it seemed to be a cluster of enclaves, working and getting along well together. She discovered a small school offering basic education, but children were mainly educated at home. *What a unique situation!* she thought. *I must spend time at the nearby library to educate myself about these various cultures. Class distinction among my own culture seemed enough to grapple with, and now a new layer of cultural variation is added to it.* Rachael could see where her writing would take her in the future.

As she looked out the front window of her tiny flat and into the bleakness of the January day, Rachael was curious to see Todd pulling up to the building on his bike. A small wooden crate on wheels was attached to the back. Within seconds, he was at her door carrying an armload of used household linens. "Mrs. Cronin sends a few things she thought you might be able to use," Todd explained, "and – there's more!" He was back again with all manner of china and flatware.

"How wonderful of her!" said Rachael. "I can use all of it, and it will certainly save me the time of browsing through second-hand shops. Please express my gratitude."

"Oh, and I have something else," said Todd. He had an armload of cut logs for her small fireplace. "I just want to see how it works," he said, as he crumpled up papers and laid the logs in just the right position. "I feel it warming the room already."

"Thank you so much, Todd, now I really do feel at home. Can you wait for tea? I will just put the kettle on the stove," she said, as Todd nodded agreement and rubbed his hands at the fire.

"Do you miss Terry, Rachael?" Todd asked. "It seemed you had spent a fair bit of time with him the months I was away."

"Actually Todd, I seldom think of Terry these days; I've been too busy getting on a new track with everything!" she said. "If you think Terry might be more than a friend, Todd, you are mistaken. Terry will never be more than that, and we both realize it. I suppose I am at the age where I might be looking at a lad as a special beau, but I just feel that I could not share my deepest feelings with just anyone – at least not yet or even for a long time." Rachael paused to gather her thoughts: "I guess I'm an older woman in life experience, if not in age. But, what about you, Todd, did you meet a lass of interest to you?"

"No Rach, there was little opportunity at the academy for socializing," he smiled. "But, like you, I have no thoughts of it at the moment. You are right: we both have a background that would be difficult to share, or if there would be any understanding of it. Better that we stay as we are for now, and rebuild what was lost."

"I'm glad we can talk like this, Todd, and you are home again. You will get tired of hearing me say that, but I can't guarantee it won't happen again and again," Rachael laughed.

"I won't get tired of it, Rach."

CHAPTER FOURTEEN

TODD FOUND THE WEEKS AND MONTHS SLIPPING BY, MID-TERMS passed, and spring was bursting out upon the beautiful University of Aberdeen campus. *Rachael should be over here,* he thought. *She will soon be seventeen, and with all her writing credits, possibly eligible for a literature scholarship.*

"I've done a bit of research, Rachael. It seems that the Carnegie Trust has a bias when it comes to granting scholarships to students in the arts. I have seen several women roaming around campus; it would seem the big breakthrough of allowing women the privilege of university education is not such a struggle as it once was."

"I have never given any thought to attending university, Todd. I would need more writing credits to qualify," Rachael responded thoughtfully. "But thank you for giving the matter your consideration. I am just finishing up the serial books, and now I can look more to serious writing. As I wander in this neighbourhood, and discover where these people have come from, and the possible reasons for leaving their homes, I feel there is an urge to write about them stirring in me. Information will not be relinquished easily," Rachael continued. "I must spend time gaining their confidences, as well as my own understanding. I am planted in this neighbourhood for a reason, Todd, if only for my own insights into another world of experience."

"Sounds like a wonderful project, Rachael," Todd responded.

"Now that you mention it, Todd, would you have any interest in coaching soccer among these lads in this community? There seems not much to do, except for games of tag, or just talking together."

"Hey now, let's not get carried away, sister! How would I know if the lads, or their parents, for that matter, would want me spending time with their children? And what about space for that purpose – is there a park nearby?" Todd asked.

"There is no park nearby that I'm aware of, but a small playground at the school might be an option," Rachael suggested. "I could drop over there this week and ask the teacher if the playground could be used. Can I say, then, that you are willing?"

"Oh sure. As usual, you can talk me into anything," Todd said with mock annoyance.

After their usual bike ride, and a tea break with Rachael's fresh scones, Todd went away smiling to himself. *Actually, coaching young lads might be fun.*

An agreement, with some modification, was struck with the teacher. She felt that the lads attending the school might find a late afternoon mid-week practise to their liking. "Another consideration, Rachael, is the children in your immediate community may not be available on certain days because of religious observations. However," Miss Conrad continued, "we need to know when your brother is available. Let me assure you, the lads here will love this opportunity, and in short time the others will follow."

"Thank you, Miss Conrad, you have been very encouraging. I believe I have my brother sold on the plan." With that, Rachael scribbled a note to Todd, and jumped on her bike to deliver it to Mrs. Cronin's home.

Tuesday afternoon became regular soccer practise. As predicted, the lads from the school were eager to get started and, one by one, children from the neighbourhood began watching the activity with great interest. Rachael had delivered a notice to each home stating boys, ages eight to twelve, would be most welcome to join in. Within a month, there were enough participants to make up two teams. As an added bonus, Todd brought along a university friend to share in the coaching. Rachael was overjoyed.

It was time to discuss a short holiday that summer of 1904. "Let's get a map to see where we haven't been. I'm sure our bikes can handle the rough trails in the Highlands. Does that appeal to you, Rach?" asked Todd.

"It does, Todd," Rachael agreed absently. "I've been so immersed in the cultures of Eastern Europe and the middle east lately, I would think a pause to learn more about our own country would be in order. So, would you say about a week to ten days in mid-July? It should be fairly warm in the mountains at that time."

Rachael was becoming a familiar face in her adopted community. She was welcomed as she entered and browsed in the shops, and with the weather turning warm in the afternoons, she would join the ladies as they gathered in groups around the open markets. The topic of food was always a faithful opener to more intimate conversation. Participating families of the Russian Christian Orthodox faith came together over the period of Lent, or *Maslenitsa*, Rachael learned. But as Easter Sunday passed, plans were being made for the day of feasting, and decorating of eggs – the tradition of *pyanka*. The young girls, with coaching from their mothers, painted the eggs with elaborate designs and brilliant colours. This was obviously an anticipated activity and Rachael was able to watch and eventually to join in. As the girls giggled at her careful brush strokes and selected colours, Rachael could see that reckless abandon was a skill to be cultivated. A wonderful array of exotic patterns and colours appeared before her eyes at an amazing speed.

With the observation of *Maslenitsa* behind them, this delightful group of neighbours broke into several days of celebration with music, dancing and feasting, until late each evening. It became a whole community outdoor event with tables and chairs moved out of the homes and lined up along the lane. There was *blini* and *kulich* from the Russian hosts, *baklava* – the sweet flaky pastry of Turkey, as well as quantities of *dolmas* – rice wrapped in grape or cabbage leaves. Treats of fresh vegetables, fruit, dates and olives were provided by Rachael's closest neighbours, Ethan and Rosalyn.

The youngest children were entertained with Hoca tales of ancient times, and the older children participated in puppet shows that presented a variety of cultural myths and songs. With fiddle and bouzouki, the singing of folk songs of both sadness and celebration began, and soon the tunes were put to clapping and round dances. An assortment of teas, served to all according to their individual customs, ended each glorious evening. Carved smoking pipes appeared, and the elaborately decorated eggs were distributed as gifts to everyone attending. "This has been such a special evening," said Rachael, as she thanked Todd for coming, and walked him to the end of the lane.

"I would not have missed it, Rachael. How interesting to find these people have so much in common. Everyone likes an occasion to celebrate, to sing, dance, and feast together. We are not so separate after all."

"We will be attempting to bike on the trails left behind by shepherds, but let's give it a go anyway," Todd encouraged. "Going as far west as Fort Augustus, we can follow along Loch Ness to the head waters at Inverness. Are you still with me so far, Rach? We might have to camp, so let's see what we can take along for that purpose. There might even be an old abbey where we can take refuge," he laughed.

Rachael was used to having Todd take charge of their outings and holidays, so she simply went along with his ideas. Their holiday turned out as unplanned, and they returned exhausted, but exhilarated.

"May I suggest," said Rachael, "since you will be returning to Dartmouth next summer for a few weeks, we meet there again for further exploration along the Cornwall coastline – complete with English tea rooms and lodgings," she smiled.

Rachael became part of the community in more ways than participating in special evemts and celebrations. Her days were filled with providing meals for the sick, caring for small children, running errands, sewing when needed, plus all the other tasks that make up a sharing and comforting community. There was joy in receiving, as well as in giving. She felt blessed and encouraged, and her writing reflected a changed spirit of openness.

As the year 1904 came to a close, it was apparent, but not openly spoken of, that many of these special neighbours were preparing to return to their homeland in the coming year. Pressure from families at home, and difficulties experienced there, made it imperative that any change would require a united front. As Rachael discovered earlier, her friends who operated the shop below her flat would not be returning. "We have been forbidden to practise our religion," said Ethan, with sadness. "Being Jewish, we were the first group to be singled out; it all began when our village synagogue was burned to the ground. Our Orthodox Christian friends in this community helped us to move west with them," Ethan continued. "But now, with unrest of the people for urgent change, together with the political climate brewing to fill the leadership vacuum, I worry that soon all freedoms will be suppressed. It is just a matter of time."

A few weeks later, as dusk turned to darkness along the neighbourhood lanes, Rachael heard the wail of prayer and crying. All were out of their homes awaiting a horse drawn vehicle that would transport three of the beloved families to the train station, and out of their lives forever. *This is their moment,* she thought. *Though I feel the pain too, I will not disrupt their sorrow in a matter I know so little about.*

"How is your submission to the Carnegie Trust coming along, Rachael," asked Todd.

"Oh finished, actually," she responded with relief. "It's being typeset and printed out just now. I will want several copies, and I would like you to have one."

"Have you decided on a title for your paper, Rach?"

That is usually the hardest part, but it will reflect all I have experienced this past year:

"Who is your Brother?" was asked. "It is You."

The Aberdeen Chronicle:

"A scholarship awarded by the Carnegie Trust for study in history and literature was awarded to Rachael Atkinson, who will attend at the University of Aberdeen, Scotland."

"I had to see it in print before I could believe it, Todd," said Rachael humbly. "I feel under-educated for such an award."

"No indeed, Rach. You are educated well beyond secondary school. Now, let's get out of here and go have a strawberry sundae in celebration!"

Beth McMurchie

The Village of Airdrie, Alberta September 01, 1905

Dear family: You will note a change in our address this time. It was finally decided by Prime Minister Laurier that this enormous piece of land be divided into two provinces south of the 60th parallel, and to be called Alberta and Saskatchewan. Alberta is named after Queen Victoria's fourth daughter. We haven't heard how she should have this honour, but we like the name anyway. When the harvest is finished this fall, I believe there will be a local celebration to mark the occasion.

As a community, our common challenge is for a school to be built which will also serve as a meeting place. As a head start, Maggie has already volunteered to be the school representative. Once the land is located for the building it will be a community project to erect it. Niall will be ready for school in another year, and we are anxious to have such a place for him. The next challenge: where to find a teacher? Joey is looking forward to a teacher being some nice, young and good-looking woman. Can you blame him? There are no single women in this countryside, and he feels a city woman would not be right for him. We will do our best to accommodate his wishes!

Rachael: Maggie, and her fellow farm ladies are loving your serial books, and hope there are more to come in the future.

Love and good wishes to you from all of us in the new province of Alberta, your brother Billy

Golden Ribbons

Dartmouth Naval Base, on board the Dreadnaught Battleship
July 10, 1906

Dear Rachael and Aggie: It's one thing to hear about this ship, but quite another to see it from afar, as well as to be on board. It is the pinnacle of the British Royal Navy! It was built in secrecy, I'm told, and was launched in February from Portsmouth. Besides its massive hulk, it is revolutionary in design, and equipped with long-range armament. It has caused a lot of excitement around here, and speculation as well. Three weeks here does seem very short, but it's good to keep in touch, and to push the training a bit farther along.

Rachael: Before I know it, my time here will be finished. Please try to be here July 31. Bikes will be ready, and we will proceed west along the Cornwall coastline for our brief holiday.

Love from your brother Todd

"Shall we shut down a bit early today, Rach? A ship mate told me about a quaint spot at Dodman's Point that's not too far away now. We can do a bit of walking there and perhaps it's a place where ideas can be hatched. I have one idea that I would like to share with you."

"You never fail to surprise me, Todd. I can't wait to hear what you have in mind," Rachael agreed with mounting interest.

"Yes Sir," agreed the desk clerk. "We do have adjoining rooms, but for one night only. I'm afraid. It's that time of year when folks find this place a pleasant retreat from the big cities, and they seem to book from year to year."

Over tea, and a welcome rest stop, Rachael was beginning to wonder if Todd had something difficult to share with her; he was less chatty than usual. "Rach," he began, "I want a home of our own. The others seem to have that now; I think it's our turn. It can be a place that is accessible to both of us, even if our lives take us away from it for periods of time. So, what do you say; would you be willing to share a home with me?"

"Are you joking, Todd? Willing is hardly the word. I can't imagine anything I would like better than a wee place we can call home. I certainly have had enough moving about. This is such a lovely thing you have come up with, my brother, and it is indeed our turn. Yes, yes!!" Rachael agreed, with enthusiasm.

"Okay, now that's settled," Todd said, straightening in his chair. "*Where* will be the first decision. You will be starting university in a month, and I will be going back for at least two more years. Later, in Edinburgh, I will be involved in the research; that has to be considered as well."

"Let's make this a planning trip, Rach. I even have a map with me, and we can scan distances and possible places we will want to look at."

"I am so excited, Todd, I can hardly contain myself! Maybe tomorrow I will be able to think straight, but for now, I simply want to think about a lovely little home."

"Alright, you go ahead and think about it," smiled Todd. "I believe I will stay up and make a list of possible locations. There are a few weeks of summer left, and we should make good use of them. This will involve a bit of travelling about as well; we might have to get some kind of motorized contraption on wheels."

"Good night, my brother," said Rachael.

Todd took no notice of Rachael leaving - he was already deep into the map, with a measuring device.

"Since our plans have now taken a turn, Rach, I think we should get back to Dartmouth right away," Todd suggested next morning at breakfast. "The earlier we get started, the sooner we will find a place that appeals to us. I believe we should look along the coast - between Aberdeen and Edinburgh; then from there, move inland a bit. I have made a list of *possible* spots. What do you think, Rach?"

"That sounds most reasonable, Todd. But let's not overlook simply *asking*, or the newspapers would be a good source of information. The right place will simply appear to us, and we will just know it is right."

"I will depend on your sense of *just knowing*, Rachael. I guess I'm more of a practical being, and no doubt I will drive you crazy checking, and double checking."

"I doubt that, Todd. I can always count on your good sense and timing. Not a small matter, though: do we have enough money to make an offer?" Rachael asked seriously.

"I have been pretty easy on Malcolm's money, Rach. I have the remainder of my annuity from last year at my disposal, and I believe Malcolm would be delighted to know we will have our own home," Todd assured her.

"That's lovely, Todd, and I have a bit too."

"We're alright then, sister! Let's have some fun with it along the way!"

Well. Malcolm, it looks like your old green chair will finally have a home. Todd reflected. *Rachael is so happy. We will think of you every time a choice must be made; that way we will know it's the right one.*

The motorized *contraption* turned out to be exactly that. "I didn't know you could drive a vehicle, Todd?" said Rachael.

"We had this type of thing at the base to fetch and carry supplies around. I'm not sure they are any handier than a dray, but we'll find out soon enough. Do you fancy village life, Rach?"

"We should certainly look into it. Yes, I think that would be nice," she replied, thoughtfully.

"We might wander in and out through the countryside," suggested Todd. "The prices might be lower than closer to the cities, but there will be other factors to take into account as well – like what services we will need, transportation being one. As soon as we are completely moved, I think we should get rid of this *contraption*, it will only break down again and again."

"I agree, Todd. If we do decide on village life," said Rachael, "there is no reason why we can't ride our bikes to the train station, and leave them there for the return home. *Home* will be a new word for us, my brother."

"Yes, my sister, and it sounds just right," Todd agreed.

The days went by, and the *possibilities* were looked over carefully. "I liked the one with lovely wood floors and such a grand fireplace, Todd. But, yes, the plumbing was a concern, and would be an expense to correct."

"The cottages with a large garden look good to me, Rach. We could try our hand at growing vegetables and small fruit, even though we have no experience."

"I know, Todd! If we did decide on a place that has a garden, we could consult with John and Rebecca over at the manor - they are gardening experts. I don't know if they are still living on the manor grounds, but perhaps we can go over there today when we get back to Aberdeen."

Rachael was happy to see John and Rebecca again, and to know that – indeed – they were able to stay on and continue their business of market gardening. John was also involved in his trade of carpentry when opportunities arose in the immediate area.

The enterprising couple were pleased to see Rachael again. It was an opportunity to get caught up with the news of each other's activities since they last met. "We would be pleased to help in any way we can, Todd and Rachael, and good luck with your search. You might have a look over Laurencekirk way," suggested John. "I've had some work over in that direction, and there are several cottages being renovated at the moment. I will draw a quick map for you, and that might save you some time."

"We will certainly take any suggestions," said Todd.

"It sounds so exciting for both of you," said Rebecca.

It was a pleasant late afternoon visit with John and Rebecca, and ideas were hatched, as well as a promise to keep in touch. Rachael took time to look toward the manor, and, with sadness, contemplate its emptiness.

An available cottage in the village of Evan Glen, close to the larger Laurencekirk, presented itself as having most of the desired features. Rachael *just knew* it would be right, and Todd, after checking and double-checking, agreed.

"We can pick up your possessions first, Rach. Then, if there is room for all I have, it will be just one load. I have asked Sergeant McTavish, again, to

Golden Ribbons

help carry Malcolm's old chair down the stairs. We should be able to handle it from the other end.

"Did I tell you, Rach? Mrs. Cronin will be selling her house and moving to live with her daughter before long. She will have furniture to sell, and other items to give away, if we are interested."

"I would say that we are interested, Todd," replied Rachael, "depending on how much room we have."

Moving the two living spaces was one load, except Malcolm's old chair took up a load in itself. When the last bundle was moved into the cottage, the brother and sister collapsed in front of the fireplace of their own home. "Hey now Rach, why are you crying? I hope it's not because you are sorry we are taking this on together," Todd asked, with concern.

"Gracious, no, Todd! It's just that I am so happy, and I guess – overwhelmed. It has been almost eight years since we lived in a home together, and I never dreamed it would happen again. It seems like a miracle."

"I sure do feel the same, Rach. Let's enjoy every fun moment of putting this place together. Just think, we can have visitors to enjoy it with us! But, for now, let's just be thankful; I can't put it another way. O.k. then, what will we do now?"

"Let's make a list: I will make us a wonderful dinner, using those delicious vegetables John and Rebecca brought over as a house warming gift. Now, what are you going to do?"

"I can move furniture around. Who gets the bedroom upstairs? We haven't discussed that."

"I know you want it, Todd, and I will take the lower one."

"Thanks, sister. It's just that I'm used to climbing stairs," he said, laughing.

"Right! You will get the visitors to sleep up there with you," Rachael smiled.

"By the way, Rach, there is a package for you in that pile by the door," Todd said, as he looked down at her from the top of the stairs. "Mavis Gibbons left it with Mrs. Cronin."

"Okay Todd, I wonder what it could be?" Rachael puzzled. "Oh, it's the fabric left over from, – well, two years ago! How nice of Mavis to send it; I remember each beautiful piece. Yes, I can use it."

The summer went quickly. Rachael tried to forget about it, but she was faced with her first day at the University of Aberdeen. "These past weeks have been like a holiday, Todd." Rachael reflected. "A holiday I don't want to end."

"It's not going to end, my sister, we'll make every day a holiday in this special place," Todd returned. "Now, off we go to catch the train. I will show you where you are to make your presence known; the faculty people will take it from there. It's a fairly small faculty, I understand, but that's good - you won't be overwhelmed by numbers."

"As long as you are nearby, Todd, I will be alright."

"I doubt we will be arriving home at the same time, Rach. We will have two schedules to juggle, but you will be just fine," he assured her. "I've learned you can handle anything."

A welcoming party emerged from the inner administrative office, and the provost, Mr. William Candish, held out his hand to Rachael and asked her to join the faculties of history and literature in a small meeting room. "Won't you have a seat, Miss Atkinson; we have all been waiting to meet the first Carnegie Trust student to be admitted to our growing history/literature faculty.

"Your submission was outstanding," Mr. Candish continued. "We also note that you have published. You are a most unique candidate, and if gender has anything to do with it, I am confident we can expect other women to follow in the future."

What has gender got to do with it? Rachael pondered.

"Thank you, Mr. Candish," she returned, with as much confidence as she could muster. "It is a great honour for me to accept this opportunity."

"Right then, Miss Atkinson," Mr. Candish continued, "we will attempt to make you feel at home here." There were introductions all around, and Rachael felt nervous to be in the presence of only men. It was like being caught with too much candy in her mouth.

I hope this attitude changes. How would any of these men enjoy being so respectfully, but warily, treated by a gaggle of women? thought Rachael, with a sudden impulse to laugh. She, however, deferred, with a warm smile - as would have been the expectation.

By the time Todd returned to the cottage, Rachael had a warm fire crackling, with the promise of a delicious meal being prepared. "Well, how did it go Rach?" Todd asked, with anticipation, as he bustled through the door with papers and packages.

"Perhaps, once you have settled yourself, Todd, I will attempt to relate my day."

"Okay sister," said Todd, handing her a package, with shyness.

"For goodness sake, Todd!" Rachael gasped, "you didn't need to get me flowers, but I love you for doing it."

"It's a special occasion, you will have to admit, Rach."

Rachael was sorry to spoil Todd's expression of pleasure. She wanted the dinner and evening to be special, as he felt her day had been; there were, however, unpleasant and puzzling impressions of her first day to be shared. "I am rather perplexed about what I faced today, Todd," she began. "I believe these men were just as perplexed - wondering what they will do with me. I have heard of *gender discrimination*, but never taken it seriously. Today was a revelation: I have never been treated with such apprehension."

"How sad, Rachael, and, here, I've been so excited for you all day. I suppose I should have a good look at myself in the mirror, my sister: how would I conduct myself if a woman suddenly showed up in one of my anatomy classes? I really must pay more attention to what's going on out there. I've been so occupied with moving forward, I haven't looked around to see who else – but men, were my mentors," reflected Todd. "You are my beloved sister, and you have a wonderful gift to share with the world. This is very hurtful for you, as well as for me."

"You don't know how it heals to hear you say that, Todd. I just feel that our time together, especially right now, is a special gift. I can endure this, my brother. With your presence and encouragement, I can endure this."

"We are together – all the way," said Todd, with assurance.

Sitting by the waning fire embers, Todd related his day: hearty handshakes, warm good wishes and slaps on the back, followed by a vigorous beginning of the term. Rachael smiled, recognizing Todd, too, was experiencing a revelation of thought.

"Good night, dear brother. The flowers are wonderful, thank you. I understand that my history pre-class interview will be with Mr. Godfrey tomorrow morning, and I must have a good night's sleep."

"Knock 'em dead, sister!" said Todd, giving Rachael a peck on the top of her head.

Rachael had never enjoyed weekends as much. *What a relief to get away from those stiff-necks,* she thought. *But I did enjoy meeting privately with Professor Jamieson of literature. He was like a kindly old grandfather, being interested in my knowledge of the classics. Perhaps I've found someone I can relate to.*

Weekends continued to involve settling into the cottage, and exploring the village. "I hope Mrs. Cronin will be in touch soon Todd," Rachael said. "A table and two more chairs would be useful, as well as some book shelves and an extra bed."

"I will drop in on Mrs. Cronin after classes next week, Rach. She must be lonely without one of us there," said Todd, with concern. "On the other hand, she may be quite happy by herself; she has a big transition ahead. Of course, I will remind her of our interest in taking surplus furniture off her hands."

"How about a walk out our back gate, and onto the meadow below," Todd suggested. "The landscape is a glorious spread now that autumn is fully here. We must not waste a minute of it, Rach. I can even look forward to seeing snow on the old stone fences and the hills. I love this village life."

"I love it too, Todd. How wonderful it is to be here."

As the weeks went on, Rachael decided to make a special effort to greet her teachers warmly. *If they don't reciprocate, well, that's their problem!* she decided. *At least, Professor Jamieson has a smile and a friendly word for me. My classmates seem to be caught up in their own world.*

Todd resurrected an old sketching book from secondary school days, and decided he would try to capture some of the beauty of pre-winter. Rachael watched from her bedroom window as he walked farther out into the meadow – toward the distant hills. *How I love to see Todd so happy,* she thought. *If there is such a destination called heaven, I believe we have a bit of it in this place we call home.*

"We should soon think about what we will do for the New Year holiday, Rachael. We are not really prepared to have Aggie and the children here just yet, and we can't afford to travel to Dundee."

"I think that is meant to be, Todd. It would be nice to simply spend the holiday here, and perhaps, on the eve, we can roam through the village and offer good wishes to our neighbours. I can have some baked treats on hand, as well as a fruit punch, in case some of them come knocking at our door."

"That's great idea, Rachael!" Todd agreed. "We should have a few lumps of coal in our pockets in case some of these folks are still old fashioned enough to observe the visiting tradition."

Rachael wrapped her wool scarf loosely around her shoulders as she headed out, with Todd, to extend their good wishes. With few exceptions, they were greeted warmly and welcomed to the village. With an invitation for tea, or in some cases a bit of sherry or whisky, they had the opportunity to return the invitation.

By the stroke of midnight there were twenty-three neighbours packed into the cottage: elderly couples, elderly singles, couples with and without children, and university students. All were eager to celebrate the New Year with the newcomers at number 63 Oak Tree Lane. Some had even thoughtfully brought extra chairs, but mainly it was standing and circulating, with exchange of stories and laughter. At midnight, the strains of Auld Lang Sine could be heard throughout the village, with hand shakes and more good wishes to welcome in 1908!

It was agreed that the first New Year in the village of Evan Glen could not have been more delightful and appropriate. Later, as Todd and Rachael tried to remember names of the folks who had been there, where they lived, and all the bits of information gleaned from the conversations, Todd suddenly leapt to his feet and dashed up the stairs. Within minutes he was back, carrying a large canvas. "With all the excitement and work of moving, Rach, I forgot your birthday. So, here it is - I made it myself," he laughed.

"This is amazing, Todd, I didn't realize you had such artistic talent!" exclaimed Rachael, as she held up the large canvas, reflecting a scene from so many of their walks together through the countryside. "It goes above the fireplace, it will look wonderful there."

"Have you seen my train ticket, Rachael?" asked Todd, as he rummaged through shelves and drawers.

"I believe I saw it stuck in one of your books as a marker."

"Thanks, sister. Now, I guess I have everything, and I will see you again in three weeks. Look after those carrots, won't you?"

"Yeees, Todd, and I will even do a bit of hoeing, being careful to only pull weeds, of course. I know I should get another novel started, but – honestly – I just want quiet."

"Okay then, I'm off! I doubt there will be an opportunity to send a note, Rachael, as I will be away from the base, but it will be good to have a wider view of the Grand Fleet and its many royal manouvers," he said smiling.

CHAPTER FIFTEEN

"Good morning gentlemen," said the Admiralty officer. "We will be heading east along the Channel to the North Sea entrance at the Strait of Dover, manoeuvring our way north along the coastline as tight as possible until we are clearly out to sea. Our destination is Scapa Flow in the Orkney Islands, chosen as our principle base of operations into the foreseeable future. It is important to control entrance to the North Sea, as well for protection of our northern trade routes.

"This will be your first long-distance assignment, Atkinson. You will be serving on a sister capital ship once we are within sight of our destination. Fog and choppy seas will be a challenge; consequently, testing the effectiveness of flagging under those conditions, will be your major assignment. Good luck to all of you. We welcome your commitment to the ongoing operations of the Grand Fleet," said the Admiralty officer.

Todd felt a tinge of excitement as he was whisked immediately onto a battle cruiser from the naval port on the Isle of Wight. *No time for niceties this time,* he thought.

"Just hang onto the clamp that holds the belt around your waist, and over your shoulders. Don't worry – it's all attached to the cable," said the shipmate, grinning at Todd. "Off you go then."

Todd did not want to look down, but he couldn't help himself. The wind was torture, and the waves seemed to be reaching up to grab his legs. *If I don't make it to the other ship,* he prayed, *I know you will look after my family, whoever you are up there!* It seemed as though he'd been dangling there for hours. There was a crash as he hit the side of the flagship, and two sets of arms reached down to pull him on deck.

"A little rough out there, Aye son," said the seaman. "It can get worse."

Village of Airdrie, Alberta May 14, 1908:

Dear family: It was interesting to hear of your unique New Year celebration, Todd and Rachael. What a great way to meet your neighbours! Maggie wants to introduce that idea into our community as the year end approaches.

We've made good use of the school building for meetings as well as social events. Niall loves school and he is doing well in grade two. We were happy to be able to keep the teacher for a second year; I believe this will be a constant challenge until one of our married ladies in the community takes on the job. Jena is a very good teacher, but her family and friends live in Calgary, so she leaves us Friday afternoon until Sunday evening – unless a school function keeps her here.

We have a wireless now, even though the reception is poor at times. It does keep us in touch with the world in a limited way. The news from Europe suggests a lot of turmoil, but hopefully the small skirmishes can be kept from spreading. You are a naval lieutenant now, Todd, and it may be hard for you to keep on task as a doctor and medical researcher. We are hopeful for you that a choice will not have to be made. It's wonderful for you and Rachael to have a warm and comfortable home to call your own. We are grateful every day for the privileges and freedom we enjoy in Canada.

Love from your brother Billy

"Well, sister, did you enjoy some peace and quiet while I was away?" asked Todd.

"Very much, Todd, but I'm glad you're home. Now the hectic school schedule can start any time," said Rachael, smiling. "How did your training go?"

"As always: interesting. I would have to say, though, not as exciting as the dream I had my first night in that land of nightmares! I was being moved from one ship to another by sliding along a cable, and all the time being scared out of my wits as I looked down at that angry sea. It took me several minutes to get my bearings when I woke up. But, yes, it's wonderful to be home again."

"This will be the last term when we can ride together on the train to Aberdeen, Todd," said Rachael, regretfully, "but how exciting you will soon be Todd Atkinson, M.D.!"

"Not there yet, sister, but – yes – it's wonderful, and even more wonderful to accept that fellowship for medical research in Edinburgh. Life is ticking along well for us, Rach."

"Yes, it's ticking along well for us, Todd", she agreed, hesitantly.

"There's a letter for you today, Todd."

"Well, it seems I am a First Lieutenant now, Rachael. If that means more torturous dreams, then I'm not so sure it's a good thing," he laughed.

"Do you think there will be war, Todd? I mean in the near future."

"There is a build up of ships and hardware." Todd returned, speculatively. "From my perspective, I would say there is a reason for it; I've heard that Germany, and others of the Balkan countries, are enlarging their fleets. Britain is the first to have a Dreadnaught battleship but, I expect the competition is becoming intense with more of them being built every day."

"It does sound like there's something to it, and it's insane to think of it as a competition."

"Yes, it is insane, my sister. Your wonderful submission to the Carnegie Trust spoke volumes about the cycle of survival and suffering, power and the powerlessness. I recall you saying your short time in that small community of enclaves was an experience meant to be." Todd continued. "I agree, and I also believe you will go on to write many more important works that will give hope and encouragement to victims of oppression. We live in a world of beauty as well as ugliness, Rachael; I guess it's a daily task to choose one over the other: which one are we going to accept."

"Well, I know what I will accept, and never give up accepting," responded Rachael. "We have to keep reflecting the beautiful back onto humanity by working, talking and moving it along. How fortunate I am to have you as a brother, and I am fortunate to have been born into the family we share. Our parents <u>did</u> show us the way through their devotion to each other, and their commitment to instil in us their own values of independence and self-respect. Remember the *loving thoughts on golden ribbons*, Todd? That bit of philosophy has been such a help to me throughout the years: though apart, we'll always be there for each other."

July 28, 1913

Under orders of Sir Winston Churchill, Lord of the Admiralty, all commissioned officers must be available for duty immediately. The Grand Fleet will be located at Scapa Flow in the Orkney Islands, placed on *preparation and precautionary*.

"Well, Rach, I guess that postpones our plans for travel across to Canada next month. But let's be hopeful this apparent problem can be negotiated away before it escalates out of control."

"I will be disappointed to see you leave, Todd, and that it disrupts your research project. But, I expect others on your research team will receive the same notice. The call is out for infantry brigades to report for duty as well; I heard it on the wireless for the second time this morning."

"I will have some time off anyway, Rach, so let's plan to have a holiday here at home – perhaps a trip over to the western isles," suggested Todd.

"That would be nice, Todd, and perhaps we can take Peter and Mary along with us. Aggie has been appointed to administer the nursing unit at a base hospital near Eastbourne. She has no plan to return home soon."

"That's a great idea, Rachael. As soon as I know of some free days, we can ask Peter and Mary to join us."

Heather Cross Road, Dundee

Dear Auntie Rachael and Uncle Todd: Thank you for the invitation to join you for a holiday on the Isle of Tiree. August 25 to 31 sounds just right for us. As mother will be home on August 31, Peter and I will have some housecleaning to do before she gets here! It would be nice if you could stay over for a visit with mother before you return home.

Love from your niece Mary

Aggie was delighted that Todd and Rachael were at the train to meet her, along with her children, Peter and Mary, who were eager to share the excitement of the holiday they had just taken with their beloved aunt and uncle. "This place is shining!" Aggie exclaimed, as she went from room to room. "What a wonderful welcome home!"

"And I have a chicken pot pie in the oven," declared Mary with obvious pride. She could not help sharing a sly smile and a nod with Peter.

Later, in the front parlour, as they shared each other's news and read the latest letter from Canada, Aggie was hesitant to relate the frantic activity that went on at the base hospital and new nursing unit. "The words *preparation and precautionary* were not used, as they were in your telegram from Mr. Churchill, Todd, but we are definitely in that mode. It was as though I should put my house in order in case of re-call at any time. But, on a positive note," Aggie continued, "I have a wonderful and enthusiastic team to work with."

Life at 63 Oak Tree Lane carried on as usual but, with longer days, and longer train rides for Todd as he travelled to Edinburgh and home again every day. "It could be, Rach, that I will be staying at the medical centre the occasional overnight but, I'm sure you will be quite fine without my scintillating company," he teased.

"I will try to bear up under the pressure of silence, my brother," Rachael returned. "Are you enjoying the activity at the research centre?" she asked.

"Yes, my sister, very much. I can only describe the time as endless," he related. "Trying to leave for the day is usually impossible. One more person will have a proposition to present, or to discount one that has just been published. It's a very exciting time to be a player in medical research. Some chap in the United States has come up with a germ theory to account for the origins of some of these deadly epidemics. There are heads both shaking and nodding over that one. But, the question remains: where do these epidemics start?

"But, how about you, Rachael?" her brother asked. "Are you getting the time you need to write?"

"Not as before, Todd. Unfortunately, thoughts of war are affecting all of the faculty positions. I will be student-teaching more as the days go by," said Rachael. "But, I enjoy that too."

"Let's, walk over to the corner pub," suggested Todd. "I love to hear the neighbourhood chatter, and take part in it as well."

"Hallo Todd and Rachael," said Gordie. "There's not much do'n tonight. Everyone's stay'in home these eve'nins, glued to the wireless in case somebody out there's go'n ta fire the first shot. What ya think, Todd, are we in for it?"

"I don't know, Gordie, it's a time to wait and see what happens."

"Ya know ma Eddie?" said Gordie, "He says: Da, I'm go'na sign up. Might be over quick, an Ah don't want ta miss ana'thing," Gordie continued. "There's nothing Ah can do to stop 'im, Aye. Ee's eighteen year old, an' there's no jobs here."

"Well, you can't blame him, Gordie. I'm sure many of the young fellows around here are thinking the same way, and Eddie wants to be part of it. Like you say," Todd continued, "you can't stop him, only give him your blessing and keep the letters and good thoughts going his way."

"Thank ye Todd. Ah knows y're right, still it's tough to let 'im go."

Sitting by their fire that evening, Todd and Rachael had little to talk about. The evening was full of apprehension, but they were careful not to let it show to the other.

August 14, 1914

The news was brief, but direct:

> As a result of their refusal to allow Germany access through their lands to enter France, the neutral position of Belgium has been violated by German forces, who have ruthlessly swept through their land, taking up strategic positions.

The wave started: Belgium occupied by Germany, France declaring war on Germany, with Britain subsequently taking aim at Germany's unprecedented attack on Belgium. The allied countries were at war with Germany.

On August 5, 1914, the proclamation of war was signed and made official by King George V.

"I will wait until I get the official notification from the navy reserve, Rachael," said Todd. "It will come very soon, I expect. But, for this evening, let's take our usual walk through the meadow, and beyond. It will be good to remember the beauty of this place no matter where we happened to be."

It was decided there would be no good-bye. *This situation will be over soon,* Rachael thought, hopefully. *Todd will be back quickly, and life at 63 Oak Tree Lane will go on as usual.*

"Please write often as you can, Todd," said Rachael. "I will let you know when Aggie is called, and I will keep track of Mary and Peter."

"Aggie will appreciate that, Rach."

"I guess Todd has already left for Edinburgh," noted Rachael, as all seemed quiet on the floor above her. She had become used to his clatter as her warning to get out of bed and on with her day. The notice from the naval reserve was lying on the table, and Todd was gone.

It was routine now: the wireless would be turned on while Rachael readied herself for the trip to Aberdeen University. That particular morning, faculty and students were moving around aimlessly, talking in whispers. The word *enemy* was hard to say aloud, but many of the lads had already decided to answer the call. Excited anticipation was everywhere. Many of the faculty members were also reservists, and there was a scuttle heard from their offices: filing records, and mumbling instructions to those who would stay behind. A meeting in the gymnasium was set for 1:00 p.m. The announcements were predictable.

"Rachael, we are counting on you to help keep this department going when there are so many of our faculty people expecting to leave within a few weeks," said the acting provost, Jim Keeper.

"I will do all I can to keep some semblance of study, Jim," said Rachael. "Count on it."

As August rolled into September, the wireless was occupied solely with news of war, and calls for more troops. "Belgium is under siege," it said. "The Belgian army is not sufficient to put up resistance, and the country has fallen. People are staying in their homes until dark when they feel safe enough to slip out for food and medicine. The Red Cross is on duty," the wireless continued, "but the need is great. The war on land has begun. British, along with French and Algerian units have dug in to hold the German line from advancing farther."

"The University of Aberdeen will be shut down temporarily until early in the new year," was the brief directive. "The conflict is expected to be over by Christmas."

 Village of Airdrie, Alberta August 30, 1914

Golden Ribbons

Dear family: Thanks for keeping in touch now that war has been officially declared. As you are experiencing over there, young fellows here are lining up to take the challenge. Joey will go with the 10th battalion from Calgary, and although we would rather keep him here, he feels it is only right that he sign up with others we value as friends and neighbours. His training will take place at Valcartier, Quebec in mid-September. Joey and Jena had begun to date seriously this summer, and we are expecting an engagement announcement any day. We have all come to know Jena as a wonderful teacher, but now she will be part of the community, and we couldn't be more delighted.

You will not be surprised to be among the first to be part of this campaign, Todd, since you are a reserve naval lieutenant, but hopefully that will allow time to go home occasionally. Our best to you, and that you will stay out of harms way. Rachael will miss you, but I expect she will be involved in the war effort in some way. Maggie says that her *Women's Institute* will help out with Red Cross supplies and packages. We are so proud of Aggie, as she heads off to be where nurses are needed most. Peter and Mary will miss her, but they are capable young people and will keep the home fires burning.

Our deepest love to all, your brother Billy

Dateline October 17, 1914:

"Allied forces have driven back the German army at Ypres, a small Belgian town not far from the English Channel," droned the wireless. "Our forces are showing their resistance to the enemy most admirably.

"And now at sea: early reports indicate British battleships and destroyers have managed to isolate four of the German

High Seas Fleet as they entered the protected zone in the North Sea. All four German ships were sunk."

As she opened the first letter from Todd, Rachael wondered where he would be at that moment. His familiar scrawl stated he expected to be home for a few days late-October, although no specific dates mentioned. *I suppose that would be a secret,* she thought, *though it will be hard to get used to.*

Writing was a difficult task for Rachael since the university closed its doors. *I can only think of my family, and all that is changing so quickly.* It was a comfort to be among the villagers as they went about their daily routines, but she noticed that posters had been placed in shop windows. The comic ones caught her attention first. *That has to be Terry's work, it's so obviously his style,* she smiled. But the subject matter was disturbing, and it took a minute to recognize. "These can only be described as satirical hate posters," she decided with horror, "and I will be very sorry indeed if I must accept that Terry is part of that campaign. Now I will wonder what a poster in Germany would say about us. What can war ever do but divide people – even to the smallest children?"

Todd arrived home unexpectedly. Rachael had been helping set up the local Red Cross station, and she was pleasantly surprised to find him in his casual clothes, asleep on the living room divan. "Are you doing a bit of sleep recovery, dear brother?" she questioned, laughing.

Todd started up quickly, shook his head, rolled over to a more comfortable position, and was asleep again in seconds.

I'm sure Todd's days and nights are muddled, Rachael thought. *I will get tea ready, and he can come to life whenever he's ready. These are moments to remember, Mr. Murray. How I wish you were here to see the lad you knew, who has become such a remarkable man.*

Rachael wakened early the next morning as she heard the click of the door closing, and Todd was gone.

Golden Ribbons

"I will simply volunteer as a person without special skills," said Rachael to the local recruiter in Laurencekirk. "I'm confident there is something useful I can do."

"Now, my lady, I'm sure you have useful skills. If you are employed outside of your home, there must be a skill, like office work, I could refer you to."

"Actually," said Rachael, responding to the cue, "I am a writer as well as a teacher."

"Well then," said the recruiter, "there is need for women, especially mature women, to help the chaplains in their work of support and comfort to the troops and their families."

Rachael's first task was to write notes to all of her family, telling them where she would report for volunteer duties. She was pleased that Eastbourne Army Hospital was her immediate destination, hoping she might have an opportunity to see Aggie. Mary's letter stated that her mother had left again, but she and Peter were doing well - there was no indication of school disruption.

As Rachael packed her small valise with basic necessities, she was thankful that relative normalcy was still available for Aggie's children. It was difficult to leave the home she loved so dearly but, as she said good-bye to her neighbours, she was assured that it would be watched over with care.

The train was crowded with young soldiers, heading back to base, after a brief respite at home. All along the way, Rachael noticed, with despair, the proliferation of posters encouraging both patriotism at home as well as hate for the enemies of freedom.

"Our need becomes greater every day, Miss Atkinson," said Chaplain Lieutenant Roger Beaton. "The numbers of wounded and dying are unprecedented at this early time in the war."

"Are you suggesting, Lieutenant, that the war can no longer be given an end date?"

"That is exactly what I'm saying, Miss Atkinson. Don't be taken in by radio reports of great gains by the allied forces. Here we are, the year end closing in on us, and very little progress has been made by either side even though the fighting is fierce.

"The role we play, as chaplains, is to give hope and console – that's what we've been trained for," continued Roger Beaton, "but, often on the front, the land troops don't see it that way. With our commission, comes suspicion we are just as much to blame for the casualties as are their senior officers. This is where we can use your help, and others like you, Miss Atkinson. Letters need to be written to families of the dead or dying, and those who can't hold a pen because of their injuries. Some will simply want you to stop and chat, and still others will need a warm hand to hold in their final hours.

"I will be joining my colleagues closer to the front line now," advised Lieutenant Beaton. "The field hospital has been set up, and that will be of enormous help but, I will be in regular contact with you.

"You might want to start with the injured, and I would recommend that. I have a notion that, with your wonderful smile, the days will be automatically brighter for them. For now, these men are in the base hospital at Eastbourne. If serious, but in stable condition, they will be eventually sent home; if less serious and still able to carry a rifle, they may be back on the line again. Good luck, Miss Atkinson, your presence here is very welcome."

As Rachael made her way to the base hospital, she felt her fortitude becoming challenged. *Still, I must, I must,* she repeated over and over.

Meeting Aggie outside the surgical ward, Rachael was given a morale boost. "Just seeing your beautiful face gives me courage to be here," said Rachael, as the sisters embraced.

"It's wonderful that you have come, Rachael, but I know it would be hard <u>not</u> to be here," Aggie said as she poured two strong cups of tea.

Rachael had images in her mind of what she might see on the injury ward: young soldiers lying helpless, their heads and bodies bandaged. What she found was a complete surprise, although the bandaged heads and bodies were evident. A group of four were playing cards: one had both legs removed to the knee, the second an arm missing, a third with open wounds to his face and torso, and the fourth lay on his front with heavy bandages over his back. The contortions required to carry out the game were arranged according to each man's disability. It was moving right along and all were laughing and making fun of each other's lack of coordination. "My name is Rachael," she said, hesitantly. "Someone sent me here to cheer you lads up. Can I go now?" she teased.

"Don't you dare, Rachael," said Bill, who had the arm missing. "Just stand over there," he motioned, "so we can all look at you. That's all, we just want to look at you, and please continue smiling, even though some of us can't smile back – like this goon over here trying to take the game," as he pointed to Rob with the face wounds. Rob waved.

Rachael was taken aback by the bravado, but she could also see there were others who were motionless and in obvious pain. She crossed the room, and stopped at a bed where a young man lay completely still. As she introduced herself again, she touched his cold hand, and realized with agony that the young soldier was dead.

"I'm not sure I can be of any help, Aggie. I was so overcome by seeing that lad – so young and dying in the midst of all the rest …" Rachael choked. "The duty nurse was just outside in the corridor. I'm sure she thought I was hopeless."

"That would not be the case, Rachael, because she would have empathised with you. We all have a *first day* Rachael," Aggie said with sympathy. "My first few days here were a kind of hell, even though I was supposed to be a nurse, fully experienced with pain and dying. No, this is like nothing else any of us has to experience. It's their youth, of course, but, it's their spirit that cuts so deeply. They see themselves as letting their buddies down, and they will minimize their injuries so there may be hope of going back to them. No, don't go home, Rachael," Aggie urged. "Stay and love them – each and every one of them. That's what they will want from you more than anything else."

"Thank you, Aggie. I needed your assurance, and I will be better prepared tomorrow."

"I'm so glad you're here, Rachael," said Aggie, "just knowing my sister is close by. I would suggest we get a room together but, I will be moving over to the field hospital now. There are some who can be saved if care is taken soon enough. On a positive note," Aggie continued, "you will be surprised how quickly comradeship develops among those of us who are here to alleviate suffering in all of its many forms. It's called: *friends for a lifetime*."

"The battle continues at Ypres," stated the wireless, "but, allied forces hold on with strong commitment, even though heavy casualties are reported weekly. The Canadian Expeditionary Force of 32,000 men has now left Canada, in a convoy of ships, bound for our shores. Their training will continue here in England until they are seen as ready to be integrated with the British divisions."

As they listened to the broadcast together, Rachael asked, "Is that what Joey would expect, Todd? I believe he thought the Canadians would fight shoulder to shoulder under their own command."

"Well, I guess the British are leading the charge, Rachael. Disappointing as it may be, the Canadians will have to prove their ability to perform as one body. All the Commonwealth countries will be expected to integrate, not that I think that is the best way, but, unity is vital if this war is ever to end."

Todd and Rachael were happy to be home again, even for such a short time, and the joy was enhanced when it was found that their leaves could be coordinated, if planned early enough.

"No war talk!" said Todd, as he tossed a soccer ball to Rachael.

"Soccer may be out," said Rachael, as she gazed at the heavy wet snow, accumulated overnight.

"Okay then, I'll just get into my wellies and go see if there is anything left of my wonderful garden. Blasted war!"

Golden Ribbons

The Canadian contingent arrived at Plymouth, unexpectedly, that October day. As the news spread of their arrival, the welcome became hysterical; the British Empire was responding to the call. As the men marched through the streets to the waiting trains, that would take them to the training fields, people walked along with them - cheering and waving hats and flags. Gifts were offered along the way: cigarettes, chocolates, and bottles of whisky. *These people are no different from those we left behind in Scotland,* thought Joey. *It's wonderful to be so welcomed.*

The Village of Airdrie, Alberta. December 10, 1914

Dear family: By the time this reaches you, it will be 1915. Jena is so lonely without Joey; she watches for the mail everyday, even though Joey's first letter was brief, stating only that the convoy of ships arrived at Plymouth October 14. Jena spends her weekends with us now. In fact, she is planning to leave her room at Donaldson's and move into Joey's old room upstairs. George and Katherine are completely understanding about this, though they love Jena and will miss her. I often wonder how the community ever managed without these wonderful people; they are like parents and grandparents to the neighbourhood.

Keeping up with the work is a daily challenge for Maggie and me, but Niall and Katherine have pitched right in and help in many ways.

Our love and best wishes to all, your brother Billy

Rachael found it easy to love the soldiers. She would have scribbled messages in her notebook to take back to her room, and evenings would be spent writing letters to loved ones at home for the following day's post. If a soldier was able to add his signature, she would hold the letter over until meeting with him again the next day.

The joy she found in her work was hard to express; the soldiers themselves kept her going. "It's just so important," she told her host. "I don't want to spend a minute doing anything else."

"I'm glad to see you are still here, Miss Atkinson," said Roger Beaton, as she was leaving the wards for the day.

"I'm Rachael to the soldiers, and to you," she smiled.

"Okay, Rachael, fair enough," he responded, "and I'm Roger to you. Now, this Roger wants to take you out of here for a decent meal this evening. You do realize it's eight-thirty, Rachael?"

"Oh, is it?" said Rachael with surprise. "I would love to join you, Roger – for maybe an hour," she stressed. "I have a lot of letters to write this evening."

"Then, let's make good use of that hour."

All the usual exchange of information, hopes and dreams, were shared over a pint and a roast beef pie, and Rachael found herself wondering if it was the war that made it easy to speak so freely with someone she had only just met. "I love this work, Roger," she shared. "The days are never long enough; there is such urgency to it all. What if that certain lad is not there tomorrow, and I didn't get to see him today? I'm sure you understand what I'm saying."

"I do understand, Rachael, and I also understand there are never enough hours in a day, or a night. Sitting at a table in a warm pub looking across at a beautiful woman sure beats eating a week-old sandwich, while holding one end of a stretcher," he laughed. "We have to laugh, Rachael, or we'd go crazy."

"This was wonderful, Roger - just to sit for a time and chat. But, I really must go now, and I'm sure you do too."

"Yes, I need to go, Rachael. But I want to meet again, whenever there's a chance. Okay with you?" asked Roger.

"More than okay."

———

Salisbury Plain is a fancy name but, it sure is an ugly place, thought Joey. It was an empty and wasted plain - no fences, houses or people. There had been more rain than was experienced in years, and the chalky soil was a quagmire. The trainees were housed in huts and tents – often overcrowded, with little provision for taking meals at regular times, and the food barely edible. With the snow and heavy mist, the camp itself began to disintegrate, and much time was spent rebuilding. Illness was widespread.

Nobody told the Canadians of these trials before they left home. Their bright-eyed eagerness soon faded, but not the cheerfulness, optimism and determination, soon was to be their hallmark. There was no complaining.

"Miss Atkinson," called Nurse Amy Rolston, from the hospital's stairway. "You have been with us for two weeks now, and we appreciate so much all you are doing. But, I wonder, now, if you would spend time with soldiers who are dying. It's becoming harder to spend the time with those frightened souls, when we are so pressed to save those where there's still hope. This is a hard thing to ask, Miss Atkinson," Nurse Rolston continued, "but, you have shown so much compassion with the seriously injured, we know you will be able to offer comfort where it is so badly needed." Amy Rolston was such a young nurse, and so very close to breaking down, Rachael would never have hesitated.

"It's *hurry up and wait*, Lieutenant Atkinson," said Captain Robert Ashley. "We're not making good use of wireless communication, in my opinion but, those are the orders: we must save the wireless unless the German High Seas Fleet is within our range of detection. There is too much fog out here for flagging, and being winter what else can we expect? This is one hell of a place in winter, Atkinson - the end of the world, so to speak. Where did you say your home was – or did I ask before?"

"I don't recall you asking, Captain," Todd responded. "I'm from Aberdeen, and it's not a great place in winter either, but, perhaps I'm used to it."

"A hardy Scot indeed," said the captain. "Got a little woman at home waiting for you?"

"No, Sir, I'm not married. My sister and I share a cottage near Laurencekirk – south of Aberdeen. My sister is a writer and student-teacher at the university there."

"It's better not to have a wife and children when we're seamen, Atkinson; I expect you took that into account?"

"Actually no, I'm a doctor – not career navy. When this is over, I'll go back to medical research in Edinburgh."

"Well, that's needed! Let's hope we both get through this without mishap. You a card player, Lieutenant?" asked Captain Ashley. "We have to fill the lonely hours some way."

"Actually, I sketch, and paint a little, Sir. I guess we could say that's my hobby."

CHAPTER SIXTEEN

RACHAEL HAD AN OPPORTUNITY TO READ THE CHARTS OF EIGHT soldiers she would see that day. "This will be useful," she said to Nurse Rolston. "I can call them by name, and I will know where they are from - making our time together more personal."

"There is no clergy available today, Miss Atkinson," the nurse said, with regret. "We just do the best we can." Rachael nodded in understanding.

As she approached Gerald in the first bed, Rachael introduced herself, and asked if he would like her to write a note to a loved one or friend.

Gerald looked at her with a frightened daze: "Please tell Mum and Dad: *I'm sorry.*"

"I will do that for you, Gerald but, I will also tell them how strong you are, and how you will never be forgotten." Rachael held Gerald's hand while she felt its pressure. He would be awake briefly from time to time but, finally, fully awake: "Her name is Rachael too," he said. Then his hand fell away from hers.

Remembering Nurse Rolston's final words, Rachael searched her memory for some appropriate remembrance to say over Gerald's frail young body. *I love what Tennyson wrote,* she thought, *and it may have been for a friend: Sunset and evening star, and one clear call for me! And may there be no moaning at the bar, when I put out to sea.* Waiting for a few minutes in silence, Rachael closed Gerald's eyes gently, and folded the top sheet to cover him, as she had been instructed to do.

It had been a long day but, Rachael left the room of the dying, with regret. Even though two men had died before she could attend them, she stopped for a few minutes and, using their first names, said good-bye.

Rachael smiled as she saw Roger waiting for her. "So good to see you, Roger," she said warmly. "Sorry to keep you waiting, and I know it's late, but, I don't feel tired - only at peace."

"I don't feel tired when I see you, Rachael," said Roger. "Same place?" he asked. "Actually, I don't need to ask, there is no other place open."

Todd had the habit of taking a sketch pad with him whenever he had watch duty. *There's not much to sketch here but the ships on either side of us. I suppose those chaps are just as bored as we are here,* he said, with resignation. There was a break in the clouds, adding bit of light.

A long stretch of grey metal suddenly surfaced in the Flow, and Todd grabbed his binoculars to take a better look. Then it was gone, the water heaving as it submerged.

"There's a sub out there in the Flow!" he said, hurriedly, "I got a glimpse of it, and again through the binoculars."

"You're sure, Atkinson? It looks pretty calm to me. This boredom can play tricks on us occasionally," replied the captain, with guarded interest.

"It's there, Sir!" said Todd, directly. "I wouldn't have come to you if I imagined it."

"Well, let's wait a bit. Maybe it will pop up again."

"I tell you, Sir, there's a sub out there! We should signal the others, and get the crew ready to drop the boats! It could be within range in, I would guess – ten minutes! We'll need that time to get as far away from the ship as possible."

"I'm relieving you of your watch, Atkinson," said the captain, with authority. "All we need is an officer to panic and take actions irrationally."

"Then, I'm disobeying your orders, Sir!" Todd yelled, as he raced down the deck, shouting orders. ". . . and close the magazine before it implodes in on us!" he added.

The boats were released in an instant, followed by a scramble to get on board, and push off at the same time. Todd jumped, hitting his head on a projected railing.

Golden Ribbons

Another day, and Rachael hoped to gain more information from Nurse Rolston. "Please provide me with everything you have about them, Amy," Rachael said, "and a few cues may help." She decided not to read through all the charts and the added information, but take each bed she came to – one chart at a time.

"Hello Bradley," she started. "I hope the medication is relieving you of some pain, but you are aware of why I am here. I will just sit with you for awhile and you can tell me, as you are able, what words you would like to leave your loved ones."

This is more difficult today, Rachael thought. *There are some who cannot speak, only holding my hand with all the strength available to them. Then, that's what my letter will contain: I was there at the end, holding hands and retelling the verse by Lord Tennyson.* She would change to the third verse as she thought of it: *"Twilight and evening bell, and after that the dark! And may there be no sadness of farewell, when I embark."*

"For tho from out our bourne of Time and Place ..." Rachael heard a familiar voice reciting faintly, and coming from a bed farther on. Presently approaching the unexpected intrusion, she was seized with remembrance. "Oh Blaine!" said Rachael, "can this really be you?"

"It is my fair rose," said Blaine. "If I must die, to be with the one I've had in my thoughts, my dreams, my hopes. Let me say it while I can, Rachael: I've loved you always, even though you maimed me for life," he said, attempting to smile.

"Blaine, Blaine! How can this be? One so full of life and energy to make people happy," said Rachael, choking back emotion.

"It's been such a long road, Rachael; a road without destination or hope. How I longed to see you again, but you know I could not go back to the manor. I just lived in hope. And now hope has come to me. Please hold my hand, Rachael. Will you stay with me until I die?"

"Yes, of course I will Blaine. Is there anyone ...?"

"Only you, Rachael," Blaine muttered faintly. "I even dreamed that we might spend the rest of our lives together. If you had refused, I would have demanded it!" he whispered with that same faint smile. "How lucky you are that never happened. Another time – another place, my fair rose."

As the moments passed, Rachael could feel Blaine's hand slipping, but reaching back again. Finally his hand was still, his eyes closed.

Rachael bent and kissed his forehead where the scar was still faintly visible. "Yes, Blaine," she said softly, "another time, another place." She wiped her tears gently from his face, as she raised the folded sheet.

Todd woke up, his head pounding. "Hold on there, Lieutenant," said a plump and rosy-cheeked nurse. "We are wondering if you had a concussion at another time, Sir?" asked Nurse Olson.

Todd looked at the friendly nurse, then at his surroundings, finally saying, "Yes, I did have – long ago. How can you tell?"

"We took an X-ray of your skull, Sir. I'm happy to say the technology is much improved since long ago. Are you amazed at the progress, Sir?" the nurse asked proudly.

"Yes, I am. I'm a doctor, as you know," he said smiling, "but, I've never had a patient. Are you amazed, nurse?" he teased back.

"As I say, Sir, with the X-ray we found a small bone chip. But, you obviously survived very well," assured the nurse.

"Well, I'm glad of that! Now, when can I get out of here?"

"A few more days should do it, Sir. There's a lovely lady outside to see you, by-the-way."

"Todd!" Rachael said with concern. "I just found out you were over here at the naval hospital. Are you alright?"

"I'm alright, dear sister," said Todd, "except for the headache no one is concerned about. So, I guess I won't be. I want to go home, sit by the fire, and sleep!"

"Can you tell me what happened Todd?" asked Rachael, as she brought her brother a cup of tea, and fussed over him.

"Lucky for me - I was correct! Most of the crew got off the ship but, I'm afraid not all. The ship was torpedoed and eventually sank. I don't know whether the captain jumped, or what happened to him. I expect a report of the incident soon," he added with impatient concern.

>Dateline April 22, 1915:
>
>"Reports that outlawed chlorine gas is being used as the enemy's last resort in breaking down the allied front line," the radio announcement crackled. "Many of the French and Algerian forces have succumbed to this brutal assault, leaving the line held by them unprotected. Newly arrived Canadian troops have joined British forces in an attempt to hold the line, but shelling and gas attacks continue."

Joey was part of the First Canadian Division who joined the exhausted remains of British and French troops, arriving to face the unprotected line at Ypres in western Flanders. The Canadians were unprepared for the raw battle they would face. "This is not modern twentieth century warfare," stated the Canadian commander, "but a throwback to medieval times."

Rachael continued her work with injured and dying soldiers at the base hospital as the second battle of Ypres carried on relentlessly. Her concern for Joey had become one more reason to keep her spirit from faltering, but reports of casualties in the thousands began to wear her down. She found that thoughts of Blaine, and his dying words, haunted her night and day. *How can one soul have only one other who cares?* she thought with sadness. *It's like we two – Blaine and I, are now locked together in an eternity all by ourselves. No one knows that we met in an obscure kitchen, or again at a fair where his caring began. But who can help me carry this pain, when there is no one with whom I can share it?*

Rachael received a letter from John and Rebecca, announcing the manor would be converted into a convalescent hospital for officers, and for regular soldiers as space allowed. They were recommending her as a person who could administer this overcrowded facility. The few nurses and doctors assigned were overworked and needing relief themselves. Someone with a clear head was needed to keep watch over the numbers of servicemen admitted, and to see that their needs could be more effectively met.

These old friends reported that their work as an ever expanding market garden operation had been the deciding feature when the manor was given the designation as a care facility. But, out of need, it was not long before Rebecca was working in the kitchen, and John given a vehicle to transport the patients from the train. No one was taking care of housekeeping.

"Please come, Rachael, we need you," pleaded Rebecca. "We are finding that we cannot juggle so many tasks and do well with any of them."

What kind of a world are we living in? Rachael pondered. *Even ordinary people are recruited to fill roles that crowd their lives into ever increasing bedlam. But, I need to go home, and I need to be there with Todd.*

Roger was waiting at the bottom of the stairs. He held out his hand and pulled her to him. "I couldn't spend another day without seeing you, Rachael."

"Roger, I'm going back to Aberdeen tomorrow. I need to go home."

"How can I take this in," Roger said in disappointment. "I love you, Rachael, and I need to know you will always be there for me - even when the war is over."

"But what you are feeling is the war, Roger! How can we think rationally with all that is going on? Emotions are pleading for solace in a world gone mad. No, I'm sorry, Roger, I can't tell you I will be there for you, or for anyone else. I need to go home," Rachael spoke softly, as she touched Roger's face. "I just need to go home."

"When do you have to go back, Todd?" asked Rachael, as the brother and sister walked the favourite trail across the meadow.

"I'm on indefinite leave, Rach, that is, until I'm called back. Does that make it clear to you?" Todd laughed.

"I'm just a bit envious of your ability to sketch and paint, Todd, and to be able to create something beautiful from nature in the midst of chaos!"

"Yes, that's true Rach, but what about you? I don't see you writing, as you did before."

"No, I can't write now, Todd. I just can't focus," said Rachael, with sadness.

"I just want to see my sister smile again."

"That army major … Oh, I can't remember his name," said Rebecca, with confusion. "Anyway, he said he would be here today to greet you, Rachael. I can't tell you how happy John and I are that you consented to come, and that you will consider taking the position. I believe the plan is that you can choose where you would like to have your office. I know Sir Gordon's old study is available, but, the adjoining rooms have already been blocked off for beds."

"It's wonderful to be near friends like you and John."

"Then, let's have dinner together in the kitchen this evening, just like old times."

As Rachael went quietly from room to room, it seemed as though a thousand years had passed: *My name is Rachael Atkinson. I am fourteen years old. My Da and Ma are both dead. I have some schooling, but not since my Da got killed in a coal mine explosion. I have cooked, cleaned, and cared for small children. I must find work to support myself.*

Rachael laughed to think she could remember the speech, burned into her mind all those years ago.

It seemed that none of the rooms had been altered to accommodate the change. She was, however, amazed to find that the kitchen was completely renovated. A huge commercial refrigerator had been installed, along with a bigger and better cooker. The counter lined two sides of the room, and another larger window had been installed beside the old long table she remembered. It was a beautiful day in late spring, and Rachael sat down in the arm chair at the end of the table to enjoy the warmth engulfing her body.

"I'm so sorry the major didn't come today," said Rebecca, with dismay. "I'm sure you had other more important things to do than to wait around here."

"It was a wonderful dinner, Rebecca, and a visit with you and John is never a waste of time."

As the friends moved from the table to say good-bye to Rachael, the door bell rang. "Who would be coming at this hour?" Rebecca expressed, with frustration.

"I'm Major Lakkey," said the upright and unsmiling visitor. "I understand there is a woman whom you are recommending as a director of this facility. I realize it's late, but could you tell me where she lives? I can call on her there. Time is of the essence," he said, importantly.

When Rachael heard the conversation from the main hall, she came forward. "I am Rachael Atkinson, the person you are referring to. I have waited all day for your arrival here, Major."

"Oh well then, we can get this over with now. What experience do you have for this position, Miss … er?"

"Atkinson, Major," responded Rachael flatly. "The answer is *no experience*, but I have worked in this manor in the past, and I am well acquainted with its attributes for such a facility – as well as its limitations, of course."

"We are not too worried about limitations, Miss Atkinson. We want to cram as many men into this place as possible, and as quickly as possible. The pay will be basic army pay," the major continued, "and you would be expected to be on site at all times – night and day."

"Now that I've heard what you are expecting, may I advise you of my expectations regarding this position?"

The major stood on one foot and then the other, stating that he didn't have time to take a seat in the parlour. "So, if you could be brief, Miss Atkinson."

"I would like to have an address where I could post a detailed proposal, Major."

"That is impossible, Madam. Do you realize how busy the war office is? We are involved in a war, Miss Atkinson, - just in case you haven't heard!"

"Major!" exclaimed Rachael. "I have just returned from Eastbourne Hospital where I have spent a month at the bedsides of dying soldiers. Oh yes, Major, I <u>know</u> we are involved in a war, as you so callously state. Now, if I may show you to the door . . ."

"Oh Rachael," Rebecca, moaned. "he was awful, and I'm so sorry. If we rattle a few chains, would it still be possible for you to come?"

"Congratulations Lieutenant Atkinson!" said the Admiralty officer. "There were many lives saved as a result of your quick and decisive action."

"Thank you, Sir."

"It has been our experience, Lieutenant Atkinson, when a subordinate officer disobeys a command, there is a good chance that, under similar circumstances, he will do it again. We can't have that Lieutenant! We have to hold complete confidence in our captains; their orders are to be the final word. Therefore, I am relieving you of your duties," the officer continued. "You will be stripped of your commission and honourably discharged from the navy. Good day, Atkinson. Your medal for bravery in the face of oncoming disaster will be mailed to you in due time."

"Thank you, Sir," said Todd. "You may keep the medal, and hang it around the grave marker of an ordinary seaman."

"I suppose I should be shocked, or grieved – or something," Todd shared with Rachael, "But, all I want to remember are the faces of those seamen who pushed their mates onto the boats before the undercurrent of the sinking ship took them along to an ocean grave."

"Oh Todd," Rachael said, with sadness, "how many more will lose their lives before this war is over?"

"I suppose these postcards will be handy," said Joey to Ted, a mate in the lower bunk. "No use trying to write a letter home when it will only be censored."

"They are called *Whizbangs*," said Ted. "Just check off the boxes with either *I am well* , or *I am injured*, or maybe both. I don't suppose the censor would mind you including *I love you*," he teased.

Dateline May 31, 1915:

"Allied troops have been withdrawn from the battle lines at Ypres. There was no decisive victory. 65,000 troops – French, Algerian, British, and Canadian, have died in this action."

"It's late for planting the garden, Rach, but, that's what I will do today," said Todd. "Perhaps June will bring showers."

"And I will get the cottage cleaned and back into the condition it so richly deserves," returned his sister, as she looked around at dust and neglect.

It was a feeble effort at light conversation between two people who were far away in their thoughts. "I want to go to Edinburgh, Rach," announced Todd. "I know the research centre is closed right now, but I just need to be there anyway. There are people I can look up, and piles of reading I can get caught up with - just to get back on track."

"I understand that," she sympathized. "I feel the village has been neglected. I want to work at the Red Cross Centre for a few days, and visit with those who have lost a family member. I love this community, Todd, and I will be more content just now in finding my way back into it."

"I guess we are lost sheep, my sister," Todd said, with sadness.

"That dreadful major came back, Rachael. He wants to see you again to apologise for his rudeness. Please consider the position again; we long to have you with us," Rebecca pleaded.

Rachael was touched that Rebecca would travel all that way to make her plea. "I will see him," she said. "You may give him my address; in truth, everyone is under such stress these days. I hear that the grocers are running out of produce for at least three days a week; your own work with John is just as important as what this major is expecting. Yes, I will consider coming back, but first, I need to get the terms straightened out with this man. Would waiting a week be acceptable to you, Rebecca?"

"Thank you so much, Rachael," replied Rebecca, with relief.

Rachael received a letter from the president's office stating that the university hoped to reopen January, 1916.

> We do not have the financial resources to simply wait and see. A definitive date has to be set, or the war will shut us down indefinitely.

Todd's letter said:

> I'm renting a room close to the research centre. This city is so beautiful, it hurts. Besides the hours of reading, I have taken to sketching again. Please keep in touch with me, Rach, I need to know you are okay. No doubt we will get Joey's news through Billy and Maggie, and we can relay any message to Aggie - keeping her in the loop.

Rachael arranged to spend weekends at home. "I will stay at the manor weekdays, Major," said Rachael, "and the medical staff must have relief for one day a week." Remaining terms of the agreement were negotiated and accepted, and Rachael began, immediately, to make a list of all she hoped to accomplish in seven months.

Patients at the old manor are largely in need of recovery from loss of arms and legs, Rachael thought. *I would think Rehabilitation Manor would be a more appropriate name for this facility, and that suggests physiotherapy. I don't see one of those specialists on the staff list, neither did the major mention the provision of prosthesis' when these men are ready to try them.*

The great room was fitted with railings and pulleys, which was about the limit of Rachael's budget. The window coverings were removed to let in maximum light; it was summer, and the grounds were glorious. Railings were also fitted along both sides of the front walk – all the way out to the main gate. "In the days to come, I hope you will have less time in those uncomfortable wooden wheelchairs," she said to a group of men in an overcrowded room. "When your families come to visit, please ask them to bring along soccer balls, puzzles, and musical instruments – just anything that may be lying around home not being used. Oh yes," Rachael continued, "and a phonograph, if one is available." She didn't know what to decide about radios. *I suppose they must know what is going on,* she thought.

Then there were those who did not speak, but stared into a space that was theirs alone. *These men are harder to reach,* Rachael speculated, *but, why are they segregated, and grouped together?* The men were divided into two groups, and the amputees became their new room mates. *I don't know how this will work, but it can't remain as it is,* Rachael sighed. *There are twelve patients here now, and there will be no more accepted until we have a lift installed to the second floor, as well as an overall plan.*

Medical staff were consulted about the changes; some were supportive, while others dubious. "These people will never get well if they don't see life beyond these walls," Rachael said, with conviction.

Sir Gordon's study was not used as an office; it was made available for more beds. Rachael decided a corner in the kitchen could do just as well, and she would be there with Rebecca as she planned menus and attended to the cooking. "It's not such a burden now that you're here," Rebecca said.

"Let's take time to decide what support you will need to keep meals prepared, and all the cleaning up that has to be done," Rachael continued. "Housekeeping is next on my list. Would two housekeepers be able to keep the manor operating? I think one of them should be a man, if any are available."

"That is doubtful, Rachael," said Rebecca regretfully. "Any that are fit will have gone into the war. The nurses are having a difficult time lifting some of the severely disabled men; that is a matter that has to be addressed. John helps when he can."

There were no men available, as Rebecca predicted, and able-bodied women were also involved in the war effort. Consulting with John and Rebecca was a daily activity. "What can we do if there are no people to help?" Rachael asked, in desperation.

"I guess we have to ask the patients that question," suggested John. "Why wouldn't problem-solving be part of their therapy?"

Wheelchairs were taken into the great room, and chairs brought in for those who could walk on their own. Rebecca offered tea or coffee, and baked treats.

"Friends," Rachael started, "We are asking for your help. There are positions needed that we can't find in the community: two cook's helpers, two housekeepers, and two people to maintain the grounds. Are there any among you who would care to volunteer?"

"Sure," said one man, with only one arm. "I like being outside, and there are a lot of things I can do with one arm. Sign me up!"

"I can wash dishes and wipe counters," said a silent one.

"I can dry dishes," said another in a wheelchair, "and I can cook a little."

"I can help maintain the grounds too," said an officer. "I never had that chance at home. We always hired people to do it." The others laughed.

"How wonderful!" Rachael said, with appreciation. "Now we know where our help is coming from. I realize housekeeping could be difficult, but give it some thought," she suggested. "Every little bit counts. How about dividing up into teams; that way, everyone gets a job. But, please, please, - suggest, invent, and – I almost forgot: I can use some help with the paper work."

The men in wheelchairs made a circle quickly, and the others joined in. Two natural leaders emerged and teams were organized, and soon Rachael was ignored as the group chattered and laughed until medical staff suggested it was time for supper trays, and the patients should return to their rooms.

"I have a suggestion, Rachael," said natural leader, Robin, from his wheelchair. "Why don't we quit the trays, and all eat together?"

"Great idea, Robin," said Rachael. "We'll make room for all of you around the big table in the kitchen. The dining room is used for storage right now, but that can change."

"It's a miracle!" said Rebecca. "We were a family before; why can't we do it again? There are no limits to the human spirit."

"You two are wonderful, you know that!" said Rachael to Rebecca and John.

Todd was curious about the new rehabilitation venture. "It's so positive," his letter read.

"May I come and visit?" he asked.

"You can come, only if you participate," Rachael returned. "Remember, my brother, you are a doctor and a soccer coach!"

As Todd posted a note in return, and walked the causeway toward the sea, he thought of Malcolm.

Where am I to go now, Malcolm?

Just be yourself, Todd boy, you can't do any better than that, came the familiar answer.

Rachael could hardly wait to share all that was happening at Rehabilitation Manor. "It's just amazing to see these men taking back their lives, but, without the will of the collective, this never could have happened. After the initial shared meal," she continued, "there was a shuffle so that each disability could be taken into account in the seating arrangement; now each man in the group knows where he is to sit and that he will be comfortable. A side bonus is that this shared meal gives the nurses more time to attend to all of their other duties."

"It's like democracy in action," responded Todd. "I'll be there tomorrow with a soccer ball, but, for now, I have a surprise for you, Rach," Todd announced, as he tore the paper from a large package.

"This painting is wonderful! I recognize Edinburgh Castle, even though I've only seen it from a distance."

"When the research centre is open again, you must come, and we'll tour it together," suggested Todd. "In some ways, it has carried right on in homes of the researchers, as well as in tea rooms. Discussions and exchange of research papers never end."

The Village of Airdrie, Alberta May 20, 1915

Dear family: The wireless keeps us up to date with the war, but I know we are not getting the full story, and certainly

Joey is not telling us anything. The Whizbangs at least let us know that he is alive and well, and they come in the mail quite regularly.

We are glad you are helping out at Eastbourne Hospital, Rachael. Aggie will be glad to have you close by. Please keep the letters coming.

Our love to all, your brother Billy

Heather Cross Road, Dundee June 15, 1915

Dear Todd and Rachael: I am taking a month leave now; it's important that I spend that time with the children, and their summer break will enable us to take a short holiday together. Aunt Mary has invited us to visit at their home in Perth early July.

It was wonderful to have you here for a month, Rachael. After you have had a rest at home, I hope you will want to come back again. The work you did was so much appreciated.

Our love to you both, Aggie

Village of Evan Glen June 30, 1915

Dear Aggie: I hope you are having a restful break, Aggie. It is unlikely I will be returning to Eastbourne Hospital. I have committed to helping out with a rehabilitation centre that has opened at the old manor home. It is coming along well, and I will stay until the university opens in January, 1916.

Todd joins me in sending our love, your sister Rachael

Dateline September 15, 1915:

"Fighting continues along the Western Front. Heavy casualties reported at Lille and Lens. Our British forces, along with French troops, have made a valiant but an unsuccessful attempt to break the enemy's hold on Vimy Ridge."

The morning rituals complete, four of the amputees rolled their wheel chairs into the great room for arm-hold exercises on the pulleys that were spaced at generous intervals. They enjoyed Todd's time with them the day before, and today they were ready to have an hour of rigorous passing. "O.k. my friends, let's not let the ball get away this time," said Todd, as he bounced to the first, the second was ready to bounce to the third, and then the fourth. Then back again, and over and over again.

"Are you ready for a little head contact?" asked Todd, laughing.

"Ready! Over and out, mate," yelled Robin, as he whacked the ball a hard one toward Ross, who quickly wheeled to position. Another whack, and Tom leaned forward as the ball sailed by. "Hey, progress!" said Todd. "Let's finish the time with some fast action;" a bounce and grab at position one, then two, three and four. Back to Todd, then faster and faster, as finally the ball crashed against an upright guard. The men were in hysterics; it was a big leap forward for them.

"That was a lot of fun today, my sister. What great chaps they are! I would like to stay past the weekend and have another go at it, but I will be meeting on Monday with John Stone, director of the centre. I'll be back, though," assured Todd.

Todd is such a faker, thought Rachael, as she caught his wave from the train. *I know he feels lost, just as I did, but I hope the next few months will bring something as satisfying for him as the manor facility has been for me.*

Golden Ribbons

With few exceptions, the patients at rehabilitation manor benefited from their time there. By the end of summer, three ambulant cases were discharged to their families.

The men who were provided with prosthesis, both above and below the knee, were the long term patients, but among the most eager to bring their disability into everyday life. Mornings and afternoons would see them testing their new appliances along the path to the front gate; it became a competition to see who could outlast the other. These men were also a source of encouragement to those newly arrived, and, as a result, benefited by adapting more quickly to their life changing circumstances.

To Rachael's disappointment, the silent ones were little improved. Eventually they moved on to a more appropriate level of care where psychological treatment was available. There was at least the comfort of knowing that the manor experience revealed the need for mental as well as physical care, and the condition of *Shell Shock* was recognized. The condition was the result of, not only the noise of battle, but the fatigue and the ever-present images of an inexpressible horror that neither rest nor time could erase.

As the year 1915 came to a close, Rachael could look at her list of items to be accomplished at the old manor with considerable satisfaction: a lift to the second floor meant more rooms were available with less crowding; the dining room was in full use as it was meant to be; and Duncan's former cottage on the manor grounds provided the needed storage space, as well as a walk-in clinic for those who needed to meet privately with their visiting care givers.

"It has been good to have you in on our discussions, Todd," said John Stone. "With the centre open again, we can look at the soldiers who are recuperating at the field hospitals along the western front, as well as at Eastbourne Army Hospital.

"We are well aware of the numbers of casualties among the troops fighting on the line, and the deplorable conditions they live with daily, but it is the numbers who are falling ill that has me worried. We need to see these lads, take throat cultures and blood samples to find out if there are any similarities, or indeed – differences in their conditions. I am particularly concerned about tuberculosis," Dr. Stone continued. "If that is the prognosis, those infected need to be removed immediately from the others who are healing from injuries."

———

CHAPTER SEVENTEEN

Dateline May 31, 1916:

"The Battle of Jutland has resulted in the loss of fourteen British ships, including the famous battleships: *Indefatigable, Invincible,* and the *Queen Mary.* This blow to the Grand Fleet was the result of inadequate and misleading wireless communication arriving too late. The use of flagging was ineffective, being lost from sight in the fog. Of the 100,000 men assigned to these ships, 6,784 were casualties."

Dateline August 10, 1916:

"Heavy casualties have been reported following the first day of fighting along the River Somme. Cold and rain is impeding progress, with trenches giving way under a sea of mud.

"The British have introduced heavily armoured tanks but, despite the obvious advantage of their mass, they have been mechanically unreliable - often snagged on broken tree trunks and, with instability of the terrain, easily tipped into muddy craters."

Rachael was glad to get back to the university. Two war casualties among the faculty members were remembered at an open ceremony. *This is so painful,* she thought, *everywhere we turn there is loss and sadness.* Rachael's regular classes had been greatly reduced with the drop in enrolment, but still she could not think of writing when there were needs to be met.

"I will either volunteer again at Eastbourne hospital, or help out at the manor as I can. There will be menu planning to help with, since Rebecca has taken over the duties of admitting new patients and discharging those ready to leave."

Tunnels covered the plants for winter, giving John extra time to work with the patients who were adapting to their prosthesis. Though fewer now, Todd's weekends at home were also spent with the amputees at the fully equipped gymnasium at the rehabilitation centre. For him, this was a time of relaxation, and an island of hope to the future.

Dateline November 25, 1916:

"Exhausted and depleted troops have now withdrawn from the battle along the River Somme. There was no clear victory. Both sides have lost much and gained little."

The coordinated efforts of the Canadian forces did not go unnoticed by allied officials. The second attempt to break Germany's hold on Vimy Ridge crumbled, and allied forces were depleted.

In April of 1917, the Canadian Expeditionary Force was assigned the task of capturing Vimy Ridge. This would be the first time all four Canadian divisions would fight together.

Vimy Ridge was one of the most strongly fortified areas of the German line. Tunnels covered with barbed wire, and a small railway provided the

Germans with a constant flow of supplies. It was an assignment that had to be carefully planned, with each soldier knowing the strategy exactly and their place in it. This was a challenge the Canadian soldiers had hoped for – to fight together under their own command.

Todd joined a small group of research scientists as they made their way from one field hospital to another. It was chaotic, with stretchers lined up back to the edge of the allied line. Todd felt it was important to spend time with each soldier, explaining the reasons for samples being taken from them before their injuries were taken care of. Most were just happy to have a friendly face address them personally. The work was arduous and heart breaking, and Todd felt he must steel himself for the task at hand; the follow up work at the centre was of immediate importance.

Dateline April, 14, 1917:

"President Wilson of the United States had managed to keep the nation out of the conflict. In early 1917, however, German aggression against American ships was beginning to wear down his stand. Two events pushed President Wilson into declaring war: an American passenger ship was attacked and sunk in the Irish Sea, and - at the same time, the publication of a secret telegram from Germany to the government of Mexico, promising support for a direct attack on the United States. The night raid on London in May moved the decision forward, and conscription followed. The first U.S. troops shipped out in June, of 1917, and American air power would soon augment the RAF and French fighting force."

Beth McMurchie

Dateline April 15, 1917:

"The Canadian Expeditionary Force captured Vimy Ridge! After a week of heavy bombardment, the main attack took place the morning of April 09. The well-planned and coordinated strike succeeded, and by afternoon the Canadians had captured the Ridge. On April 12, they had secured Vimy Ridge and their victory."

Joey had been part of the First Canadian Division to go over the top that cold and wet day of April 09 - the day after Easter Sunday. Three minutes to go. Two minutes now; and the order came to fix bayonets. One more minute passed – a single gun fired, and the field of battle burst alive as a single organism. The artillery barrage found the enemy unprepared for such a massive assault. The Battle for Vimy Ridge had begun. There were four simultaneous mini-battles on the Canadian front that morning – all interconnected. The First Division, under veteran Arthur Currie, held the extreme right of the line and the longest advance of all.

Joey put the present out of his mind. The task at hand was all there was, and to allow other thoughts to creep in would endanger, not only his life but, those along with him. Almost there … Farbus Wood was the objective. The noise was deafening, and, as Joey plunged forward, a bullet reached out from somewhere and caught the back and below his knee. He was knocked to the ground, and the unit pressed on over him. Crawling to the side as far as he could, he then lay still and the mud soon covered him. The pain in his left knee was excruciating, and he became unconscious for an indefinite time.

When Joey regained consciousness, all was quiet around him, and he shoved himself free of the mud blanket to see the dead all around him; stretchers laden with the injured and dying, moving away. He tried to shout, but he could not be heard, and the blackout came again.

He could remember being lifted high over a shoulder, and a voice saying "Hey Joey, we almost passed you by." He was in the field hospital – still hearing shots being fired far away. There were voices heard from all directions, and mass confusion – pushing and shoving of beds to make room for those arriving. A doctor came at last to have a look at his leg. "This one's got to go," was all he heard, and the blackout came again, as a mask was held over his mouth and nose.

Rachael and Todd found their time with the recovering soldiers, at the old manor, was the highlight of each week. But there was also a day, at least once a month, when they would be together at the cottage in the village of Evan Glen. The tasks of cooking, house cleaning and gardening took on a sense of normal life, and there were letters from family to read and to answer. With sorrow, but also hope, they read that Joey was listed as missing in action following the battle at Vimy Ridge. The battle took more than 11,000 Canadian lives.

Aggie left the Eastbourne hospital, and its connecting field emergency treatment centres. Fatigue and sorrow had taken their toll, and her need to spend time with Peter and Mary became evident with their loneliness and fears. After a short rest, she would return to the Home Road Hospital in Dundee - filled beyond capacity with soldiers needing further treatment for their injuries.

The information gained from visits to soldiers who had fallen ill did not have the outcome of a tuberculosis connection; it was seen that these men were fatigued, ill fed and dehydrated – most seriously enough to require a period of several months in recovery.

Some interesting facts from the tests, however, gave reason for Todd to examine and re-examine the results. He spent more and more time at the research labs, drawing diagrams of cells and their relationships to one another. He found that blood samples from several of the soldiers contained more than one type of antibody, and in other samples the antibody was not present. Each discovery led to more questions, and the main one for Todd was: what is the role of these unusual protein shapes, and what function do they perform?

As Rachael made her way to her classroom along the corridors of the university, she passed Professor Jamieson's door - left open and inviting. "Come in Rachael," Doctor Jamieson called. "I have missed our discussion times together."

"As have I, Doctor Jamieson. This war has disrupted and changed the way we live to a point where it will be difficult to find our way back."

"But finding our way back is a must, Rachael. I need to hear your feelings about it but, more importantly, I need to read what you have to say about our future here at the university and about how we must come back – for ourselves, and for the generations who will be counting on us to lead. I have heard about the wonderful program that has been set up for rehabilitation over at the old manor site, and I also know you have had a lot to do with its success. I can't commend you enough, Rachael, but don't forget about your role here or you may be passed over by your perceived lack of interest."

"I don't understand, Doctor Jamieson."

"I want to encourage you to start writing again, Rachael. After all, that is what gave you a position here. I know you are a good teacher, but there are lots of qualified teachers out there. If we run short, we can always import one or two. I believe that process is already underway."

"What I am trying to convey to you is that your position here depends on your writing. You must get started again, or your position could very well be in jeopardy. I give you this advance warning, not only because I care about you, but because you are wasting your own abilities and your own future."

Rachael was shocked. She did not expect to hear this message. "Thank you, Doctor Jamieson. Perhaps I have been blocking: where to start when there is so much ending? Does that make any sense to you?"

"No Rachael, it doesn't make sense. If it adds anything to your resolve, I want to share with you the confusion and uncertainty I have been facing, and continue to struggle with, being of a nature that I can hardly get out of bed in the mornings. You see, Brian – our grandson, who Mother and I have raised since he was three years old; our Brian is gone – lost to us in that horrible battle of the Somme. This young man was our hope for the future, Rachael. He was very precious to us. Were we to sit together with the hopeless and let our life blood drain away?

"One evening as we stared blankly at his wonderful photograph, it dawned on us that we have memories of him. This is all that we have, and we don't want to lose him again. We are going away, perhaps to the Isles somewhere, where we can spend endless days remembering and writing down every word he uttered, every smile. And we will cry until all is left of us is the joy of remembrance, and to make that remembrance our soul companion.

"You are carrying sadness, Rachael. No one writes like you without having had life experiences that are painful. Go back, Rachael. Pull it all out and let the sadness go. Instead remember the joys, and make pain and remembrance a fellow companion. That's the only way any of us can move ahead."

"Thank you for sharing your pain and loss, Doctor Jamieson. I will remember you and Mrs. Jamieson while you are away, and encourage you in my thoughts."

"You know that Mother and I both love you, and we don't want to lose you. In my absence, a chap from London – Robert McLaren, will act as department head. I know him well, Rachael, and he can help you."

As Rachael left the university that afternoon, she decided to walk to the train instead of riding in a hansom to the station. *I have been found wanting today. Thank goodness Todd is staying in Edinburgh this weekend; I need to hold my own counsel with all my doubts and confusions. I will begin writing,* she pledged. *We can't tie ourselves down to the war any longer; even Aggie has left Eastbourne Hospital to go home.*

"A Mister Joshua Karim is here to see you, Joey. Can I send him in?" asked the young and pretty nurse.

"I don't know anyone by that name, nurse. Tell him this is not a good day for me; he can go see someone else."

"Are you sure, Joey? He looks a most handsome and friendly fellow. And he says to tell you he was the one who carried you off the field following your wonderful victory at Vimy Ridge."

"I still don't recognize the name but, o.k. let him come," said Joey without interest.

"Hello Joey!" said Joshua as he came forward, with outstretched hand. "How's the time going for you? Sorry I couldn't make it earlier; it was a bit of a mess to clean up after you guys raised hell out there and did such a terrific job. You still don't remember me, do you?"

"No, afraid not." Joey moved awkwardly in the bed, and turned to face the wall.

"O.k. then, you're not going to get rid of me that fast. I did carry you off the field, and so glad I did. After all the kindness you, Billy and Maggie showed me way back on the old homestead near Calgary, I was just in a fit of happiness to find your name on the list of front line chaps to pull off that battle in such a splendid way."

"What? Homestead? Calgary? What are you doing here? I have only faint recollections."

"It's been a long seventeen year journey, Joey, and I want to tell you all about it one day but, for now, I will tell you that I've been living in Algeria for quite some time - my roots are there. I finished my medical training with the army, and then was sent off to war in Britain. I just can't believe that I've found you. It's a miracle!"

"This is hard to digest. What did you say your name is?"

"Just Joshua, that's all I ever shared with you wonderful people. I should leave you now so you can rest, and not be bombarded with facts that are not adding up. But keep me in mind, I'll be back again in a few days." Joshua smiled at Joey, giving him a quick wave as he left.

Joshua . . .Joshua, the homestead, and Calgary. Joey could only think of his miserable condition. He would no longer be fit for combat, and he wanted to finish the war off in a flurry of Canadian victories. "Hadn't the Canadian combat troops already been picked to take Passchendale? And hadn't Arthur Currie been around to congratulate him? The Canadians were now at the forefront of the battles, and here he lay with one leg missing."

Golden Ribbons

"So what's the mood for today Corporal Atkinson?" asked the young and pretty nurse.

"I'm angry, Amy, and full of self-pity. Does that mean you medical experts will call in all the shrinks you can find?"

"Not on your life, Joey; you are going to be up and at it in no time. But, of course, there's rehab. We're not going to let you off without that. You've got two roommates coming today; one chap I think you know – Ted, I believe he said his name was."

"Ted was with the second division; we were going to meet for a pint at Farbus!"

"All the best laid plans, as they say," mumbled Amy. "Better you than he, who lost both legs at Vimy Ridge."

"Oh God, No!" said Joey, as he sank down into the pillows.

"We're going to have you up and into a chair sometime today, Joey, and you may sit for a short while. The stump is still very tender, but we'll watch it and get you up for longer periods every day. A brand new set of crutches await, my friend."

"How can anyone who is so pretty also be so cold?"

"It's my Irish disposition – tough as nails," nurse Amy Rolston laughed. "I understand you have relatives in Scotland, Joey. They must know by now that you are no longer missing in action. Would you like word be sent for them to come and visit with you?"

"Please no, Amy. I haven't seen them in almost seventeen years. I couldn't stand it. So, no, not yet. My oldest sister, Aggie, is a nurse. She has worked in one of the field hospitals in France, but I don't know where. I wouldn't mind seeing her."

"I'll see what I can do, Joey. But you must, at least, send a Whizbang home today - your family will be going crazy, wanting to hear from you."

Aggie had barely unpacked her bags when she heard from Eastbourne Hospital. A nurse, Amy Rolston, requested that she come to visit her brother, Joey, who is recovering from injuries sustained at the battle of Vimy Ridge. She further explained he was not ready for his younger brother and sister

243

to come just yet; he hoped they would understand, but they to be thanked for the cards and letters.

Aggie lost no time in making the return trip to Eastbourne Hospital, finding a room with six amputees on the second floor. Joey was in the chair, and made an attempt to stand – forgetting his handicap. "Stay still, Joey," said Aggie, rushing toward him. "It's so good to see you, and I came immediately after I receiving the letter from Nurse Rolston." She bent to gave her brother a robust hug; then they were both in tears.

"I can't believe I'm seeing you, Aggie, after all these years, and so much has happened. You look marvellous, my sister. Your new life must be agreeing with you," observed Joey.

"Yes, Joey, I suppose – sadly, it agrees with me very much. Peter and Mary send their love, and hope you can come to Dundee when your injury heals."

"I will want that very much, once I'm able to make my way around."

"Are you glad that your combat days are over, Joey?" asked Aggie, with some doubt.

"No Aggie, I would give anything to be out there with my buddies. But at least I am close by and I can keep in touch with what's going on."

"I suspected you would feel that way. I have treated so many young soldiers, and they all felt as you do."

"It's the intensity of the operations; the life and death of it all, making us closer than any family member could ever be, Joey shared. I'm not a *young soldier*, Aggie, but, as you said, the feelings are the same. Perhaps over the years this will fade … I'm not betting on it. I start rehab next week - Sergeant Major Amy Rolston will see to it! It will at least keep my body in shape."

"Actually, Joey, you look wonderful to me," said Aggie.

Heather Cross Road, Dundee May 30, 1917

My dearest family in Canada: I know Joey is not up to sending letters home, so I will simply let you know that he consented to see me, and I went to Eastbourne Hospital last week. He is understandably shaken by the prospect of spending the rest of his life with only one leg - and he envisions the *only one leg* quite literally. In actual fact, I have spoken to his resident doctor, and the surgical team feel there is hope in saving his knee, but, it will take time and several procedures to accomplish. All this must precede fitting of prosthesis. He is most anxious for rehabilitation to start, and that is a good sign; it will keep his body strong, and his mind alert.

I must now tell you about Joshua Karim, and his devotion to Joey's welfare. I was not fortunate enough to meet Mr. Karim when I went to the hospital, but he visits Joey regularly.

He is an army doctor from Algeria and very familiar with post-trauma among the soldiers from his own country. He does plan to write all of you. He feels that this connection to Joey is also a connection to all, and has expressed his gratitude for the kindness he received from you, as three brave pioneers, making a home and a farm on the prairies of western Canada. These coincidences seem to occur regularly among the soldiers, and others connected to the war. Mr. Karim feels this connection with Joey is a miracle.

I have now left the field hospitals, and have taken up my duties again at the hospital in Dundee. It is wonderful to be home again, and close to Peter and Mary. Peter is finishing secondary school this summer, and there is a possibility he could be conscripted into the war, along with many of his school mates. We can only hope the war will be over before that happens.

Rachael and Todd are very busy people; Rachael is attempting to retain her position at Aberdeen University and Todd is immersed in medical research in Edinburgh. His specialty is Immunology. There is so much danger of an epidemic of some sort coming out of this influx of soldiers from so many parts of the world that his work is vital. Both Rachael and Todd are anxious to see Joey whenever he feels he would like to see them. But, they do understand Joey's position and they will be patient for his sake.

Peter and Mary join me in sending our love to all, your sister Aggie

---

A heavy snowfall blocked roadways, and rail travel was at a virtual standstill. *This will be a quite new year,* thought Rachael, as she read Todd's greeting with a note saying he would be spending the New Year holiday with John Stone and his family just outside of Falkirk. "Barring further weather problems with travel, I will be home for a weekend in mid-January," he wrote. "Doctor Stone has more than a social reason to invite me to his home; he wants to discuss my observation of blood samples taken from the soldiers recently."

---

63 Oak Tree Lane, the Village Evan Glen December 26, 1917

Dear Joey: With winter-related problems, it will be impossible to get to Eastbourne before the holiday is over. I hope your recovery and rehabilitation is going well, and you are encouraged by it. I'm sure you are hearing from Todd; he is extremely busy testing for new treatments should a new strain of influenza become evident among the troops this bitterly cold winter.

I will be at home alone, but I am making good progress with an autobiography I was encouraged to write before the spring term commences at the university. I hope to see you soon.

Love from your sister, Rachael

Golden Ribbons

The Village of Airdrie, Alberta November 30, 1917

Dear family: It was wonderful to hear from you, Aggie. We had two letters from Joshua, and it was helpful for us to know more about how the war is going, and, as well - how Joey is feeling about the loss of his leg. It is understandably a shock, and he will reflect on all the tasks in life he will have to by-pass or adapt to. Niall is especially anxious to have Joey at home, and we are trying, gently, to prepare him for a different Joey.

Jena has decided to apply for another teaching position in the Calgary region. Although we have come to feel that she is part of the family, we do understand her feelings at this time; she does not want to assume that her relationship with Joey can carry on as before, recognizing he will have so much to connect to when he gets back. You did not mention a time for his release from treatment but, I suppose that is uncertain.

We hope, as you do, that Peter will be spared from going to war. At this time, the perceived adventure of it all has come down to resignation. Conscription is in place in Canada too but, if it helps end this war it may be the only thing that will do it. Niall is not so anxious to go now that he knows Joey is alive and will be home soon. Our Katherine Rachael is now fourteen; she is such a help to Maggie, and Niall will be eighteen Christmas Eve. Both, he and Katherine attend high school in Airdrie. We are blessed with beautiful children, and blessed with each other.

Our love, and best wishes for the New Year, your brother Billy

Rachael ended her autobiography on a hopeful note. She expressed her gratitude in being of help to injured and dying soldiers, but it was the sense of truly being useful that brought the rehabilitation centre to mind. The combination of nostalgia for the manor, and the friendship of John and Rebecca, but finally - support from the army, made her realize *they* (the army) cared too, wrote Rachael. *I never wanted to leave there, not expecting the rehab centre would one day end its usefulness, and go back to being an old worn out manor again.*

As Rachael slipped the manuscript into her brief case, she paused to send loving thoughts to Doctor and Mrs. Jamieson, and their travail into remembrance.

Entering the printing shop to have her work typeset for review by the interim department head, Mr. McLaren, Rachael was surprised to find a new proprietor greeting her, and three ladies seated at desks operating typewriters. *Goodness, I'm really out of date!* she thought. *I must get a typewriter, and learn how to use it.*

CHAPTER EIGHTEEN

AFTER THE NEW YEAR HOLIDAY BREAK, RACHAEL ENTERED HER classrooms with a new energy. The weather had cleared and there was a spark of optimism among faculty members.

"Good to see you, Rachael!" said acting Provost Jim Keeper.

"It's good to be back Jim. I'm hoping to find more students enrolled in my first-year classes; any indication of that?" she asked.

"So far, yes. You will find five more in literature, and ten more in history."

"That's encouraging," said Rachael. "I have reserved space for a monthly article with the Aberdeen Chronicle, Jim; do you have any suggestions regarding a topic? There are so many issues, it's hard to choose."

"I would suggest, initially, a commendation to our soldiers for upholding freedom and opportunity for our young people. The victory at Vimy Ridge is certainly something to feel good about, and we need to know more about our Canadian relatives. This could be a new course in the future – like, *How Canada Became a Nation.*"

"I like that a lot, Jim. My brother, Joey, was part of the four divisions to fight, and win, the battle of Vimy Ridge. We are all so proud of him, as well as his pioneering spirit - settling in western Canada at the turn of the century."

"I didn't realize that, Rachael! These topics are made for you."

"Thanks for the suggestion, Jim. I will get right on it."

"That's wonderful, Rachael. We were all beginning to think you might have abandoned us, but, welcome back indeed!"

As Rachael rapped on the office door of interim department head, Robert McLaren, she was surprised to simply hear - "Enter."

"Good morning, Mr. McLaren", she said, enthusiastically.

"Doctor McLaren," he corrected her, without looking up.

"Yes, Ah, Doctor McLaren. I'm Rachael Atkinson, faculty writer and teacher."

"Yes, Doctor Jamieson told me about you."

Rachael decided to skip the usual – 'I hope it was favourable.' *This one is rude, if I ever saw one!* she thought, as she sat down opposite his desk, and said nothing.

"Do sit down, Miss Atkinson," said Doctor McLaren. As he looked up, Rachael noticed a tiny flush of embarrassment; still he covered it well, and carried on with a handful of items he expected of her.

Trying again, Rachael stumbled, "We are pleased to have you here, Doctor McLaren; Doctor Jamieson spoke highly of you."

"Indeed," the interim department head said, without interest.

"I'll just get along to my classroom then, Sir. Do you have a meeting of the faculties of history and literature planned in the next while?"

"No. Just get on with what you have planned. I'll catch up later."

"Good day then, Doctor McLaren." There was no response.

Rachael left her manuscript with the secretary, and asked that she pass it along to Doctor McLaren. "Right then, Rachael." said Violet, with a sly smile.

It would appear this man has made his miserable presence known, thought Rachael, with amusement, but also a sense of wariness.

Robert McLaren shifted uneasily in his chair. *The old man didn't tell me she was gorgeous,* he muttered to himself.

As signs of spring descended on the ruins of the French and Belgium landscape, Joey found his confinement even more tedious. "Amy," he asked, "do you know when that next procedure is scheduled? I'm beginning to think this hold-up is for nothing."

"I will ask again, Joey, I know you are becoming fed up with this routine, but I believe the best effort is being made for your benefit. How about joining me for a walk in the garden, it is a glorious day - the first sign of spring. I'll get your coat and we can take the lift down to the main floor."

"I can't wait to get out of this room," agreed Joey.

Golden Ribbons

"I'll pick up some cushions and, if we find a bench in a sunny spot, we can sit awhile and soak up the energy." Amy walked carefully beside Joey, pretending not to watch that he might fall.

A spot was found, in full sunlight. Joey let Amy assist him to sit on the cushion, resting the crutches out of sight. Joey lifted his head and closed his eyes. "I had forgotten how it feels," he said.

"You mean, how it feels to have the sun on your face, Joey?"

"Well, . . . that too. I was referring to falling in love." Joey turned to Amy's slightly flushed cheeks. "I could never have made it this far without you, Amy. YOU are the sun that breaks through for me every morning, otherwise I would go stark raving mad."

"Perhaps any *angel of mercy* would make you feel the same, Joey."

"No, that's not true, and you know it. I feel you love me too."

"I could have fallen for any soldier I've cared for, Joey. But yes, I am in love with you — against all warnings and good judgement," she said, with reluctant tears forming.

"Has this revelation marred the day, Amy?" said Joey, as he took her hand.

"Yes, in some ways it has. We can never meet each morning now without it being so obvious how we feel. Then the matron will have a *little talk* with me. Besides that, Joey, you are doing well, in spite of how you feel about it, and you will be leaving soon. Now, I have to bear the burden that you love me; it was bad enough when I felt I was the only one to love you."

With spring, came the troubling news that a deadly strain of influenza had suddenly struck many of the soldiers stationed at Camp Funston in Fort Riley, Kansas. Within a week of the first symptom, five hundred men had become infected. Just as the wave of illness was hitting Camp Funston, another two hundred thousand troops were preparing to ship out to Europe.

It was July before a widely circulated bulletin was sent out from the Philadelphia health authorities to the effect that a deadly virus was on the move. It was called *Spanish flu,* named for inaccurate reports about the virus's place of origin. Before the American troop ships arrived in Europe, widespread infection had spread among the soldiers, many dying before reaching the far shore. Popular opinion, at this stage of the war, suggested that Germany was using germ warfare against the Allies; this speculation ended, however, when the Germans also began falling to the disease.

With protective masks, the scientists again approached the front line hospitals in France and Belgium. The virus had already taken hold. "We are back again to examining the influenza outbreaks of 1833, and again in 1890," stated Doctor John Stone to his group of research scientists. "The first emerged out of Asia, with the elderly among the most common to die of the illness; then again in 1890, it was the same – but a more virulent strain that struck down people of all ages: 250,000 in Europe and a similar number in North America.

"So, what do we have to go on?" Doctor Stone asked. "In the past, theories such as bad air or drinking water seemed to be a consideration in addition to the reality of population growth and rapidly increasing migration. Groups of people living in close proximity to one another was certainly noted as cause for spread of disease. But, I believe," he concluded, "we must move on the theories of Koch and also of Pasteur, and the *germ theory* – that microorganisms passed to humans through water, food, or even the air, can cause these epidemics.

"I'm interested in what you are discovering, Todd. You have carried on with probing the properties of blood, while the rest of us have given up, following the raid we made on the injured last month – taking throat and blood samples from those poor young lads."

"I am investigating, not only those who have fallen ill," said Todd, "but, also those who have not fallen ill, under similar conditions. It was unfortunate I had to go back to find the soldiers who were in that negative category but, it has led to some interesting observations. I have a paper underway that I hope might clarify what I've been up to. But, to me, it is significant."

"If it is significant to you, Todd, after all your hours of leaning over a microscope, then it is significant to the medical research community. Absolutely nothing should be discounted."

"Doctor McLaren wishes to see you after your afternoon class, Rachael," said Violet.

Oh, great! thought Rachael. *I will be treated to another batch of rudeness no doubt,* thought Rachael. *How can such an ogre be a friend of Doctor Jamieson? This is something I cannot understand.*

"I have read your manuscript with great interest," said Robert McLaren, without first greeting her. "It is an autobiography for sure, Miss Atkinson, but it is also Scottish history! Where is your passion, Miss Atkinson? Your anger, your stiff-necked pride, your bent toward the sentimental? Your Scottishness, for heavens sake? You are a writer, not a newspaper reporter! There is still a lot of work to be done to get this manuscript fixed up, Miss Atkinson. I have a notion to see it is put on a reading list for first and second year history majors. But, it is of no consequence as it is. Have another go at it, and I'll see you later - after you have done so."

"Thank you, Sir," said Rachael, with pursed lips. As Robert McLaren got on with other matters, Rachael assumed she was dismissed. She rose and departed swiftly.

A smile crossed Robert McLaren's lips, as he watched Rachael go. *I'll have that one some day — see if I don't!* he mumbled.

The third and final procedure, to ensure a measure of mobility to Joey's knee, was scheduled for that morning. Joey watched for Amy before he was whisked to the surgical theatre, but she had not come. "We're closing in on this Joey," assured the head surgeon. "It will take approximately half an hour and, once you are fully awake, we will get you to give bending your knee a go. It will be tough at first as your brain has not been conditioned for it, so don't think, after one try, it's over. It will take concentration and your full cooperation. Off to sleep you go then, and we'll meet again in a half hour."

Joey's senses were dull. *I just want to get this over with, and I want to see Amy's face again — like, for the rest of my life.* But, he was scared. As the anaesthetic wore off, he wondered: *What if this doesn't work? Will my knee have to be hacked off too? Then, for sure, I'll be like Sam Snider, hobbling along for the rest of my days.* But, after first, second and third trys, Joey was surprised to find he could bend his knee - just a little. There were cheers and smiles all 'round, claps on the back, and congratulations to Joey.

"You did it, man!" said assistant Miles Connor. "Just take it easy, and we'll get you in a good sitting position for a bending every few hours."

"Do you realize what this means, Joey?" asked the head surgeon. "We can do this again and again. Yours was an experiment that has paid off. Thanks for your patience, a pint awaits you in the staff room a bit later."

Joey felt at peace as he was wheeled away to his room, and a rest to get his thinking back in order. Amy was waiting for him. "I'm so happy for you Joey, I'm going to hug you - and I don't care who is watching."

"I love you, Amy," whispered Joey, as he fell into an exhausted sleep.

Joey would now be facing the final stage of his rehabilitation. Resident surgical assistant, Miles Connor, was his constant companion; they were spending full days in rehab, going through details of the prosthesis that would be attached top and bottom of Joey's knee as a solid brace.

"By the time you leave Eastbourne, Joey, you will be walking with a cane, moving up and down stairs, and we will even take a tour of Eastbourne itself. You will be walking over pavements and rough ground - even adapting to jostling crowds. I am assigned a week with you, and we want to make the best use that time; your Canadian commander will be around shortly to arrange passage to your home. I realize this is all coming to an end very quickly Joey but, by the time you've had me hanging around you for a week, you will be glad to be a free man."

As predicted, Amy was summoned to see the matron and nursing supervisor, Mrs. Adamson. "Amy!" Mrs. Adamson began, "you have been one of our outstanding nurses, and I can now tell, though I've had to keep it secret: you have been selected to move on to St. Thomas Hospital in London, and from there to specialization within the Cambridge University Community at the Florence Nightingale School of Nursing. This is a special honour, and I hope you will find it exciting and challenging.

"I did expect you might protest, Amy, saying there is much work to do here, and I agree. But, other nursing sisters are following your example, and I believe we will do our best to adjust to your leaving. This will come as a surprise to you, so give it your deepest consideration, and let me know if you are willing to make this move, and how quickly. We will certainly miss you, no doubt about that."

"I am overwhelmed!" said Amy. "This is indeed a wonderful opportunity for me, but I must get my house in order, so to speak. Thank you, Mrs. Adamson; you have been my inspiration – along with so many of the medical staff, and that includes the doctors, though they can be pushy at times."

"This is so true, Amy," laughed Mrs. Adamson. "But, as we move toward professionalism, we will have the confidence to meet those challenges effectively."

"I will let my family know about this, of course," said Amy, "and there will be other matters to consider. But, with your indulgence, I will be back as soon as I possibly can to confirm."

As Amy rose to leave, Mrs. Adamson came to put her arm around Amy's shoulders. "It's alright to fall in love with a patient, Amy. Most of us have been down that road; it's almost predictable. But, beyond that, it's good for us to reach out with loving compassion as part of our role in good nursing, and as normal human beings. God bless you, Amy."

Amy hurried down the corridor and into the small nurses lounge, where she might sit for a moment to digest all that had just happened. *Mrs. Adamson is right,* she reflected. *Nursing has always been a first love, and I must follow it – wherever it will lead. Joey will go home now to challenges I'm sure he would rather avoid. But, we have loved, and I hope he will carry that love with him as a source of strength, as I will.*

Rachael was sitting by the fire in her home, this flight from the world, that she loved so much. The manuscript was in front of her and she must go back, page-by-page, to see where she had glossed over opportunities for showing anger, stiff pride, a bent for sentimentality, and – *Oh yes, my Scottishness! I'm not a poet, for heaven's sake, and what does that conceited hunk of humanity know about any of that anyway? He's a bully in the broadest sense of the word and, being so put out as I am right now, I don't see I can 'fix' my manuscript, as he so crudely put it.*

Rachael heard a scuffle at the door, and when it opened she was delighted to see, not only Todd, but Joey - standing there, both smiling like two satisfied cats. "Surprise!" said Todd. "I found this long lost relative on the station platform in Edinburgh!"

Joey moved to Rachael giving her a bone-crushing hug. "My little Rachael!" he exclaimed. "How the years have changed all of us, and how beautiful you've become. But, here now, what a great little cottage!" Joey moved around room to room, with Todd and Rachael looking on in amazement. "I hope I get to sleep upstairs, I'm a whiz at climbing stairs."

"You will indeed have that opportunity, my man," said Todd. "You'll be up there with me, and the guest bed awaits you."

"While you two make yourselves comfortable," Rachael said happily, "I will pull a late dinner together for us. Then, we can sit down and get caught up with the news from both sides of the Atlantic."

"Terrific!" said Joey. "I never dreamed I'd see my family over here. It's so *normal,* compared to the intensity of southern England. I just want to soak it up."

Todd and Rachael were fascinated by Joey's stories of the farm and how it developed, of Maggie and Billy, Niall and Katherine.

"We had a plan mapped out to make a trip to Canada," explained Todd, "then the war interrupted everything, as it did for you. But, we'll come as soon as possible, of that you can be sure."

Joey continued to look around the cottage, in amazement, as they moved over to chairs closer to the fire. There were more stories, back and forth, until Joey was ready to drop with exhaustion.

"I will show you to your room, my brother," said Todd. "The morning will come too soon, and we must be on our way again. I will try to be at the boat at Liverpool to wave you off, Joey, and hopefully Rachael will come too."

"No question, I'll be there," agreed Rachael, "and I will notify Aggie, Peter and Mary. Let's make it a grand send off. But, do waken in time for breakfast tea: fresh scones and finnan haddie!"

"How wonderful!" said Joey. "A proper Scottish start to the day, for sure!"

―――――

CHAPTER NINETEEN

JOEY WAS HAPPY HE HAD MADE THE TRIP TO SCOTLAND, AND NO problems with his knapsack. It was a wonderful weekend. But now it was time to say good-bye to all of those mates he had come to know so well. He was going home, but they would stay on for more recovery time. Gathering up all the letters he would to mail for them, he hurried to the second floor rehab. He would see Amy last. The thought of parting with her was painful, and he steeled himself for it. She had shared her future plans to train in London, and farther at the nursing school in Cambridge. He was so proud of her.

They went out to the garden spot where they had confessed their love to one another, but neither spoke. Their embrace was long and tearful; there were no promises made. Joey turned to go, and Amy hurried back to the hospital. A car was waiting for him and the long journey back home began.

Todd made further observations and notes to be included in his research paper. This would be his first submission to the medical community that circled the globe. He paused to think of the people who might read it, and that someone – out there – would be able to carry it farther along the road to new insights into the radical viruses that were now taking a heavy toll of lives in Britain, and throughout Europe.

The heat of summer was approaching and, although the influx of soldiers from all over the world would bring an end to the war, their departure could also mean the spread of disease to every corner of the earth. Reluctant to leave the research centre at this time, Todd also knew he needed some rest and renewal at home.

"There!" said Rachael, "I've done my best to make changes that should satisfy *His Majesty*, and I can do no more. Wish me luck, Todd, I may be late getting home this evening; I'm picking up a surprise. No guesses now!"

Todd smiled as Rachael hurried down the path toward the train. "My sister still loves to surprise, and I guess I do too. It seems to be something we're good at and it brings so much joy, we must never let it go." But Todd also savoured the thought of a day all to himself; he would pack up his sketching tools and wander through the village and the countryside.

The party of five were there at the Liverpool dock to see Joey off. As he had not seen Aggie's children since they were babies, Joey was shocked to see that Peter was shoulder to shoulder with him, and Mary a comely young lady. There was nervous chatter, and pictures taken of Joey with each one, and the group together. "We'll see that you get these pictures as soon as possible, Joey," Rachael assured.

"A trip to Canada is high on our agenda, Joey," added Todd. "Watch for us soon."

Then it was time to board the ship and there were hugs and hand shakes all around. The group hung together, in mute sadness, until Joey appeared on deck and the waving began, Mary blowing kisses. "God, bless him, and keep him safe," murmured Aggie.

"This is more like it, Miss Atkinson!" said Robert McLaren. "I can recommend this manuscript as a reading resource now, and I will do that at the open session on Friday."

"A forward is still to be written," reminded Rachael. "I would have thought that Dr. Jamieson might . . . "

"I will be writing the forward, Miss Atkinson."

"Oh, I see . . . thank you Mr., I mean Doctor McLaren."

Rachael was nervous about presentation. She felt, sadly, it would be up to Doctor McLaren to explain the contents, and to outline his reasons for recommendation. *He doesn't even know me,* she reflected. *He barely looks up when I enter his 'royal presence'. I feel like an object and a mere onlooker. I do wish Doctor Jamieson was here.*

The administrative group were gathered at the front of the gymnasium, and Rachael took her place with students on the risers. But where was Doctor McLaren? "Good morning, students and administration," greeted Jim Keeper. "This is to be an informal gathering, not only to meet Doctor McLaren who is filling in for Doctor Jamieson at this time, but to hear what Dr. McLaren has to say about a modern historical account written by our own Rachael Atkinson. Doctor McLaren is recommending this manuscript be accepted as a reading resource for history students and, if his recommendation is approved, it will be submitted for publishing, and displayed as a *first* in a very long time to be written by one of our own.

"And now, at this time, may I introduce Doctor Robert McLaren." Jim Keeper led the applause as Doctor McLean wheeled his way down the aisle to the front of the gathering.

Rachael was shocked, dismayed and humbled. *Oh no! He's a paraplegic! No wonder he never left his chair in greeting, or moved about when I was with him!* Rachael felt like crying, but she smiled at Doctor McLaren, and joined the applause with the others as enthusiastically as she didn't feel.

"Thank you for your kind greeting," said Robert McLaren, with a smile that lit the room with warmth, and displayed a handsome face and confident manner. "I was honoured to be chosen by Doctor Jamieson for this short assignment. Doctor Jamieson is one to be greatly valued at this university. In fact, it was with his encouragement, I turned to history and literature as a teaching profession after my personally devastating accident with a major soccer league in England.

"This is work that I have learned to love, and to make my own. It is especially rewarding when I have the opportunity to review a most insightful and moving account of our modern day life in Scotland. Without shame in poverty, this author has gone on to climb heights that would be impossible to many of us who would need time to wallow in self-pity, and to have a crutch to lean on. No, this has been a Robbie Burns transition if there ever was one. But it is rare that anyone, in these modern times, can meet his claim that personal ability alone is enough to achieve success in life. This claim of Burns' is not a Victorian Myth, as I'm sure many of you students have been told. You, as an educational institution are fortunate indeed to have such a person among you and, as you have had the opportunity to read Miss Atkinson's manuscript, I now recommend it as a permanent reading resource at this university."

As the applause now turned to Rachael, Jim Keeper motioned her to move to the front of the room. *You will make it Rachael, you will, you will,* she encouraged herself, as she moved forward and extended her hand to Robert McLaren. "Thank you, Doctor McLaren for this generous endorsement," Rachael began. "I came to this university with the help of a Carnegie Trust scholarship, and I was the first of my gender to have a recognized faculty position. It was tough going and many times I wondered if it was my place to be here. It was Doctor Jamieson who encouraged me along the way, and I am gratified to have led the way for several other women to follow. I have never been a raving feminist ." (laughter). "I believe that we are given doors that open to us and we can enter or back off in fear. I encourage all of you, my beloved students, to enter the doors that are opened to you. The corridors can be frightening, but the rooms await your gifts, and the gifts are eventually returned in full measure." Enthusiastic applause followed.

Rachael wondered if her wobbly knees would get her back to her seat, but she was stopped mid-way by Robert McLaren's wheelchair swinging toward her. "May I ask, Miss Atkinson – are you free for dinner this evening?"

The Atkinson farm, near the town of Airdrie, Alberta July 16, 1918

It was one of those balmy late summer afternoons, and Billy looked up from his work of digging fence post holes. Niall was not that far behind him – stringing barbed wire fencing along. With three rows of fencing, they were pretty evenly matched as far as getting the job finished before harvest.

The crops looked fine, the growth about what one would expect for this time of year. Barring a hail storm, it would be a good year. *I wonder if Joey will be home for the harvest?* Billy mused, as he brushed away the tears that came every time he thought of what Joey had endured these past months. Then he looked at Niall. *What a fine looking lad he is; Joey will be so proud. Niall suffered a lot more than we realized when we first heard Joey was missing in action. I believe he still wonders if Joey will really be coming home, and I often catch him looking off in the distance as if he were looking for an answer.*

They were like buddies, Joey and Niall. Right from the time Maggie brought Niall home to us, we all just fell in love with him, - but, especially Joey. His eyes would wander everywhere the little tyke went.

Then there's Jena. I believe, at times, she felt Joey had abandoned her. He'd been gone for three years, and here she is – not getting any younger. I suppose women look at it that way - the child bearing years are closing in. Maggie has never said anything, but I think she kind of felt that way for Jena. But, Jena decided to move back with her family in Calgary, and she will be teaching in some other lucky school. Everyone loved her. We have a replacement now, but I doubt he will match Jena's ability to keep the kids interested. But, then again, we didn't blame her. She wonders if Joey still feels the same as before.

Maggie is such a fine woman. How could a funny-looking Scot be so lucky to have her as his wife? I think she loves me, she says so once in awhile. We Scots are not the mushy kind, but Joey has admired her so much – like she is some kind of Madonna.

Well, there's no use thinking too much – just get on with the job. But, who the heck would come bungling along the road like that? Maybe it's old Sam Snider, he always told everyone he had one leg shorter than the other; I think it was so's we'd all feel sorry for him, Billy concluded. *No, it's not Sam ... but limping like that ...* "Oh, my God!" shouted Billy. "Am I getting so old I'm see'n mirages – whatever they are. No, it's ... No, it can't be. But, it IS Joey!" Billy threw down his spade and jumped across the ditch to get a closer look. And it WAS Joey! "Joey's come home, Niall! Come quick! See what I see! It's Joey!"

When I think back on it, thought Billy, *we all piled up in the ditch like a bunch of new puppies. I sure didn't want to hurt Joey; I knew he would have one of those artificial legs. But we would talk about that later. Then Niall ran to find Maggie and Katherine. We were all so thankful Joey was home.*

Beth McMurchie

It was a sparkling evening. Rachael was fascinated with this man who had hidden his real life situation from her so cleverly.

"I wanted nothing to distract from your flow of writing, Rachael. I don't apologize for my rude behaviour, it was what I had to do."

"I have to admit, Doctor McLean …"

"Robert, please," he emphasized, "as we are getting to know one another – and away from the university. I am taking the liberty to ask that we <u>do</u> get to know one another while I am filling in for Doctor Jamieson."

Rachael began again. "I have to admit, Robert, I had to spend some time in the staff room after the open meeting – just to *read* the situation more carefully. I do understand why you presented yourself as you did, and I expect this may be the case as we continue to work together in the coming weeks. I do not want, or expect, an apology; in fact I may learn from it as I continue to find a pattern of relating to the students I teach. I have experienced so much kindness along my journey, a good jolt is refreshing and new," she laughed. "And, yes, I would enjoy getting to know you better."

"Then let's, as much as your time permits, make it a Friday evening event. I will need to check back with my job in London occasionally, but that will be on weekends."

Joey was dazed as he found his way to the farm home, the others trailing along and trying not to crowd him. "I had to walk from town," he explained, "just to be by myself and to feel the country again. It's so open, and the cool breeze intoxicating," he laughed. "But, I have to tell you I am very tired and in need of a very long sleep. I hope you will understand that I am not up to talking just now."

"We certainly understand," said Maggie. "We have an adjustment to make too, a very happy adjustment. Words can never express how lovely it is to have you home, and – well, just to see you!" Maggie was smothering tears. "Billy and I can exchange rooms with you, if it …"

Golden Ribbons

"No, Maggie. I am just fine on stairs; besides I will be close to Niall across the way so we can have the odd pillow fight."

Niall was also in jubilant tears. "Sure, Uncle Joey," he said.

Katherine finally broke the deadlock, and rushed to embrace Joey; the others would follow as the days went on. *Ah, the Scottish reserve,* thought Joey. *It's so good to be back with my family.*

In the following days, Joey would strike out, on his own, to walk the perimeter of the property - wandering into the fields to get a closer look at the cattle and the wheat now coming to full fruition. His strength and mobility improved, and occasionally Billy or Niall would accompany him. They would chat about the coming harvest, and Billy and Maggie's plans for future improvements. "Now that our partner is back with us again," said Billy, "we can get serious about what needs to be done."

"Let's make that soon," said Joey, putting his arm around Billy's shoulder.

As they wandered along the road back to the house, a car drew up close and a voice called, "Welcome home, Joey!" It was Jena.

"Good to see you Jena," Joey smiled. "I understand you will be teaching at a new school, with, no doubt, a lot of new challenges. So, let's get together when you've settled into it, and the dust settles here."

"Sure, Joey, whenever the dust settles," agreed Jena.

An autumn glow began to settle on the village of Evan Glen once again. Rachael and Todd decided to take a break from sanding the front room floor. "It's looking good under all those years of wear and tear," said Todd, as they walked out toward the hills. "Now the new telephone will make us seem positively modern. Thanks for the surprise, sister.

"Rachael, I sense you are finding this Robert McLaren very attractive. Is my crystal ball giving me reliable information?" he asked, as he smiled down at her.

Rachael smiled back up to him. "Yes, Todd, I'm finding Robert attractive. Our Friday evening dinners together are becoming very important to me, and – he says – very important to him. Doctor Jamieson will return for the fall term, and now the time has come to ask ourselves and each other: Are we falling in love? And will this feeling last after we are separated?"

"Are you going to let me meet him, Rach? Or do I have to sneak onto the railway platform to check him out as he leaves?"

"That should not be necessary, Todd. In fact, he is anxious to meet you. After we get the mess cleaned up, and the floor back to its original beauty, I would like to ask him out to our village. I might even be calm enough to cook the meal myself."

"An old chef like you should not have a problem with that. Have you ever heard me complain, Rach?"

As arranged, Robert would take a hansom from the train and arrive the following Friday evening. Todd was first out to greet him. "Welcome Robert! I'm Todd, as I'm sure you have guessed. Rachael is still fussing around in the kitchen, but I'm sure she is calm enough now to sit with us. I will see what we have in the cupboard for something cool to drink." Todd opened the front door, and stood to one side, allowing Robert's wheelchair to pass through.

"Ahh," Robert said, "just made it! Often, I have to be lowered down from a hole in the roof. I would not want that to happen here," he laughed.

Rachael relaxed. *I think these two are going to get on just fine,* she decided, as Todd did the fussing with settling the seating arrangement and fixing cocktails. She smiled at Robert as he drew her down to him. "I love your cottage, Rachael," he said. "I can't remember when I've felt more at home."

The evening was taken up with soccer talk between Robert and Todd. *I might as well not be here,* Rachael thought happily.

Later, as Rachael accompanied Robert to the train, and he was left to wash the dishes, Todd was filled with a feeling of peace and contentment. *Gosh, I like that guy,* he mused, *how perfect he is for Rachael.*

A rap came to the door, and Todd quickly dried his hands with a tea towel before answering. A dishevelled young man was standing outside. "I understand you are a doctor, Sir. My name is Walter Scott. My wife is in premature labour, and I wonder if you could possibly help us. We have just moved into that cottage at the end of the street, number 56."

"It's good to meet a new neighbour, Walter and, yes, I will certainly do what I can. Are the pains coming regularly, Walter? Sometimes, a period of relaxation will slow things down a bit. Did you say number 56? What is your wife's name?"

Golden Ribbons

"Her name is Jennie," said Walter, "and it's number 56. Thank you, it is a relief to know you will help."

"I will be down your way just as soon as I get a few items together," Todd responded. He did not want to show any nervousness; he had not actually assisted in a birth all by himself – only as an intern. "Oh well," he said aloud to himself. "No time like the present." He went upstairs to get his bag of necessities, and to write a note to Rachael. She must come to number 56 immediately.

Todd found that Jennie had already relaxed, knowing help was on the way. "I'm pleased to meet you Jennie, and perhaps you can tell me everything that is happening so far: how close together are the pains, and are there any feelings of pushing?" Todd asked.

As he washed his hands in the new neighbour's tiny bathroom, and shrugged on a wrinkled lab coat, Todd was back at Jenny's side, taking her pulse and blood pressure, and coaching her to breathe slowly and to relax between pains. *It's all coming back to me now,* thought Todd.

Rachael arrived at number 56 just as a perfect baby girl was delivered. She was surprised and pleased to observe Todd in his professional role. After quick introductions, Todd smiled up at her, asking her to go home and bring back as many towels as she could find.

Walter and Jenny were glowing with happiness as they listened to Todd's capable directions regarding baby Alice's first few hours of life. "Hold that pose," said Rachael, as she found the new parents proudly holding their new little daughter, and smiling broadly. She was back in an instant with a camera to snap a family picture. At the parent's insistence, another picture was taken with Todd beside them. It was a wonderful occasion, and the beginning of a special friendship.

"I'm so proud of you, Todd," said Rachael, as they walked home together. By this time, it was fully dark and the stars were out, producing a glow that seemed to engulf the entire village.

"It feels wonderful to bring a new life into the world. Perhaps this is where I belong. It just seems right."

"It does seem exactly right, Todd," said Rachael, linking her arm with his.

CPSIA information can be obtained
at www.ICGtesting.com
Printed in the USA
LVHW031932280319
612217LV00002B/25/P

9 781525 536861